A Thread of Evidence

By

Joanne Connors-Wade

authorHOUSE™

1663 LIBERTY DRIVE, SUITE 200
BLOOMINGTON, INDIANA 47403
(800) 839-8640
WWW.AUTHORHOUSE.COM

First published by AuthorHouse 05/03/05

ISBN: 1-4208-3856-3 (sc)

Printed in the United States of America
Bloomington, Indiana

This book is printed on acid-free paper.

DEDICATION

"A Thread of Evidence"

is inspired by a true event

It is dedicated to the families of the two victims

FORWARD

"A Thread of Evidence" transpires in the 1950's.

It has been written fictitiously, inspired by an actual, true event.

The story has been carefully researched for accuracy. Portions are taken from actual court transcripts and records, as well as newspaper accounts. Additional information has been obtained from the personal recollections of the author and several individuals who lived in the area at that time.

All names, including that of the city have been changed respecting the privacy of the true characters and their families, living or dead.

As you read *"A Thread of Evidence"* you will detect some remarkable, sometimes unbelievable facts. The author has adhered as close as possible to the actual facts, and these 'remarkable, unbelievable' portions of the story are factual, and actually occurred as the story unfolds.

'A THREAD OF EVIDENCE'

PART I

Friday, September 24, 1954

The alarm rang, and the young girl rolled over as the sun flooded over her face. It was Friday, September 24, 1954 and Lynn Ann Clarke was now finishing up the third week of her freshman year of high school. What an exciting time! Every day a new adventure.

She lay awake, mentally deciding what to wear. Her new back-to-school wardrobe was much more elaborate than in previous school years. Now she was in high school, and everything was different. Clothes had to be just right. She began piecing together her outfit for the day. A white angora sweater hadn't been worn yet.

September in New England can be very warm, and this year was one that everyone referred to as an "Indian Summer." Unseasonably warm temperatures, breaking records set back as far as 1920. Lynn wanted to wear that sweater. She turned on the radio and listened for the weather forecast.

"Another sunny and warm day folks. We're anticipating record-breaking temperatures. Could reach 80°." The weatherman went on to forecast the progress of "Hazel" a hurricane that was slowly moving up the east coast.

"Expected to hit Western Massachusetts around late tomorrow," he warned. "By then, it should be classified as a tropical storm. Enjoy today, you know how New England is!" He said jokingly.

Lynn popped out of bed and headed for the dresser, took the sweater out and decided she'd held off long enough. Today she was going to look particularly nice. A white angora sweater and a light blue skirt. She shuffled down the hallway to the bathroom and looked into the mirror. She was always searching She splashed the cool water over her face and patted it dry with a thirsty towel. Smooth as satin she thought. Then she brushed through her light brown hair and pinned it up into a pert pony tail. As she donned her robe, she heard her mother calling from the kitchen.

"Lynn, honey, you up? Breakfast is ready."

Lynn answered with a cheerful, "Yup, I'll be right there."

As she entered the kitchen she reached into the refrigerator for the orange juice and poured a glassful. She couldn't start a day without that refreshing glass of fresh squeezed orange juice.

Barbara, her nine-year-old sister was already seated at the table. Barbara poured the Cheerios into a bowl and covered them with sugar.

"Hey, their kiddo, take it easy on the sugar! You're sweet enough," her mother warned.

Barbara reached for the milk and picked up the section of the Stanfield News her father had laid aside on the table for her. She liked reading the paper at the table like her dad did every morning. The news seemed boring for her, and she hardly understood it anyway, so she read the 'funnies'.

As Lynn passed Mr. Clarke, she leaned over to give him a peck on his cheek.

"'Morning Dad," she said cheerfully.

Phil Clarke grunted, which was his customary reply, not looking up from his paper. Lynn slid into her place at the table and spread her favorite strawberry jam over the hot toast.

Elaine Clarke was dressed in a flowery dress with a yellow apron. Her hair was twisted into a perfect chignon that she seemed to manage effortlessly every morning. She leaned across the table to refill her husband's coffee, and poured one for herself.

4

Lynn began announcing her plans for the day. She was always excited about one thing or another. As she began, Phil put his paper aside, giving his oldest daughter his undivided attention. Elaine looked at Lynn and thought how pretty she looked today and how grown up she had become just over this last summer. She's becoming quite a young lady.

Lynn had many friends and cherished them all. Not only were her friends in her freshman class, but also the upper classes. Lynn's friends had brothers or sisters that were older, and Lynn was the sort of girl that everyone took a liking to. Lynn was sure she would be with them throughout her school years, and how exciting it would be sharing all the experiences high school girls go through. The boys, the crushes, the heartbreak, the dances and today the cheerleading tryouts!

Ever since sixth grade she had dreamed of becoming a cheerleader. She would spend countless hours practicing the cheers, the form, and the agile moves it takes to gain a position on the squad. Ginny Poirier, a senior at Lincoln High School had spent hours with Lynn over the summer. Ginny was confidant Lynn would be a tough competitor.

Phil took a final sip of coffee, folded his paper and got up from the table.

"Have to get going," he said. "What a beautiful morning. I love the fall." He started to reach for his hat, "Oh, Lynn. I've got something for you." He reached into his pocket. "These are for a little extra luck at the tryouts." He handed her two shiny 1954 pennies.

"Gee thanks, Daddy," Lynn replied. She raised her head toward Phil with exaggerated puckered lips. Then she slipped off her loafers and placed the pennies into the slots.

"Now you have a good day young lady, and don't forget, right home from school."

"I know Daddy. You always say that!" Barbara answered. Elaine handed Phil his car keys and kissed him on his cheek.

"See you tonight, Hon."

Phil was on his way. He worked at Boman Manufacturing. It was a large plant and provided employment for a large percentage of Stanfield. Boman produced military airplane parts and components.

Phil was never drafted for WWII or Korea but he believed he did his share of the war effort by working for a manufacturer that supplied machine parts to the military, including the gigantic B-52's.

As Phil drove to work, he found himself reminiscing. Upon graduation, class of '32, he started at Boman's as the 'mail boy'. In a short time, he worked in the tool crib. Within a year he was training in the 'time study' department, and eventually became manager of quality control.

When Phil was 21, he met Elaine Stringer, a bright young secretary. Elaine worked in the Personnel Department at Boman. Phil was head over heels for her, right from the start. His shift would end at 4:00 and he would wait outside for Elaine to appear in the doorway of the office building at precisely 5:00. They would walk a couple of blocks to the bus stop. Elaine would catch the bus for home. Phil would walk the remaining four blocks home, barely touching the ground. He was in love.

They soon began dating, and after a year, they were engaged. Six months later they were married, on September 24, 1939. The following July they were blessed with a beautiful baby girl they named Lynn Ann. She was named after Phil's father, Lyndon and Elaine's mother Ann.

Shortly after Lynn's birth, Phil moved his little family to 48 Lynndale St., Stanfield, MA What a lucky man I am! He thought. A year ago he had been promoted to Production Manager. He had everything he wanted, and it seemed like it kept getting better! He was thirty-eight and had moved well through the company. His pension plan was in place and he hoped to retire at age fifty-eight.

Now, as he pulled his shiny black Buick into the parking lot and rolled into the spot marked Management Parking Only, he remembered, September 24th, his 15th anniversary! He made a mental note to stop by the flower shop on his way home.

Another day had begun for Phil Clarke.

Stanfield, Massachusetts, 1954

Stanfield is one of the larger cities of Massachusetts. It is located in the Western part of the state and quite unique. The downtown, or hub of the city, is surrounded by four well-defined sections. "The Meadows" to the north, "Springdale" to the south, "East view" to the east and "Breckwood" to the west. The Clarke's moved from the Meadows to Springdale.

Springdale, still in the confines of the City of Stanfield is best described as a self-contained community. On the main artery of Springdale are the R & S Market, Blocker's Cleaners, Tony's Barber Shop and a Rexall Drugstore with a soda fountain where the teenagers gather after school. The Loews Poli Theater and the Springdale branch of the public library are also a part of the community's make up. Springdale has a house of worship for every denomination, including a synagogue. Three elementary schools, Gifford Elementary, Proctor Elementary and a parochial school, St. Joseph's. All house Kindergarten through eighth grade. Cathedral High School, located in the Breckwood section boasted the highest percentage of graduates going on to college. Lincoln High was a very close second. There was a healthy rivalry among the Stanfield High Schools. Springdale was in every sense of the word, a nice, safe community for a family in 1954.

E laine busied herself clearing the breakfast table. The girls had left for school and Elaine had a busy day ahead. Four years ago, when Barbara started school, Elaine took a job shuttling nursery school children to and from the Community Sunshine Nursery School. It was the ideal job for her. She would leave her house at 8:30 A.M., pick up the children and deposit them at the school by 9:15. At 1:15, she would leave to pick them up and return them to their homes. The schedule was custom made for Elaine. It allowed her to be home in time for Barbara's arrival at 3:15.

At 2:30, Elaine was just arriving home. She heard the telephone ring and struggled with the bags of groceries, not wanting to miss the call. She placed the groceries on the table and reached for the phone.

"Hello?" She said, a little out of breath.

"Mom, Mom! Guess what! I made the squad!"

"Slow down Lynn. I can hardly understand you. Now what was that?" Lynn could hardly contain herself.

"Mom, I'm on the cheerleading squad! The student body voted, and I made it! I'm the only freshman. Mom, I'm so excited!" Elaine tried to squeeze a word in, but it wasn't possible.

She finally managed, "Congratulations honey, tell me all about it when you get home!"

"Okay, Mom. I'll be home right after school. See you then. I love you," she said.

"I love you too, baby," Elaine replied, and hung up the phone. Elaine barely placed the phone on the receiver and it rang again. She answered, "Hello?"

"Hi Hon.," a deep familiar voice replied. It was Phil.

"I'd like to take my favorite girl out to dinner and a movie tonight. What'd say?"

"Oh Phil, that would be so nice. What about the girls?"

"I thought maybe, because it's a special occasion, Lynn might stay home with Barbara. Do you think she'd mind, being Friday night?"

"I just spoke to her. She was so excited. She made the cheerleading squad!" Answered Elaine.

"That's great! See what she has planned. I'll see you around 5:00. Don't make supper!" Phil replied.

"Okay, I'll see you in awhile, bye." She hung up. Elaine smiled. He never forgets. In fifteen years, he's never forgotten their anniversary. It will be nice to go out. They hadn't had dinner out in months, except for countless summer picnics, and you could hardly call that dining out! .

She rushed into the bedroom to her closet. A quick glance and she instantly decided on her favorite plum dress. It was Phil's favorite too.

Barbara came rushing through the kitchen at precisely 3:20.

"Slow down, where's the fire?" Elaine asked as she caught her younger daughter around the shoulders.

"I have to hurry, Mattie Jansen is coming over to Timmy's house and I want to get changed so I can be there before he gets there!"

"Soooo, what's so important about being at Timmy's? I didn't think you even liked the Connor boys."

"Well, I like Matt. Besides, he has a new bike, and he said I could ride it!"

Barbara slipped out of her mother's grip and rushed toward her room. As she passed Lynn's room, she spotted the red and white pom poms in the corner. She couldn't resist. She knew she was not allowed in her sister's room without permission but, she just wanted to wave those pom poms around once. After all, she had watched Lynn practice enough, she knew all the cheers.

She picked up the pom poms and started, "One-Two-Three, Who are. We...."

When Mrs. Clarke heard her young daughter, she stood in the doorway and laughed.

"You've got a few years before you start that! One cheerleader in the family at a time is quite enough! Lynn called, she made the squad!"

"Wow!" Barbara replied. "She's so lucky! Does that mean I get to go to the practices? Can I go to the games?"

"Hey, wait just a minute, you won't be going to any practices. But, I'll bet Daddy would love to take you to the games. Now put those pom poms back and scram out of your sister's room." Barbara placed the pom poms back in the corner, just as she found them, and as she passed Elaine, she gave her a hug.

"I love you Mom." She said and continued on into her room to change. Elaine leaned against the open doorway and enjoyed the moment. She felt a warmth from those words that came spilling out for no apparent reason.

Lynn was anxious to get home and tell her mother all about the tryouts and voting. She was so excited. It was a dream come true.

She arrived home at 3:45. She was full of energy and bubbling over with excitement as she met her mother in the kitchen. She plunked down at the kitchen table where her mother was glancing through the entertainment section of the Stanfield News.

"I'm so excited," she began. "Can you imagine? I made the squad!" She leaned over and gave Elaine a squeeze. Elaine had never seen her so happy.

"You worked hard, sweetie, and you certainly deserve it! I'm really happy for you. Barbara can hardly wait to go to the games to watch you! She's so proud of you!" Elaine genuinely shared in her daughter's moment of glory.

"Lynn, can you do me a great favor?" She asked.

"Sure Mom, anything." Lynn answered, sneaking a sip of milk straight from the bottle. She liked the cream that floated to the top.

"Will you watch Barbara for a while tonight, would you mind?"

"Well, I was going to go over to Lisa's tonight. You and Dad going somewhere?" She asked.

"We'd like to. It's our anniversary. Dad wants to take me out to dinner and a movie. Why not ask Lisa to come over here instead. She can stay over. I'd really appreciate it, Lynn."

"Oh Mom! I completely forgot about your anniversary! I'm really sorry. I guess I was so excited about the tryouts. I'll call Lisa right now. I'm sure she'll come over. What movie are you going to?" She asked.

"I've been looking through the paper and Marlon Brando's new movie, 'On the Waterfront' is playing at the Bijou tonight. He's playing the non-contender, Terry Malloy. Everyone's been talking about it."

"Then, it's all set. You have a date!" Lynn replied with an authoritative tone. She was already dialing Lisa's number.

"Thanks Lynn, you're a real doll!" Her mother answered.

Because the Clarke's were of the Catholic faith, they were in the practice of abstaining from eating meat on Friday. Mrs. Clarke had a tuna casserole all prepared.

It was nearly 4:30 and Barbara returned from Timmy Connor's.

"So how's your little boy friend?" Lynn teased. "Mattie and Barbara sitting in a tree, k-i-s-s-i-n-g," she chanted. Barbara was annoyed.

"Cut it out Lynn. You're not funny."

"Did he ask you to go steady?" Lynn continued taunting her little sister.

"You're stupid!" Barbara shouted back and went to the sink to wash up. She spotted the casserole on the kitchen counter. Eh, she thought, I hate Fridays! I really hate tuna casserole!

Then she announced, "When I grow up, I will never make my kids eat tuna casserole."

"Oh well, until then, it is tuna casserole Friday for you. Besides, Mattie probably loves tuna casserole!" Lynn laughed, her voice trailing off as she headed for the living room.

Phil Clarke arrived just as Barbara was drying her hands. He was carrying a large bouquet of red roses, tied with a gold satin ribbon. In the center of the bouquet were two white carnations, symbolizing the two girls.

Barbara greeted her father with a hug and asked what the occasion for the flowers was.

Phil bent down and whispered in Barbara's ear, "It's a surprise for Mommy. It's our anniversary."

Barbara wasn't sure what an anniversary meant, so she asked, "Do I get an anniversary too?"

"Not yet baby. Anniversary means celebrating a special occasion. Mommy and I have been married for fifteen years. So this is our 15th anniversary. Sort of like a birthday."

"Oh, I get it," Barbara answered.

Just then, Elaine appeared in the kitchen doorway.

"Oh Phil, they're beautiful." She picked up the flowers from the table and through her arms around her husband's neck.

"Thank you so much, and happy anniversary to you!"

Barbara giggled as she witnessed her mother and father's display of affection. It made her feel good. She wasn't exactly sure why, but it did.

"Did you talk to Lynn about babysitting tonight?" Phil asked.

"Yes, and she's fine with it. I've got supper all ready to just heat in the oven and . . . "

"I hate it when you call me a 'baby'!" Barbara exclaimed, interrupting her mother in a sudden outburst.

"I'm nine and I don't need a babysitter!" Elaine remembered this subject coming up not too long ago.

She replied, "Oops, sorry Barb. I meant you and Lynn will be having supper together and Lynn will be in charge because she's older. Okay?"

"Okay." Barbara answered with a scowl.

Phil picked up the evening paper and went into the living room. He noticed the paper had been opened to the entertainment section.

He was quite sure he would be seeing Marlon Brando tonight. He checked the starting time. 7:30 at the Bijou. Plenty of time for dinner before the movie. Besides, if they were a little late, they'd only miss the newsreel and previews of coming attractions.

Barbara turned on the TV. She sprawled out on the carpet, her hands clasped together under her chin. She was just in time to hear Bob Smith, 'Buffalo Bob' charging the Peanut Gallery with his familiar, "Hey kids, what time is it?"

Barbara chimed in with the Peanut Gallery's response, "It's Howdy Doody Time!"

Lynn waited until her father got comfortable in his easy chair and said, "Happy Anniversary Daddy."

"Thanks Lynn," he replied, "and thanks for changing your plans for tonight. We shouldn't be too late. Probably about 10:00."

"That's fine. Lisa is coming over and she's going to stay the night. Mom said it was okay."

"Oh, congratulations to you! Big news today I hear!" Her father exclaimed.

"Yup," replied Lynn with a big smile, "isn't it the greatest?"

"I guess those lucky pennies worked?" Phil laughed and turned back to the paper. A few minutes later, Elaine announced she was ready to go. Phil looked at his wife and smiled.

"You look great! Did you have me or Mr. Brando in mind when you dolled yourself all up?" He chuckled.

Elaine struck a mock pose, one hand on her hip, the other behind her head and laughed,

"I had my date in mind. So you like?"

"You bet I do! Let's get going."

Phil slipped a light coat over Elaine's shoulders. It was a balmy night on September 24, 1954.

Lynn placed the casserole into the preset oven. She returned to the living room with Barbara. As Barbara continued watching TV, Lynn turned to her book, Emily Bronte's classic, *Jane Eyre*. It was a class assignment to read the book and then compose a book report by the end of the semester. Lynn was an avid reader, but she dreaded writing the book report!

At 6:15, Lisa knocked on the back door and let herself in.

"Mmm mm, smells like tuna casserole! Must be Friday!"

"Hi Lisa," called Lynn. "Come on in." Lisa was concealing a small bag behind her back.

"Guess what I brought?" She asked. "I stopped by the record shop today and look!"

"What is it?" Lynn asked. She took the bag and squealed with delight.

"I don't believe you got it!" She jumped up and down waving a record in the air. Lisa had the latest recording of the newest heart throb. A young recording artist was soaring to the top of the charts with his newest release, *"It's All Right Mama."* Elvis Presley had the teenagers going wild with his sensational style and the new craze, Rock 'n Roll.

The girls engaged in conversation. It was a wonder they had anything to talk about. They saw each other just about every day. But, they always seemed to have some new gossip.

Occasionally an outburst, "Isn't he the coolest?" or, "I really dig that, it's so groovy!"

Lynn announced, "Supper's ready." Barbara didn't respond.

Lisa sat at the table and teased Barbara calling, "Come and get it, it's your favorite, Barb!" Finally Barbara took her place at the table just as Lynn was spooning out a portion onto Barbara's plate.

"Do I have to eat this stuff?" She whined.

"Yes you do, so get going," replied Lynn.

Barbara began rearranging the tuna, peas and noodles in her plate. She rested her head on her hand and fiddled with the food.

"Elbows off the table, Barbara. You know better." Lynn said, sounding a little irritated at her sister's behavior. She was losing patience with Barbara.

"If you don't eat, you can go straight to bed," she warned. Barbara scowled and took a few tiny bites. She divided the food into three equal portions on her plate and asked,

"If I eat one of these piles, can I be excused?"

Lynn gave her a look to say, 'don't push it' and replied,

"Eat two piles." Barbara quickly ate the two small portions, and excused herself. She placed her dish in the sink and returned to her place on the living room floor.

14

Lisa and Lynn cleared the table and washed the dishes. The two girls decided to make a surprise anniversary cake for Mr. and Mrs. Clarke. Barbara chimed in and the three got busy. They found a Betty Crocker chocolate cake mix in the pantry, mixed the ingredients and baked it. After it was cooled and frosted, Barbara made a colorful sign.

"Happy Anniversary Mom and Dad,
Love, Barbara and Lynn xxxooo"

Lisa took the red crayon from Barbara and in small letters added, "and Lisa too!" They placed the cake with the sign in the center of the kitchen table, stood back and admired their masterpiece.

Barbara busied herself with a jigsaw puzzle she had spread out on the coffee table. Lisa and Lynn went to Lynn's room to listen to records and paint each other's nails.

Just before 9:00, Lynn announced, "Barbara you've got to get ready for bed."

"Aw, come on Lynn. It's Friday, no school tomorrow. Mommy lets me stay up."

"Okay," Lynn agreed. "But get you p.j.'s on and you can stay up and listen to Amos and Andy on the radio."

Barbara rushed down the hall and into her bedroom. In a flash, she was back, carrying her pillow and Raggedy Ann doll. She lay on the sofa and Lynn turned on the Philco in the corner. The three sat, laughing out loud at the outrageous comedy of the famous Amos and Andy Show.

It wasn't long before Barbara was asleep. Lynn took the throw cover that was draped over the chair and covered her sister. She turned down the radio and dimmed the light. Then she and Lisa went back to Lynn's room. They began setting each other's hair in pin curls.

At 10:10 Phil and Elaine returned. Quietly they tiptoed into the living room, expecting to find Barbara asleep on the sofa. There she was, curled up, cradling her Raggedy Ann. Phil gently picked her up and brought her to bed.

Elaine poked her head into Lynn's room announcing they were home.

"Hi Mrs. C, Happy Anniversary!" Exclaimed Lisa.

"Thanks Lisa." Elaine replied.

15

"How was the movie?" Lynn asked.

"It was great. That Marlon Brando is so handsome! The cake is lovely Lynn. You're so thoughtful!"

"Oh it was nothing," Lynn replied.

Then Mrs. Clarke said goodnight to the two girls.

Saturday, September 25, 1954

It was raining. Lynn and Lisa decided to sleep in. Lynn turned over and tried to go back to sleep but couldn't. She playfully nudged Lisa.

"Come on Lis, let's get up! You've got to get home by 10:00 don't you?" She reminded Lisa she had promised her mother she'd help with the usual Saturday cleaning. Lynn had hers to do also.

"Aw come on Lynn, five minutes, that's all I ask. I'm begging!"

"Well, if you put it so pathetically, I'll give you ten minutes. Then, I'm throwing you out!" She laughed and jumped out of bed. Lynn headed for the bathroom, calling over her shoulder to her sleepy friend,

"I'm going to get washed up, Lisa, and when I'm done, I'm dumping your sorry body out of that bed!"

"Yeah, yeah, yeah," answered Lisa.

Tonight, like every other Saturday night, since she had turned fourteen, Lynn had a regular babysitting job at the Rosen's. She had promised to take Barbara to the movies in the afternoon, just as she did most every Saturday. Lisa and some of her other friends would be there with their younger brothers and sisters. They usually met at the movies and all sat together.

After about fifteen minutes, Lynn returned to her bedroom. Lisa had gone back to sleep. Lynn thought of waking her up with a cold water treatment, but decided that would be a bit drastic. She also knew Lisa well enough to know she was not in her best humor in the morning!

She nudged Lisa, and pulled the blankets off her. "Okay, time's up. Rise and shine. Time to greet this dreary, rainy day!"

"Okay, Sarge, I'm up!" In half an hour, Lisa was on her way home.

Lynn sat in the kitchen and listened to her mother recount the movie she'd seen the night before. Lynn was pleased she had such a good time. The Clarke's didn't go out much, and they really enjoyed themselves on the occasions they were able.

"Where's Barbara?" Lynn asked.

"She's down in the cellar bundling up all her newspapers. The rag man will be here by 11:00 and you remember how grumpy he can be. She wants to be sure she has all her newspapers out on the tree belt when he comes by. He doesn't wait for anyone. Poor kid, she works so hard and I know that old man takes advantage of the kids. He cheats them out of the little bit he pays them."

"I know, I remember, a nickel a pound! I can't believe I did all that work for a nickel a pound!"

"What are your plans for tomorrow?" Asked Mrs. Clarke.

"Nothing special, why?" Replied Lynn.

"I know you've been wanting a permanent, so I picked up a Toni. I thought we could get that done tomorrow. Of course, that will chase your father right out of the house! He can't stand the smell, but he'll probably do something with Barbara while we stink up the house!"

"Sounds great Mom! Let's do it." Lynn replied enthusiastically.

Elaine noticed Lynn's fingernails.

"You're finally letting your nails grow. No more biting, what a difference. They look so nice."

"Thanks. Lisa and I did each other's last night. She's really good at it, maybe she will go to beauty school. Then she can give me my permanents in her very own shop!" Lynn laughed, "I'll have my very own personal beautician."

At 1:00 Barbara and Lynn were standing in the long line outside the Loew's Poli theater. The line extended around the corner just like any other Saturday. It seemed the whole neighborhood gathered to see the next exciting episode of the cliffhanger, serials, short subjects and the main feature. Today featured Dean Martin and Jerry Lewis.

By 3:45 everyone poured from the theater. The rain had continued all afternoon with no sign of clearing up. Lynn, Barbara, Lisa and her younger brother Matt headed for home. Matt was ten and Barbara thought he was 'okay for a boy'. They walked ahead of the two older girls, skipping and jumping over the puddles that had welled in the cracked asphalt sidewalk. Lisa and Lynn walked behind the two younger siblings. They discussed their plans for the evening, and the next day.

"I have to watch Mattie for a while tonight," said Lisa. "Mom and Dad are going out."

"Oh, too bad." Replied Lynn. "I was hoping you could come over to the Rosen's and keep me company. The Rosen's have a new TV. It's huge!"

"Maybe later, depends when my parents get home." Lisa said. "And by the way, Lynn, I have to tell you again, you looked great at the tryouts, congratulations pal!" She gave her friend a little squeeze.

"Thanks Lisa, but you're the 1st sub. If anybody gets sick, or their grades slip, you're in! I'll bet you'll be subbing practically every game!"

"Yeah," Lisa mocked, "and maybe the moon is made of green cheese!"

Maintaining at least a "C" was very strictly enforced at Lincoln High School for anyone participating in extra curricular activities. Lynn and Lisa were potentially straight A students.

Before they knew it, they were at the corner of Dorset and Archer. Lisa lived on Dorset, so they said their goodbyes. Lynn and Barbara continued walking along Archer Boulevard. Only a few more blocks to their house on Lynndale Street. They passed the Rosen's house on the way. It was rainy, so nobody was out. Mrs. Rosen often sat on the front porch, but it was getting close to supper time, and the rain was persistent.

The two girls turned onto Lynndale Street. It was a pretty street, lined with ancient Maple trees and the leaves were just beginning to turn to their autumn hues. Fall was just beginning and with the rain and wind, many of the orange, red and yellow leaves had fallen, blanketing the sidewalks.

Lynn and Barbara had lived there all their lives. When Lynn was younger, she believed the street was named after her. Phil and Elaine let her believe this was true. It made her feel special.

When Lynn was five, Barbara was born. Lynn was so excited to have a baby sister. She did everything just like her mother. She bathed and fed her dolls when Elaine bathed and fed Barbara. She seemed to grow up quickly once Barbara arrived.

One day, Lynn went with her father to get his haircut. From that day on, she was sure they had named her beautiful baby sister after the barber. That became a family joke. Lynndale St. was named after Lynn, and Barbara was named after the barber!

All the houses on Lynndale St. looked pretty much the same. Two family houses with two porches, one on the first floor, one on the second. The only exception was the house directly across the street. It was a one family. That's where Lynn's friend Brenda Chapman lived. Brenda was a year older than Lynn and starting her sophomore year.

When the two girls attended Proctor Elementary School they were close friends. However, when Brenda entered her freshman year at Lincoln, they seemed to drift apart. Now that Lynn too was at Lincoln, they seemed to bridge that gap and saw each other more frequently. They walked to school together and both were members of the choir at St. Michael's, so they would always attend mass together. It was a more casual friendship than Lynn had with Lisa.

Brenda had an older brother, Karl. He was pretty much of a loner. He seldom had friends around and kept to himself. He was eighteen. A junior and he didn't even have his driver's license! Lynn thought that was just unthinkable. In two years she'd be sixteen, and she would surely have a driver's license!

Most of the families that lived in Stanfield had lived there for generations. People weren't transient in the '50's. Neighbors enjoyed the security of knowing who lived in every house on the street. They weren't close friends, just neighborly. Nodding a hello in the morning, chatting occasionally when they were in their backyards, and just going about their own business while their children played together.

The stores were accessible to the neighborhoods. All the kids knew each other and all played on their own block. A playground was only a block away, with swings and jungle gyms. In the summers, college students would volunteer as councilors and conduct arts and craft sessions for the neighborhood kids. Life was very simple, and very safe at that time.

When school was back in session, the kids walked, starting out in small groups, and collecting more and more walkers on each corner, until they all arrived at school. The high school students did the same. Some had cars, but most walked.

Barbara attended Proctor Elementary just as Lynn had from kindergarten through eighth grade. She repeated the same route her sister had. After school, there were hours of sidewalk roller skating, jumping rope, riding bikes around the block and being in the house when the street lights came on. The rules were simple.

Saturday Evening, September 25

Lynn finished dinner at 6:00. She was usually excused from doing the dishes on Saturdays. She got up from the table and went to her room to get ready to go to the Rosen's. She pulled on a pair of blue jeans and rolled them just below her knees. That was the way all the girls were wearing them. She put on a blue and green plaid shirt and glanced in the mirror. She looked fine. She wasn't one for make up, besides she was only going babysitting.

As she was about to leave, she realized it was still raining. It was only a short walk to the Rosen's but she thought it best to wear her hooded raincoat. She picked up a book from the dining room table and tucked it inside her coat to keep it from getting wet.

As she was leaving, she shouted "Bye everybody, see you later."

Elaine called back to her, "Did you change your shoes? You'll ruin those loafers in this rain."

"Oh, I'll be careful. I don't go splashing through puddles like some people I know!" Lynn replied, giving her sister the eye.

The radio was announcing the progress of hurricane "Hazel" moving toward Western Mass. Only two weeks before, the area had been hammered with a severe hurricane. It had left a lot of destruction in its wake, throughout the state. It was hoped Hazel would be a bit more merciful. It was hard to predict a hurricane pattern in New England. September was a hurricane season. The weather was warm. Hazel was expected to hit within twenty-four hours. Fortunately, it was predicted to lose its hurricane status and be nothing more than a storm.

Lynn decided to stop by Brenda's house for a few minutes. She had time. Brenda and her mother were just finishing up the supper dishes. Lynn knocked on the back door and heard Marge Chapman call,

"Come in! Get out of that rain!"

"Hi Mrs. Chapman." Lynn replied and plunked herself down at the kitchen table.

"Hi dear, you off to the Rosen's?"

"Yes, I just thought I'd stop in and see what's up with Brenda tonight." Brenda was rushing around getting the dried dishes put away.

"I've got to get ready." Brenda sounded excited. "Paul is picking me up at 7:15. We're going to the movies."

Brenda and Paul had been going steady for about two months. Brenda had just turned sixteen and was allowed to go on real dates now.

"What movie are you going to?" Lynn asked. "My parents went to see Marlon Brando's new movie, *On the Waterfront* and they said it was great! Of course you know how my mom is when it comes to Marlon Brando!"

Brenda laughed, "I guess I'll leave that up to Paul."

"And don't forget, no later than 11:00!" Marge Chapman warned her daughter, "That means in the house at 11:00."

"I know Mom. We're only going to the movies and then to get something to eat. I'll be home by 11:00, I promise." Brenda answered, rolling her eyes at Lynn.

Brenda knew if she was not home by 11:00 she wouldn't be going anywhere for a long time. Mr. Chapman didn't listen to any excuses. Maybe she'd talk her mother into just about anything, but not her dad!

Brenda's brother Karl came into the kitchen.

"Hi Karl," said Lynn.

"Hi," Karl answered as he reached into the refrigerator for a Coke, and left the room.

Just then Lynn looked at the clock and jumped up.

"Oh! I didn't realize how late it was. I've got to be at the Rosen's in 10 minutes! I'll see you tomorrow for church. Mom, Dad and Barbara are going to 8:30 Mass, so they'll give us a ride."

"Okay, see you in the morning." Brenda answered.

"Have a good time with Paul tonight!" Lynn was smiling. "See you Mrs. Chapman."

She hurried along Lynndale Street, onto Archer Boulevard and finally arrived at the Rosen's. As she approached the front door, she saw young David's tricycle tipped over in the middle of the sidewalk. She placed the bike upright and rolled it over to the hedges at the side of the porch steps.

Lynn pressed the ivory doorbell. Mr. Rosen answered the door and as she stepped inside, she knew she was right on time. The antique grandfather clock that stood in the entrance way chimed, indicating seven o'clock.

"Hi Lynn, come on in." Mr. Rosen said. Lynn stepped inside. Mr. Rosen took her raincoat and hung it on a hook by the door. Lynn slipped off her shoes and placed them by the door. In her stocking feet, she proceeded into the living room where David and Daniel were playing with tinker toys on the living room floor. Mr. Rosen returned to his overstuffed easy chair. He puffed on his pipe. Lynn had detected the familiar cherry aroma.

As she walked into the living room, David jumped up and grabbed her around the legs. He always looked forward to Lynn's arrival. She was his only babysitter, and that was just fine with him. He was clad in his Roy Rogers pajamas. Lynn lifted him up as high as she could and swung him around.

"I'm an airplane!" David shouted. Daniel looked up and gave Lynn a little wave acknowledging her arrival.

"What are you making?" Lynn asked.

"We're trying to make this Ferris wheel." Daniel replied, pointing to the diagram on the tube the tinker toys came in.

"I can't find the spool that makes the wheel go around."

"Well, I'll help you Daniel," Lynn replied. Just then, Mrs. Rosen came bustling into the room. She was fussing over a locket, trying to fasten it.

"Oh hi Lynnie," she said. She always called her Lynnie. "Can you do this for me? I just can't seem to get the clasp to close."

"Sure, you look so nice, Mrs. Rosen. Where are you going?"

"We'll be at Antonio's for dinner, then at the Carlson's to play cards. Their telephone number is on the pad beside the telephone. We won't be too late."

"Oh, don't worry about the time." Lynn replied. "I've got this book I have to read for English Literature and the boys are never any trouble. Have a good time and don't worry."

"Don't forget you guys, in bed by 8:00, no later!"

"Oh Mom," cried Daniel, "can't I stay up later? David is only four and he gets to stay up. That's not fair," the six-year-old protested.

Mr. Rosen interrupted with, "You heard your mother." That's all Daniel needed. Besides, Daniel knew that after David fell asleep, Lynn would let him get up for a while.

Mrs. Rosen conducted her usual cursory check of window and door locks. It was her habit, and once she was assured all was secure, Mr. Rosen walked her out the front door. She stopped just outside the door and waited for the familiar 'click'. As she had always been instructed, Lynn turned the dead bolt.

Lynn returned to the two boys sitting in the middle of the living room. Daniel was getting frustrated with his Ferris wheel. David had lost interest and was busy with his coloring book and crayons. Now Daniel was on his own.

Lynn searched around the pile of spools and dowels and after a few minutes, she declared, "Aha! Here's the missing pin!"

She handed it to Daniel, and he inserted it into the proper place. Lynn put the remaining pieces in place and voila! The Ferris wheel was spinning around! Now David joined in the celebration. Lynn carefully picked up the Ferris wheel and placed on the coffee table.

"There," she said, "now that will be the first thing your Mom and Dad will see when they get home. A nice job! Let's get the rest of these picked up and put away."

David went back to his coloring and Daniel picked up the remaining pieces, placing them into the tube and putting them on the shelf in his room.

"Can we have a snack now?" Asked Daniel.

"Sure, David, put your coloring away and I'll make some popcorn," she called to the four- year-old.

"Will you read us a story?" Asked David.

"Go pick out a book, and we'll read it while we have our popcorn." David ran to his room and returned with a small Golden Book.

"Ah, that's a baby book!" Daniel teased his younger brother. "I'll pick one."

"But I like this story, Daniel," David whined.

"Let me pick a story you will both like, and one that I like too." Lynn suggested. She went to the big mahogany bookshelf in the den and selected Black Beauty.

"I'll read you a few chapters of this one, and then the next time, I'll read some more." The boys agreed that would be a good idea.

They curled up on the sofa, each with a small paper bag of popcorn. David leaned his head on Lynn's left shoulder, and Daniel's head was in Lynn's lap. They really liked Lynn, and she thought of them as her little brothers.

After less than a chapter was read, she felt David getting heavier on her shoulder. He was nodding off already. She gently nudged Daniel.

He looked up and she held her fingers to her lips,

"Shhhh, he's asleep." Daniel took the book from Lynn's lap and Lynn cradled David in her arms. She slowly stood up. He's really getting heavy, she thought. Seems like he's grown so much since she started babysitting.

When Lynn was thirteen, she started babysitting the two boys occasionally for about an hour, while Mrs. Rosen ran errands. In time, she was given a little more responsibility, caring for the boys in the summertime, while they were at the playground, or even just in the backyard. Mrs. Rosen was a very protective mother, and seemed to have her eye on David and Daniel at all times. It was a nice break for her to have Lynn around.

On July 8th, Lynn turned fourteen. She had gained the trust of the Rosen's and became their official babysitter.

Now, she placed David in his bed. Daniel followed closely behind her and whispered, "Can I stay up? He's asleep."

"You get into your bed for a few minutes, until we're sure he's sleeping soundly. I'll come back and check in a few minutes. If he's still asleep, then you can get up for a little while."

Daniel knew she would let him up. She always did. He shuffled across the hall to his room, closed the door behind him and slipped into his bed. He never needed a night light because the street lamp shone through his window. It illuminated his room just enough. He was a sound sleeper and he liked the door shut.

Lynn leaned over the sleeping little boy and turned on the dim night light on the night stand. She brushed the wispy curls from his forehead and kissed his plump rosy cheek. Before she covered him, she removed the little cowboy slippers and placed them on the floor beside his bed.

Lynn tiptoed out of the room, leaving the door open. She felt better with David's door open. He was in the habit of waking up, sometimes to use the bathroom, sometimes for a drink of water. In any event, she wanted to be sure to hear him.

She went into the kitchen to refill her bowl of popcorn and get a cold drink. When she opened the refrigerator, she smiled and thought, nobody would ever starve in this house. An assortment of snacks filled the lower shelf. She was sure Mrs. Rosen made a special effort to be sure there were ample snacks when Lynn was babysitting. She was really a nice lady. Lynn was happy with the Rosen family, and they were delighted to have Lynn!

Before Lynn, there was Patty, the girl next door. Patty lived at 421 Archer Boulevard. She was in high school when the Rosen's moved in next door, seven years ago.

Mrs. Rosen became acquainted with the Brazzini's and Patty was more than happy to babysit for Daniel. Patty Brazzini was a responsible, 15-year-old girl and right next door. Daniel was just an infant, and David arrived two years later. It was a perfect arrangement.

When Patty started dating, Mrs. Rosen allowed her boyfriend, Ted Rossi to come over after the children were settled. When an important affair came up and Patty was not available, Patty's mother, Theresa Brazzini was always accommodating. She had gotten acquainted with the Rosen boys and they often frequented her kitchen on days she would bake cookies.

Patty was an only child and she was grown. The Brazzini's enjoyed having the small boys around. When September 1953 rolled around, Patty was off to college and the Rosen's were looking for a suitable replacement.

Daniel had started first grade, and David was attending Community Sunshine Nursery School. Lynn's mother, Elaine Clarke, was the driver for the nursery school. Little David was one of the nursery school students she picked up and brought home every day. Mrs. Rosen was always out on the sidewalk in front of the house to greet her little boy. She and Mrs. Clarke would exchange greetings and pretty soon they discussed babysitters.

Gail Rosen asked Mrs. Clarke if she knew anyone that might be interested. At first, Brenda Chapman came to mind. She was comfortable about recommending Brenda. She also mentioned her daughter, Lynn. Although Lynn was only thirteen, and in the eighth grade, she'd been looking after her sister occasionally and perhaps Mrs. Rosen would like to meet her also.

Gail Rosen called Brenda. She told her she had been referred to by Elaine Clarke. Brenda arranged to meet Mrs. Rosen, and agreed to babysit the boys.

After a few weeks passed, Gail Rosen was pleased with Brenda, but Brenda had other ideas. She didn't like babysitting. That's when she spoke to Lynn about her dilemma. She wanted to tell Mrs. Rosen, but she didn't want Mrs. Rosen to be left without a babysitter. Lynn told her mother about the conversation with Brenda and asked what she should do.

"Why don't I call Mrs. Rosen. If she's not busy, we'll go over and talk to her about you replacing Brenda. You're a little young to sit at night, but maybe you can get to know the kids, and when you turn fourteen you'll be ready to stay in the evening. Won't hurt to talk to her. What do you think?"

"Sure, I'd like that." Lynn replied.

So, from there Lynn eventually became the official babysitter. Brenda was relieved that she hadn't left Mrs. Rosen stranded and she no longer had to babysit. It worked out well for all concerned.

Mrs. Rosen watched Lynn interact with the boys, and liked what she saw. Daniel and David liked Lynn, and Mrs. Rosen had the assurance that the Brazzini's were next door in the event of any emergency. She instructed Lynn to call Mrs. Brazzini if she ever needed to whenever she was caring for the children.

Lynn picked up the book she had brought. Great, I'll have a chance to read a few chapters and then have all day tomorrow to do whatever I want. She turned the TV down, and curled up on the sofa.

As she reached for the soda she had placed on the coffee table, she inspected the Ferris wheel Daniel had built earlier. With closer examination, she thought, not bad! He really put some work into that. Pretty smart kid for six. That reminded her, I'd better go check to see if David is asleep and let Daniel up for a while. He's probably wondering what's taking so long!

As she walked down the hallway toward the bedrooms, she sensed a quiet. Everything seemed to be still. It was almost eerie. She peeked into the bedroom. David had turned over and was curled up into a ball, sound asleep.

She went across the hall to Daniel's room. When she opened the door, she was surprised to find Daniel asleep also. Well, the little builder must have worn himself out. She closed the door and returned to the living room.

Ateenage boy paced back and forth in his small upstairs bedroom. He sat on his bed. Think, think, he told himself. Don't do anything stupid. She'll never talk to you again. She probably thinks you're a jerk anyway. If only he could get her to let him in while she babysat. She'd see him differently.

He'd walked past the Rosen's house almost every Saturday night. He'd arrive at 425 Archer Boulevard, watch Lynn Ann and the inner voices would start taunting him. He would give into the voices and continue walking up the boulevard to his grandmother's house.

She was always delighted when he stopped by. She always welcomed the company of her grandson. He was so kind and thoughtful. The young man would visit, she would make a snack and they would play gin rummy. He enjoyed his grandmother, but missed the hours of playing chess with his grandfather who had passed away a few years before.

Tonight, he would go to the Rosen's, only it would be different. He'd devised a plan. Surely, it would work. The porch light would be on. He would tap on the window, and when Lynn answered the door, he would scare her! That's it, I'll scare her he thought. Then, when she realized it was just a joke, she'd laugh and invite him to come in.

He prepared himself for his scheme. He donned an old jacket that belonged to his father. The teen was over six feet tall, but he didn't have the bulk of his father. The jacket hung on him. He looked into the mirror. Not much to be afraid of here, he thought. He placed a hat over his dark wavy hair and turned the brim downward. It cast a shadow over his face. Needing a shave, his face looked dark and mysterious. That's the look he was after. Surely, with the porch light behind him, standing in the doorway, he would look frightening to the young babysitter.

It was 9:00 and very dark. The masqueraded teen reached up to the shelf in his closet. On the shelf was an assortment of shoe boxes containing memorabilia he had collected over the years. Baseball cards he had collected throughout his younger years filled another. Tucked back into the far corner, out of reach of his 5'3" mother was a knife wrapped in a towel.

He took it down and unrolled it onto his bed. It was a carbine type bayonet he had purchased at an Army surplus store a few weeks before. He had wrapped the blade of the bayonet with a piece of brown paper. He wound a piece of thread around the paper and secured it with a tight knot.

Now, as he picked the weapon up from the bed, he slid the paper from the blade. He stroked the shiny blade, and replaced it into the make shift sheath and tightened the string. With a twist of his wrist, he slid the bayonet up the sleeve of the oversized jacket.

When he came downstairs, it was not difficult to leave the house unnoticed. His mother was watching TV. The living room was at the front of the house, and he slipped out the back door.

The rain was steady now. He turned up the collar of his jacket and hunched his shoulders, trying to avoid the rain. After he walked the first block, his shoes were soaked, but he had made up his mind tonight he was going to tell Lynn how he felt, and no rain storm was going to discourage him. He was driven by the thoughts of being with Lynn, the girl that was everything he could ever want a girlfriend to be, and after tonight, everyone would know, they would be a couple!

When he arrived at 425 Archer Boulevard, he was apprehensive and anxious. He took a deep breath and stood silently in the shadow of the street lamp. As he had expected, the porch light was on. He'd walked by so many nights before. Never having the nerve to stop. The wind rustled in the trees and cast an eerie shadow over the house. That voice inside him began to taunt him.

"You're nobody, why should she let you in? She'll probably laugh at you and tell you to get lost!" He couldn't bear that, so he decided to follow through with his well-thought out plan.

He walked up the front porch steps. His stomach ached. Again, he took deep breaths. As he stood at the door, headlights of a car turning onto Archer Boulevard scanned across the porch and the bulky figure standing there. He froze in place, fearing it may be the Rosen's returning early, but the car continued north up the boulevard.

Slowly, he walked to the window. There she was, curled up like a little kitten. She was reading. The console television across the room was on, but he couldn't hear it and she wasn't watching it. The volume was turned down.

As if some inner power took control, he moved closer to the window and tapped on the glass. She didn't move, so he tapped again using his ring to make a louder sound. She turned, and drew her face closer to the window to see past the reflection of the light. Lynn expected to see Lisa, but she recognized the night visitor. He smiled and gestured, suggesting she open the door to let him in.

She placed the open book on the table beside the sofa. A red tasseled bookmark served to mark the page. She was not frightened, but she was annoyed. What is he doing here? I'll just tell him I'm not allowed to have anyone in while I'm babysitting and he'll just go on his way. He's probably just passing by anyway, she thought.

As she approached the front door, she reached for the dead bolt. Turning the lock and door knob simultaneously, the door opened. Quickly, the intruder pushed the heavy door in and knocked Lynn off balance. In an instant, he slid the weapon from his sleeve, and yanked the paper from the blade.

Lynn was frightened and shouted, "What are you doing here? Get out!"

Then she saw the shiny blade. She screamed, "No, no, please no!"

The cruel, vicious attack began and Lynn felt the first thrust into her side. She gasped, and turned to run. She managed the few steps into the living room and he grabbed her hair. She was no match for her attacker as he continued pulling her toward him.

She grasped her side and felt the warmth of her blood between her fingers. Her attacker was frenzied by now. Although she had suffered at least four stabs to her arms, side and shoulder, she fought and kicked. He continued to deliver blow after blow, five, six . . . the deed had become euphoric to him. He couldn't stop. He struck a mighty blow with the handle of the blood soaked bayonet. It was so powerful it broke her neck. Like a lifeless rag doll, she crumbled to the floor.

He could hear the silence. It was dead silence now and he couldn't move. He stared at Lynn's lifeless body, now in a half sitting position, propped up against the blood spattered walls.

The silence was broken by a whimper of a small child. Suddenly the whimper became a deafening cry of fear and panic. The deranged attacker snapped out of his reveries and the cry became real.

He followed the crying and entered the bedroom of little David Rosen. By now, David was standing on his bed calling out to Lynn.

Between the sobbing, he called, "Lynn, Lynn!" Then he froze in place and looked into the eyes of the monster.

The helpless four- year- old backed into the corner of his small bed. The butcher took only two strides to reach the tiny figure and struck again. He plunged the knife into the four-year-old's tiny chest and the crying subsided. Again and again, he repeated the savage stabbing and the blood puddled onto the sheet.

Droplets of blood trickled into the little slippers on the floor. The killer was excited. His mind raced. He backed out of the dimly lit room, leaving little David Rosen crumpled between the bed and the corner. He shut the door, separating himself from the gore and carnage he had created.

The killer followed his bloody footprints back down the hallway and into the living room to his beloved Lynn. Did he think he had just imagined it all? It was done, all in less than ten minutes. Two beautiful lives ended in just ten minutes. It was like a lifetime passing before him.

Suddenly, the light from the television flickered onto Lynn's bloody body. He thought she moved. Could she still be alive? The brutal, indiscriminate butcher stood towering over Lynn's crumbled body. He became enraged, and repeated the stabbing until she lay motionless surrounded by the blood that had already began soaking into the vivid colors of the oriental carpet.

In silence he stood, mentally assessing his gruesome deed. He felt a slight gust of air and realized the front door was still open. Stepping over Lynn's body, he made his way to the foyer where the deadly struggle had begun. The bright light from the porch shone through the open door. He spotted his hat on the floor. It had fallen off during the struggle. As he reached for it, he noticed the brown paper he had wrapped around the weapon. He picked up the hat and wrapped the paper around the bloody knife. He slid the covered knife into his blue jeans pocket.

He felt a crunching sound under his feet as he walked toward the door. It was the light that had broken when he delivered the first blow. He had raised the knife above his head and hit the globe of the overhead light. It shattered on the floor. The foyer was dark. Silently, he closed the door and turned the dead bolt.

The porch light remained on. To passers by, everything would look normal. Hardly anything in the living room had been disturbed. The open book with the scarlet bookmark was just as Lynn had left it.

Beside the book, an opened box of Fanny Farmer's chocolates. His bloody hand reached into the box and removed two foil-wrapped morsels. Again, he stepped over Lynn as he would a sleeping dog. He exited through the side door, off the kitchen being careful to lock it behind him.

The rain was steady now. It felt exhilarating. He removed his hat and lifted his head to feel the rain pouring over his face. He was devoid of remorse, sorrow or regret. He was consumed in self gratification and justification of his horrendous deed. He began babbling out loud.

"She shouldn't have screamed. I wouldn't have hurt her if she had just let me in. They'll find her, and that will end all the torment she's caused me for so long. I'll be free from her. She's a demon, and deserved to die." In his own mind, his savage act was justified. He was convinced he had done what needed to be done.

At no time did his thoughts turn to little David Rosen. David was simply collateral damage.

The rain was cleansing. He felt the knife he had shoved into his pocket. It had pierced his denim pants and slightly punctured his thigh. He drew it out. Lynn and David's blood had started to cake on the shaft and into the ornamental etching at the hilt. The brown paper wrapper fell on the sidewalk and washed into the overflowing catch basins and sailed along the flowing gutters, taking all traces of the two innocent victims with it.

Suddenly the sound of sirens pierced the silence of the night. The killer looked down the boulevard and saw the flashing lights getting closer. An ambulance followed closely behind.

His heart was pounding. Thoughts raced through his head. The exhilaration of his deed vanished, transforming into panic. He put the hat on, pulling the brim down to shadow his face. He slouched and pulled the collar of the oversized coat up and stepped into the dark shadows of a large maple tree at the tree belt.

How could they have found her so quickly? Had he left just in time? Did the Rosen's return early, just as he was leaving and discovered the gruesome scene? Maybe a neighbor saw him. Every conceivable conclusion flashed through his now, throbbing head. He was certain Lynn was dead, and the little boy could never have summoned the police.

The cruisers raced past him with lights flashing and the deafening sirens blaring.

The teenage killer was petrified. He froze in place until he was sure the police and ambulance were unable to see him as they continued north, up the boulevard, passing the Rosen's house.

Once he was sure they were at a safe distance, he slipped from behind the tree and stepped up his pace. In minutes, he was jogging toward his street. Taking no chances of being seen, he cut through backyards, ducking clothes lines in an effort to avoid the light of the street lamps.

When he finally arrived at his house, he could hardly breath. He could hear the television on in his house as he stepped onto the front porch. He sat on the front porch taking deep breaths and tried to clear his thoughts. There was no doubt. This was surely clear consciousness of guilt. He began mentally concocting an alibi. It didn't take too much imagination. He would keep it simple. After all, he couldn't have been gone for more than an hour.

He sat a few more minutes and then walked in the front door. He slipped out of his shoes. He had deliberately walked through the puddles knowing the blood would be washed away. His shoes were soaked, but not with his victim's blood. He headed for the stairs leading to his bedroom. His mother called,

"Where have you been?" She asked. "It's really nasty out there."

"I was sitting on the porch." He replied, continuing up the stairs. That was it! No more questions!

He went directly to the bathroom. The blood soaked clothing had become heavy, drenched from the downpour. The blood seemed to be everywhere. He stripped to his underwear. He scrubbed his hands and face and noticed a small scratch on the back of his left hand. It wasn't bleeding, but it stung. It was the only defensive mark Lynn had inflicted as she fought for her life.

The clothes lay in a heap on the cold tile floor. The knife was on the porcelain sink. He quickly rinsed off the knife and placed it in the midst of the soiled clothing. Then he rolled the stained wet clothes into a bundle, with the knife inside. He took the cord from the bathrobe that hung on the bathroom door and tied it tightly around the gory bundle. Looking around his room, he decided to toss the bundle into the bottom of his closet.

It was then, he realized how tired he was. He was exhausted. The adrenalin rush had subsided. He turned down the blanket on his bed and slipped between the freshly laundered sheets. Briefly he recounted the deadly scene. It was over. Finally he was free of the torment that Lynn had caused. He turned out the light. The rain pelted against his window as he drifted into a deep sleep.

At 425 Archer Boulevard, the murder house was silent. The pendulum of the majestic grandfather clock standing in the foyer, was still. The time read 9:35. Never again would it mark time in the Rosen's home. The television displayed a test pattern indicating programming had ended for the day, precisely 11:00 P.M..

Daniel slept undisturbed in his room. His door had remained closed, and he slept unharmed, unaware of the macabre events that had taken place just across the hall. He had been spared.

At 11:30 a tan Chrysler pulled up directly in front of 425 Archer Boulevard. Mr. Rosen remained in the driver's seat as his wife exited and walked toward the front porch. The rain had let up and there was a refreshing night breeze. As she did every other Saturday when Lynn babysat, Mrs. Rosen would send Lynn out and Mr. Rosen would drive her the short distance to her house.

Gail Rosen approached the front door. She immediately noticed through the leaded glass, the foyer light was not on, but supposed it had burned out. She had her umbrella in one hand and her purse in the other, as she fumbled with her key.

She opened the door and took a few steps into the dark foyer. She heard the crunchy sound as she turned the corner toward the living room. On the floor was Lynn's lifeless body.

Mrs. Rosen gasped, and tried to scream, but no sound would escape. She struggled to breathe, gasping, fighting to make some sound. Finally she screamed, again and again,

"Oh Ben, Oh God! Ben, Ben!"

She rushed down the hallway toward the boys' rooms. By then Ben was racing through the front door. He could never have imagined what he was about to witness.

He knelt beside Lynn and searched for a pulse. She was cold, and he knew. As he stood to find his wife, his head whirled. He raced down the hallway and got to David's room.

From the doorway he saw Gail Rosen draped over the dead boy's body. She was moaning. She sounded like a wounded animal.

Ben turned to Daniel's room. Fear gripped every part of him. He began to perspire. What horror would be lying on the other side of the door? He opened the door and flipped on the overhead light. Daniel was sitting on his bed, rubbing his eyes trying to adjust to the sudden brightness in his room. He looked confused, but he was unharmed.

Gail picked up David and raced down the hallway screaming, "Call Dr. Frazier! Call Dr. Frazier. He's breathing. Call Dr. Frazier!" Her trembling blood-covered hand reached for the phone on the kitchen counter.

Mr. Rosen instructed Daniel to stay in his room and then ran to the kitchen. His wife was trying to dial the phone. Mr. Rosen took the limp body of David from her and she managed to dial.

A sleepy voice answered on the second ring.

"Hello. This is Dr. Frazier."

Before he could say anymore, he heard the wailing. He had never heard such terror, such anguish.

"It's Gail, David . . . Lynn. Come quick. My baby is dying! Please hurry. David is dying!"

The doctor had been their family doctor since Daniel was born. He was also a friend of the Rosen's and lived only two streets away.

"Gail, where is Ben?" Asked the doctor. Again, the only reply was hurry, David is dying.

"Gail, put Ben on the phone. Gail, get Ben on the phone." He wasn't getting anywhere. Mrs. Rosen became more and more hysterical.

The doctor, in a firm controlled tone said, "Gail, hang up the phone." Again, "Gail, hang up the phone."

He heard the click, and when he was able to get a dial tone, he immediately called the police and requested an ambulance to the Archer Boulevard address.

By then, Liddy Frazier was fully awake and getting dressed. She instinctively knew something was dreadfully wrong, and when she heard the name Gail, she knew it was Gail Rosen.

The doctor pulled his clothes on and grabbed his medical bag. His wife snatched the keys and followed behind him. When they got outside, Tom Frazier started racing up the street toward Archer Boulevard and the Rosen's house. Liddy was only a few paces behind him.

As they reached the house, the first person they saw was an elderly woman seated on the front steps. She had her arms around two young boys. One, six-year-old Daniel Rosen the other ten-year-old Peter Griffon. The elderly woman was Mrs. Griffon. She lived upstairs with her son, his wife and her grandson Peter. She was recently widowed, and often sat with Peter when his mother and father went out. Tonight was one of those Saturday nights.

It was obvious to the doctor this woman was on the verge of shock. The two boys huddled close to each side of the sixty-eight-year-old woman. Dr. Frazier gestured to his wife to stay with the three on the steps. He had no idea what was about to unfold inside. Until he was able to assess the situation inside, he preferred to spare his wife. She was an R.N. and he was confident she would be more helpful outside for the time being.

Just as the doctor entered the house, the sounds of a police siren and ambulance were heard. Steadily they grew louder and louder. They appeared, rounding the corner of Elm Street onto Archer. Their lights whirled. The cruiser pulled into the driveway beside the house. The ambulance backed up to the front steps.

Two uniformed police exited the cruiser, lights still flashing. They hurried to the four people sitting on the front steps. The first officer asked them to identify themselves. The second officer proceeded into the house. Mrs. Griffon gave the officer her name and stated she lived upstairs. She had heard Mrs. Rosen's screams and ran downstairs to see what was happening.

"It was horrible, so horrible!" She said sobbing. The police pressed her for more information. She told them, the front door was open and she walked inside. She saw Gail Rosen and Ben Rosen.

Ben was holding the bloody body of little David and Gail was screaming into the phone, "David is dying, David is dying."

She said she became faint and nauseous and started to back out the door when she spotted Daniel coming toward her with outstretched arms. She grabbed him and brought him out onto the porch. Then, she instructed him to stay on the porch while she went upstairs and woke Peter. With Peter in tow, she came back and sat with the two boys. She hoped someone would come. She knew her son would be home soon.

The officer asked if anything unusual occurred earlier in the evening. Mrs. Griffon thought carefully and said that she had heard a scuffle downstairs around 9:30. She wasn't particularly concerned about it. She thought the boys may have been up later than usual and were rough housing. She admitted she was watching TV and that she was a bit hard of hearing so the TV was probably a little louder than it should have been.

That was about all Mrs. Griffon was able to offer. Liddy identified herself and the two boys. She told the officers about the phone call to her husband and that the doctor was inside. She still did not know what had occurred inside.

All Mrs. Griffon would say is, "It's horrible, I can't believe it, poor Gail, it's so terrible!"

The officer told the four to remain on the porch. Liddy wanted to get into the house. She needed to know what was going on. She needed to be with Gail. Mrs. Griffon sat quietly. She knew Donald would be home soon.

Mr. and Mrs. Brazzini came rushing from next door. They asked Liddy, but Liddy was unable to relate anything to the concerned neighbors. One patrolman came out of the house and headed straight for the cruiser. He was calling in a double homicide and he needed detectives and backup on the double.

As he returned to the house, he briefly questioned the Brazzini's. Theresa Brazzini identified herself and her husband Mario. They had been home all evening and noticed nothing unusual.

Theresa asked the officer if she could take Daniel to her house next door until everything was sorted out. She was trying to shelter Daniel from as much of the mysterious events that had occurred inside the house. The officer agreed and Mrs. Brazzini took Daniel's hand and walked him to her house. Mr. Brazzini stayed behind. He needed to know what exactly had happened at his neighbor's home.

Donald Griffon pulled up behind the Rosen's Chrysler in front of the house. Donald and his wife leaped from the car and ran to the three on the steps. Liddy assured them that Mrs. Griffon and Peter were fine. Again, the officer approached the new arrivals and asked them to identify themselves.

Mr. Griffon told the officer that he and his wife had just arrived home. He and his wife lived upstairs with his mother and son. The officer had no reason to detain the distraught woman any longer and suggested Mr. Griffon take his family upstairs. Mr. Griffon took Peter's hand and Janet Griffon helped her trembling mother-in-law upstairs.

Sargent Detective Steven Logan had just finished his paperwork. He had stayed late, but had the next two days off. He looked at his watch, 11:55 p.m. The dispatcher handed him a message that had just come into the station.

"Just my luck! Looks like my weekend is shot!" He grumbled as he dialed the phone to reach Ray Gage, his partner.

"Ray, meet me at 425 Archer Boulevard." He said.

"Sounds like it's going to be a long night, pick up a couple of coffees on the way." He hung up the phone, grabbed his sports jacket from the back of the swivel chair and signed out.

Immediately, the dispatcher notified Police Chief Paul McNamara. This was the standard practice of notifications. In turn, the Chief would contact Captain Jack Mahoney.

The detective's car turned into the spot at the front of the house that had just been vacated by the ambulance. A few minutes after Steve had entered the house, Ray Gage arrived. He too, avoided the questions from the on lookers and went directly into the house.

By the time the detectives arrived, spectators were beginning to gather in small groups up and down the boulevard. It was obvious this was a very serious matter. Four patrol cars with flashing lights, followed by two detectives and the ambulance was leaving without picking up anyone. After the Griffon's had returned upstairs and Daniel was taken by the Brazzini's Liddy entered the house.

She asked the police officer at the door the whereabouts of Gail Rosen. He informed her she was in the living room. Liddy brushed past the officer to be at Gail's side. She looked to the left and saw the body of Lynn Ann Clarke, lying on the floor, surrounded by her own blood. Liddy didn't know Lynn, but she felt a sickening feeling in her stomach.

She went directly to Gail. Mrs. Rosen was very calm. She sat on the couch, with David still cradled in her arms. If Liddy hadn't seen the blood stained pajamas, she would have believed David was sleeping, but he was covered in blood. His light curls were matted in the dried blood. Mrs. Rosen was rocking back and forth and speaking in a soft soothing tone.

"It's okay baby, Mommy is here. Mommy is here baby, it's okay." She rocked and rocked. Liddy wasn't sure what to do.

Gail Rosen looked at Liddy and simply said, "I've got to put him back in his bed. He's fallen asleep."

As she stood, still clutching to the little boy, she started to weave. Liddy steadied her and held her as she walked slowly down the hallway toward David's room. As she passed the small group that had gathered in the kitchen, Liddy looked at Dr. Frazier with a questioning expression. Her husband gestured to her, to go along with Gail, so she continued walking with the grieving mother.

Upon the Frazier's arrival, the doctor had examined the young girl and the Rosen boy. He had confirmed they were both dead, the result of multiple stab wounds.

The autopsy report would later determine that David died after the first thrust, piercing his heart. It would also report the little boy suffered a total of twenty eight- stab wounds, twenty-seven of them, post mortem and a fractured skull.

Lynn's autopsy report would determine she had died after struggling with her assailant. Her death, the result of several stab wounds to her vital organs. Her heart and lungs were pierced several times. Her neck was broken. Both her wrists were bruised, and six of her fingernails were broken.

Gail placed David into his bed. The sheets were drenched in his blood. The walls were splattered with blood, and yet she seemed to be oblivious of any trace of the horrific scene. She placed a light blanket over David and left the room.

Liddy walked up the hallway with Mrs. Rosen and it was then the doctor approached the two women. He guided Mrs. Rosen to the sofa where he had prepared a hypodermic needle. The doctor administered the sedative and instructed Liddy to bring Mrs. Rosen into her bedroom and to have her lie down in her own bed. The sedative would take affect very soon. Liddy stayed with Gail until she fell asleep.

Liddy joined the others in the kitchen where the detectives were questioning all. The patrolmen had obtained as much information as they could, now the detectives would question everyone once again, hoping someone could offer something new.

A short time later, Captain Mahoney arrived. He entered the house, and spoke with the two detectives. Captain Mahoney was the Captain of the Detective Division. After assessing the situation at 425 Archer Boulevard, the Captain would assign Logan and Gage to the case.

The Captain looked at the bloody body of the teen, then, asked to see the second victim. Ray Gage led the Captain to David Rosen's room. The officer stepped aside to allow Gage and Mahoney into the guarded room.

The Captain was visibly shaken as he lifted the blanket that Mrs. Rosen had placed over the dead boy. Quietly, the detective and the Captain exited the room, leaving instructions to the officer guarding the room that no one was to be allowed inside.

The officer closed the bedroom door and positioned himself in front of the door.

The Captain returned to the group huddled around the kitchen table. He reached for the phone and called for the Medical Examiner then, the funeral director.

Four patrol officers were posted outside. They had secured the perimeter of the house, and prevented anyone from approaching within fifty feet. Four patrol officers were inside the residence. They had ushered everyone inside into the kitchen area in an attempt to prevent contamination of the murder scene.

Outside, flashbulbs were lighting up the entire vicinity. The media was no exception to the restrictions of the roped off area, they were not allowed inside. They were unable to get any information from the officers stationed at the exterior of the murder house. They would have to wait for the detectives to obtain any information.

Captain Mahoney informed the detectives that Dr. Paul Chapman, Medical Examiner would be arriving soon and that James & Ryan Funeral Home would remove the two victims. He ordered Gage and Logan to notify the girl's family as soon as possible.

Steven Logan was directing his questioning to Benjamin Rosen, while Raymond Gage concentrated his efforts on the remaining persons present in the house.

A newsman was seen trying to peek into the bedroom window where little David lie dead. The newsman was removed from the premises.

The media snapped pictures of the house, as well as the neighboring houses. Pictures of little David's abandoned tricycle parked beside the porch steps. Side view, frontal views of the house. They would be included in the feature article of the Sunday edition of the Stanfield Republican.

Mr. Rosen sat at the table, his head in his hands and tried to answer. Ben Rosen had telephoned his sister and her husband, Gordon and Millie Schaeffer. The Schaeffer's lived in the nearby town of West Stanfield. They had hurried to be with the Rosen's. They had arranged to take Ben, Gail and Daniel to stay with them.

Ben Rosen got up from the table. Steve followed him as he made his way into the living room. As they walked, Steve prodded him with questions that needed to be asked.

"Were the doors and windows locked when you got home, Mr. Rosen?" Asked Logan.

"Yes, Mrs. Rosen always checks everything before we leave. She's very careful about those things. She locked the back door, and when we left, she instructed Lynn to lock the front door behind us. She even waited to hear the dead bolt snap into place behind her."

Again, Steve Logan repeated his question. "Was the door still locked when you got home?"

"Yes," replied Ben.

"Would you mind taking a quick glance around? Is anything missing?" The detective continued.

One of the officers had placed a clean sheet over the butchered body of Lynn. They were still waiting for the Medical Examiner. The presence of Dr. Frazier at the scene did not preclude, nor negate the need for the medical examiner to confirm both dead at the scene.

Ben Rosen glanced at the young girl and covered his face with his hands. Steve Logan, gently put his hands on the fragile shoulders of Mr. Rosen and guided him to the further side of the room. There, Mr. Rosen saw the finished Ferris wheel on the coffee table. It had not been disturbed. It stood as a testament to the activity that had taken place only hours earlier. The last time he saw David alive.

He walked to the table, and gently touched the tinker toy structure. With a slight flip of his finger, it spun around, and then toppled to the floor. Steven bent to pick it up, but Ben waved him away.

"It doesn't matter now. It just doesn't matter." He continued to walk around the living room in a daze.

The blood spatters on the walls seemed to take on a bizarre pattern of their own. He walked into the foyer, and realized the familiar ticking from the old grandfather clock had subsided. It was an eight-day clock. He had wound it that day as he had done every Saturday since it was put in place seven years ago. It never stopped, but now it was silent. On a closer look, he could see it had been moved. Only a few inches. The marks from the clock's feet were visible. Small black circles on the polished hardwood floor that was now strewed with broken glass.

He mumbled to the detective, "Time stopped at 9:35."

He had no idea the significance this slight observation would have on the investigation.

As Steve Logan examined the small marks that Mr. Rosen had pointed out, he spotted a piece of string. It looked like string, looped and tied with a square knot. Using his pen, Logan picked it up. He held it up to the light. At closer examination, it was a blue strand of crochet thread. He removed a small brown paper envelope from his jacket pocket. The envelope had EVIDENCE boldly printed on it. He slipped the thread into the envelope and put it into his pocket. Mr. Rosen confirmed that nothing seemed to be missing.

The police photographer had arrived moments before and waited for specific instructions from the detectives.

Captain Mahoney and Sargent Raymond Gage walked through the house with the photographer. He took pictures of the first victim, lying on the living room floor. Next, they walked down the hallway that led to David's room.

The police officer stepped aside to allow the Captain, detective and the photographer admittance. When they entered the dimly lit room, the photographer looked at the little boy. He looked like he was sleeping, until Ray flipped on the overhead light.

The photographer took a couple steps back and audibly gasped. The flash bulbs started popping as he shot the blood-covered walls, the floor, the little cowboy slippers, the night light beside the bed and finally the little boy lying in the blood-soaked bed.

Captain Mahoney leaned over and pulled the light blanket off the boy. It was shocking to the photographer. There was little David, butchered. The photographer took a couple of photos and had to leave the room. He handed the camera to Ray and rushed down the hallway, through the kitchen and out the side door. Ray and the Captain stood behind holding the camera and looking around the room.

The photographer's reaction was understandable. Never had he been called to photograph anything like the massacre he was witnessing now. Ray looked up and spotted the blood on the ceiling. Actually on the ceiling! Cast off spatters. He was no pro, but he snapped a few pictures of the ceiling.

The photographer returned after a few minutes and assured Ray Gage he was able to finish up. He shot pictures of the bloody footprints that led to and from the bedroom. In the living room he took shots of everything he could. Flash after flash.

In the foyer, the clock, the broken light. Then he followed the footprints to the side door. A small wadded piece of foil lay just inside the back door. He photographed the bloody doorknob, both inside and outside. He followed the footprints to the small porch, down the four steps leading to the black top driveway. Then they vanished! The rain had washed every trace of the night marauder's visit.

The medical examiner finally arrived. It had been over an hour since the detectives arrived at the scene. Dr. Paul Chapman, M.E. met the detectives at the front door. After a short update, Captain Mahoney advised Logan and Gage it was time to notify Lynn Ann Clarke's family. The Captain would oversee the crime scene in their absence.

The two detectives walked to Ray Gage's car. The media held microphones over their heads and shouted questions to the detectives. Neither commented. By now, nearly one hundred neighbors had gathered outside. Their suspicions were confirmed when they saw the medical examiner arrive.

The doorbell pierced the silence at 48 Lynndale Street. Elaine Clarke rolled over and peered at the illuminated dial of the clock on the bed side table. It was 12:30 AM. She gently nudged her husband.

"Lynn must have forgotten her key again, will you go let her in?" Phil slid out of bed and headed for the front door.

Again, the bell rang. "I'm coming, I'm coming," he grumbled. He casually opened the door and was surprised to see two men standing on the front step. They held up their badges to identify themselves, and asked if they could step inside. Phil Clarke was wide awake now, and baffled. He stepped aside allowing the detectives' entry. As they stepped past him, he peered over their shoulders, expecting Lynn to be trailing behind them. For what reason, he had no idea.

"What's this all about?" He asked. "Is Lynn all right?" The detectives were somber and grim.

"Is Mrs. Clarke here?" Asked Steve Logan.

"Yes, she's in bed, what is going on?" Phil was starting to feel panic welling up.

"Could you ask Mrs. Clarke to come in here? This concerns your daughter Lynn Ann."

By then, Elaine had heard the voices and was already entering the living room where the three men stood.

"Please have a seat." Steve said, gesturing them to the sofa in the living room. Without a word, the two sat down.

"I'm sorry to have to inform you, there's been a terrible incident on Archer Boulevard this evening. One of the victims has been identified as your daughter, Lynn Ann." Steve Logan's voice was cracking, his mouth was dry. The couple looked at him in disbelief.

Finally Phil Clarke stood up in defiance and replied,

"You must be mistaken. Lynn was babysitting at Gail and Ben Rosen's all night. She should be home any minute now. You must be mistaken."

Ray Gage stepped forward and placed his hand on Mr. Clarke's shoulder, indicating that he should sit down.

"Lynn Ann and David Rosen's bodies were found about an hour ago, at the Rosen's. Positive identification has been made. I'm very sorry."

Phil Clarke dropped back onto the sofa where his wife had remained. Her only reply was, "No! No! No! It can't be!"

Phil wrapped his arms around his wife and she fought to free herself from his strong hold. Steve Logan and Ray Gage stood helplessly by. Phil had choked back the tears as best he could, but now with his wife on the verge of hysteria, he could hold back no longer. The two were wrapped together sobbing.

Phil managed, in a soft almost inaudible tone,

"Where is she, what happened? Who did it?" His demeanor changed abruptly. Now he was visibly angry. Angry at the detectives for delivering such a horrific message, angry and confused.

Steve began to answer his questions as briefly as he could. After all, he didn't have any answers. He tried to keep his voice steady, and hoped he would have a soothing affect on the anguished couple.

Just then, Barbara appeared. She was rubbing her eyes and trying to adjust to the bright lights in the living room. Her father's voice had awakened her. She had a questioning look on her face. Who were these men? Why were her parents so upset? Mr. Clarke rushed to Barbara's side, not knowing what to say, or do. He picked her up and held her. His grip was so tight she squirmed to free herself, for unknowingly he was hurting her.

In an effort to take charge of this dismal situation, Steven Logan asked,

"Is there anyone that she can stay with until we finish here?" It sounded cold, unfeeling, but he knew it would be better to get the young girl somewhere else as soon as possible.

Barbara started. "What's wrong Daddy? Who are these men? Where's Lynnie? Why is Mommy crying?" She fired one question after another, not waiting for any answers.

As best he could, and as calm as he could Phil answered,

"Lynn has had an accident and we have to go see her."

"I want to go too!" Answered the little girl. "I want to see Lynn!"

Searching for a reply, Phil looked to the detectives, silently asking what to do? Just as Ray Gage was about to speak, Elaine answered in a soft voice.

"I'm going to call Mrs. Chapman across the street, to see if you can stay there for just a little while. That way, you'll know when we get back, and she'll send you home right away. Okay Sweetheart?"

Reluctantly, Barbara agreed, but only if she could come home as soon as they returned.

Ray Gage caught Mr. Clarke's eye and signaled him to follow him into the next room. With Barbara wrapped in Elaine's arms, Phil walked into the kitchen with detective Gage.

"Can you call someone to stay with your daughter?" He asked.

Phil nodded and picked up the phone book. His hands were trembling. He could hardly read the pages through the tears he was trying so hard to hold back.

Ray took the book from him and asked the name. "John Chapman," was Phil's reply.

Ray made the call on behalf of the Clarke's. He tried to be as brief as possible when Mrs. Chapman answered the phone. After a short barrage of questions, she said she would be right over and take Barbara to her house. It would be a long night.

After Barbara had left, Steve Logan sat with Elaine in the living room. Ray asked Phil to join him in the kitchen.

Steve began, "I know this is painful, but we must ask you some questions.

"Please, please, not now!" Cried Mrs. Clarke. "I want to see Lynn! How can I answer any questions when you haven't told me what has happened to Lynn?"

Steve Logan tried to answer Mrs. Clarke gently, but there was no 'gentle' way of explaining to a mother that her child had just been butchered!

Still, he tried, "Mrs. Clarke, Lynn was the victim of a stabbing. The Rosen boy was also killed. Can you think of anyone that would want to harm your daughter?"

"You're asking me who would want to kill Lynn? Are you insane Detective?"

Logan began again, "I need a list of Lynn's friends. Please Mrs. Clarke. A list of friends and we'll continue this tomorrow. I need something to start with. It's very important."

The first name that came to mind was Lisa Jansen. "Oh God! Poor Lisa!"

"Where does Lisa live?" The detective pushed on.

"Dorset Street," answered Elaine.

"Anyone else Mrs. Clarke?"

"Yes, Brenda, she's right across the street. Brenda Chapman."

"Would that be the family who came for Barbara?" Asked the detective.

"Yes," she replied.

Again, Logan pushed for more names. Elaine was gathering her thoughts and started naming all the friends she could think of. There were so many. Lynn was so well liked. Names came pouring out, "Ginny, Frank, Warren, Susan, Pamela...," the detective stopped her.

"Can you give me the last names of these people? I'll need last names."

Elaine slowed down and repeated each name in full as the detective had asked. Some addresses, but mostly just names.

"I'm sorry Detective, that's all I can think of." Elaine said apologetically.

"You've done fine Mrs. Clark," replied the detective. Steve knew he could inquire at the school for the addresses. This would be a start. He and Ray Gage would follow up on Monday, at Lincoln High School. He hoped Ray was able to get something from Mr. Clarke.

Steve placed his notepad in his jacket pocket and began talking to Mrs. Clarke in a calming nature. Ray Gage was conducting a similar interview with Mr. Clarke in the kitchen.

Gage directed his attention to any acquaintances of his that might have a 'grudge' or any reason for wanting to harm his daughter. Mr. Clarke was unable to come up with any names. It seemed inconceivable that anyone would want to harm his daughter.

Then, as if something suddenly occurred to him, he mentioned the name 'Randy.'

Ray pressed on, "Who is Randy?"

Phil went on to tell the detective about the annoying telephone calls Lynn would receive from Randy. These calls went on over several weeks.

The detective asked, "Do you know his last name?"

"I don't know. Lynn didn't say. I know she was irritated that Randy wouldn't take no for an answer. Lynn would tell him she was not allowed to go out with boys." Phil shook his head in frustration.

"I don't know the kid. I should have asked, I should have taken more interest in what was going on. I just didn't think Lynn was that bothered by him." By now, Phil was getting weary.

Still Ray pressed for more. "Anything else you can tell me about this Randy character?"

Phil answered, "Lynn said he wanted her to meet him at the movies. Lynn takes her sister nearly every Saturday afternoon to the Loew's Poli, down on Archer. She said he would hang around at the theater, and she just ignored him. She never said that he approached her. She didn't seem upset or concerned. Mostly annoyed. I think he goes to Lincoln. I'm not sure."

Ray Gage noted Randy's name and underlined it. He would definitely be a 'person of interest'.

"You've been very helpful Mr. Clarke. We'll talk again tomorrow."

Phil Clarke joined his wife in the living room. Steve Logan was sitting with Elaine Clarke. By now, Mrs. Clarke was insistent on going to the Rosen's to her daughter. The two detectives advised against it, but the Clarke's would not be dissuaded.

Mr. and Mrs. Clarke were escorted to the unmarked detective's car that had been parked at the front of their house. They huddled together in the back seat. Each trying to console the other, still not comprehending the magnitude of what was to lie ahead of them.

The James & Ryan Funeral Home hearse rolled to the front of the murder house. There was a hush throughout the spectators that had gathered.

The funeral director stepped out accompanied by two assistants. All were dressed in black suits, black overcoats and all wore black leather gloves. The crowd murmured in disbelief as they watched, first Lynn Ann Clarke's body being delivered to the awaiting hearse, then little David Rosen. What they had suspected, was now confirmed. A double homicide at 425 Archer Boulevard, Stanfield, MA. The crowd parted to allow the hearse to slowly pull away with the two small victims.

Next to leave was the medical examiner, then the police photographer.

The Clarke's arrived at the Rosen's at 1:30AM. The street had been partially blocked off and traffic was reduced to one lane, keeping everyone a distance from the house. The crowd had grown substantially since Gage and Logan left for the Clarke's. Passing cars had pulled over and watched as police arrived and left.

Ray Gage jumped from the car to take a position in front of the Clarke's. He knew they were not prepared for what they were about to see. He wanted to be close by their side at all times.

Flashbulbs were popping as the Clarke's emerged from the detective's car. Microphones were held high above their heads, hoping to pick up even the slightest comment. The police weren't sharing any information. Rumors were already starting, but nobody actually knew.

As the Clarke's entered the house, they expected to see Lynn. They had missed her by only minutes. Dr. Chapman, the medical examiner, had left and informed the officers remaining at the scene that the two victims were transported to James & Ryan Funeral Home, where the autopsies would be performed by Dr. Chapman, the following day.

This was standard procedure at that time. The hospitals were equipped with a morgue, but did not have the facilities to perform autopsies. The funeral homes were equipped and the medical examiners performed the autopsies at the funeral homes.

The Clarke's went directly to Mr. Rosen who had returned to the kitchen. Elaine Clarke asked where Daniel and Gail were. Ben Rosen told her Daniel was safe next door with the Brazzini's and that Gail had been sedated and asleep in the back bedroom. The Captain approached the grief-stricken parents of Lynn Ann and spoke briefly, offering them comfort, but his words fell on deaf ears.

Mr. Clarke was aimlessly walking around the living room. He saw the huge stain on the carpet, where his daughter had been lying. The sheet she had been covered with was beside the bloody mass. He glanced over at the sofa area. There was Lynn's book, opened to page 46, Jane Eyre. A half-filled bottle of Coke was on the coffee table. His heart ached, his entire being ached. How would he ever get through this? How would Elaine be able to manage? And what about Barbara?

The sedative was beginning to wear off. Mrs. Rosen was groggy, and it was of utmost importance to escort her out of the house as soon as she woke. Mrs. Schaeffer went to the Brazzini's to get Daniel. He was asleep, and she was able to get him into the car without waking him.

Mr. Rosen picked up his wife's purse and coat and guided her to the front door. She was weak and barely able to walk on her own. He put her into the back seat of the Schaeffer's awaiting car and joined her, holding her every second. The Schaeffer car pulled away.

Next, Dr. Frazier and his wife Liddy prepared to leave. The detectives spoke to them briefly, but the Frazier's were not able to add anything significant. The doctor advised that, upon his arrival, both victims were deceased, regardless of what Mrs. Rosen had claimed.

She was hysterical and on the verge of shock. He would visit her again in the morning to evaluate her condition and recommend any further treatment. Then, without anything further to contribute, they left.

At 2:00AM, the only persons remaining in the house were Steve Logan, Ray Gage, Elaine and Phil Clarke and Captain Mahoney. Outside, two police officers remained to deter any curiosity seekers from nearing the house.

The Captain took Steve Logan aside and indicated that any further questions to the distraught Clarke's could wait. Nothing would be gained tonight. Phil and Elaine Clarke wanted to go home. They wanted Barbara close to them.

Ray Gage walked them through the blood-stained foyer toward the door. Just as they were about to step out onto the porch, Phil Clarke saw the tan raincoat, splattered with blood. He reached for it. Gage asked him to leave it, possible evidence, but Steve Logan signaled to let him take it. Then the grievous father looked down at Lynn's loafers just below the raincoat. He picked them up and rubbed his fingers across the shiny pennies. He began to sob as he rolled the raincoat around the shoes. He tucked the bundle under his arm and took his wife's hand. She leaned on his shoulder and the two walked to the detective's car.

Steve Logan and Captain Mahoney remained at the scene. Ray was to return after he delivered the Clarke's to their home and assisted them in any way possible. He wanted to be sure Barbara was safely home with them. Surely there would be phone calls to be made. Relatives needed to be contacted.

Gage knew for certain the Stanfield Sunday Republican would carry this murder as their lead story. Ray could envision the headlines now. He wished he could shield the Clarke's and Rosen's from the media and the heart wrenching agony they would have to bear.

The bizarre, clues and turn of events that would develop in the next two weeks would be far beyond anything even a seasoned detective could have possibly imagined.

As the unmarked car pulled into the Clarke's driveway, Gage looked in his rear view mirror. Elaine and Phil Clarke were huddled together. He hadn't spoken to them since they left the Rosen's. They had driven the short distance in total silence. Ray cleared his throat and turned to the couple in the back seat.

"Would you like me to stay with you? Is there anyone I can call?" His voice seemed strained. He didn't have the right words. What are the right words?

Mrs. Clarke was amazingly gracious. She answered,

"Please come in Detective. It's been a long night for you. Phil will get Barbara, I'll make coffee."

She stepped out of the car, and the balmy air seemed refreshing. There was a gentle breeze and at 2:00 AM there was a lull. The early morning hour was peaceful.

Ray took Elaine's keys from her hand and hurried to the door. Phil Clarke remained in the car. Gage opened the door for Mrs. Clarke and waited outside for Mr. Clarke. He looked toward the parked car and after a few moments, started walking back.

As he approached, the car door was still open and he bent to look in. Phil Clarke was sobbing. He saw the sweat beading on his forehead and for a few seconds considered calling for medical assistance. Ray handed Phil a handkerchief and Phil wiped his drenched forehead.

Then he straightened his posture, and softly said, "Thanks Detective."

"Are you okay?" Ray asked with genuine concern for the bereaved father. "Do you want me to call anyone? Do you take any medication?"

Mr. Clarke took a deep sigh and leaned back onto the seat.

"No, I'm all right. Where's Elaine?" He asked, looking toward the front door of the house.

"She's inside. Do you need any help?" Asked the detective.

"No, I just needed to catch my breath. I have to get inside. Will you come in for a few minutes?"

"Sure, anything you want Mr. Clarke," answered Gage. With the rolled-up raincoat and shoes still under his arm, Phil and the detective walked up the front walk. When they got inside, the telephone was ringing.

Ray asked Mr. Clarke,

"Do you want me to answer?" Phil nodded and Ray picked up the phone.

"This is the Clarke residence." He spoke into the receiver.

"This is Marge Chapman. Whom am I speaking to?" She asked.

"This is Detective Sargent Gage." Replied Ray. "Can I help you?"

Marge Chapman was silent for a moment. She wasn't sure what to say.

Finally, she said, "This is Marge Chapman, is Elaine able to come to the phone?" Ray placed his hand over the mouthpiece of the phone and asked Elaine if she wanted to take the call from her neighbor.

"Yes." She replied. Ray handed her the phone.

"Marge? This is Elaine. Is Barbara awake? Phil will be right over to get her." Elaine spoke rapidly. She was trying to avoid questions that she knew Mrs. Chapman would ask.

Mrs. Chapman answered, "Barbara is asleep on the couch. Would you like me to wake her or do you want her to stay? Oh Elaine, I'm so sorry. I'm so sorry."

Mrs. Chapman was crying and Ray heard Elaine's voice suddenly sound soothing.

"I know Marge. Please don't cry. I know." Mrs. Clarke was actually trying to be a comfort to her neighbor!

"Phil will be over in a couple of minutes. Don't wake Barbara. Maybe we can get her to bed without disturbing her. Marge, where is Brenda? Are John and Karl there with you?" She asked.

"John is out of town. An emergency in Connecticut. Karl is sleeping and Brenda is here with me. Brenda is pretty upset. She heard the phone ring when you called earlier. I had to tell her what I knew." She started crying again.

"I'll put the porch light on for Phil. Is there anything I can do? Please, anything..." Elaine cut her off in mid-sentence.

"No Marge. Please come over here with Brenda.?" She asked and placed the receiver back on the hook.

Ray watched as Elaine returned to the kitchen. She had coffee on the stove and began putting cups on the table. Ray had witnessed this behavior before. She was finding her 'comfort zone', a temporary 'fix'. It was a protective shield that some people find to get through traumatic events. If he was correct in his observation, she would postpone her grieving. She would somehow find her way through all the tragedy, but for how long? There was no way of knowing. He saw her pick up a piece of cardboard from the counter. She pressed it against her breast. Ray went to her. It was a hand made "Happy Anniversary" sign. Ray placed it face down on the counter beside the half- eaten cake.

Ray Gage and Elaine were seated in the living room sipping their coffee when Marge Chapman opened the front door and Phil came in carrying Barbara. Brenda followed behind. It was clear, she had been crying. Phil went directly to Barbara's room and Marge Chapman rushed to Elaine.

"Oh Elaine, I'm so sorry!"

Elaine stood to allow room for Marge to sit down beside the detective. She went to Brenda who had remained in the open doorway. Elaine wrapped her arms around the teenager and hugged her as hard as should could. They didn't say anything. For several moments, they just held onto each other. Then Elaine took Brenda's hand and led her to a chair in the living room.

"Marge, let me get you some coffee. Thank you for minding Barbara. I just don't know what I'm going to tell her. I just don't know how to tell anyone. It's all such a blur. The Rosen's are with Ben's sister in West Stanfield. Daniel is okay, but little David..." Elaine seemed to be almost babbling as she spoke to Marge Chapman.

Marge took the coffee pot from Elaine's trembling hand and told her to sit down, she'd get the coffee herself. She poured her coffee and refilled Ray Gage's empty cup. Brenda sat, her legs tucked under her and her head rested on the arm of the overstuffed chair. Her eyes were swollen, and she just stared across the room.

Phil returned to the small group. "She's still asleep," he reported. He picked up the bundle he had carried. Lynn's raincoat and shoes.

"What do I tell Barbara? How can I explain her sister has been murdered? God, I don't even understand it myself. "

He clung to the bundle. No one answered. Phil joined the others in the living room. As he passed Brenda, he gently touched her shoulder.

Ray thought of questioning Marge and Brenda Chapman but thought it better to wait until the next day. By now, it was 2:30AM. Ray knew he should be back at the crime scene with his partner. He placed his cup in the kitchen sink and handed Mr. Clarke his card.

"I have to leave. Call me anytime, day or night if you need anything. My home phone is on the back of the card. Please don't hesitate."

The detective drove directly back to 425 Archer Boulevard. As he arrived, the Captain was leaving.

"I'll see you at the station in the morning." He addressed the two detectives. "Go home and get a few hours sleep."

There was a police cruiser still parked in the driveway. The upstairs apartment was dark. Steve met his partner in the doorway.

"What have you got?" Asked Ray. His partner looked exhausted. Ray was tired also. The uniform police joined the two detectives. They had been posted outside the house until now, watching for any curiosity seekers who might be trying to get a closer look at the grizzly aftermath of the horrific scene.

"You guys can go. Looks like we've got everything covered. Thanks, get some sleep." Steve dismissed the two officers.

Steve and Ray went through the house room by room, all the shades were drawn. They turned out lights, locked doors and windows and finally, locked the front door. The house was secure. They sat on the front step.

Steve Logan broke the silence.

"I don't have much Ray." He said, almost apologizing to his partner. " The place was clean. Except for the blood."

"What the hell do you suppose we're dealing with here? This had to be a demented son-of-a-bitch! Did you see those two kids? This butcher has to be a nut case. I just don't get it. Why them?" He asked, not expecting an answer.

The elder detective ran his fingers through his slightly graying hair. He shook his head.

"It's going to be hell. I can't even think of a motive, it's senseless!" He was tired, but more angry! He'd been up for nearly twenty- four hours, and fatigue was starting to take its toll.

"Come on pal," Ray broke in. "Let's swing down to Stella's and get something to eat. I'm starved."

Stella's was an all night diner in the Breckwood section of Stanfield. It was a well-known stop for most of the dog watch of the Stanfield police.

"You're on. Let's go!" Steve answered pulling himself up with the aid of the wrought iron railing. "And you can buy!"

"My pleasure." Ray answered, as he slid into the driver's seat. Steve Logan started his car and followed Ray to Stella's.

They pulled into a parking spot in front of the old diner. At 3:00 Sunday morning, the parking lot was almost empty. The only patrons of Stella's at this hour were truck drivers and police. Fridays and Saturdays were a different story. The bars closed, and Stella's filled up. The two detectives were relieved when they drove up to the desolate eatery.

Ray Gage slid into a booth and reached for the menu. Steve walked directly to the restroom. A splash of cold water would work wonders for him right now.

A middle-aged waitress approached the booth.

"You guys look like something the cat dragged in. How's it going Ray?" She asked in her usual cheerful tone.

Steve returned and slipped into the seat across from Ray.

"Betty, make it hot and black!" He ordered.

"That's it? You came all the way down here just for coffee and to see little 'ole me?" The stocky waitress joked.

"We'll be ready to order by the time you get that coffee over here."

Betty was accustomed to Steve's usual abrupt manner, but tonight she sensed this was not a night for joking with her favored detective.

"You got it honey, I'm all yours tonight!"

Steve looked around. She wasn't kidding. The only ones in the place were the two detectives, a tired short order cook and good 'ole Betty.

Ray leaned over the table and started. "So what'ya think partner?" He asked.

"I think, I'm going to eat a very large omelette, drink my coffee and go home." He replied.

Betty placed the heavy worn mugs of coffee on the table. She pulled a pencil from behind her ear and waited for the order.

"Two bacon and cheese omelettes, and white toast." Ray responded to the waiting server.

"You got it!" She answered, and shouted the order back to the cook. She returned to the counter and continued filling the salt and pepper shakers.

"You must have something, Steve. That place looked like a butcher shop. There must be some kind of lead, anything?"

"Nope. Nobody saw or heard anything. Like somebody just dropped in, hacked the hell out of two kids, and went home to bed. What have you got Ray?"

"Got a name from the father. Kid by the name of Randy. He says the kid's been trying to get Lynn Ann to go out with him. According to the father, he didn't want to take no for an answer. Kept calling, hanging around the movies, you know the type, pain in the ass."

Ray continued, " The father didn't seem to be concerned about him. Lynn never indicated she was afraid of him, just that he was irritating." Ray didn't have much. He knew that, but the difference was, this was not a friend of Lynn's.

His partner's list would surely be helpful, but only if one of them could provide a last name for Randy. Otherwise, it would be like interviewing Lynn Ann Clarke's fan club. Nobody would have a harsh or negative word to say about her.

The two detectives knew they would have to follow through on anything that even resembled a clue or lead. They ate, without much conversation. Both were mentally laying out some type of plan.

Finally, when they were finished eating, Steve handed a small envelope to his partner. Ray recognized it. No detective worth his salt ever left the station without a few of those tucked away. He took the envelope from Steve.

"What's this?" He asked as he opened the flap.

"Found that in the entranceway at the Rosen's." Steve replied.

"What do you think it means? It's a piece of thread, am I missing something?" Ray asked.

"I asked Mr. Rosen if his wife did any type of knitting or sewing. Maybe some of that fancy stuff with colored yarn, you know, crocheting." Steve answered.

"Guess what? Ben Rosen says his wife never sewed in her life, never mind anything fancy. He said he never saw any thread like this." Steve sounded a little excited.

"Well, maybe the girl did. Maybe she brought over some of that crocheting with her, you know, to have something to do while watching the kids." Ray replied.

"Nope, asked Mrs. Clarke, she says no." Steve took the envelope containing the blue crochet thread from his partner.

"This case is going to be tough my friend. What we have here, is a thread of evidence. That's it, a single thread of evidence."

The two detectives stood up. Ray picked up the hand-written slip the waitress had left on the table and walked over to the counter. Betty took the bill along with the money. Ray leaned over the counter and kissed her on the cheek.

"Cheer up honey, Mr. Personality needs some sleep." He said, trying to apologize to the waitress for his partner's behavior.

Steve was in the parking lot standing by his car. Ray joined him and both decided to go home, get a little sleep and agreed to meet at the station by 9:00. It was close to dawn when they drove away.

Detective Raymond Gage and Detective Steven Logan were about to launch the most intensive murder investigation in the history of Stanfield.

Detective Raymond Gage was 42 years old. He'd joined the Stanfield Police Department in 1942, twelve years before. He was promoted to Sargent, and was selected to serve under Captain Jack Mahoney, in 1946. Eight years of experience in the detective division.

Ray pulled into his driveway on Apple Orchard Lane. His house was modest, but adequate. Ranch style, two bedrooms and comfortable. His wife decorated the simplest room to look inviting and warm.

His daughter was attending a local college, so finances were stretched to the limit. Mrs. Gage made do, and seldom complained. Ray's work worried her but she knew if she discussed it with him, nothing would change. He was dedicated to the department and would not consider any other profession. She worried quietly, but daily. It was nights like this, she tossed and turned, and slept very little. She heard Ray as he placed his keys on the kitchen counter.

Linda Gage was an attractive blonde. Every year, she turned heads at the Policeman's Ball. Ray was pleased with the way Linda took care of herself. She still had the figure of a twenty-five-year-old. She still 'turned him on'.

Now, Linda was up, making coffee.

"God, Linda, it's dawn. Go back to bed." Ray said, wrapping his arm around his wife's neck.

"I know Ray, but I haven't slept all night, so, I might as well get up and find out what's kept you out all night. You'd better make it good!" She jested, poking him in the arm.

Ray sunk down on the kitchen chair. "You don't want the details of this one, Hon. Really." Linda detected a serious tone in her husband.

"Pretty bad one huh?" She asked. "You going to the station later?"

"Pretty bad," Ray repeated, then gave Linda a brief run down of what had taken place earlier.

"I'm going to lie down awhile. Will you wake me by 8:00? I told Steve I'd meet him at 9:00."

Linda turned off the coffee and followed Ray into the bedroom. He stripped to his shorts, and crawled into bed. In minutes he was asleep. Linda cuddled up beside her husband. Ray was safe, Mary Ann, her daughter, was asleep in the next room, and now, she would sleep peacefully.

Detective Steven Logan was 52. He had joined the Stanfield Police Department twenty years ago, 1934. He was a seasoned detective with fifteen years experience.

Steve was home and flopped on the sofa. His shoes were in the middle of the room, his jacket flung over a chair and pockets emptied on the coffee table. He felt like he'd been awake for three days.

His mother-in-law had undergone surgery the week before and his wife was in Connecticut nursing her back to health. Steve and Katherine had no children. Katherine had wanted to have at least three, but was unable to conceive. After ten years of trying, Steve and Katherine had resigned to being childless. Between the two of them they had eight nieces and nephews, and they were the favorite aunt and uncle to each of them. Their lives were full.

Steve Logan didn't enjoy the bachelor's life he'd been experiencing for the last week, but after tonight's bloody scene, he was happy to come home and not have to relive it with Katherine. She insisted on knowing every detail of every major case Steve was involved with, but she was way too emotional to handle it. He hoped he would be through the investigation by the time she came home.

Stanfield Police Department:

For nearly a decade, the Stanfield Police Department was recognized as the finest in the Commonwealth of Massachusetts.

The Stanfield Police Department, from the Chief to the Patrolmen, were plain, friendly people. They were the guardians of their city. Most (four out of every five) were born in Stanfield. They were bonded to their communities, and dedicated to the safety and welfare of the people who lived there.

The patrols worked three shifts.

There was a time, when a lone constable would have handled Stanfield's crime problems. By 1950, the police department had grown to over 300 officers, and 125 auxiliary police. There were countless specialists to solve complex crimes and maintain law and order.

The number of vehicles on the streets of Stanfield had doubled in a short 15 years. This created a traffic problem. The police department developed a Traffic Division, headed by a Traffic Specialist. It was the Traffic Specialist's responsibility to study the layout of the city and develop plans to accommodate the growing number of motor vehicles, including the large trucks, an industry that the city had become dependent upon.

In 1950, the city boasted that there had not been one traffic related fatality in over 2 years! Soon, the division developed into the Traffic Bureau, a division within the Police Department. The Bureau was headed by the Traffic Specialist. The bureau studied charts, statistics and reports. All working towards a common goal; to keep people out of the hospitals and ultimately, out of the morgue.

In the 1952 the Vice Squad was replaced by the Crime Prevention Bureau.

The objective of this bureau, again, a branch of the police department was to prevent crime, before it occurred.

Targeting young people with problems and women who were treated as social outcasts, the CPB developed a procedure to accomplish this goal. It was staffed with experienced policewomen, juvenile officers, a medical doctor and a psychiatrist.

The police department evolved from guns and blackjacks adding wisdom and sensitivity. Each officer was schooled in every phase of police operations. Each police officer was periodically tested and retrained.

The Stanfield Police Department became visible in the 50's. They participated in community activities, and visited the schools, instructing the elementary school students in safety, forming a common bond. The police were friends of the community.

The police department consisted of one generation following the next. In the 1950's, ten officers had fathers on the force, thirty had brothers on the force.

There was a 'brotherhood' among the men in blue. They were extended family, and displayed genuine concern for their fellow officers and their families. They were a benevolent group who had advanced far beyond the beat-pounding, crime-smashing days.

The efforts of the restructured police department resulted in a considerable decline in crime. Stanfield, per capita, proudly boasted the lowest crime rate throughout the Commonwealth from 1950 through 1955.

Every candidate was afforded equal opportunity to advance through the ranks, from patrolman, to sergeant, to lieutenant and rising to captain. Deputy Chief and Chief of Police were always in a young rookie's sights.

By 1954, Chief Paul McNamara had become a national authority on criminology and a regular lecturer of the F.B.I National Academy. The Chief had come up through the ranks. He encouraged every member of his department to further their expertise whether it be police lab work, ballistics, or investigations. He welcomed all new ideas and gave each careful consideration. He held informal interviews with his men, and made it a point to know each one.

When the Chief detected a trace of 'extra perception' in one of his patrolmen, he called him into his office. He had detected this in one other young patrolman a few years earlier.

Steven Logan had been promoted to Sargent, and had become part of the detective division. Steve worked with several other detectives, but did not have a permanent 'partner'.

Raymond Gage walked into Chief McNamara's office as patrolmen and exited as a detective, and Steven Logan's permanent partner. They were given no assigned beat. They were to cruise the city on their shift. Soon, their arrest records would pay tribute to the Chief who had recognized their ability and created the "Free Lance Patrol."

The Stanfield Police of the '50's made their city a better and safer place to live. Raymond Gage was quickly promoted to the rank of Sargent.

Sunday, September 26, 1954 AM
Stanfield Sunday Republican

BABYSITTER, 14 AND 4-YEAR-OLD MURDERED

The editor had stopped the presses, and the reporters turned in their full stories. The headline originally laid out by the editor was knocked down below the fold of the front page.

The reporters had done a thorough job with the limited information they were receiving at the scene. A picture of the Rosen house spanned across four columns of the page. The lead story described the gruesome scene.

Logan and Gage arrived at the police station at 9:00 Sunday morning. Each carried a copy of the morning paper and a cardboard cup of steaming coffee.

The station was buzzing with detectives and patrolmen. Chief Paul McNamara was meeting in his office with Captain Jack Mahoney.

Steve and Ray went directly to their desks. Both detectives' 'In' boxes were filled with the police reports that had been compiled from pages of notes. Most were flagged, *'priority'*. The police photographer had deposited dozens of 8 x 10 glossy photos on the two detectives' desks.

Steve Logan began sifting through the mountains of paperwork. Ray Gage leaned back in his chair and examined the photos, one by one.

As Logan scanned his own notes, he hoped something would match up with the reports now spread across the surface of his desk. He needed something, and he found it.

One of the reports recounted an interview with a man by the name of Charles Latham. Mr. Latham had approached one of the officers at the scene and reported he had witnessed a man standing on the front porch of the Rosen's house at about 9:30 Saturday night. He described the person on the porch as at least six feet tall. He wore a hat and a heavy jacket.

When asked what drew his attention to this individual, Mr. Latham said 'because the house stood out among the others'. He stated that the houses on either side were not 'lit up' like this one. The porch light was bright and as he turned onto Archer Boulevard, the house was 'directly in line of his headlights'.

Maybe it would be the clue he was looking for. He flipped through his own notes. When he got about half way through the scribbled notes, there it was.

"Bingo!" He shouted. Ray Gage along with most of the others in the room looked over at Logan. "That's it! The time of the murder."

Ray was up and walking toward his partner. "What the hell are you talking about?" He asked.

"9:30, that's when it all came down!" Steve Logan answered. "Take a look at this Ray." He directed Gage to the police report, and his own notes.

"Mr. Rosen noticed the clock had stopped. He said it never stopped. I know how those grandfather clocks work. They're very sensitive. If they get bumped, or moved, they stop. They have to be perfectly level. The clock stopped at 9:35. It had been moved about an inch or so, Ben Rosen pointed it out to me." Steve was excited. It wasn't much, but it was a start.

Ray was sifting through the police reports on his desk.

"Look at this!" He shouted to Steve. "The woman upstairs reported she heard a scuffle downstairs around 9:30."

Steve felt a surge of energy through him. Time of Lynn Ann's murder, 9:35. Description of her killer, six-foot male, wearing hat and heavy jacket. Those two leads in addition to the thread he had picked up in the hallway, was the basis of their investigation. Not a whole lot to go on, but it's all they had.

Ray's thoughts turned to Randy. Randy who? How tall is Randy. Where was Randy at 9:30 Saturday night?

Maybe there would be a speedy arrest. His mood swung from dismal to optimistic.

The Chief called the two detectives into his office. Captain Mahoney stood and shook hands with Logan and Gage.

"I'm going to call everyone into the squad room in a few minutes." The Chief started. "I'd like to have something to give them. What have you got gentlemen?"

"Well, Chief," Steve Logan began, "not much, this guy's like a phantom. All he left behind was a trail of blood, all belonging to the two victims I'll bet." Steve searched the face of the Chief. He wanted something, and he didn't look like he was about to settle for little else.

Ray could sense Steve was groping for something to add. He wasn't sure how Steve was going to handle the newly discovered lead, but one thing was certain, Steve Logan was not one to hold back. He shot a look at Steve. Logan took the cue from Ray and added,

"We think we know the time of the murder. At least the time the struggle started in the front foyer."

Steve went on to explain how he had arrived at this bit of information. Then he took the small evidence envelope from his pocket and marked the date and time and location it had been collected.

"I picked this up in the front hallway at the Rosen's. Nobody connected with these victims, that is neither the Rosen's nor the Clarke's recognized this thread as anything they would come in contact with."

Steve continued, "The perpetrator must have had it on him. He must have dropped it. Maybe it was wrapped around the weapon in some way. I say, find the thread that matches and you've got your killer."

Captain Mahoney was listening very intently. He was impressed with the deduction Steve was exhibiting.

"That everything Logan?" Asked the Chief. "Can we let this out to the media? It's your case now."

He spoke to Captain Mahoney. "I want Logan and Gage on this. Give them all the backup they need."

"You heard the boss, gentlemen. It's you're baby. I'm putting two additional teams on with you. Connelly, Broderick, Morgan and Mallory. Now let's get to the briefing and find this bastard!"

The Chief led the three men through the large room. He summoned all to the 'squad room' and disseminated all the information he had collected from Gage and Logan.

All patrolmen, on all watches were directed to be looking for anyone that could be a possible suspect. Nothing was to be left to chance or overlooked. All information was to be shared throughout the department. All districts on every shift would be alerted and given the same instructions. All shifts would be updated on a daily basis. Reports were to be detailed and turned in at the end of every watch.

This one was definitely 'by the book' and anything short of superb police work would not be tolerated. Gage had deliberately kept his suspect to himself. Only Steve knew he was on Randy's trail. He didn't want it out for fear Randy would run.

The Chief announced he would hold a press conference to be aired on the 6:00 Tuesday evening news. By then, he hoped he would have a little more to pass on to the frantic citizens of Stanfield. The autopsy reports were due later today, and the bodies would be released to the families once the reports were in the hands of Captain Mahoney.

Dr. Chapman, M.E. had scheduled the autopsies to be performed at the James and Ryan funeral home.

The Clarke wake was to be held at that funeral parlor and the Rosen's arrangements would be made with their Rabbi. David Rosen would be buried on Monday morning. Lynn Ann Clarke would be waked on Monday evening and buried on Tuesday.

The switchboard at the station was hot. Incoming calls were being handled as quickly as one operator was capable of. Tips were jotted down, and handed to the nearest officer or detective. It was like a relay race. Passing and running. Some tips were unsubstantiated, but still needed to be followed through. Direct orders, every lead or tip would be investigated.

Steven Logan approached the desk. The police log was opened to Sunday, September 26, 1954. The detective flipped the page to the previous night's log. He ran his finger down the numerous calls that had been recorded.

Motor vehicle accident called in at 21:45(9:45 P.M.). Location, intersection @ Archer Boulevard and White Street

Time: Officers arrive at the scene, 21:52 (9:52P.M.) Ambulance transports two male victims, Mercy Hospital. One passenger refuses treatment. Driver and one passenger admitted to hospital with multiple injuries. No fatalities.

That was the report, in brief. It caught the detective's attention because of the time and location. 9:52 P.M. and just up the street from the Rosen's. It was worth checking out.

When Logan arrived at the hospital, he asked to see the admittance records from the previous night. The names of the two young men were listed. He strolled to the elevator and pushed the illuminated #3 on the panel.

The first patient was in room 304. He entered the four-bed room and walked to the bed to the far right. He looked at the young man laying in the bed. He appeared to be about 5'7, with a slight build. His head was heavily bandaged and he appeared to be sleeping. The detective glanced at the chart clipped to the foot of the bed. Taking out his notebook, confirmed the name of the sleeping patient and left the room.

His next visit was in room 320. This room was a six-bed room. A nurse was administering medication to one of the six patients. Logan waited at the door for the nurse to finish and then approached her. He identified himself and asked which patient was brought in last night, a victim of an automobile accident. The nurse turned and pointed to bed #4. It was the middle bed to the right.

Steve approached the side of the bed, and greeted Michael Sampson.

"Good morning Michael, how you doing?" He began.

"I'm okay, who are you?" Answered the boy.

"I'm Detective Steven Logan, Stanfield P.D." Steve replied, displaying his badge.

"I'd like to ask you a few questions, do you mind?"

"No, I don't mind, I'm a little groggy, they gave me something for the pain, actually, I'm feeling pretty good right now!" The injured boy replied.

"Yeah, I'll bet you do. Some of that stuff can do that to you. Looks like you got pretty banged up. You the driver?" Steve asked casually.

"Nope, Frankie Bailey, he was driving. He's in worse shape than me from what I'm told. I was sitting in the front seat, passenger. Boy, don't know what happened! I just remember the crash. Anyone else get hurt?"

"Not that I know of Michael. Just you and Frank." The detective answered.

"Where were you headed Michael? Actually, where were you coming from?" Steve was trying to get to the 9:30 time line.

"It was my birthday, 18 yesterday. Frank and Bobby Nielson picked me up to go out and celebrate. Some celebration! They picked me up in front of the drugstore on Archer Boulevard, just before the accident. We got as far as White Street, and, well, you know the rest."

Steve was looking his 'suspect' over carefully. It was difficult to determine if he had scratches on him. He was pretty bruised and his right arm was in a full cast. His face had a few minor cuts but didn't appear to be scratches. More likely the result of shattered glass. He was a big kid though. At a guess, he'd say, over 6 feet, broad in the shoulders. Steve asked him if he'd heard about the murders on Archer Boulevard the previous night.

"No, haven't heard anything. They knocked me out last night, slept right through until about 9:00 this morning. No, what happened? You looking for witnesses? Sorry, I guess you got the wrong guy. I don't know anything about a murder on Archer."

"Just want to know what you were doing before your friends picked you up Michael. You said you were waiting for them by the drugstore. What time did they pick you up?"

"I don't remember, exactly. It was after nine, about 9:20? I really don't know Sargent."

The boy thought for a moment, "You don't think I had anything to do with a murder, do you?" Michael asked, suddenly realizing what the detective was driving at.

"Don't know, Michael, just following up all possibilities. You were in the vicinity of the crime. You were there at the estimated time of the crime. Have to cover all leads. You understand?" Steve spoke in very serious tones.

"Yes, sir. I understand, but you've got to understand, I don't know anything about any murder. You believe me, don't you? I swear, Detective, I don't know what you're talking about. Talk to Frank and Bobby. They can tell you. God, I don't believe you think I had anything to do with a murder!" The boy was getting louder and showing signs of panic.

"Calm down Michael. I'm only doing my job. I'm not here to arrest you, or even accuse you. I'm just asking questions. It's my job. Now, calm down. Maybe you saw somebody hanging around while you were waiting for your friends?"

The boy thought for a few seconds and said, "No, I don't think so. It was raining pretty hard. Don't think too many people were out just 'hanging around'.

"Yeah, you're probably right about that. Sorry to have bothered you."

Logan looked around the room. All eyes were on him and the young man in bed #4. Logan reached up and pulled the privacy curtain around the bed. He spoke softly to Michael. He's not going anywhere by the looks of him, he thought. I'll check him out for previous offenses.

"Okay, Michael. I'm leaving. Get some rest and hope you get out of this place real soon. Thanks for your help, and just calm down. Nobody's accusing you of anything!"

"Okay Sargent, but believe me. I'm not your guy! I was just out trying to celebrate my birthday with some friends. That's all, just celebrating!"

Steve left, noting the name and address of the two hospitalized accident victims. He was able to obtain the third passenger's name and address also. He was pretty sure Michael was not his man, but he couldn't disregard anyone that could be a possible suspect.

He stopped at the nurse's station on his way to the elevators. A nurse was attending the desk, crocheting. He knew that was not a likely suspect, but it struck him as ironic. When was the last time he'd ever seen anyone crocheting? Maybe he'd just never had reason to notice before.

"Excuse me, madame." He addressed the nurse. He displayed his badge, and introduced himself.

"I'd like to see the clothing of one of the accident victims, Michael Sampson. Would you have access to those items?" He asked, with a warm smile.

"Why, I think so, Sargent. They should be in a bag labeled 'personal items'. The bags are usually in the closet in their rooms. Do you want me to get them?"

"I'd sure appreciate it, ahh, Shirley." He replied, reading her name tag. Steve had a way of getting people to cooperate. He had a gentle nature and usually it was very effective in these types of situations.

"I'll be right back." The nurse replied, placing her crocheting aside.

Steve waited at the nurse's station. The nurse returned carrying a bag marked, PERSONAL ITEMS, and Michael Sampson's name written on it.

She handed the bag to the detective and stood watching, waiting for him to search through it. Steve looked at Shirley and she realized, this was none of her business. She returned to her place behind the desk, as Steve walked across hall to an empty bench.

He sat down and reached for the shirt that lay on the top of the remaining clothing. It was a solid color, light brown, and showed no signs of any stains whatsoever. He reached for the blue denim pants and they too were devoid of any sign of blood. He was not surprised, but he had to follow through and check it out.

"Thank you Shirley." He spoke to the nurse as he handed the bag to her. "I appreciate your help."

"You're very welcome Detective, anytime." She replied.

Monday, September 27, 1954

Again, the double homicide dominated the Stanfield News:

POLICE INVESTIGATION PROBES NEIGHBORHOOD
Police searching around the clock for killer of 14 year old girl and 4 year old boy..

The article went on to report the clues and evidence the police had to this point, including the blue crochet thread found at the scene.

A small white coffin was placed on the emerald carpet of grass. It was 10:00 Monday morning. At sundown, the solemn observance of Rosh Hashanah, significant of the religious New Year in the Jewish Faith would begin. Normally, the burial would take place the day after the death, but the autopsy was incomplete, and the medical examiner was not able to release the tiny body.

The one hundred twenty five mourners gathered. Among the friends and relatives in attendance was Mrs. Myra Trudeau. Myra was the owner/founder of the Community Sunshine Nursery School. She was flanked by two of the teachers of the school. The three women clasped hands.

The loss of David was quite profound to the staff at the nursery school. David was an exceptionally warm and well-liked little boy. Mrs. Trudeau had closed the school for the day, in respect to the Rosen family.

The Rabbi positioned himself at the head of the coffin. Gail Rosen sat, her shoulders bent. Elaine Clarke sat to her right, clasping Gail's hand. Two grieving mothers. Benjamin Rosen was seated to the left of Gail. He wrapped his arm around his wife's trembling shoulders, her head rested on him. Ben Rosen, the father was also grieving, but sat stoically, void of any expression.

Phil Clarke stood behind his wife Elaine. He wanted to console the grieving parents of four-year-old David Rosen, but he felt helpless. He hoped his presence would convey the sorrow he was feeling.

The Rabbi began, *"Dark are Thy ways and hidden Thy messages..."*

His words trailed off as Mrs. Rosen sobbed uncontrollably. She felt the grief known only to a mother who has lost a child and her grief engulfed all at the grave site. Elaine squeezed Gail's hand a little tighter. There were no words.

While the Rabbi presided at the grave site of the little Rosen boy, Frank Tallman, the principal of Lincoln High School, scheduled an assembly for the entire student body. It was imperative the horrific murders of Lynn Ann Clarke, a freshman and David Rosen be addressed and validated to the students.

Sharing the stage, was Detective Gage. Gage and Tallman had met briefly before the assembly and agreed to continue their meeting after the assembly was dismissed. Ray Gage had questions for the principal that couldn't wait. He had a strong feeling about 'Randy' and was sure he would get additional information from the principal.

Mr. Tallman had watched the students as they arrived that Monday morning. He had instructed the faculty to do the same. This was traumatic to these kids.

Small groups gathered in the hallways, whispering, recounting what they had read in the paper, what they had heard on the news, and all the unsubstantiated rumors that had began to spread throughout the city. It was the principal's responsibility to lend some type of support and assurance and some semblance of comfort to these young people.

The students filed into the assembly hall. The overflow were instructed to go to the gymnasium. They sat on the bleachers waiting to hear Principal Tallman's familiar voice.

The public address system crackled and Frank Tallman began,

"Students, this is a solemn occasion, as I'm sure you are all well aware. The news of Lynn Ann Clarke's death has been a tremendous shock to all of us hear at Lincoln. The entire faculty has asked me to express our concern and we are available to you if you need to talk about your feelings and concerns."

"Also, we have requested the assistance of Dr. Dennis Aldridge, a psychologist and chairman of Mayor Gardner's Commission for the Study of Juvenile Delinquency. Dr. Aldridge has agreed to assign members of his staff to assist you in any way necessary. Dr. Aldridge's staff member will be temporarily sharing an office with Mrs. Stone, the guidance councilor, and strongly encourages each student to take advantage of his services."

"Sign up sheets will be posted on each of the bulletin boards throughout the school, as well as on Mrs. Stone's office."

"Detective Sgt. Raymond Gage, of the Stanfield Police Department would like to say a few words."

Raymond Gage stood at the podium. He looked over the student body. He cleared his throat, adjusted the microphone and began,

"You may notice the presence of police officers in the building over the next few days, during our on-going investigation. You need not be alarmed or concerned. In addition to a citywide search, we are focusing on the entire student body."

"Please cooperated with them if you are questioned. They are diligently pursuing every avenue to get information that could shed light on the case, and will be very interested in any information you are able to share with them. All information will be kept confidential. We are counting on your cooperation.

"I am available, after this assembly if anyone would like to meet with me." He stepped back and turned the assembly back to Mr. Tallman.

"I've been informed, the wake for Lynn Ann Clarke will be held this evening at James & Ryan Funeral Home. Visiting hours will be from 7:00-9:00 PM. The funeral will be tomorrow. An 11:00 Mass will be held at St. Michael's Cathedral, burial immediately following the Mass. Any student who wishes to attend the funeral will be excused for a day of bereavement, and the absence will not be recorded on your school records."

"Before you are dismissed to return to your regular classes, I'd like to share a moment of silence in the memory of Lynn Ann Clarke. Thank you."

The students bowed their heads. Many cried. After a few minutes, the silence was broken by the 10:45 bell. Slowly the students responded, shuffling into the hallways.

The usual hustle and chaos that students displayed as they moved from one class and hurried to the next was not there. Instead there appeared to be a reverent silence among the saddened student body.

Detective Raymond Gage and Principal Tallman exited the assembly hall together. They were headed for the principal's office. Gage was armed with a list of names that Steven Logan had turned over to him. Steve had elicited names of Lynn's friends from Mrs. Clarke. Ray had to interview each one hoping one would lead him to a suspect.

As he looked through the list, he saw the name Randy. He had underlined and circled it. This was the individual he wanted to know more about. This was actually the only one on the list he considered a possible suspect.

As they entered the modest office of the principal, Ms. Brock was straightening the papers and files on Frank Tallman's cluttered desk.

"Have a seat Detective." Tallman said, gesturing to a straight back wooden chair placed directly in front of the oaken desk. "Coffee?"

"I could use one, black, thanks." Ray answered.

He was anxious to get to his list, particularly Randy. He didn't have a last name, so he was prepared to wait until he questioned some of Lynn's friends. Surely someone would know who he was.

Ms. Brock returned with the two cups of steaming hot black coffee. She placed them before each of the men.

Raymond Gage began, "I've been told that Lynn Ann Clarke was a very well liked girl, and had many friends. I have here a list of students I'd like to interview. How would you suggest we go about that?"

Mr. Tallman thought for a few seconds, and glanced at the clock.

"The first period lunch begins in about forty-five minutes. We could check the schedules of the students on your list and ask them to come to the office," he suggested. "Do you want to talk to them one-on-one?" He asked.

"I think that would be best." Replied Gage. "Each one shouldn't take long. Once I've had a chance to talk to each one, I can narrow down the one's I'll need to question further."

"Hopefully, someone will add substantial information, and I'll have something to follow up. To be honest with you Frank, I have nothing! Day three, and nothing but a list of kids I can be pretty sure will tell me Lynn had no enemies, and surely nobody would want to harm her." He sounded discouraged already.

Frank Tallman called Ms. Brock into his office. He explained what Raymond Gage had just told him, and asked her to check the schedules of the students Detective Gage was about to hand over to her. Ms. Brock scanned through the list.

"Most of these girls are in gym class right now. I can notify Janet Cross and ask her to send them directly to your office at the end of that period. I'll have to check the other schedules. We have a slightly higher absenteeism today. Should I schedule them tomorrow?" She asked.

"No, Ms. Brock, just do the best you can with the students that are here today. Detective Gage will need all the cooperation you as well as the rest of the office can extend to him. Please provide him with any information he needs."

Mr. Tallman was quite somber in his tone. Ms. Brock had been his assistant long enough to know, he meant there would be no exceptions. Ms. Brock glanced at the time. By now, it was 11:45. She rushed out of the office and began her task. Within the next twenty minutes, six young girls were seated in the outside office of the principal. They looked nervous. They'd never been questioned by police before. What did the detective think they had to tell him? Did he think any of them had any involvement with the murders? One girl was noticeably missing. Lisa Jansen, Lynn's best friend.

One by one the girls were summoned into the principal's office.

First was Sarah Broughton. The detective stood as Sarah entered the room. He pulled a chair up, placing it directly in front of him. The principal had left, so the detective could do his job uninterrupted.

"Good morning Sarah." He began. "My name is Sargent Raymond Gage." He handed her a card. "Try to relax, I just have a few questions to ask you. Nothing to be nervous about." Sarah straightened up in the wooden chair.

The detective began gently prodding for information. The answers were pretty much as he had expected. After about ten minutes, he excused the young girl and asked her to send in Jeannie Tuttle on her way out.

Detective Gage went through the same interview with Jeannie as he had done with Sarah. He mentioned the name 'Randy,' and she had the same reaction as Sarah. Don't know who he is. Jeannie offered the names of a few other friends of Lynn's that Ray didn't have on his list, but beyond that, he wasn't any further ahead as he was when he began. As Jeannie was leaving, Ray looked at his list and asked her to send in Suzanne Porter.

In total, Detective Gage interviewed six girls. None that could shed any additional information. Ms. Brock entered the office and announced that she had scheduled another group of Lynn's friends. Would he like to see them now?

Ray took a deep sigh. "Thank you Ms. Brock. I'd like a couple of minutes to put my notes together. Will you ask them to wait?"

"Certainly Detective. Just let me know when you're ready. Would like more coffee?"

"That would be great, thank you," Ray replied.

He sat back and put his feet up on the empty chair in front of him. Who is this Randy that nobody knew?

After about ten minutes, he pressed the intercom on the principal's desk.

"Yes, Detective?" Came the formal voice of Ms. Brock.

"Please send in Brenda Chapman," he replied.

Brenda entered the room. She had met Raymond Gage and Steven Logan that horrible night. She could barely remember what she had been asked, let alone what her answers were. Brenda was still visibly shaken. She had contemplated staying home today, but she wanted to be among friends, especially Paul. She couldn't bear staying home and looking across the street at her friend's house, knowing the pain and agony the Clarkes' were going through.

Brenda sat down. She took a deep breath and hoped she would keep her composure through this interview. Ray started his questions as gently as he knew how. All Brenda's answers were pretty much the same as the previous students. Then he asked, "Did Lynn know anybody by the name of Randy?"

Brenda's expression changed. She looked surprised that Randy's name would be brought up. What could he have to do with anything?

"Yes, she knew Randy. She thought he was a creep. He was always pestering her. Calling and showing up at the movies on Saturdays."

"Do you know Randy's last name?" Gage pressed on. He was leaning forward, and was literally sitting on the edge of his chair.

Brenda thought for a moment, "Yes, its Crowley, no wait, I'm not sure. Something like that."

Gage tried not show his excitement. "Take your time Brenda, was it Crowley?"

"No, it's Crawford. Yes, that's it! Crawford." She was certain. Now the mysterious Randy had a last name. Ray Gage felt a new surge of hope.

"Do you know where he lives? Does he go to this school?"

Brenda thought and replied, "I don't know where he lives, but I think he might be in this school. I really don't know him, except for what Lynn would say about him."

"Thanks' Brenda. You've been a big help."

"Do you think Randy did this horrible thing to Lynn and David?" She asked sounding frightened.

"I don't know Brenda. I do need to talk to him." Brenda stood. "Can I go now?" She asked, feeling relieved.

"Yes, Brenda, and please tell the others that are waiting they are excused."

After Brenda left, Ray pressed the intercom and asked Ms. Brock to come in.

"Is Principal Tallman in the building? If he is, can you page him to his office?"

"Yes sir," she answered and left the office.

"Mr. Tallman, Mr. Tallman, please come to your office." Ms. Brock's authoritative voice broadcasted throughout the school.

In a short time, Mr. Tallman appeared in the doorway.

Ray stood as the principal entered and walked to his desk. "Is there something I can do for you Detective?"

"Yes, are you acquainted with a Randy Crawford? Is he a student here at Lincoln?"

The principal thought for a few moments and answered,

"I don't recognize the name, but I'll have my staff check the records. It might take a few minutes, do you want to wait?"

Ray could hardly hold back his excitement. He glanced at his watch, suggesting he might be pressed for time, but he would wait.

One of the staff members appeared within ten minutes carrying a manilla folder. She handed it to the principal and exited the office. Frank Tallman looked through the file and turned it over to Ray.

"Here's your boy. Not very impressive," he stated. "It appears that Mr. Crawford enrolled at Lincoln at the start of the semester. He has a total of four days of attendance. On September 14th he turned seventeen and quit. He enrolled as a Freshman. As you can see from his records, he wasn't doing very well throughout his school years. The average freshman is fourteen to fifteen. He could have quit when he was sixteen."

As the principal went on about the obvious delinquency of Randy Crawford, Ray Gage was most interested in obtaining an address. He jotted it down. He would be paying Randy Crawford a visit within the hour.

As gracious as he could possibly be, Ray thanked the principal, Ms. Brock and the entire staff for all their cooperation. He assured them he would be back to follow up on any students he was not able to interview today. Frank Tallman shook Ray's hand and walked him to the door that led to the parking lot. Ray walked to his unmarked car and waited until the principal was out of sight.

He checked in with the station for any messages. He listened and mentally prioritized the exorbitant amount of messages. His partner, Steve Logan was the first call back. He would wait until he found a diner with a phone. He was famished.

He had to get a quick sandwich and needed to talk to Steve before he contacted Randy Crawford. This was his only suspect, and if all went as Ray was beginning to suspect, the double homicide of last Saturday night could be blown wide open in record time.

Steven Logan had returned from the Rosen's funeral and found himself buried in paperwork at the station. The patrol officers had completed their reports from Saturday's homicides and they were stacked on Steve's desk. The medical examiner's autopsy reports had been submitted, and there were more 8 x 10 glossy photos that the photographer had delivered that morning.

"Logan," his voice sounded tired as he answered the phone.

"Steve, I've got the kid's name, Randy Crawford!" Ray answered. "He lives down on Water St. Ext." He went on. "I'm on my way to the station, I'll pick you up in twenty minutes."

Steve was waiting outside the police station when Ray pulled up. "Hop in Partner, I've got a good feeling about this."

"Where the hell is Water St. Ext?" Steve asked.

"It happens to be down by the tracks behind the Rosen's place. You know, the place the kids go parking. Water St., then over the railroad trestle it turns into Water St. Ext."

Ray was getting excited about this lead. "There are row houses down there. He lives at 36, Unit B, Water St. Ext."

Water St. Extension consisted entirely of row houses as they were called. They were six-plexes. Six units per building, similar to duplexes. The row houses were owned by the mills in the area and were constructed to provide housing for the workers.

Water Street Extension was not the most impressive address. It was referred to colloquially as 'the flats." The apartments were adequately maintained and provided affordable housing for the employees of the various mills.

The two detectives drove north on Archer Boulevard. They passed the Rosen's house.

"Can you believe people?" Ray asked, in a disgusted tone. "There are curiosity seekers trying to peek into the windows. What do they think they're going to see?" Ray sounded discussed with the behavior of a couple of people he spotted on the porch of the Rosen's house.

"Can't do anything about that now, Ray" Steve answered. "It's private property, the barricades have been removed. Technically, no longer our crime scene."

After passing the Rosen's they turned right onto Dorset Street. Steve noted Lisa Jansen lived at 94 Dorset St. He asked Ray if he had talked to Lisa at school today. Ray informed him Lisa was not at school.

"Slow down here, Lisa lives in that green house, first floor, #94. Let's see if she's got anything to tell us."

An attractive middle- aged woman answered the door.

"Can I help you?" Mrs. Jansen asked.

The detectives identified themselves and asked if Lisa was home. Mrs. Jansen knew why they were there. She hesitated for a moment and replied,

"Yes, she's in her room. She's been there all day. She's taking this very hard."

"We understand, Mrs. Jansen. We'll try to be as brief as possible," Ray assured the concerned mother.

Mrs. Jansen invited the two men to sit as she went to get Lisa.

After a few moments, Lisa appeared in the doorway of the dining room, still in her robe. It was obvious to the detectives she was upset. She took a seat at the dining room table where the two men were seated. Mrs. Jansen stood protectively behind her daughter. Steve Logan took out his notes and began gently.

"Lisa, I know Lynn was your best friend. I'm sorry to have to put you through anything as unpleasant as this, but we need your help." Lisa looked puzzled. What could she offer to the police? She listened to the detective very carefully.

"Can you tell us about Lynn? What she liked to do. Who some of her other friends were? Did she have a boyfriend? Someone that she liked, and maybe confided in you. Did she keep a diary?"

Lisa bowed her head, and shrugged her shoulders. Obviously, she just couldn't grasp this line of questions.

"She just liked everyone. Everyone liked her. I don't know why anyone would..would.." she finished her sentence sobbing. Her mother cradled Lisa's head. She handed her daughter a tissue, and Lisa slowly composed herself.

"I just can't even think of anyone who would want to hurt Lynn. She didn't really have a boyfriend. She had friends that were boys, but they were just friends. Frank was her friend."

Steve Logan asked, "Frank Jablonski?"

"Yes, he's Ginny Poirier's boyfriend. Ginny helped Lynn with her cheerleading practices," Lisa replied.

"Who else, did she know a boy by the name of Randy?" Ray couldn't hold back any longer.

"Randy Crawford? She knew him, but he surely wasn't Lynn's boyfriend. He wasn't even a friend! Lynn thought he was a creep!" Lisa answered looking directly at Ray.

"Do you know Randy?"Asked Steve.

"I've seen him a few times at school. Not this year, he was in Proctor with us last year. I thought he quit this year. We saw him at the movies last Saturday, the day..."she faded off again covering her face.

"Go on, Lisa, last Saturday, at the movies, and?" Ray pressed.

"And nothing, Lynn just ignored him. We saw him when we were going into the show, I don't think he was around when we got out." Lisa answered. Then, as if reality snapped into place, she shot back,

"Do you thing Randy killed Lynn and David! Oh God!, Randy Crawford?"

Ray answered as calmly as possible,

"We're checking out everyone Lisa. We don't know, we just want to talk to Randy as well as anyone else that knew Lynn." Then Ray pushed a little farther.

"Could you tell me what Randy looks like? Is he tall, his hair color, anything you can think of that would describe him?" Lisa thought for a moment,

"He's about your height," she answered indicating Ray's six foot two stature. "He has brown hair, it always looks greasy, and he's always wearing a black leather motorcycle jacket, even when it's warm out."

"Good girl, Lisa. You've been a big help." Ray replied. "Will you be at school tomorrow?" Ray asked without thinking.

"No, I'm going to the funeral." Lisa answered, sniffing into the tissue. "I have to go to the wake tonight. I've never been to a wake before. It must be terrible!"

Mrs. Jansen looked at the detectives searching for an indication the interview was over. Steve Logan caught the look and stood up. Ray followed his partner's lead.

"We'll be on our way." Steve spoke directly to Mrs. Jansen. Lisa ran from the room. Mrs. Jansen walked the two detectives to the door. Ray Gage handed her a card and asked that she call him if she had anything further to add. She assured him she would and said goodbye.

"Well, what do you think?" Asked Ray.

"About what, this Randy character? I think you have to keep an open mind. What if this goes sour? I'm looking for a depraved psycho, a little more than just a 'creep'." Steve was concerned his partner might be too focused on this one suspect.

"Yeah, I know. Well, we'll know as soon as we get to talk to him."

They continued down Dorset St. a short distance and took a right onto Water Street. About 2/3 of a mile they crossed the railroad tracks and arrived at 'the flats'. The houses were clearly numbered, they easily found #36, Unit B.

The two detectives walked up the few steps onto the porch and Ray knocked on the door. They waited, and knocked again. They looked around the premises. A man was painting the porch railings on the house next door. He was wearing a green shirt with stenciled letters that read 'Maintenance.' The detectives walked to the neighboring house toward the worker. As they approached, the painter stood up and acknowledged the two men.

"Can I help you?" He asked.

"Just looking for Randy Crawford, you know him?" Ray asked, casually.

"I know Emily, his mother. She's probably at work now. She works at the North Plant." The maintenance man volunteered.

"Do you know whose car that is parked beside Building 36?" Ray asked pointing to a 1949 Ford coupe.

"Yeah, that belongs to the kid. Don't think he's around. Ain't seen him for a while. His mother should be home soon. What time you got?"

Ray looked at his watch, "3:45," he answered.

"She'll be home around 5:00. The whistle at the plant blows at 4:30. They all get out at 4:30 over there."

"Thanks for your help." The two detectives walked back to the Crawford's apartment.

"Well, what do you want to do? Want to wait? It's your call Ray." Steve asked.

Ray was busy jotting down the registration number from the Ford. He noticed the car's right rear tire was flat.

"Let's give Mrs. Crawford a call later, find out where her boy is. Don't want to spook him," Ray replied.

They drove back to the station.

Detectives Sean Connelly and John Broderick were on their way out as Logan and Gage arrived.

"Hey you guys, where have you been? John and I have been really busy here." Sean Connelly reported.

"We've been questioning and releasing suspects all afternoon. I can't believe the response from the public. Tips have been coming in you wouldn't believe. Nothing to hang our hats on yet, but we're a long way from running out of suspects."

"You guys got anything?" Connelly was pressing for some good news. He and his partner were part of this team, and expected to be kept up to date on any leads or clues.

Steve filled in the detectives concerning his visit to the hospital earlier in the day. He assured them that Michael Sampson along with his two companions were checked out and turned out to be a dead end.

Steve Logan had already decided to disclose the 'thread' to the media. He couldn't think of any logical reason to withhold anything from the public. They had the gruesome details of the scene to hold back in the event they got a solid lead, or suspect. Some things had to be kept within the department, but the citizens of Stanfield were frantic, and needed continuous updates. The story would dominate the front page. Reporters were camped on the steps of the station.

They had to be informed of the progress, if any, regarding the search for this predator. The public had the right to know.

Chief McNamara had scheduled a press conference for Tuesday, to be aired on the 6:00 news. He'd be breathing down Captain Mahoney's neck, and in turn, the Captain passed the 'heat' onto the whole department. The public was demanding something that would indicate the intensity of the search.

We've got a kid on the line." Ray replied. "Nothing yet, but looks like we might be on to something."

Detective Connelly reported that the clothing, blood samples, bed sheets and fingernail scrapings had been dispatched to the State Police Laboratory, Boston for analysis. Should be a couple of days for the reports.

All the detectives, on all watches were jointly sifting through every bit of information coming in. The murder weapon was still missing. It was an onerous burden.

"We've got to get together with Dr. Aldridge. Maybe he can give us a profile of what type of demented individual we're looking for," suggested Connelly.

"Good idea. Get the autopsy reports and crime photos to him first thing in the morning." Steve replied.

"Ray and I will be at the Clarke's funeral at St. Michael's tomorrow morning. Let's get Morgan and Mallory in on this. We'll get with you at the station right after the funeral. Should be about 1:00."

"You got it boss," replied Sean. "I'm headed home. I'll be home all night. Call me if you turn up anything, otherwise, I'll see you tomorrow." He left the three detectives.

John Broderick finished filling in Logan and Gage. "Morgan and Mallory have been on the street most of the day. They visited the Rosen's this afternoon. Really lousy detail, but they were following up on maybe somebody was after the boy. You know, David Rosen. Thought maybe the revenge angle."

Steve asked, "So, what did they find out?"

"All I know is that Mr. Rosen and his brother-in-law, Gordon Schaefer are partners. Did you know they own the R & S Markets?"

"No kidding, both locations?" Ray asked, in surprise.

"You mean all three markets?" Broderick corrected. "That's where the R & S comes from, Rosen and Schaefer. I don't have all the details, but Sargent Mallory left his report on your desk. Rosen's going to turn over his employee's list to him by tomorrow. See if anyone might have a reason to harm the family," Stan filled in as much as he could remember.

"See you tomorrow, 1:00." John said, as he turned and headed for his car.

All shift commanders were keeping their patrolmen updated almost hourly. They were instructed to bring in anyone they thought suspicious. The evening watches, dog watches were particularly aggressive. Six foot tall, walking the streets in the predawn hours were worth checking into.

Logan and Gage were focusing on the student body. They didn't have a lot of faith in the revenge angle. If that were it, why not both the boys? Why just one? They were certain the girl was the target, the boy must have been killed to avoid identification. They were pretty sure the girl knew the killer. If not, he contrived a clever rouse to get her to open the door. There were no signs of forced entry. They had to conclude she let him in. Once they had the opportunity to meet with Dr. Aldridge, they would have a better picture of what kind of monster they were searching for.

Ray and Steve went into the station. Steve wanted to look over any new reports that were turned in and check all his messages.

Ray reviewed the registration number, Massachusetts 11234, he had copied from the Crawford kid's car. After a few minutes, a response came in. Registration Plate #11234: Owner, Emily Crawford, 36B Water Street Ext, Stanfield, MA Expiration: December 31, 1954.

Well, nothing remarkable about that report. Makes sense, the mother registered the car. Where's Mr. Crawford? Ray wondered. Well, his questions would be answered in a few minutes. He picked up the heavy telephone book. Turned to the C's and ran his finger down the page to Crawford, Emily. He copied down the number RE8-8081. The phone rang and on the second ring, he heard,

"Hello?"

"Hello, Mrs. Crawford please?" Ray asked

"This is Mrs. Crawford, who's calling?" Her voice sounded very soft and pleasant.

"This is Detective Raymond Gage, Stanfield Police Department," Ray replied. "I'd like to talk to you about your son, Randy Crawford."

There was a noticeable change in Mrs. Crawford's tone.

"Randy's not here." She stated.

"Do you expect him home tonight?" Ray asked.

"I don't know when he'll be here. What's this about?" Mrs. Crawford demanded.

"I'd rather not discuss this over the phone, Mrs. Crawford. Would you mind if I stop by this evening? It won't take long, just a few questions."

Ray was trying to be as casual as possible, but he needed to talk to her now that he had made the initial contact. He didn't want Randy to get any idea he was under suspicion.

"Okay, when will you be here?" She asked.

"If you don't mind, I'll be there in twenty minutes."

"I'll see you in twenty minutes Detective." She agreed, and abruptly hung up the phone.

Ray waited for Steve to finish up his telephone conversation.

"I've just talked to Randy's mother, I'm on my way down there. You want to come along?"

"Nope, you can handle it. I'm going to finish up a few things here, grab something to eat, and get a good night's sleep. You seem to forget, I'm a bachelor these days, nobody's cooking supper for this tired dog! See you in the morning. You going to the funeral home first, or straight to the church?"

Ray thought for a moment,

"I'll probably be here first thing. Got a lot of paperwork and reports to look over. Hopefully, I'll be filing a report on Randy by morning. See you at the church. St. Michael's 11:00?

He thought for a moment and added, "Think we should go to the funeral home first?"

"Could be a good idea. Might get a better chance to talk to some of the people there. Okay, how about 9:30 at James & Ryan Funeral Home?" Steve asked.

"Okay, funeral home, 9:30. Have a good night."

Ray Gage arrived at Randy Crawford's house at 5:45. As he was about to knock on the door, Mrs. Crawford opened it. She was a small woman, and looked older than her years. She had the appearance of a woman who has been through some hard times.

"Hello, Mrs. Crawford?" Ray asked in the most pleasant tone he could muster.

"Yes, Detective Gage is it?" She asked.

"Come in." She was far more cordial than Ray had anticipated she would be.

"Now what's this about Randy? Has he gotten into some sort of trouble?" She asked.

"We don't know. That's why we would like to ask him a few questions." Ray replied. "Will he be home tonight?"

"I don't know, I doubt it," Mrs. Crawford answered. "I haven't seen him since he left yesterday morning. He asked me for ten dollars, and was out the door. Didn't say where he was going, or when he'd be back."

"Is he in the habit of just 'taking off' like that without telling you where?" Ray asked.

"Look Detective. Let's get one thing clear. Randy has been doing what he pleases since he was fifteen. I know, I should have more control over my own kid, but I don't. His father left three years ago, and I haven't heard from him since." She stopped to take a breath then continued.

"Randy is not your average 'All American Boy', I'm afraid. He's never been in any serious trouble with the police, just he has a mind of his own, and frankly, I haven't the time to keep him under my thumb. I work at the mill long hours, and put food on the table as best I can..."

"Wait a minute, Mrs. Crawford," Ray interrupted.

"I'm not here to pass judgement on how you raise your boy. I know it's got to be a difficult job, you being a single parent an all. I just need to ask a few questions that will help with my investigation."

"What kind of investigation? Oh, no! You don't think Randy had anything to do with those two children being murdered last Saturday, do you?" Ray could sense a genuine panic in the mother.

"That's what I want to clear up. I think you can help." Ray answered.

"Do you know where Randy was on Saturday night?" Ray was trying to be as casual as possible.

"Saturday night I think he was home. He spends most of his time upstairs in his room. He doesn't always let me know when he's going out, unless he needs money." She replied.

"Has Randy ever mentioned Lynn Ann Clarke?" Ray asked.

"Look, Detective, you have to understand one thing. Randy does not have much to discuss with me. He calls this his home, but he's more like a boarder around here. He comes and goes, and we don't exactly have warm and cozy chats. I don't mean to be laying my problems on you, just want you to understand the situation." Mrs. Crawford came across as very straight forward and Ray appreciated her frankness.

"Is that your car out there?"

"Yes, but Randy's the one that drives it. I mean, I only registered it for him. His father left it, I guess that was a small price for him to pay. Randy hasn't driven it in over a week. The tire is flat and he hasn't gotten around to fixing it."

"So, he must be with someone if his car isn't running, and he's not home." Ray pressed.

"I don't know. He left on Sunday morning. He probably hopped the train. He does that often you know. The train travels slowly through the city. He rides the train to New York, upstate, Albany, I think. I know he has some friends that go with him, or he meets them there."

"He just turned seventeen a few weeks ago, quit school, against my wishes, and he's turning into a bum." She was noticeably saddened by the story she was relaying to the detective.

"I just don't know what to do with him. I suppose if his father was around, he'd be better equipped to handle him, but I just don't know what to do."

Ray felt a certain sympathy for this distraught mother. She obviously worked hard. He glanced around. Her home was modestly furnished, but clean and well kept. He had no advice to offer. What this Randy kid was lacking was a good kick in the ass.

"So you haven't seen or heard from Randy since Sunday morning?" He asked.

"That's right, he left around 11:00 A.M. I'm sorry, that's all I can tell you." She sounded apologetic.

"Do you get the Sunday paper delivered, Mrs. Crawford?"

"Yes, I do. Why?" She asked.

"Do you think Randy saw the paper before he left?"

" I doubt it, he never reads the paper. I'd be happy if he just looked through the help wanted section once in a while. If he's not going to school, he should be working. Don't you think so, Detective?" She asked.

"Yes, I'd say that's pretty much the way it works!" Ray tried to make the conversation a little lighter.

"I know my folks would have had me out there picking up garbage if that's all I could do!"

Ray stood up to leave. Mrs. Crawford quickly changed her demeanor and asked,

"Would you like a cup of coffee, or a cold drink, Detective?" She seemed to want company.

"Sure." Ray replied."If it's no bother, I'd like that." He felt a certain empathy for her.

"Do you mind if I use your phone?"

"Help yourself, I'll fix the coffee." She said, almost cheerfully.

Ray went to the phone and dialed his home number.

"Hello?" A cheerful voice answered. It was Mary Ann.

"Hi there stranger!" Ray replied. "Long time no see. You're mom there?"

"Yup, just a minute Dad." She shouted to Linda, "Mom, it's Dad."

"Hi honey, what's up?" Linda always had that up beat attitude.

"Just wanted to know if the 'Gage Dining Room' was still open for dinner." He joked.

"Well, for you, Mr. Gage, of course. What time will you be here?"

"About half an hour. See you then." He hung up.

By then, Mrs. Crawford had placed the coffee on the table and sat down to join Ray. She looked like she needed somebody to unload her burdensome life on. Ray was not in the mood, but he could not find it in his heart not to give her at least a few minutes. Besides, he wanted her on his side when he finally caught up to Randy.

"How long have you been at the mill?" Ray asked, trying to keep the conversation general.

They chatted for about a half an hour. She was a very interesting lady and it was such a shame she hadn't done more with her life.

As he was leaving, he handed her his card and asked that she contact him as soon as she heard from Randy, or when he returned home.

Tuesday, September 28, 1954
The Stanfields News Headlines:

POLICE REPORT MURDER CLUE
Crochet Thread Found on Floor of Death House Believed to be Once on Knife

Loops of blue crocheting thread fastened with a square knot may have been secured on the murder weapon. A major clue in slaying investigation. A Stanfield Detective, Sgt.. Steven Logan revealed that a piece of blue crocheting thread in several loops tied with a square knot was the only piece of evidence found after the babysitter and the four-year-old in her care were knifed to death at the Archer Boulevard home. The department has released this information to enable the public to help run down the killer. The thread was found on the floor, not far from the body of Lynn Ann Clarke, at the Rosen's home.

The police theorize that the thread was wrapped around the murder weapon. Upon entering the home it dropped to the floor. It is likely the murderer comes from a home where someone crochets..."

The full-length lead story continued to state that this horrific crime was a premeditated act and the killer had concealed the weapon which had not been found.

The sub headline followed:

Four-Year-Old Murder Victim Buried

Below the headline was a picture of David Rosen and a biography of his abbreviated life.

Steve Logan and Raymond Gage arrived at the James & Ryan Funeral Home at 9:45. Outside, the funeral director was speaking to six young men. He was giving them instructions. These were to be the pallbearers for Lynn Ann Clarke.

After about ten minutes, the funeral director walked back into the funeral home. The six boys stood in a group. Steve, with Ray following closely behind, approached the group. The two detectives separated the boys into two groups, three with Steve, three with Gage. They took advantage of the opportunity to question the boys.

The detectives asked the whereabouts of each on the night of the murders. They looked the boys over for any visible scratches. The detectives let the boys do the talking, listening for some sign of guilt. Each took notes, they would compare notes and talk later.

Throngs of mourners climbed the stone steps of St. Michael's Cathedral. In silence, they filed into the great stone building. They were grieving, but their faces were blank. Fear had partnered with disbelief and confusion. Some were strangers, and yet there was a unity. They shared the same fear. A common denominator. A ruthless, demented predator was loose in their city. Families clung tightly to each other.

The bell tolled. Hundreds gathered to say their final farewell to 14-year-old Lynn Ann Clarke.

In the vestibule of the church stood a middle-aged man in a brown gaberdine suit. His hands were folded in front of him as he watched the endless line of mourners file into the church. Detective Steve Logan searched the faces of each, looking for that someone who didn't seem to fit. A few exchanged perfunctory glances, otherwise they seemed absorbed in their own sorrowful thoughts. It was difficult, but it was a police procedure.

This was the third day of the investigation. His partner, Detective Raymond Gage stood at the side entrance, scanning the crowd. It seemed the entire city had come to mourn on this sorrowful September morning. The two detectives stood like centurions at their posts.

Logan and Gage were veteran homicide detectives. In the thirty-two combined years of their careers, never had anything so gruesome, or meaningless challenged their detective skills as this case was about to. This was the work of a powerful maniac, still loose somewhere in their midst.

Only yesterday, Steven Logan had attended the funeral of little four-year-old David Rosen. Gail and Ben Rosen had requested privacy from media coverage. The reporters stayed back. No pictures, no microphones for grave side interviews. It was a show of respect and sorrow to the Rosen family.

Gail and Ben asked that family members and close friends be present as they lay their precious baby to his final rest. Steve Logan had to attend. Steve felt he owed the family his attendance, without being obtrusive.

Less than a week ago, David's older brother, Daniel was teaching David to tie his shoes and how to whistle. David was a year away from going to kindergarten. He was excited about a loose tooth. His first one!

He squealed with delight as he ran with Daniel and jumped into the gigantic pile of leaves his father had raked in the backyard. His short life was over. Merely a flicker, and now darkness forever.

Steven Logan was professional. He had arrived at the boy's funeral as a seasoned detective. He walked away with sadness and gut wrenching sorrow that comes with witnessing parents burying a child.

Now the Clarke's. The deafening bells rang as the dirge beckoned all. Every row, every pew was filled. The overflow stood in the rear of the church and spilled out onto the steps. All stood with heads bowed and eyes avoiding each other.

Slowly, six young men grasped the polished rails that flanked the blanketed casket. Trying to prevent their gloved hands from shaking, they held tightly to the rails. The six pallbearers were friends of Lynn Ann Clarke. Children themselves. Their faces reflected no emotion. They walked stiffly down the center aisle toward the altar. Three pallbearers flanked each side.

The first on the right was Robert Jansen. He was a handsome six foot junior at Lincoln High School. His sister, Lisa Jansen was

Lynn's best friend. His thoughts drifted to the countless hours Lynn had spent with Lisa. They were inseparable. They slept over each other's houses on Friday nights. They laughed, cried and shared every experience with each other.

The day of the murders, they had been at the movies together. They had plans to see each other the next day. How could they know, when they gave a carefree wave at the corner of Dorset Street, that would be their last farewell?

Lisa had been out of control upon learning of Lynn's murder. It was doubtful she would be able to get through the wake and funeral. But she did get though the wake the night before and now she stood along side Lynn's classmates.

Following Robert was Karl Chapman. He too was a tall, lanky 18-year-old junior. Karl had known Lynn all her life. The Clarke's moved into 48 Lynndale St. about six months after the Chapman's. Karl was only four, Lynn was an infant. They lived directly across the street.

Karl's younger sister Brenda was a year older than Lynn. Lynn and Brenda played together as little girls, but once Brenda entered high school, they started to see less of each other. Over the summer preceding Lynn's freshman year, they seemed to bridge that gap and rekindled the friendship they once had.

Finally, Frank Jablonski. Frank was a stocky, ruddy faced senior. His 'steady' girlfriend had coached Lynn throughout the summer, preparing her for the cheerleading try-outs.

Ginny was also a senior and had been a cheerleader throughout her high school years. Lynn was a natural, and before long, Ginny became somewhat of a mentor to the young freshman. Ginny Poirier was an honor student, and an excellent role model.

Lynn admired Ginny. Frank was like an older brother to Lynn. Several times during the summer, Ginny and Frank would stop by to pick up Lynn on their way to the beach. Frank would miss her. Ginny Poirier was taking the loss very hard. Frank was worried about her.

The first pallbearer on the left was John Brady. The death of Lynn was especially bitter to him. John was only sixteen. The youngest of the bearers, but the closest.

John was Lynn's first cousin, the favorite cousin. She'd team up with John at family gatherings. She looked forward to the weddings, family picnics and all the family functions that teenagers usually come to dread. She knew John would be there and he would make it fun.

The thought of Lynn at the hands of a monster was too much for John to even image. How frightened she must have been, and he couldn't help her. He felt like he had let down.

Walking behind John, was Warren Couture. Warren, was a sophomore and had harbored a secret crush on Lynn. He never made his feelings known to her, but they were always there. He was sixteen, and over the summer had sprouted up to a full six feet tall.

Lynn hung around with Warren throughout her elementary school years, and this year they were re-united as she entered high school. They had started school together. Lynn in kindergarten, Warren in first grade. Warren would have to continue without her. Lynn was Warren's confidant as well as his best friend. They shared secrets, and now, she was taking all the secrets to her grave.

The last pallbearer followed Warren. Paul Thibadeau. Paul was a junior, and spent a lot of his time at Lynn's house. He was Brenda Chapman's boyfriend. It was Lynn who played 'matchmaker.'

Paul was shy, and with the coaxing of Lynn, he finally got the nerve to ask Brenda to the movies. Little by little, their friendship blossomed and they were a couple. Paul nicknamed Lynn his own 'cupid.' Now his cupid was gone forever. Never to attend her first prom, fall in love. She had so many dreams. He remembered the gnawing feeling he felt in his stomach when he heard the gruesome news. Last night, at the wake, seeing her surrounded by more flowers than he had ever seen, she looked like 'Sleeping Beauty.' If only he was her prince charming, merely a kiss would bring her back.

He had hoped by morning, he would wake and find it was just a terrible nightmare. But, as he walked beside her, he was living the nightmare.

Lynn Ann Clarke's final escorts were stoic, as they walked slowly toward the altar and the awaiting priest. Passing the pews filled with classmates, Lynn's family, they reached the front rows. The journey down the aisle became the most agonizing walk these young boys would ever take.

They passed Phil and Elaine Clarke. Gail Rosen sat to the left of Elaine, and Ben Rosen sat to the right of Phil. Only yesterday, they had attended little David Rosen's burial, and now, they were here, to bury their own daughter.

It was bright and sunny that September morning. As the casket neared the altar, a ray of sunshine filtered through an open stained glass window. It flooded over the casket like a shroud. Some believed it to be Lynn's spirit. It was the last time the sun would shine for Lynn Ann Clarke.

The six escorts took their places in the pews at the front of the church. The priest, wearing the appropriate deep purple vestments, gestured for the congregation to sit. He addressed the multitude. His booming voice echoed throughout the ancient church.

"As we gather here, I know the question in most of your hearts and minds is, where was God? Where was God on the night Lynn Ann Clarke was taken from us? Taken from her friends, teachers, the community and sadly from her loving family."

"We've all been taught, God has a plan, and only He knows or understands it. We are all in agreement, this horrible crime should never have happened, but it did, and we cannot let the seeds of dissension affect us all."

When his brief address was ended, he invited all to kneel as he was about to begin the Requiem of the Dead.

The sound of wooden kneelers dropping into place and the rustle of the mourners leaning forward to kneel was heard throughout the cathedral.

The priest walked up the three carpeted steps to the altar and began,

"Deliver me, O Lord, from eternal death in that tremendous day when the heavens and the earth shall be shaken When Thou shalt come to judge the world with fire."

As he continued with the ritual of the Mass, Mrs. Clarke fought back the tears that welled in her swollen eyes. She closed her eyes and was lost in the flashbacks. It was like watching a movie on fast forward.

She pictured Lynn first as a baby. What a joyous occasion it was when Lynn was baptized here. Then, when she made her first communion kneeling at this very altar railing. She remembered her entering junior high school, and finally, how excited Lynn was only three days ago!

Tuesday PM September 28, 1954

At 12:50 P.M., Gage and Logan pulled into the police station parking lot. They were still somber from the funeral. They didn't have much to say from the church to the station. They did not attend the grave side service. They were able to pay their respects to the Clarke's following the Mass and assured them they would keep them informed throughout the investigation.

It was close to 1:00. They headed straight for the squad room. Each detective poured a cup of coffee and joined the other detectives, shift commanders and supervisors already seated.

The Captain, Medical Examiner, Dr. Aldridge and Chief McNamara walked through the room directly to the elevated platform at the front of the room. They sat at a long table, facing the group of law enforcement personnel.

It was anticipated Dr. Aldridge would offer a profile of what this killer was made of and what to look for. To now, all were merely drawing at straws.

Also, on the platform was a stenographer. She was to take notes of this meeting and make transcripts to be circulated to all police personnel of all shifts. All information was to be shared. That was imperative. Captain Jack Mahoney was the first to speak.

"I'd like to start this meeting by consolidating all tangible information we have. Any evidence, solid leads, tips, everything. We all need to be on an equal playing field. We're a team, and we have to perform as one."

"Who's first?" He looked over the group.

Detective Morgan stood. He read from his notes.

"Mallory and I worked the streets yesterday. We questioned neighbors of the Rosens's. We inquired about the blue thread."

"We questioned Mr. Rosen regarding anyone he could think of that might have a 'grudge' against him. Someone who might be trying to get revenge."

"Mr. Rosen and his brother-in-law, Gordon Schaeffer own three businesses in Stanfield. The R & S Markets. They employ several people. Some on part-time basis, some have been with them since the beginning. However, we asked him to make his employee's files available to us. It's probably a long shot, but we'll be checking through that. We've picked up a few tips that were called into the station, checked them out but nothing came of them. So far, we haven't had enough cause to hold anyone. No arrests."

Detective Connelly was next to summarize what he had. It wasn't much. He had questioned several potential suspects that had been picked up overnight. He couldn't find anything to hold them on. He too had canvassed the neighborhood following up on the 'thread of evidence'. Both Broderick and Connelly reported they contacted neighboring states, requesting information from crimes that were similar in nature to this one.

Connecticut reported a 'slasher' who had killed an elderly lady in her home a week before the Smith/Rosen case. The individual was sent to Bridgwater State Hospital for ten days observation. After checking the record, seems he's still there. That turned out to be a dead end.

Finally Ray Gage stood. He related the information he had regarding Randy. He stressed that he intended to seek a search warrant for the Crawford residence that afternoon and he would like this information withheld from the media.

"I've notified the Albany police," he continued, "and provided a description. I have reason to believe he will be making the bar scene. Drinking age in New York is 18. This kid is 17, but I believe he can and does get served."

He flipped through his notes and continued,

"The NYPD has been advised to keep an eye out along the tracks. Check anyone hopping on and off the trains. Randy Crawford is pretty accustomed to riding from Stanfield to Albany. I've got a unit watching the tracks down at the flats. He should be coming home any day now."

With that, he sat giving the floor to his partner Steve Logan.

Steve stood. Steve Logan was the senior detective and well respected among his peers. He had a presence that quietly demanded the attention of all.

"Ray and I have been keeping close to the Clarke's and Rosen's from the beginning. Through a report from one of the officers that was also on the scene, along with a witness who saw a six foot man on the Rosen's porch at approximately 9:30 Saturday night, we have established the time of the intrusion to be 9:30. This is also fortified by the fact that the Rosen's have a grandfather clock in the foyer to their house. The clock coincidentally stopped at 9:35. So, we've concluded the killer is about 6 feet tall, wore a heavy (unseasonable) jacket and a hat. According to the crime scene photos he wears a size 11-12 shoe."

"Another thing, I'd like you to take particular attention to. It may not seem like much, but it could be. I know we've discussed this thread evidence, but I cannot stress it enough. I believe the thread could have been tied around the weapon in some way."

He continued, "When questioning anyone, particularly if you are at their home, keep your eyes open for evidence of some type of knitting or sewing. If you don't see any indication it is present, ask. So far, the victims families have no association with this thread. It has to have come from the killer."

"Sorry gentlemen, that's about it. We have no motive, no murder weapon. Until the reports come back from the lab that's all. We've questioned students at Lincoln High and according to everyone we've interviewed, she was a terrific girl, one of the nicest girls in the school."

The Captain stood and asked if there was anything else to be added. Seeing no hands, he continued,

"Well, I can tell you that the clothes of the victims, bed sheets, fingernails and blood samples have been sent to the State Police Lab in Boston. We should get the results of that within the next two days."

"Now, I'll turn you over to Dr. Dennis Aldridge. As most of you know, Dr.Aldridge is a highly respected psychologist, specializing in criminal behavior. He is the founder of the Mayor's Committee of Investigation of Juvenile Delinquency. Dr. Aldridge has reviewed the crime scene photos, and the autopsy reports. He is confident he can draw some conclusions and explain just what we're dealing with."

All eyes turned to the doctor as he walked to the center of the platform. They were counting on him to shed the light that was going to get this monster into custody.

"This is not the act of a sane person." The doctor began. "He probably has a record, not a criminal record, but of a long history of peculiar or eccentric behavior. These are the acts of an unbalanced mind which has been unbalanced for some time."

The doctor continued.

"He doesn't know he's sick. He has been able to keep out of mental hospitals. I have been able to conclude by the materials I have been given, this individual shows every classic sign of being a psychopath. Now, this term has been used loosely in our everyday conversations. But, believe me, there is a defined, clinical profile of a psychopath, and this individual seems to fit perfectly."

The doctor paused briefly.

" This person is incapable of feeling or displaying emotion. He feels no remorse, no sorrow, no regrets for his actions, regardless of how despicable they may be. A few of the characteristics, are; he will be void of any discomfort when confronted with the crime. If you interrogate this individual, you will not witness the signs of discomfort you are trained to watch for such as body language, perspiration, shifting positions while being questioned.

None of these signs will be visible when you confront a true psychopath. He will have no difficulty maintaining his usual daily behavior.

If he is a student, he will continue to maintain his regular schedule, while listening eagerly to the horror stories from the other students. He will be unaffected. He does not believe he is capable of anything wrong. Chances are, he has few friends, but also few enemies as well. He is incapable of forming or maintaining meaningful relationships."

The doctor had the full attention of all. He continued.

"If he is a single adult, he probably lives alone. If he is married it is likely his family is unhappy or maladjusted. Psychopaths tend to be in a constant state of boredom. They seek self gratification, and portray a shallow affect."

"That's about it gentlemen, any questions?"

The room buzzed, most were still jotting down notes. Captain Mahoney was listening intently at every word. He was preparing notes for the Chief's press conference. It was imperative, the Chief be kept informed. The public was hungry for up-to-date progress of the investigation. This crime crippled an entire city.

Detective Logan stood up, "Doctor," he began.

"what are the chances this 'psycho' will strike again?"

The doctor thought for a moment and addressed the detective,

"He may quiet down after a double murder. Similar to blowing off steam after a temper tantrum. I don't mean to sound 'trite' about this. Keep in mind, this individual has been harboring these urges for some time. He will be carrying on, appearing as normal as any one of us in this room. This type of individual is very cunning."

The doctor's words were chilling.

The doctor added.

"I have recommended to the Chief, as well as Captain Mahoney that the mental institutions in the area be contacted. You should be looking for any inpatients that may have been on furlough, or escaped."

"If there are no further questions, I'd like to turn you over to Dr. Paul Chapman, the Medical Examiner."

Dr. Chapman stood. He had photos and paperwork in his hand.

"I've completed the autopsies on the two victims. You are well aware, they both suffered from multiple stab wounds."

"The younger victim, male, age four and one half years, David Rosen sustained a total of twenty eight-stab wounds. He died as the result of the first one, which penetrated the aorta. Twenty-seven stab wounds were inflicted post mortem. He also suffered a fractured skull."

Dr. Chapman continued, reading from his notes.

"The female, fourteen years, Lynn Ann Clarke, sustained a total of thirty-eight stab wounds. Examination reveals she fought her attacker. This is indicative of the bruising on both wrists, six broken fingernails on what appeared to be a fresh manicure. She possibly fought after sustaining at least five stab wounds. It is probable that the sixth stab wound was the fatal one. It pierced her left lung and the aorta. Her neck was broken, post mortem, the result of a heavy blow from a blunt object. The girl sustained a total of thirty-eight stab wounds, thirty-two of which were post mortem."

The doctor continued.

"The weapon appears to be some type of a Bowie or butcher knife, with a tapered point. The wounds on both victims were 3/4 to 1 inch wide, and one to two inches in depth. This was clearly a case of overkill. It appears this was a frenzied attack. At some point, the killer was totally out of control. There was no evidence that would support a sexual assault occurred."

"You should be looking for a person who has sustained scratches on his face, hands, or any exposed portion of his body. Flesh scrapings from under the female's fingers have been forwarded to the Crime Lab. These scrapings will indicate the color of the offender. That will be helpful to your investigation."

The Medical Examiner's report ended the one and one-half hour briefing.

By now, it was nearly 3:00. Ray Gage was still waiting for the search warrant that would allow him to search Randy Crawford's residence and car.

Suspects from throughout the city were brought in, questioned and released. The interviews and questioning were unending. Every available means was being extended.

A seventy- man police squad was assigned to comb the nearby park area for the murder weapon. None was found. Every trash container, every imaginable place that one would likely discard a weapon was searched.

The seventy-man squad walked the miles of railroad track that ran behind Archer Boulevard, and through most of the city. They came up with nothing. Police squads and detectives were coming up with countless dead ends.

Detectives as well as patrolmen continued to canvass the neighborhood, looking for a match to the crochet thread. Some residents were reluctant to open their doors to the detectives. The plain clothes detectives displayed their badges, but that did not sway many of the women who were home alone. If they did talk, it would be through a locked door.

"Come back when my husband gets home." They would say. At times, the detectives would bring a uniformed patrolman. The citizens seemed to be more receptive when they saw a squad car and a patrolman.

Cleaning establishments were visited, looking for blood stained clothing. None were found. Teenage girls were banned from babysitting until this maniac was apprehended. A City Councilman proposed an ordinance prohibiting babysitting under the age of 18. This was not passed, but it was clear indication of the fear that captured the citizens of Stanfield, MA

The newspapers carried the story daily, giving it front page coverage. The reporters were kept abreast of any progress, any suspects being held, any arrests, and evidence obtained. The Chief had opened all means of communication. He believed it would be advantageous to the investigation if the public was kept informed, and encouraged to call in any tips they might have.

A tip line was installed at the station, as well as at the newspaper.

The Stanfield News reporters were working in unison with the police department.

The police Chief met with the Editor in Chief of the Stanfield News. The Chief assured the Editor that he would be privy to all information from the police. The Editor instructed all reporters and staff they were to turn over all tips, or information that came into the newsroom. All information was to be turned over to the SPD immediately. Anyone trying to get a 'scoop' would be dismissed.

The police became the conduit to the newspapers. It was unprecedented. The Police Department and The Stanfield News would be working in unison for the common good. The Stanfield News stated there would be no sensationalism, strictly facts verified by the police before anything went to press.

A system was devised for potential claimants of the reward money. It was referred to as 'Operation Clues'.

The plan guarded the identity of the informants but left them eligible for the mounting reward. By the time the plan was implemented, the reward money had grown to $2,500.00. The reward was donated by private citizens as well as business owners. It was offered for information leading to the arrest, and conviction, of the killer.

On the first day, of Operation Clue, thirty tips on the murders were received.

Any person with a tip on the double murders who wished to remain anonymous, yet still be entitled to the reward money was to send the tip to P.O. Box 308.

This plan was devised by the Citizens Crime Committee of Massachusetts and approved by Police Chief McNamara along with the contributors to the mounting reward.

If a person had information that may be helpful to police, but feared retaliation, the person was instructed to write the clue on a piece of paper. Then, print any five digit number in the top right as well as the lower right corners.

They were instructed to tear off the lower right corner containing the duplicate number and retain it as a receipt. Then, they were to send the tip with the other number to the post office box.

The tips were to be turned over to the police and kept in a separate file. Finally, when the case was solved and the murderer convicted, the police, along with twelve reward officials would meet to decide which, if any, was the tip that had lead to the conviction. The number on that particular tip would be announced publically. The person who supplied the tip was instructed to go, with the corner that fit into the letter, to a local bank to obtain the reward. There would be no questions and no publicity. It was similar to a lottery!

After the information delivered at the earlier briefing, investigators were forced to return to the theory that a maniac killed Lynn and David.

The Chief announced to the reporters. "We're concentrating on finding a demented killer."

He added, that a thorough police campaign in which all mentally-ill persons of potential homicidal tendencies would be quizzed. These statements would be tomorrow's headlines, along with Dr. Aldridge's profile of the killer.

Finally, at 4:30, Ray Gage, armed with the search warrant, signed out of the station.

Steve Logan went back to his desk to gather any new information that may have developed. Information was coming in on an hourly basis. He picked up a report flagged priority. Two men were found with blood stained clothes in their car. They were being held at the station.

Captain Mahoney and Steve Logan would conduct the questioning. The officers that had apprehended the latest pair of suspects were called into the Captain's office. The Captain was briefed with every detail.

Steve walked to the Captain's office. The two proceeded to the interrogation room. It was no secret, the Captain was not one to be reckoned with when he conducted an interrogation. Captain Mahoney was from the 'old school' and tolerated very little from suspects. He asked the questions, and the suspects had best come up with suitable answers.

They entered the small room. One of the two suspects was seated, leaning his chair back against the wall. He was puffing on a cigarette and smirked at the two officers as they entered the room.

"Sit up and listen!" The Captain spoke, without any introduction. He was in control and the suspect was going to know it right from the start.

The suspect, Ronald Prescott was not impressed by the Captain. He continued to tip his chair back and puff on his cigarette.

"Mr. Prescott, I've asked you to sit up and pay attention to what I've got to say to you."

"Who the hell are you?" Came the reply from Prescott.

"Captain Mahoney," replied the Captain as he stepped closer to the suspect. He gave the chair a kick out from under the suspect.

"What the hell do you think you're doing?" Shouted Prescott.

Captain Mahoney reached for the overturned chair as Prescott, still on the floor, instinctively raised his arm to shield himself. The Captain righted the chair and addressed the cowering suspect.

"Now, we can do this one of two ways, Mr. Prescott. The hard way, or my way. Do we understand each other now?"

Steve Logan stood leaning against the wall. His arms were folded. He'd seen the Captain's methods before, and seemed to enjoy the manner in which the Captain effectively operated.

Captain Jack Mahoney was 6ft. 2. He had served in the Marine Corp., and upon his discharge, took the civil service examination to become a police officer. He was a handsome, rugged man who looked like a character straight out of a John Wayne movie.

The detectives were proud and honored to serve under Mahoney's command. He was a cop's cop. He too had come up the ranks and possessed a though understanding of his detectives. He considered his command one of the finest in the Commonwealth.

Steve raised one hand to cover the grin that was slowly creeping across his mouth, as he watched the unique style of his Captain. This would be an interesting interrogation.

Ray Gage pulled up to 36 Water Street Ext. a little after 5:00 P.M.. He knocked on the door and Mrs. Crawford answered with a cordial greeting.

"Well, Detective, this is a surprise," she commented.

"I haven't heard from Randy, so what's the purpose of this visit?"

Ray pulled the search warrant from his jacket pocket.

"I have a warrant, Mrs. Crawford, to search Randy's room and the car."

Mrs. Crawford stepped back and seemed to be speechless. "A warrant, for what? Do you think Randy killed those two kids? What do you think you will find here?"

"I'd like to search his room and the car," Gage repeated, in his most professional tone.

"Could be nothing. His actions are very suspicious, and maybe this search will clear him of any suspicion. One way or the other, I need to execute this warrant."

"My God, Detective, should I call someone? Should I call an attorney? I don't know how to handle this."

"I don't think an attorney will be necessary, Mrs. Crawford. Can you show me to Randy's room?"

Mrs. Crawford stiffened and led him upstairs to Randy's room. Ray could see she was visibly shaken, and he genuinely felt bad for her. After all, she's the mother, and if Randy's the monster, they'd been scouring the city for, she would take personal responsibility. It would devastate her, of course. She didn't deserve the anguish she would bear should Randy be responsible for this atrocity.

As they walked toward Randy's room, they passed Emily Crawford's bedroom. Ray glanced into the room, and spotted a sewing machine in the corner.

"Mrs. Crawford, do you do much sewing?" He asked as casually as the situation would allow.

"Yes, I do alterations, for a little extra income." She answered.

"Do you knit, or crochet?" Ray asked.

"Oh, heavens no. I hardly have time to do that sort of thing. I don't even know how to do that type of work. No, I just do alterations."

"Well, that must help with your expenses."

"Yes, I do what I can, and when I have the time." She answered, and appeared more at ease.

As they entered Randy's room, Mrs. Crawford quipped, "The maid has the day off." The room was in total disarray. Clothes were strewn everywhere. Bags of empty soda bottles were stacked in the corner. An ashtray on the night stand was overflowing with cigarette butts. There wasn't a surface that was clear. Ray had seen teenagers' rooms before. He wasn't as shocked as Mrs. Crawford was embarrassed.

"Don't concern yourself, Mrs. Crawford. They're all alike." Ray tried to put Mrs. Crawford at ease.

"I have a teenage daughter, you'd think a girl would be a little more tidy, well, she's not." Ray lied.

As he continued to speak casually to Mrs. Crawford, he began looking around the room for some evidence of Randy's involvement in the double murders. He searched the closet, the dresser and the night stand. He lifted the mattress on the bed. Nothing. He looked up at the ceiling. The light fixture was covered with a large globe. Using a chair to stand on, he reached inside the globe. Nothing.

Mrs. Crawford followed his every step. She was silent now. Finally, Ray went back to the closet. There was an assortment of shoes on the floor. He searched them one at a time. As he reached into a black boot, similar to that of a motorcyclist, he felt something. He tipped the boot upside down, noting size 11 ½, on the sole. As he shook the boot, a switchblade dropped to the floor. Ray reached for the handkerchief in his back pocket. Carefully, he picked up the knife. Giving the knife a cursory look, he wrapped it up in the handkerchief and put it into his jacket pocket.

By now, Mrs. Crawford was starting to cry. Every thought ran through her mind. It just isn't possible, she thought. Ray said nothing as he continued to retrace his steps. He opened the dresser drawer that he had previously looked into. He began to move the contents around. At the bottom of the drawer, he found a picture of Lynn Ann Clarke. He removed the picture and turned it over. On the back, in childish handwriting, 'Lynn, my angel' and on the lower left corner of the picture, 1953.

"Do you know this girl?" Ray asked Mrs. Crawford.

"No, I don't know who she is. Do you?" She asked, knowing the detective's answer.

"This is the girl that was slain last Saturday." Ray said, almost apologetically.

"Looks like her school picture from last year."

Ray continued to look carefully for anything else that might link Randy to Lynn. He saw a small notebook. It looked like the proverbial 'little black book' that most keep pages of telephone numbers in. He leafed through it. Most of the pages were blank. A few telephone numbers scribbled, without names. Closer examination, he spotted the name Lynn, followed by RE8-0878 Lynn's telephone number, no doubt. He would check it out.

"Well, that's about it, Mrs. Crawford," he said. "Do you have the keys to the car? I'd like to check it out."

Mrs. Crawford led the detective out of the bedroom and downstairs to the kitchen. On a hook beside the back door was a set of car keys. She handed them to the detective.

Ray Gage went to the car, as Mrs. Crawford watched from the kitchen window. Ray looked through the glove compartment. Registration, pen, sunglasses, gum, bottle opener, the usual contents. He searched under the seats. With the exception of a couple of empty beer bottles and crumpled Lucky Strike packs, he found nothing he could connect to the murders.

Next, he went to the trunk. Inside he found a rolled up bundle of heavily soiled clothes. Beside the clothes, a tire iron. Could that be how the girl's neck was broken? Could that be what delivered the savage blow to fracture David's skull? He couldn't determine what the stains on the clothes were, could it be blood? Could this be the clothing of the murderer?

Returning to the kitchen, he asked Mrs. Crawford for a paper bag. Without hesitation, she obliged, handing him a brown paper bag. The sides of the bag read, R & S Market.

Ray carefully placed the clothing into the bag, along with the tire iron. He removed the knife, still wrapped in his handkerchief and placed it in the bag along with the little black book and photograph of Lynn Ann. Mrs. Crawford remained silent as Ray Gage sat at the kitchen table and filled out an official form.

He listed the clothing, the knife, the tire iron, the picture of Lynn and the small black book as 'evidence seized', and handed it to Mrs. Crawford.

"What am I supposed to do with this?" Mrs. Crawford asked.

"It's only a receipt, listing what I've taken from your premises." Ray answered.

"I'll be in touch with you after I've had these items analyzed."

"Analyzed! Analyzed for what?" Suddenly the quiet mother was enraged.

"What are you saying Detective? Are you saying Randy is the monster the whole city has been looking for? I can assure you, Randy is no saint, but I think you've gone too far. Randy is not a murderer!" She was shouting and sobbing.

Ray attempted to calm the woman down.

"Mrs. Crawford, I have to check everything out. This may be nothing, and if that's the case, we can eliminate Randy from the suspect list once and for all. Let's hope that's the way this turns out. Again, please contact me if you hear from him, or if he returns home."

With that, Ray left. He felt like a heel for leaving Emily Crawford in the state she was in, but he had a job to do.

By the time Ray returned to the station, it was nearly 7:00. He called Linda.

"Did you watch the press conference on the news tonight?" He asked. Linda said she had, and it was very impressive.

"I'll be home in about ½ hr. Do you want me to pick up anything at the store?"

"No thanks, just come home. Supper will be ready. I've been missing you this past week. See you soon."

"I've missed you too, Hon. I'll be home soon." Ray replied and hung up.

He picked up the paper bag on his desk and carried it to the evidence room.

"Sully, I'll need a couple of evidence bags for this stuff," he said to the officer behind the plastic window.

Ray placed each item into a separate bag. He marked each with the date, time and place it was collected from. Then he sealed it and scribbled his initials across the sealed flap.

"Will you give them all a number and check them in with the Rosen/Clarke case? Has the courier been by for his pick up yet?"

"Nope, you just made it. He should be here any minute now."

"Send these three to the crime lab," he said, indicating the soiled clothing, the knife and the tire iron.

The courier was scheduled daily to pick up evidence and deliver it to the State Police Lab, Boston for testing. Hopefully, Ray would have results of this evidence this time tomorrow.

"You wrapping it up for the day?" Asked the clerk.

"Yup! Have a good night Sully."

Ray quickly checked his messages, and decided they could wait until tomorrow. Nothing looked pressing and he was anxious to get home. Today's report could wait until morning. He would get in early.

The Chief's press conference was well received. The public needed an indication that these murders were still top priority and investigations were on going around the clock. Until they could feel safe, nothing short of the apprehension of the depraved monster would do.

Maybe then, they could continue the secure and safe life they had enjoyed prior to September 25, 1954.

Wednesday, AM September 29, 1954

Stanfield News Headlines:

POLICE ASK FOR RUSH ON TEST OF SKIN UNDER NAILS OF BABY SITTER

Detective Broderick Sent to Boston in Effort to Speed Up Report

Police sent an officer to Boston to get the state pathologist's report which may reveal the color of the maniacal killer who knifed Lynn Ann Clarke and David Rosen.

"Impatient" over the delay in receiving an analysis of skin found under Lynn Ann's fingernails, Captain Mahoney finally dispatched Detective Broderick to the state laboratories at Harvard University in an attempt to get the reports right away.

Detective Broderick has been instructed to get all information about the skin particles by this afternoon and phone immediately to local police headquarters. Police said determination of the color of the assailant would be of great help in the stalemated murder probe.......

Lynn Ann Clarke's picture, along with statements from her friends that had attended the funeral were spread across three columns. Friends described the fourteen-year-old as the nicest girl in school. Teachers commented she was potentially a straight A honor student. All expressed shock and horror over the young girl's gruesome death.

Sub headlines followed the featured story:
"DEATH HUNT CONTINUES, SUSPECTS QUIZZED"
'Murder Area Searched; Early Suspects Brought in For Extended Questioning'

The murder probe turned back to original territory The investigation of the latest suspect looked promising...

Logan and Captain Mahoney had questioned the two suspects for nearly hours. The headquarters became alive with activity unequaled since the intensive probe had gotten underway. Logan believed he had obtained enough cause to hold this suspect.

Logan was quoted, "One looks promising. The suspect was picked up as a result of re-questioning of persons queried earlier and a new check of homes in the area."

Logan hesitated to answer any specific questions. Logan added, "Several persons who were grilled immediately after the September 25th murders have been brought in for intensive re-examination."

He believed he had enough information to at least hold this suspect until he was able to track down the alibi, and hopefully the evidence reports would be delivered today. They could shed some light on this new suspect.

When Ray Gage arrived at the station, the reporters rushed to him, microphones held overhead, and cameras rolling. "Detective Gage, can you tell us of any progress in your investigation?"

Ray was cautious. He didn't want to give Randy's name. Randy hadn't been apprehended, and if his name got out, he'd run for sure.

"Nothing today," he replied.

"Hopefully, we'll know more when the evidence is returned from Boston, later today."

He continued to walk toward the station. The camera crews and reporters walked hastily along with him, firing questions. Most of the questions went unanswered. They were looking for the lead story for the evening news.

Ray entered the building, and the media retreated to their vehicles. They would return later that day. The newsroom was equipped with the Associated Press ticking continuously as well as police scanners constantly monitoring the police calls.

Detective Connelly was summoned into the Captain's office. The Captain had received information from Hartford, Connecticut

Police Department. An elderly woman had been stabbed, 18 times in her home only one week before the Clarke/Rosen murders. The perpetrator was in the custody of the Connecticut State Police. Connelly was directed to question this individual at the Hartford Police Headquarters.

According to the Hartford P.D., the suspect was six foot one, 225 lbs., and had visual scratches on his neck and chest. The suspect was unable to remember where he was at 9:30, Saturday, September 25. Also, the suspect was employed at the Eastern States Exposition, located in West Stanfield, Massachusetts. This was certainly enough to send the detective to Hartford.

Upon his arrival at the Hartford P.D., Detective Connelly was led into the interrogation room. Within a few minutes, Samuel Reynolds was led in, flanked by two uniformed Hartford Policemen.

Reynolds plopped down at the table in the center of the room. He gave the impression he'd been through this routine before, and showed no signs of being edgy or nervous. Connelly pulled his chair up closer to the table, directly across from Reynolds. He went through the usual introductions and began his questioning.

After several hours, Connelly was getting nowhere. Reynolds had his story wrapped up in a neat little package, with very few holes in it. He had worked at the Exposition in West Stanfield. He ran the Ferris wheel on the midway. He was at the Exposition working the ride on the night of the murder. No, he didn't know anyone that could back up his story. He didn't have any friends on the grounds. He was paid in cash by the company that provided the rides. He was what was referred to as a 'floater'.

"How did you get those scratches?" Connelly asked.

"I met a broad, after I got off. We drank a bottle of whiskey, and she got a little out of hand. The broad went nuts!" He claimed.

"What was her name, Sam?" Connelly asked.

"How in hell do I know? She was a 'carni' you know, just travels around with the fair." Reynolds was getting annoyed.

"According to the Hartford Chief, you couldn't remember where you were on that night."

"You know, the week before you cut up the old lady."

"Well, I thought about it, and remembered, I was with this chick, from the fair."

It was all Connelly could do to even bear being in the same room with Reynolds. The odor emanating from him made Connelly nauseous, and he knew Reynolds wasn't going anywhere. Hartford had him booked for the murder of the old lady. He would be available for further questioning, after Connelly checked out the story Reynolds told him.

While Broderick was on his way to Boston, Morgan continued questioning the countless suspects that had been brought in overnight. Most were questioned, and released. Some were held, pending the results of the lab reports.

Steve Logan was getting impatient. He needed the results of the testing. Legally, he could only hold a suspect for twenty-four hours. The clock was ticking. He sifted through all the reports he had read over and over, hoping he might have missed something. He still believed he was going to find the killer by focusing on the student body of Lincoln High School. It was a gut feeling. Revenge directed toward the Rosen's didn't seem likely, but he would certainly check it out. Nothing was to be left to chance.

Logan picked up the list he'd received from Ben Rosen. It included past as well as present employees. Mr. Rosen and Mr. Schaefer had employed several high school boys over the summers. They stocked shelves, bagged groceries, made deliveries and generally cleaned up at closing. Most were only 'seasonal employees'. They were hired for the summer and when schools resumed in the fall, they left to go back to school.

The detective looked for the list of 'former employees' that had been fired. It was a very short list. Reasons for firing were the usual. Three for not showing up, two for not performing satisfactory, and one for stealing. Jack Foster, dismissed for stealing products from the store. Could that be the motive for these savage murders? Logan shook his head. He could not bring himself to buying that as a motive. He decided to give the list to a uniform officer. It would take little time to run down this handful of unlikely individuals, but they had to be checked off as contacted.

Steve Logan got up from his desk and stretched. He'd been clocking sixteen to twenty hours a day since this investigation began, and didn't see any light at the end of the tunnel. He poured two cups of coffee and walked to Ray's desk.

"So, how'd you do with the search warrant? Has the kid gotten home yet?" Steve asked.

"I've got the report right here," Ray answered, holding up the freshly typed report.

"I'm going to let the press know we've got serious interest in this boy. I don't want to release the name, but I think we have enough to constitute further investigation."

Ray continued, "I do have a feeling about this Crawford kid. What do you think, Steve?"

"You may have something." Steve replied, then he filled his partner in with the activities of Detective Connelly.

"The elderly woman was stabbed 18 times. Same as these kids, 'overkill' as Aldridge put it.

"He's been working right in West Stanfield at the Exposition. The suspect showed up at the Exposition last Sunday morning with scratches on his face. The man left town the same day.

The General Manager of the Exposition was questioned by the newspaper. He reported he knew nothing of this report until he saw today's newspapers. He said he was positive the man wasn't a regular Exposition employee.

The man probably was employed by the company who ran the midway at the fair. The manager said to make sure, however, he was going to check the regular payroll to see if any regular workers left the job on Sunday.

The manager described the man as a 'floater'.

" People of that type are not hired for regular Exposition jobs. Transients are employed by concessions and amusement ride companies."

The two detectives were interrupted by the phone. "Gage, line three," came over the intercom. Ray pressed the flashing button on his phone.

"This is Sargent Gage," he stated.

"Is this Detective Raymond Gage?" A woman's voice asked.

"Yes, who am I speaking to?" Asked Gage.

"This is Emily Crawford. I just wanted to let you know that Randy came home sometime last night, or early morning. I don't know exactly when, but he was here when I got up this morning. He's here now, sleeping. But I won't be here. I'm already late for work." Mrs. Crawford spoke almost in a whisper.

"Thank you, Mrs. Crawford, I'm on my way right now."

Gage and Logan were on their way. They headed north up Archer Boulevard. As they passed the 'murder house' they saw a large moving van backed up to the front porch.

"Hey, what's going on there?" Steve asked.

"Pull over, let's check this out."

Ray pulled the black sedan to the curb directly in front of 425 Archer Boulevard. A burly man, clad in white coveralls was standing on the porch reading paperwork that was clipped to a board.

"Hi there," Steve said casually. The mover looked up, and didn't reply.

"Rosen's moving out?" Another attempt to be casual.

"Yup, who are you?" The mover asked.

"Stanfield Police Department, Detective Logan." Steve answered, displaying his badge.

"Moving everything?"

"Yup, got the orders right here, you want to see 'em?"

"Yes, I would, if you don't mind." Steve reached for the clipboard.

The work order was signed by Benjamin Rosen. The instructions were clear. All contents, including all clothing and personal items, to be transported to Burgess Storage, Jackson Ave., Stanfield, MA.

Mrs. Brazzini was walking to the detective's car where Ray waited patiently.

"Is anything wrong?" She asked. "The van got here about an hour ago. Frankly I was shocked to see it."

"No, nothing to be concerned about, ahhh, sorry, I can't recall your name." Ray felt a little awkward.

"Its Theresa Brazzini, I live next door. I met you the night, well, when you were here." She couldn't say the words.

"The past couple of days, Mr. Rosen's sister and brother-in-law have been in and out. Looked like they were picking up clothing for the Rosen's. Some boxes that looked like paperwork. I haven't seen the Rosen's. I spoke to Gail Rosen on the telephone. She didn't sound good. Of course she wouldn't, but she sounded like she's heavily medicated. Poor thing."

Ray listened, but was becoming impatient. He looked at his watch. It's been nearly 15 minutes since they stopped here. He pictured Randy, slipping out of the house and hopping another train.

"Mrs. Brazzini, I'm glad you've been keeping an eye on things. Did Mrs. Rosen tell you what her plans were, where they were moving?" Ray asked.

"No, she just said she would never step foot inside this house again. I didn't take it serious. You know, people say things when they're upset. It appears she meant it. As far as I know, the Rosen's are still staying with Ben's sister in West Stanfield."

Steve Logan was walking toward the car. Finally, Ray thought.

"Well, Mrs. Brazinni, if you see anything out of order, feel free to call us at the station." Ray handed her his card.

"Good morning," Steve greeted Mrs. Brazinni, as he got into the car.

"Good morning, Detective." She replied.

"Thanks. Mrs. Brazzini." Ray gave the woman a quick wave and they were off.

"Christ, Steve, that couldn't wait? I've got to get this kid into the station before he skips."

"Take it easy, Cowboy! That kid isn't going anywhere. You'll be lucky if he's even seen the light of day yet." Steve gave his partner a little jab in the arm.

"Loosen up a little, Ray."

They took a right onto Dorset, and then Water Street, over the tracks and onto Water St. Ext. The Ford sedan was still disabled beside Building #36.

Ray pulled up in front of Unit B. Both men exited the car. Instinctively, Steve walked to the side of the unit, where the back door was located. Once he was positioned, Ray knocked on the door, and waited for an answer. Nothing. He waited and knocked again.

Still, no answer. Keeping an eye on the front door, he walked to the side of the building, in view of his partner.

Steve walked to the front.

"I've got an idea." Ray said.

"Take the car, go to the phone booth up on Dorset, and call this number." He handed him a piece of paper with Randy's telephone number written on it.

"He's probably scoping us out right now. Figures we'll just go away if he doesn't answer." Ray replied.

"So what do you want me to tell him?" Steve looked a little baffled at his partner's scheme.

"Just get him to answer the phone. When he does, tell him who you are, and that you want him to answer the door, or you will, well, just tell him whatever comes to mind. Tell him you'll break the damn door down! Just get him to answer the door. I'll be here when he does."

"Boy, Ray, you come up with some beauties, okay, I'll be right back. Don't get crazy. We're just taking him in for questioning. Remember, this is not an arrest. Go by the book, no grandstanding!"

"You worry too much," Ray laughed. "I know the drill!"

Ray watched Steve head toward Dorset St. Any minute he should hear the phone ring.

Within a couple of minutes, the phone rang. Come on, pick it up! Come on, Randy, answer the damn phone! After about six rings, it was quiet.

Ray waited, not sure whether Randy answered, or Steve gave up. All he could do was wait for his partner to return. He lit a cigarette and sat on the front steps. No sound came from inside the house. He walked to the side where he had view of the side door as well as the front. Still, no sign of anyone.

Five minutes went by. Another five, and he saw Steve approaching the house. Ray met Steve as he got out of the sedan.

"Well, did he answer?" Ray asked.

"He answered," Steve replied. "I told him we wanted to talk to him. He didn't seem to have too much objection to that. Of course, he wanted to know what we wanted to talk about."

"So, what did you tell him?" Ray pressed.

"I told him to just put some clothes on, and answer the front door. He said okay." Steve replied.

"Frankly, I was surprised he didn't put up a fuss."

"Well, I guess we should be knocking at Mr. Crawford's door." Ray said as he stepped up onto the porch.

Ray knocked loudly. It was as if Randy were just waiting for the knock. He opened the door immediately.

"Randy Crawford?" Asked Ray.

"Yes, what do you want me for?" Randy answered. He looked pretty disheveled. Heavy 'five o'clock shadow' for a boy his age. He was over six feet tall. Ray assessed his suspect from head to toe in a matter of a minute.

"We'd like to take you down to the station for a few questions, you have any problem with that?"

"Well, I'd like to know what it's about. What kind of questions?" Randy asked, almost childishly.

"We're investigating the murders of Lynn Ann Clarke and David Rosen." Ray replied. "Have you heard about the murders?"

"Yeah, pretty gruesome from what I heard." Randy said.

"No, I haven't got any problem with that. I wasn't even around when they got killed. I'll answer your questions. Give me a minute to get my shoes on. I'll be right with you." Randy shut the door.

Steve and Ray exchanged looks. They were both thinking the same thing. Steve raced around to the side door, and Ray stepped back to the street where he could see the entire house.

Shortly, Randy stepped out onto the porch. Ray and Steve took a sigh of relief!

The three walked to the detective's car. Randy rode in the back. There was little conversation on the way to the station.

Upon arrival, Steve went directly to his desk. Ray walked Randy into the interrogation room.

"Have a seat Randy." Ray said, directing the boy to the empty chair at the battered wooden table.

"Want something to drink, soda, coffee?" Ray asked.

"No, I'm fine." Randy was getting uncomfortable already.

"What's this all about anyway? Why are you questioning me?" He was getting more and more anxious.

"Want to tell me where you were Saturday, September 25 around 9:30 P.M.?" Ray was going straight for the juggler. No sense dancing around. Either he had an alibi, or he didn't.

"I was home," was Randy's answer.

"Your mother says you were out." Ray shot back.

"She doesn't know when I'm home half the time. I was home!" Randy was shifting in his chair.

"You got a cigarette?" He asked. Ray tossed a package of Lucky Strikes across the table.

Randy picked it up, his hands were visibly shaking now. He searched his pockets for a match. Ray leaned over and lit the cigarette. Randy leaned back in the chair, crossed his left ankle over his right knee and took a long drag. Ray waited. Those long pauses in an interrogation can be agony for the suspect. Ray was playing every card he had. He fired questions at Randy,

"Anybody you can get in here to verify you were home? Talk to anyone on the phone? Maybe you called Lynn Ann Clarke that night?"

Randy shot a look at Ray. His deep-set eyes seemed to bore into the detective. He was getting angry. That's what Ray was hoping for.

"No, I didn't call her. I never called her! She wouldn't talk to me if I did!" Randy shouted.

Ray was taking notes. That was the first lie.

"Ever stop by when she's babysitting Randy? You know, just to keep her company?"

"No, never!" Randy shot back.

"Well, you liked her a lot though, didn't you Randy? You had her picture, her phone number. But you never called her? Come on, you called her, didn't you? I know you called her, Randy."

"No, I never called her!. I didn't even know her that much. She was kinda of 'stuck up' you know what I mean?"

He was grinding the cigarette butt into the ashtray and reaching for another. Ray snatched the pack from his shaking hand.

"Let's think about this Randy. Tell me the whole story, then we'll figure out what we can do about it."

"There's nothing to think about." Randy folded his arms across his chest. He was making a statement. He was about to shut down. Ray had seen this before.

"Well, I'll tell you what. I'm going to get a cup of coffee. You think about that Saturday night, and when I get back, we'll take it from the top. Fair enough?"

Randy didn't answer. Ray left the room. He went directly to his partner. He had to come up with something that would make Randy tell him the whole story. So far, he'd caught him in one lie. He knew there was more.

He brought his partner up to date. Could he hold Randy pending the results from the lab on the soiled clothing, knife and tire iron he had sent for testing?

Ray poured a cup of coffee and went to the vending machine. He pressed the button for a Coke.

"Well, here goes, round two!" Ray said, giving Steve a thumbs up.

The detective placed the bottle of Coke on the table and tossed Randy the pack of cigarettes. Randy grabbed the cigarettes and Ray reached over to light it. Again, Randy took a long drag on the Lucky Strike, and leaned back on the wooden chair.

"Well, Randy, tell me again. Where were you on the night of the murders?"

"I told you, I was home." Randy shot back. "My mother was there, she'll tell you."

"I've talked to your mother, she says you weren't home." Ray boldly replied. "She says you come and go from that house like you were a boarder. I don't think she's going to be able to back you up on this one."

"What you talking about? When did you talk to my mother?" Randy asked. "You got no right bothering her. I had nothing to do with that murder."

"Two murders, Randy. Two people dead. These were real people. Lynn Ann Clarke had a mother and father and a little sister. David Rosen had parents and a six year old brother! For God's sake, Randy, why? A four year old boy? Why the boy Randy?"

124

"I don't know what you're talking about. When did you talk to my mother?" He asked again.

"Well, Randy, I spoke to her when I searched your room and car." Ray was pushing the boy now. "Didn't she tell you?"

"I haven't seen her. I've been out of town since Sunday." Randy shot back.

"Where'd you go?"

"I was with some friends of mine. They'll tell you. I was home on Saturday night. Left Sunday morning with some friends. Ask them, they'll tell you."

"I'm asking you Randy. But if I asked them, can they tell me where you were Saturday night around 9:30?" Ray pressed on. "Can they tell me what you did with the murder weapon? Come on, Randy, what happened, she let you in, and what happened? How'd you get her to let you in?"

"I told you, I was home. I wasn't anywhere near Archer Boulevard. Never been to that house."

"Well, Randy, I don't believe you. That's all you have to tell me?" Ray asked.

"Yes, that's all. I don't know anything else." Randy answered as he reached for the Coke.

"Then, I guess it's only fair that I tell you what I think." Ray watched the boy. No signs of discomfort, but he remembered Dr. Aldridge's comments, "the suspect will probably show no classic signs that you are trained to watch for."

"Do you want to tell me how you got the picture? It's unlikely Lynn gave it to you. She didn't sign it. Usually, people sign the back of a picture when they give it away. Lynn didn't sign that picture. You did. You went to the Rosen's house. You really like her, and you wanted to babysit with her. You waited until the kids were sleeping, and then what Randy? When did you decide to cut her up like a piece of meat? Did the boy see you? Is that why you killed the boy? What kind of person are you Randy? Maybe you're sick. Tell me what happened, maybe I can help you."

"Hey, Detective, you've got it all wrong! I'm telling you I wasn't anywhere near that place. I never touched any boy, or Lynn Ann either."

"Tell me again, Randy, where did you get her picture?"

"I got it off a friend of mine. Is that a crime?" Randy was starting to perspire.

"Nope, but what about the phone number. You said you never called her, but you had her phone number in your 'little black book'. Now did you call her or didn't you Randy?"

"No I never called her. I haven't even seen her since last year in school."

Ray knew the boy was lying. He had seen her at the movies the afternoon of the murder!

"How about the clothes in your trunk? That's right, those are at the lab for testing as we speak."

"What clothes, I don't know anything about any clothes. I don't know what you're talking about."

"Come on Randy, I got the bundle of soiled clothes from the trunk of your car. Now, am I going to find Lynn's blood on them? Maybe the Rosen boy's blood? Is the knife from your boot the one you used Randy? The tire iron what you whacked them with?" Ray was firing questions at Randy faster than the boy could answer.

Randy put his head in his hands. He ran his fingers through his greasy dark hair. He was tired, it had been hours since they started and Randy was not going to answer any more questions.

Ray leaned back, put his feet up on the table and lit a cigarette. The detective waited for Randy to say something. The silence just hung there. One minute seemed like five. The only sound was the old Seth Thomas ticking away the minutes.

Finally, Ray broke the silence.

"Well, Randy, tell you what I have to do now. You've had all the opportunity to tell me everything you know about this case. I have enough evidence to hold you until I get the test reports back. Now, anything else you have to tell me?"

Randy sat up and was visibly shaken.

"You going to arrest me? You going to lock me up? I didn't do anything. Those clothes you found belong to a friend of mine. He got into a fight with a guy on the street. The guy cut my friend up pretty bad. We went to my house, and he cleaned up. I gave him a shirt and pants to change into. That's it. I swear!"

126

"Well, then when the clothes come back, we'll see whose blood is on them. If it checks out to be true what you've told me, you have nothing to worry about. Meanwhile, you'll be a guest of the City. I can keep you in custody for twenty-four hours, then, I've got to turn you loose, or arrest you. Do you understand?"

"But, I didn't do anything. How can you keep me? I didn't do anything!"

Ray stood up and took Randy by the arm.

"Just come with me. Let's not make this difficult. Just twenty-four hours, and we'll see."

Ray was surprised that Randy didn't resist. He stood up, his head down, and he looked like he was about to cry! Ray walked him to the processing room.

The officer instructed Randy to empty his pockets, remove his belt and shoes. Ray filled out some paperwork, and left Randy to officer Gammon. He would take it from there. Randy would remain in custody overnight.

Reports were coming in every hour. Suspects were questioned, some released. Tips were being followed up, and the patrol officers continued to canvas the neighborhood, looking for that one piece of thread that would match the one held in evidence.

At five o'clock, Connelly returned from Hartford. He had spent several hours questioning the 'knifer' but determined it was a dead end.

Broderick was still in Boston, and had reported no progress on the submitted evidence. The Commissioner was calling the Chief, and the Chief was handing down the heat to Captain Mahoney. It was frustrating. They needed something!

What was taking so long? Their hands were tied. The Chief called in Mahoney. He was putting pressure on the Captain, and in turn, the Captain pressured his men. He told Baldwin to remain in Boston overnight and perhaps he would get the reports in the morning.

Gage and Logan visited the families of the victims. Mrs. Clarke was sinking deeper into depression. Mr. Clarke was worried about her. The detectives gently prodded Phil Clarke, hoping for something more. He had nothing to add. Barbara had been sent to spend a few days with her maternal grandmother. The detectives answered all of Mr. Clarke's inquiries regarding any progress on the investigation. Unfortunately, they had little to tell him, but assured him it was top priority throughout all districts. They were confident the killer would be apprehended.

Later, Gage and Logan visited the Rosen's in West Stanfield, at Mr. Rosen's sister's house. Mrs. Rosen was unable to speak with them. She remained in the guest room, and Mr. Rosen wasn't much better than his wife. Mr. and Mrs. Schaefer made an effort to put the detectives at ease.

The two detectives inquired about the abrupt move from Archer Boulevard.

"Gail will never go back to that house. She's very adamant about that. Can you blame her? She's not doing well at all. I'm worried about her."

Mrs. Schaefer was very concerned for the welfare of her sister-in-law.

"She won't let poor Daniel out of her sight. She's heavily medicated and sleeps a lot. When she sleeps, we take Daniel out. He's very confused. We've not been able to tell him everything. I don't think he can comprehend the horrible truth. We've told him David is very ill, and has to stay in the hospital." Mrs. Schaefer felt helpless.

"I don't know how long we can go on like this."

Ben Rosen joined the four seated around the kitchen table. Mr. Schaefer had nothing to say. Occasionally he nodded in agreement with his wife, otherwise, he said nothing.

Mr. Rosen asked about the progress of the investigation. He only knew what he read in the papers.

"I feel like I'm on an emotional roller coaster! One day I read you've arrested a suspect, only to read the next day, he's released. I haven't even read the paper this morning. I can't go through this much longer. My wife is very ill. Daniel is asking too many questions and I have no answers for him."

He looked at the detectives for answers. They had none.

"What are your plans, now that you've moved from your house?" Asked Gage. "Will you be looking for another soon?"

"No, not in Stanfield. I don't know what we are going to do. I'm working out something with Gordon, that's my brother-in-law. We have a business to run, and I'm not in any condition to be useful right now."

"Ben, that's the least of your worries, you know that." Replied Gordon Schaefer.

"You take whatever time you and Gail need. The important thing is to get your lives and that of Daniel back to some kind of normalcy."

Ben Rosen reached over and laid his hand on his brother- -in-law's arm. He gave it a squeeze and replied,

"What would Gail and I do without you and Millie?"

Steve Logan reported that the list of employees of the R&S Markets had been thoroughly check out and everyone on the list was cleared. There were no suspects. He went on to tell Mr. Rosen he didn't believe the motive was revenge, and that the girl was the intended victim.

Both Ben and Gordon seemed to show a sign of relief. It wasn't someone they knew, let alone an employee.

Gordon had re-opened the stores the day after David's funeral. It was a business, and it had to be conducted as such. Business was noticeably increased. Odd how people, no matter how sad, or shocked they are, become drawn to the people close to the gruesome crime. Gordon believed the unfamiliar customers were there out of curiosity. He tried to dismiss the thought. He had more important things on his mind.

As was his custom, he visited each store daily. Checking the overall appearance, cleanliness and fully stocked shelves. The employees all reacted the same. They were uncomfortable. Should they ask Gordon about the investigation, about Ben and Gail?

Some of the employees had begun working for R&S Markets when the stores first opened. They were treated well by the two owners and felt like extended family. They were never faced with anything so horrendous as this.

Gordon sensed their discomfort, and felt he needed to put them at ease. He broached the subject. He spoke to the men and women at each store. Better it was out and all would be able to get back to work feeling more at ease.

Gordon Schaefer was liked by most of the employees. Of the two owners, Gordon was the one who had a personal contact with the help. Ben was the man behind the scenes. He took care of the bookkeeping, and administrative business. Gordon was the more visible of the two. It was a well-matched partnership.

Steve Logan and Ray Gage finished their coffee, and graciously said their goodbyes, with a promise to keep Ben Rosen informed of any progress.

By the time they returned to the station, it was after 7:00. Steve drove to where Ray had parked his car earlier.

"Well, another day, you going home?" Asked Steve.

"I think I'll go over some reports." Ray answered.

"Going to tuck in Randy?" Steve chuckled.

"I'm going to check my messages. His mother's probably been calling. She must know we picked him up. I guess I owe her at least a phone call." Ray sounded like he was feeling the mother's pain. Ray had a soft side and sometimes, he forgot to keep it hidden.

"Look partner, I know what you're thinking. You're right about giving her a call, but you did the right thing bringing the kid in. If all checks out tomorrow, he's only spent the night. God knows, he's a street wise kid. He's not a mommy's boy. She'll probably be relieved."

"Thanks Steve. I just hate to see a hard-working woman get stuck with a kid that doesn't give a damn about anything. She's really a nice person. But, I know what you're saying. I'll see you in the morning."

"Yeah, Katherine should be home tonight. Finally, I'm getting tired of cooking. You know my best recipe is grilled Spam. I'm looking forward to Katherine's cooking!"

"I'll give her a call. Let her know you just can't make it on your own!" Ray laughed.

"You know Linda would have been happy to have you over anytime, but you're just a stubborn pain in the ass! Go home, relax, and tell Katherine I said hi."

Ray gave the hood of Steve's car a rap, and Steve drove off.

First stop when Ray entered the station, the evidence room.

"Hi Sully, courier been here yet?" He asked the officer behind the plastic window.

Officer Michael Sullivan had been sitting in that very seat for almost fifteen years. Anything coming or going in the line of evidence, Officer Sullivan would be the one to ask.

"Just left, Ray. You got something to check in, or you looking for a delivery?"

"A delivery. You got something for me?"

"Sorry, nothing on the Clarke/Rosen case. Only things that came back today was on that burglary down on Valley Circle. You working that one?" He asked.

"Nope, I think that's Broderick. Thanks. See you tomorrow."

Ray went to his desk. He drew a deep breath and sighed. His desk looked like it had been ransacked. Piles of reports spilled over his 'in' box. Photos spread across his desk. Telephone messages were impaled on a metal spindle.

He took his notebook from his pocket, and flipped through the pages until he found Emily Crawford's telephone number. He dialed, RE8-8081. The line was busy. Damn! He hung up and flipped through the phone messages. Three from Mrs. Crawford. He wasn't surprised. He expected she would be calling. He dialed his home.

"Hello," answered Linda.

"Hi Hon." Ray always got a lift when he heard Linda's voice. She was such an 'up' person. Just what he needed after the day he had put in.

"Ready to come home? I've got a couple of messages for you from that Crawford woman."

"Oh, she called there? What did she say?" Ray asked.

"Not much. She wanted to talk to you. I asked her for a number you could reach her at later. She said she would be home, and you had the number."

"Yeah, I just tried her. I'll give it another try, and then I'll be home. Should be leaving in a few minutes. Make yourself perty for me you sweet thang." Ray joked, using an exaggerated southern drawl.

"You got it Cowboy!" Linda answered. "By the way, Mary Ann is out tonight! See you soon."

Ray dialed Mrs. Crawford again. This time she answered, "Hello?"

"Mrs. Crawford? This is Detective Gage. You called me?"

"Yes, of course I did. I expected you would have called me long before now! I've been frantic. Where is Randy?"

"We picked him up this morning, Mrs. Crawford. He's fine. I questioned him, and just want to hold him overnight." Ray replied.

"Overnight! On what charge. He's only seventeen years old Detective. You can't hold him, he's just a boy!" Mrs. Crawford was shouting. She was displaying a side Ray didn't expect. He had gotten the impression she was pretty passive when it came to Randy. Well, he was mistaken.

"Mrs. Crawford, Randy is a minor, but not a juvenile. Do you understand?"

"I certainly do not. Suppose you explain that one to me!"

"Your son is over sixteen. That gives us the right to question him and take necessary action without the presence of a parent or guardian. If he were under sixteen, that would make him a juvenile, and an entirely different story."

Ray tried to explain to Mrs. Crawford that the police were, in fact, within their rights to question and hold a 'minor' up to twenty-four hours.

"Well, can I at least see him? I am his mother you know. I should be able to see him."

"You can see him tomorrow. If all goes in his favor, he'll be home tomorrow." Ray tried to sound optimistic to the frantic mother.

"If what goes in his favor?" She questioned. "What are you holding him for?"

"I'm waiting for the lab reports on the items I took from your home the other day. I have to check everything out. Surely we talked about that. I can't take a chance he'll skip on me."

"I'll be there in the morning, and you damn well better let me see my son!" She warned.

"If he is not out of your jail by tomorrow, I will be contacting a legal representative, and we will see what you have the right to do and not do. I don't know about the laws, but I can promise you I will have legal advice by the time I get there tomorrow. Good night Detective!" She slammed the phone down.

Well, I guess I had that coming, Ray thought. He put his notebook back into his pocket and left.

Thursday, September 30, 1954

Stanfield News Headlines:

NEW SUSPECT IS QUERIED IN ARCHER BLD. MURDERS
Local Teen Picked Up Evidence Points to Possible Killer, Police Wait for Lab Results

Latest development was the pickup of a tall, slim youth who lives in the 'flats' behind the Archer Boulevard murder house. Police obtained warrant to search the teen's house and confiscated evidence which could lead to the arrest.

Police declined to release the name of the teen, but confirmed he was acquainted with the murdered girl. An arrest could be as soon as today. Police are confident they are on the right track The teen returned yesterday, after being out of town since the morning following the double homicide of 14 year old Lynn Ann Clarke and 4 year old David Rosen....

As the intensive investigation continued, Lincoln High School began to slowly get back on schedule, and pick up where it had stopped. The student body got busy selecting a dance committee and selecting a date for their first 'sock hop' of the year.

The available councilors at the High School were well received. Several students scheduled appointments to talk one to one. This program was winding down. The first week was very busy then, it began to drop off. The plan was to discontinue the availability within the school at the end of the second week.

The basketball schedule was posted, and the first game of the season, Lincoln High vs. Cathedral High was scheduled for October 13th. A pep rally was to take place the day before the first game. The faculty was instructed to encourage participation, and adhere to the curriculum as closely as the conditions would allow. The students resumed congregating in hallways, and the familiar buzzing of conversation between classes was beginning to pick up.

Investigators continued to place the Clarke/Rosen murders top priority, some working as many as eighteen hour days.

Barbara Clarke was scheduled to go back to school on Monday. She had completed several sessions with a child psychologist, and was considered a remarkable little girl. She was aware of the loss of her sister, and the pall that it left over her family.

The Clarke's had made a concentrated effort to shield Barbara from any graphic details of Lynn's death. The presence of Barbara was, in the opinion of the therapist, an enormous value to the Clarke's ability to cope. After all, they had to concern themselves with Barbara's emotional well being.

Lynn Ann's best friend, Lisa was 1st sub on the newly selected cheerleading squad, and was being fitted to her new uniform. It was bittersweet. Lisa remembered Lynn's last comment to her had been. 'You're the 1st Sub, you'll probably be cheering every game!' Lisa never expected this prediction would ever become reality. She never imaged it would come to be for the reasons it had.

Lisa was falling into a depression which concerned Mr. and Mrs. Jansen. She refused to talk to a professional about her feelings, and spoke very little to her parents. She isolated herself from her friends and seemed to just go through the motions of being sociable. The Jansen's hoped that once the school activities were in full swing, perhaps Lisa would start getting back to her usual outgoing self, but they knew it would take time.

Brenda Chapman was slowly pulling herself together. Paul was a tremendous help. They both shared the same grief, and it seemed to help, although Brenda could not avoid seeing the grief stricken family across the street every day.

Mrs. Crawford entered the police station and boldly approached the officer at the counter.

"My name is Emily Crawford, and I believe you are holding my son here. I want to see him!" She was close to shouting.

"When was he brought in?" Asked the officer.

"Yesterday, and I spoke to Detective Gage last night. He told me I would be able to see him today. Now, I want to see him!" Answered the angry mother.

"Do you mind taking a seat over there?" Replied the officer, indicating an empty bench across from the counter.

"Yes, I mind, when can I see him. His name is Randy Crawford. If Detective Gage is in the building, I'd like to see him also!"

"Yes, Madame, I'll see if the Sargent is in. Now, please take a seat. I'll be with you as soon as possible." Again, he pointed to the empty wooden bench.

Mrs. Crawford sat down, reluctantly. She had taken the day off from work, and she was determined it wasn't going to be for nothing. She removed a pair of reading glasses from her purse and tried to concentrate on the newspaper that had been left on the bench. All she could see were the glaring headlines. No names mentioned, but of course, she knew who the "tall teen from the flats' was. All she saw were articles concerning the murders. Sure, there were other bits of news to read, but the double homicide articles seemed to jump out of the print at her. Finally, she folded the paper and set it aside. Just as she was about to inquire about seeing her son, Ray Gage appeared in the lobby.

She rose to her feet.

"I want to see Randy, and I want to see him right now!" She shouted at the detective.

"Now, Mrs. Crawford, calm down. You'll get to see Randy. They're bringing him up right now. It'll only be a couple more minutes." Ray replied in that calming voice he was so noted for.

"You won't be doing Randy any good if he sees you this way. Just calm down."

"When will he be able to get out? You haven't charged him with anything have you? How is he, has he had anything to eat?" Mrs. Crawford shot questions at Gage faster than he could answer.

"Yes, he's had plenty to eat. He's in a cell by himself, and as far as I know, he slept like a baby last night."

At that point, the sound of the latch on the swinging door of the front desk clicked. There was Randy. It was obvious he had slept in his clothes, and was in need of a shave. Mrs. Crawford rushed to him.

"Randy, are you okay? Randy, I'm so sorry."

"Mom, it's okay. I'm fine. Can you get me out of here?"

Mrs. Crawford turned to Ray. "Well, Detective, can we go home now?"

"Not yet. You see, I'm still waiting for the reports from the lab in Boston. Should be coming in any time now. Meanwhile, Randy will have to stay. We need the reports to clear him once and for all."

The detective directed his attention to Randy.

"We talked about this yesterday Randy, remember? Once that evidence comes back, we'll have a better picture. If the reports go well, you'll be walking out that door, and that will be the end of it."

"But I told you Detective, I had nothing to do with anything! Call my friend that I told you about. I'll give you his name, telephone number, anything you want. He'll tell you about the fight he got cut up in. Honest, he will!" Randy was shouting at the detective.

"Only a few more hours Randy, then we'll know one way or another. Meanwhile, why not take a few minutes to visit here with your Mom. She's worried about you. Just talk to her and assure her she has nothing to worry about." Ray answered.

Mrs. Crawford shot a look at Detective Gage. She was angry, yet she did understand about the 'evidence' matter. She was sure, it would come back and exonerate her son.

Randy and his mother had a brief conversation, and Mrs. Crawford turned to leave. She stopped at the door and looked back at her son. He looked so like a child right now. She walked back to him and reached up to give him a kiss. There were tears welling in Randy's eyes as he kissed his mother goodbye.

Throughout the day, suspects were brought in for questioning, their statements checked out and subsequently, they were released. Before the investigation was completed, there would be in excess of one hundred suspects questioned!

By late afternoon, Gage and Logan were buried in more paperwork. The reporters were milling around a make shift press room, hoping for some information that would be tomorrow's headlines.

The familiar courier arrived at the station at 6:30 P.M.. Reporters surrounded the courier.

"Sorry folks, I'm only the messenger." Said the courier as he opened the back of the state police van.

"You'll have to talk to the 'big guys' for any information. I only pick up and deliver."

The reporters had a feeling this was it. On previous days, the courier arrived empty handed, and left with more evidence bags to bring to the lab. Today he was unloading several bags. He'd take the brown bags marked boldly, 'EVIDENCE', lock the van and carry them into the station, depositing them at the appropriate window with Michael Sullivan. He would return and bring in another load.

Mike Sullivan received the bags in their proper order. He logged them in and sorted them by their respective cases. Then, checking the roster, he would page the appropriate officer or detective working the cases.

"Detective Raymond Gage, Detective Steven Logan, please report to the evidence room." Came the booming voice of Sargent Sullivan. The reporters were on their feet, and waiting for the latest news to come from the two lead detectives of the double homicide.

Michael Sullivan made it a practice to personally deliver any reports or returned evidence to Captain Mahoney. He locked the 'cage' and proceeded to the Captain's office. Once he was there, he placed several official manilla folders, stamped in red, 'evidence' on them. The Captain received them with the comment,

"Well, I'd say it's about damn time! Thanks for bringing them down Sully."

"No problem, Cap," replied the Sargent.

The Captain picked up the folders and hoped for something solid to go on. It was time for a break in this case. He read the outside of the first envelope. CLARKE/ROSEN File #340372, then the date and time.

In regards to the fingernail scraping: The tests indicate male Caucasian. Noted, one small hair, color: Dark Brown. Source of hair appears to be from a limb, (arm or leg) possibly the chest.

Blood on clothing: Pajamas, size 4. Type: AB

Blood on bed sheets: Type: AB

Blood on Slippers: size child's 12, Type: AB.

Blood on Green & Blue Shirt: Girl's size 12: Type: B

Blood on Blue Trousers: Girl's size 10: Type: B

Girl's underpants: Matter, vaginal secretion: No semen present

Blood on 3' x 3' section of oriental multi colored carpet: Type: B.

Note: Regarding Blood Type AB Positive, very rare. Persons with this blood type are advised to **register with national blood banks**. Also, refrain from donating blood. Blood should be **donated upon request only!**

Well, thought Captain Mahoney, Type B, the international donor. Of particular interest, was the Type AB Positive. This could be very helpful information.

He searched through the mountains of paperwork on his desk until he found the Rosen boy's autopsy report. Just what I figured, he thought. The Rosen kid's blood type, AB Positive. Surely that would link the murder weapon to the boy. The killer's clothing should be covered with blood. All they needed, was to locate the weapon, or clothing. He set them aside and continued opening the remaining envelopes he had received from other cases.

Ray picked up the packages at the evidence cage. Attached to the bundles he had sent to the lab were the test results.

He placed the packages on his desk and called his partner over.

"Well, this should give us something to hang our hats on," Ray said, as he opened the manilla envelope marked, CLARKE/ROSEN File #340372, date and time.

Man's red plaid shirt, size L: Stain, right front: motor oil

Stain, right sleeve: Blood, Type A

Stain, right shoulder, below collar: Blood, Type A.

Note: second and third buttons, missing. Right arm torn.

Tear at right arm: appears to be inflicted by knife: downward, right to left

Tear at right chest: appears to be inflicted by knife: upward, right to left

Tire Iron: Fingerprints, not determined. Smudged not able to read no foreign substances found

Re: Knife: Type switchblade, does not appear to have been used. Appears new no foreign substances found

Ray slammed the reports down on his desk. He was so sure he had his killer. Now, he'd have to start all over again.

Steve walked to his desk. He picked up the evidence reports he had submitted to the lab on the two suspects he was holding.

The reports did not substantiate Steve's suspicions either, and both detectives were forced to release their suspects. Lack of evidence.

The reporters had camped just outside the detectives' office. The Captain buzzed on the intercom summoning Gage and Logan to his office. The reporters rushed to the detectives as they emerged from their office. The lights were glaring, and the microphones were everywhere. The two detectives declined to comment until they had the opportunity to talk to their Captain.

"We'll let you know as soon as we have all the information," Steve addressed the reporters.

"Please, just wait until we talk with Captain Mahoney."

They walked down the hallway, passed the door marked "Office of the Chief of Police" Paul McNamara, and on to the Captain's office.

Gage and Logan stepped into the Captain's office. They knew, he didn't have any good news to share. The evidence envelopes and reports were spread out before him.

"Well gentlemen, I hope you've got something to tell me. Here are the reports from the scene." He handed the reports to Logan.

"Not as much as I had hoped for, but you'll find one interesting clue. The boy had a rare blood type. That's going to be very helpful. What have you got?" He asked Gage.

Logan was reading the reports the Captain had handed him.

"We've got to turn the kid loose." Gage replied.

"Nothing in the reports that will justify keeping him, unless the victims have Type A blood."

"Nope, AB Positive, and B," Logan answered, looking up from the reports.

"Well, the kid gets turned loose. Sooner, the better. The mother is throwing a fit!" Ray sounded discouraged.

"The shirt, motor oil and blood. Type A. No fingerprints were lifted from the tire iron, all smudged. No blood either. No blood on the knife. Appears it was new, no indication it was used on anything, let alone our two victims!"

The detective sounded tired and fed up. He knew this would mean starting from the beginning and looking over everything that had already been examined over and over. Maybe something was overlooked.

Steve reported the evidence he submitted was also unsubstantiated, and he would be releasing the suspects within the hour. Mahoney stated he would speak to the press, and advised the detectives to take care of the matter of releasing suspects.

"Well, Steve, Emily Crawford will be happy. She was pretty upset earlier." Ray replied.

"I just thought this kid was it! Damn how could I have missed it. I can't even imagine how the press is going to handle this one. We're going to look pretty bad in tomorrow's paper."

Steve shrugged his shoulders and gave Ray a gentle pat on the back.

"Hey, it's part of the territory. Back to square one. You know the drill. Not the first time we jumped and nothing was there!"

They looked over their shoulder down the hallway. The Captain was addressing the small crowd of reporters that encircled him.

"Well, glad I'm not facing them. They're getting pretty restless. So far, they've been kind, but they can get ugly pretty fast!"

Ray was concerned about the press coverage. He didn't want the public getting the impression the police were not on the job. He was particularly concerned for the families of the two victims. He felt he owed them a solid arrest, and conviction.

Each day that passed there seemed to be more distance between the police and the killer. The monster was winning, and he was the one making the rules. Tomorrow's headlines would add to the police's discouragement:

Friday, October 1, 1954:

Stanfield News: Headlines:

LOCAL COUPLE KILLED
Bodies are Located in Burned Bed

Couple dies early today in unexplained blaze. Fire of undetermined origin swept through the 1 ½ story frame house on Woodside Terrace. The bodies were found in a bed which was located among the embers in the basement of the house. Arson is suspected. The Deputy Chief LaValley, has ordered an investigation......

This was the first day the double homicide did not dominate the headlines. Instead, it was dropped below the fold of the front page.

Murder Probe Bogged Down to Long Shot
Quiz of Witness Proves to be Mistaken

A prominent local woman said that news reports that she had seen a man believed fitting the description of the killer was false. The woman told the police the man who looked like the suspect was seen in the dairy store where she works, three different times during the week of the Archer Boulevard crime, but not on the same day of the murder. Originally she had claimed the man she saw, 'hanging around the store' located across the street from the Rosen house. She further claimed he had been at the store the night of the murders. After careful questioning by the police, she later recanted her story...

This story ran beside a news item with a picture of former President Herbert Hoover and President Dwight Eisenhower enjoying a fishing trip.

On page five, a short poem was submitted.

MURDER

Two innocent lives were taken away
Two children were brutally slain
There are no words which I could say
Every solace would be in vain.
Two mothers were left in unthinkable grief
The townsfolk in panic and horror
Was it a maniac? Was it a thief/
Let's find him, to end all this terror.

It was signed, A Mother

In addition to the police, the reporters were getting edgy. They had deadlines to meet, and nothing to report on the big story that had dominated the Stanfield News for over a week.

They were beginning to seek other resources, looking for the next story that would deem worthy to become tomorrow's headline.

The Commissioner began making daily calls to the Chief. In turn, the Chief would call the Captain. They wanted answers. The Chief fielded the demands of the public. The city was beginning to fear this maniac would strike again! No one was safe until the butcher was apprehended.

There wasn't a deadbolt, or any other type of lock available in any hardware store throughout the city. "Operation Clue" was diminished to about three tips a day. A substantial drop from the previous week of as many as 30 in a day!

S teve Logan and Raymond Gage had resigned to starting from the beginning. Ray would sift through the paperwork, and Logan would hit the streets. He was determined to retrace his and all the police investigators' steps.

He started up Archer Boulevard, parking his car and walking a few blocks at a time. He knocked on doors, some would not answer, others would, at least talk through the locked screen doors.

As he approached 407 Archer Boulevard, he rang the doorbell. A small, elderly woman answered. She was very small in stature with pure white hair. Steve was surprised she opened the door.

"Hello, I'm Sargent Steven Logan, Stanfield Police Department." He greeted her, displaying his badge as he introduced himself.

"Yes sir, can I help you?" Asked the elderly woman.

"I'm investigating a case. You must be familiar with the incident at 425 Archer Blvd., just down the street from you?"

"Oh heavens yes! So frightening that was. My Lord, who hasn't heard about it?"

Steve looked past the small women. He spotted a crocheted throw cover on the sofa in the living room.

" I couldn't help but notice, that's a beautiful throw cover you have on the sofa. My wife is very good at that sort of thing." He commented.

"Oh, well, I made that. I've been making those throws for years, but, I haven't done any crocheting in some time now. You see, my hands are arthritic, and I'm not able to handle the needle any longer. I was cleaning about a month ago, and gave all my material to my daughter. She's very talented also."

"You gave away your crocheting thread?"

"Yes, only a few weeks ago."

Steve glanced at the name on the mailbox. Gladys Wayland.

"Mrs. Wayland, do you live here alone?" He asked.

"Yes, my husband passed away four years ago. This house is so big, I know I should be thinking of a smaller place, but I've lived here for nearly 50 years! It's very difficult for someone my age to change. My daughter's always asking me to move in with her and her family, but, I don't want to be a bother. You know what I mean."

"Yes, I surely do, Mrs. Wayland. Where does your daughter live?"

"Oh, not far from here. She lives on Lynndale Street. Right across the street from that poor family. You know, the Clarke girl, that was murdered. What a terrible thing..."

Steve cut her off. He was trying to back off graciously, but, his thoughts were racing by now.

"Thank you, Mrs. Wayland. What is your daughter's name?"

"Marge Chapman. Why, detective?"

"Just want to continue my investigation. You've been very helpful. Thank you, now be sure to lock your door when I leave."

"Yes, I will. But..."

Steve walked back to his car. Chapman, he said over and over in his mind.

He drove directly to 51 Lynndale Street. It was the single family house across from the Clarkes.

Since the murders, Marge Chapman had visited with the Clarke's on a daily basis. She would bring casseroles so Elaine wouldn't have to cook. Sometimes she would stop in twice in a day. Some days she just dropped off a casserole and leave. She would see how Elaine was feeling and if she was in the mood to visit, Marge would stay. Phil Clarke had gone back to work, part time at first, little by little getting back to his normal schedule.

Elaine encouraged Brenda Chapman's occasional visits. She liked to have Brenda around. At first, Brenda was uneasy, but soon became a regular visitor.

On this day, Elaine was in the mood to talk extensively about the investigation. She had a way of putting everyone at ease when referring to Lynn Ann. As Marge and Elaine discussed the progress of the investigation, the matter of the blue crocheting thread was brought up. The investigators had placed a lot of weight on that one clue, a single piece of thread. They had assured Mrs. Clarke they had canvassed the entire neighborhood, inquiring about the mysterious clue. But, to no avail.

The unmarked detective's car pulled up to 51 Lynndale St. Marge greeted Steven Logan at the door. She recognized him from the night of the murder when she had gone to the Clarke's to pick up Barbara.

"Hello detective, what brings you here?" She asked

"Mrs. Chapman, I've just come from your mother's house and..."

"Oh, my God! What's happened?" Mrs. Chapman turned ashen.

"Nothing's wrong, Mrs. Chapman, your mother is fine." Steve answered as quickly as possible. "She's fine, Mrs. Chapman."

"Oh, I get so frightened. She insists on staying in that house alone. I keep telling her she should move in here, but, she's so stubborn. Oh, I'm sorry, Detective. I didn't mean to go on, what can I do for you?" She asked as she opened the screen door to allow the detective in.

Steve stepped inside and Mrs. Chapman showed him to the living room.

"Would you like something to drink? Coffee, tea?" Asked Mrs. Chapman.

"No thank you madame. I just need to ask you a few questions."

"Why of course, anything." She replied.

"Is Mr. Chapman home?"

"No, he's working."

"Where does Mr. Chapman work?" Steve Logan asked.

"Well, he's a lineman, and this week he's been working in West Stanfield. Why do you ask?"

"Maybe you can fill me in. Was Mr. Chapman at home the night of the murders? It was Saturday, September 25th."

Mrs. Chapman looked very confused. She thought for a moment and answered,

"No, he wasn't. He was out of town that night on an emergency call. He was in Connecticut. Power lines were down, because of the storm. He came home on Sunday." Mrs. Chapman continued.

"I called him and asked him to come home. Brenda was so upset. So was I. Why, Detective, why would you be interested in John's whereabouts?" She was getting very nervous.

"Just routine, Mrs. Chapman. Just like to check out everyone's whereabouts on the night of the murders. You mentioned Brenda. I believe we met her the night you picked up the little Clarke girl."Steve continued.

"My partner spoke with her at school also. Don't you have a boy too?"

"Yes, Karl." Mrs. Chapman replied.

"Do you happen to know where Karl was that night?" Asked Steve.

Mrs. Chapman thought and answered cautiously, "Gosh, I don't remember. I know he was home when we went to get Barbara. He was sleeping. He's a very sound sleeper."

"How about earlier that evening Mrs. Chapman. Do you remember if he went out earlier? It was a Saturday night, most teenagers have something to do on a Saturday night." Steve pressed. "Does he have a girlfriend he might have been out with?"

"No, Karl doesn't have a girlfriend. He doesn't drive. But I think he was home. Yes, now I remember. It was that rainy night, and I remember him coming in from sitting out on the porch. It wasn't very late because Brenda wasn't home yet. Brenda has to be home by 11:00."

"And you say he was sitting out on the porch?" Asked Steve. "Do you remember what time it was?"

"No, I was watching TV and just heard him come in. I remember commenting on how hard it was raining."

Mrs. Chapman was taking on a noticeable change of tone in her voice. She seemed to realize what the detective was getting at. Until then, she hadn't thought of Karl. She didn't know what she was thinking. Could he be actually thinking Karl had anything to do with that horrible murder? Why would he suspect Karl? What was he doing at her mother's house?

"Detective, you don't think...."she couldn't finish the sentence.

"I don't know, Mrs. Chapman. The truth is, your mother says you're very handy with crocheting. Is that right?"

"Well, I do crochet. See, here are some of my pieces. This is a little sweater set I'm making for my sister's baby. I just love the color. Don't you?"

Steve looked at the partially made sweater. It was blue. A very distinct blue. He felt a chill come over him.

"Do you have any more of that blue yarn, Mrs. Chapman?" Steve asked, trying to keep his voice steady.

"Well, yes, just about enough to make a bonnet also. Why?"

Her face dropped in an instant. She was piecing together just what Steve Logan was getting at.

"Detective, you don't think..."

"I don't know, Mrs. Chapman. I would like to take the thread in as evidence, to see if this matches the piece of thread we picked up at the scene. We'll go from there. I have to check it out. It's probably not even close to what we're looking for." Steve Logan replied.

"Would you mind if I take a look around, while I'm here? Could I look around Karl's room? You don't have to, but if you wouldn't mind, it would save some time, seeing that I'm here." Logan was hoping for the 'go ahead' from the nervous mother.

"I guess it will be all right. I don't know what you'll find, but, I suppose you can." Mrs. Chapman answered.

She led the detective upstairs to Karl's bedroom, and stood in the doorway as he entered the room. Unlike Randy Crawford's room, Karl's room was exceptionally neat. Logan tried to be casual, not wanting to alarm Mrs. Chapman only to have her change her mind. He looked under the bed, and slid his hand between the mattress and box spring. Nothing. He walked to the closet and nodded to Mrs. Chapman.

"Do you mind?" Asked Logan as he reached for the closet doorknob.

"No, go ahead" Mrs. Chapman replied. She had just hung Karl's freshly ironed shirts in the closet, and didn't notice anything out of place.

Steve Logan looked in the closet. It was as though Karl was a neat freak! His shirts were hung all facing one direction. His pants, neatly draped over hangers and separated from the shirts. He looked up and saw a shelf with shoe boxes lined up. One by one, he removed the boxes and examined their contents. Nothing of any suspicion there. He replaced the boxes and walked to the dresser. The contents were neat and orderly. He passed his hand under the cushion of a chair beside the bed. Nothing. The detective looked down at the shoes aligned on the closet floor. Everything was in order. Was this kid excessively compulsive? Nothing out of place.

He closed the closet door and looked at Mrs. Chapman. "Well, everything here seems to be in order Mrs. Chapman, thanks for your help. I'm going to stop by the school, and talk to Karl. Just routine. I've talked to several other students. Nothing to be alarmed about, if you have no objections?"

Mrs. Chapman seemed to give a sigh of relief.

"No of course not," she replied.

Steve Logan left carrying the small ball of crocheting thread. When he reached his car, he called into the station and alerted Ray Gage he would be by to pick him up within 10 minutes.

As the two detectives drove, Steve filled Ray in on his activities of the past hour. How he just 'stumbled' over Mrs. Wayland, and subsequently his visit to 51 Lynndale Street.

They drove directly to Lincoln High School. Upon their arrival, they went to Principal Tallman's office. Ms Brock greeted Ray with a smile and a friendly hello. Very out of character for the stern spinster.

"What can I do for you Detective?" Asked Ms. Brock.

"Is Mr. Tallman in? How are you today, Ms. Brock? This is my partner, Sargent Steven Logan."

"My pleasure, Detective. Yes, Mr. Tallman is in, I'll tell him you're here."

Ms. Brock appeared in the doorway of the principal's office. "Go right in, would you like coffee?"

"No, thank you," replied Ray.

The principal stood behind the old desk and greeted the two detectives with an outstretched hand. The men shook hands and Ray introduced Steve to Mr. Tallman.

"We'd like to talk to one of your students, Karl Chapman."

"Chapman, oh yes, I believe he's a Junior. Probably in the gym about now," he replied, glancing at his watch.

"I'll walk you down there. How are you doing with the investigation? All I know is what I've read in the papers, and frankly, it doesn't seem to be getting anywhere."

"Well, it's still priority. I have to admit, it's baffling, but I'm confident it will not go unresolved." Ray answered.

The three men walked toward the gymnasium. All classes were in last period and the hallways were deserted.

As they entered the gym, the boys were lined up practicing 'free shots'. The sound of bouncing basketballs on the hardwood floor echoed throughout the room.

Coach Falcone spotted the men entering the gym, and walked toward them. He was very sensitive when it came to anyone entering his sanctuary with hard soled shoes, regardless of whom it was!

"Hi there Frank," the coach said, approaching the principal. "What you doing down here?"

"Hi Mark, these are detectives Ray Gage and Steve Logan. They'd like to talk to Karl Chapman." The detective's badges were clearly displayed.

"Sure, he's right over there, sitting on the bench. I'll get him," the coach replied.

As the coach approached the gangly teenager, Karl looked over at the three men and stood. He walked to them and said,

"Hi, I'm Karl Chapman, you wanted to talk to me?"

Ray looked at Karl and tried to remember when he had spoken to him before. He looked familiar and he was sure he had talked to him.

"I'm Detective Gage, this is Detective Logan. We'd like to ask you a few questions."

"Sure, I talked to you the day of Lynn's funeral. Remember, at the funeral home, just before we left for the church." He spoke directly to Ray Gage.

That's right, now I remember, Ray thought. "Yes, I remember, could you step out here in the hallway?"

The teenager, flanked by the two detectives walked out into the hallway. The principal excused himself and headed back to his office.

The coach's shrill whistle sounded, followed by "Okay let's get back to practice. Line up and start shooting some baskets."

Karl was the first to speak. "What do you want from me? I've already answered your questions, told you everything I know."

"Well Karl, tell us again. You don't mind, do you?" Asked Gage. "How about telling us where you were the night Lynn Ann Clarke and David Rosen were killed."

"I told you, I was home." Karl answered, calmly. "I was home all night." He added.

"Anybody at home with you?" Asked Logan. "Your Mom, Dad, how about your sister Brenda?" Logan pressed.

Karl hesitated for only a moment, and answered, "My Mom was there, and Brenda too."

"Think carefully Karl, you're sure about that?" Again, Logan pressed the teenager.

"I don't have to think, I'm sure! What's this all about, what are you getting at?" He was getting angry, just enough agitation to make the detectives start to believe they should pursue this line of questioning a little bit further.

By now, the two detectives had positioned themselves, one face to face with Karl, the other behind him. Ray stood behind, and nodded to Steve, indicating he should hit the boy with the thread evidence. See how he reacted.

"Well, Karl, we think you were out that night. We think you were on Archer Boulevard and paid a visit to the Rosen's."

"Well, you can think what you like. I wasn't there." Karl replied, in a very controlled manner.

"We think you dropped something while you were there, Karl." Steve produced the embroidery thread that Marge Chapman had handed over to him.

"This came from your house, Karl. I think it gives us a good enough reason to take you in for further questioning. We'll compare this to the piece found at the murder scene. If it matches, then we'll need to talk a lot more."

"I don't care what you think, I'll go to the station. I don't have anything to hide." Karl was becoming almost cocky with his attitude.

"Good, then, go change your clothes, we're going to take a ride."

Ray Gage accompanied the six- foot- two teenager through the gym and into the locker room. He positioned himself at the door and waited for Karl to change his clothes. The gym class was over. Steve Logan asked the coach to detain the class until Karl was escorted out. The coach ordered the class to run laps around the gym.

"What's going on? Where's Karl going?" The coach asked Logan.

"Just a few questions we need answers to, nothing to get concerned about yet. Just want to get him in an appropriate environment, you understand." Steve Logan was trying to be casual, but the coach wasn't buying it. He shook his head and returned to the class.

Chapman and Gage appeared in the doorway of the boys' locker room. The room became silent, as the boys stopped running and stared at their classmate being led out by the police. They were curious, and stunned. They'd never seen anyone in custody before. Not in real life, and certainly not anyone they knew!

Karl climbed into the back seat of the detective's car. He was somber, but still unshaken. It was a short ride to the police headquarters, and the three remained silent. Ray Gage looked in the rear view mirror. Karl was sitting back on the seat, relaxed and staring out the window.

The throngs of reporters had considerably decreased as the days stretched farther and farther into the investigation. Some were assigned different stories, others returned to their regular beats. A few stragglers kept a vigil in the temporary press room that had been made available for them.

Karl was ushered into the station without handcuffs, and without any noticeable fuss. The reporters paid little attention to what appeared to be just one more suspect to be questioned, and most likely released within a short time.

Gage and Chapman went directly to the interrogation room. Steve Logan to Captain Mahoney's office. He wanted the Captain filled in on their latest suspect.

"Gage has him in the interrogation room right now. I'm going down to 'evidence' and see how this thread matches up with the one we've got. Not sure I'll be able to tell exactly, but I'll sure know if it's a possibility!"

Ray was seated directly across from Karl. He remained silent for a few minutes, to get some reaction from the teen. Karl leaned back in the chair, removed a pack of Chesterfield's from his shirt pocket and lit a cigarette. He offered one to Ray. The detective declined.

"I'm going to get a cup of coffee. Can I get you anything, Karl?" Asked Gage.

"Yeah, I'll have a coffee too." Karl answered in a casual tone. He was beginning to irritate Ray. Just as well Ray leave the room for a few minutes. He had to collect his thoughts and come up with a line of questioning that would force Chapman to confess.

"Sure, cream, sugar, how you want it?"

"Just sugar, thanks."

He's one cool character Ray thought as he left the room. He met Steve at the evidence counter. Steve was examining the thread of evidence he had from the crime scene and the piece he had collected from Mrs. Chapman.

"Sully, you got a magnifying glass in there?" He asked the Sargent.

"Yeah, hold on, I got one here somewhere. Ah, here it is." He handed the instrument to Steve.

"Boy, my eyes are shot! Here Ray, take a look," he handed the threads and magnifying glass to his partner. "You're younger than I am, what do you think?"

Ray examined the evidence carefully. "I'm no pro, hard to tell. The color sure matches, can't be sure. We'll have to get someone in here that can determine that with certainty."

The wrapper on the thread revealed it was manufactured by American Thread, Newton, MA.

"Well, I'm going back to Chapman and telling him it's a match. See how that swims."

Ray turned to leave. "Careful, Partner, don't push too hard. We don't want him clamming up. And keep this one under wraps until we know one way or another. The public doesn't need another dead end!" Steve warned.

"I'll be in to hand you a note." Ray knew exactly what Steve was up to. It was a ploy they had used many times. Ray nodded and waved over his shoulder. He proceeded to the interrogation room and his waiting suspect.

He placed a cup of coffee in front of Karl and sat across from him. He looked in the ashtray. This kid must be nervous. In the short time he had left him alone in the room Karl had smoked three cigarettes!

"Okay, Karl. Let's start over, okay?"

"Sure, whatever you say Detective," Karl answered very matter of fact.

"Tell me how you felt about Lynn, you knew her pretty well, right?" Ray began.

"Sure, I knew her, she lived right across the street. She was a friend of my sister's. Yeah, I guess you could say I knew her pretty well."

"Well, how did you feel about her, you like her?" Ray asked.

"Yeah, she was all right, just a kid. Just started high school this year. Her and Brenda were pretty tight, I guess."

"You guess, I'd say you knew her better than anyone, fourteen years, a long time for someone your age." Ray prodded.

"What exactly are you getting at? I knew her because she lived across the street, yeah, fourteen years, so what?" Karl was getting agitated. Ray tried a different approach.

"Suppose you tell me again, where you were on the night of the murders. Your mother and sister came over to the Clarke's to get Barbara, where were you?"

"I was asleep, didn't even hear them. Found out the next morning about what had happened. Brenda and my Mom were up all night, I guess. Never heard them. They were talking about it and reading the paper when I got up. That's how I found out what happened."

"Well, how did you feel when you heard about how Lynn and the little boy were killed? Must have been pretty shocking, I mean, you ever heard of anything so terrible in your life?"

"Yeah, it was pretty shocking. I figure she must have known the killer. You know, letting him in like she did. Mom and Brenda were pretty upset. Mom even called my father. He was working out of town. She was pretty upset and asked him to come home. He got home Sunday afternoon."

Ray continued the interview along the lines of just general conversation. No interrogation. He wanted to make Karl comfortable, and get a good feel of which 'buttons' to push. So far, Karl was pretty smooth. He showed no real signs of being particularly nervous. Human nature, didn't matter guilty or not guilty, it's been Ray's experience that an average person tends to show some signs of discomfort when being questioned regarding a double homicide!

The desk Sargent buzzed the interrogation room. Ray picked up the black wall receiver,

"This is Gage," he replied.

"A Mrs. Chapman is on the phone, wants to talk to you about her son. What do you want me to tell her?" Ray thought for a moment. He looked at his watch, it was nearly five o'clock. He'd had Karl for almost three hours.

"Tell her I'll be right there, Mike. Thanks."

Karl shifted in his chair. He was getting stiff from sitting, and probably hungry.

"Have to take a call, Karl. Relax, I'll be right back." The detective left the room.

"Hello, Mrs. Chapman, this is Detective Gage."

"Yes, Detective, what are you doing with Karl? Brenda came home very upset. Seems the whole school is talking about you picking

Karl up from school. Took him out in front of all his classmates. Was that necessary? What's taking so long? Mr. Chapman will be home soon. He will want some answers."

"We're asking Karl some questions. At the moment, he is free to leave, but he hasn't indicated that he desires to. If you and Mr. Chapman would like to pick him up, I don't see any reason why you can't. So far, I have no reason to detain him. We're just going over a few matters of concern. Just want to clear a few things up."

"My husband and I will pick him up as soon as he gets home. I expect that will be within the hour. Thank you." Mrs. Chapman hung up.

Ray got the impression she was more concerned about Mr. Chapman's reaction to her son's whereabouts, than the reason he was picked up in the first place. Brenda was confused, and probably put in an embarrassing position. He was sure Mr. Chapman would not be as understanding as Marge Chapman.

On his way back to Karl, Ray stopped by Steve Logan's desk.

"Anything on the thread match?" He asked. "I'm not going to be able to hold this kid much longer. His old man will be here, and I don't think he's going to be too pleased. I need something to hold him, even just overnight!"

Steve nodded. "I know what you're getting at. We'll get it dispatched out there as soon as possible. Meanwhile, I thought we'd try Grouse Thread, right here in Stanfield. They should be able to give us a preliminary evaluation.

I called down there, and got lucky! One of the foremen answered. Seems he's got his crew working overtime on some special order. He said he'd take a look at it. Got someone on their way right now. This could be our lucky Friday."

"That's great Steve, but I've got to have something now!"

"Okay, Ray. Let's try the note." Steve replied.

"Good, make it quick!" Ray turned and headed back down the hallway to the interrogation room.

"Sorry about that, Karl. Some people just won't wait. Now, where were we?"

Karl did not reply. He sat with a look of boredom.

"Are we about done here? I'm getting hungry, and I'd like to go home. Any reason I have to stay here? I'm not under arrest or anything am I?"

Karl knew he wasn't, he was simply making conversation.

Just then, Steve Logan came into the room. He shot a serious look at Karl, and handed Ray a folded note. After he delivered the note to Ray, he stepped back against the wall and folded his arms.

Ray opened the note. He deliberately took his time and read it, refolded it and placed it into his breast shirt pocket. He sat back, lit a cigarette and looked Karl directly in the eye.

"Well, Karl. Not too good news for you." He said.

"What, what are you talking about?" Karl shot a look at Steve and then back at Ray.

"What's that note about?" He asked.

Ray removed the note from his pocket and slid it across the table to Karl.

"Read it for yourself, Karl. Looks like you've got some explaining to do." Karl grabbed the note. It was on police stationary, date, time, and in bold letters typed;

Evidence Report:

Description of evidence: Embroidery Thread - Manufacturer: American Thread

Requested: Match single thread with full skein. Color: Cobalt Blue

Findings are conclusive, single thread cut from full skein.

All threads submitted obtained from Dye Lot #4597

Steve and Ray watched closely as Karl read the bogus report. Karl tossed the 'report' back across the table to Ray.

"So, what does this have to do with me? What did you mean, explaining to do?" He asked, leaning forward in his chair.

"You tell us Karl. It'll be a lot easier. Do you read the papers?" Asked Ray. "Watch the news?"

"Not much of a TV fan. Yeah, I read the paper once in awhile, why?" Karl asked.

"You been keeping up with the news about Lynn's murder?" Ray coaxed Karl. "You know, the investigation, clues, suspects?"

"Nah, I read it when it first happened, mostly the kids at school are all talking about it." Karl answered.

"Well, let me tell you about this blue thread, Karl. This blue thread belongs to the murderer. You know how we know that?" Steve joined in.

"No, well, yeah, I guess so. Someone said something about a clue or something." Karl was getting a little less comfortable.

"We got this thread from your Mom, Karl. It matches the thread from the scene of the murder. We found the thread on the floor right beside Lynn Ann's butchered body. It was left there by the killer. How do you suppose that could be, Karl? How do you suppose your mother's thread got from her sewing basket to the scene of a double homicide?" Steve pressed.

The detectives were getting more and more aggressive with the young Chapman. The teenager took a deep sigh, leaned back in his chair and hung his head. An inaudible mumble came from the slumped teenager.

"What? Speak up Karl, I can't hear you!" Steve Logan was practically shouting.

Ray leaned over and tapped his partner, indicating, slow down. He nodded to Steve to follow him to the other side of the room where he could speak to him out of ear shot of Chapman.

"Steve, I think it's time to get the Captain in here. Get a pad of paper, pencils, everything. I don't want this kid to clam up! I think we've got him!" Steve nodded and left.

Ray returned to the table where Karl sat, still slumped and his head bowed. Ray removed his jacket and tie. He unbuttoned the top button of his shirt and rolled up his sleeves.

"Karl, you want something to drink?" Ray asked. Karl didn't answer.

He reached in his pocket and took out a pack of Chesterfield's. He lit the cigarette and took a long drag. Then he looked directly at the detective across from him and said,

"I did it. I didn't intend to have it go that way. I just wanted to scare her, but she screamed and I just went a little crazy."

Ray was dumbfounded. He wanted to hear the whole story, but he wanted the Captain and Logan there. What was taking so long?

Ray lit a cigarette and tried to be casual. He felt he was sitting on a time bomb. If he pressed too much, the kid might just clam up. If he didn't probe, then it was anybody's guess.

Finally, the door swung open and there was Captain Mahoney, Chief McNamara and Steve Logan, carrying paper and pens.

The Captain sat at the head of the table. He folded his hands, and said nothing. The Chief stood leaning against the wall as Steve Logan placed the thick tablet of paper and a pen in front of the teen. Gage sat directly across from Chapman. He nudged the pad of paper closer to Karl, and handed him the pen.

"Karl, we're going to talk about the day of the murders. This is Captain Mahoney, and over there," he pointed to the Chief, "that's Chief McNamara." Ray began.

With his index finger, Karl began tracing the rim of his coffee cup. Around and around the lip of the cup. The strange idiosyncracy caught Ray's attention. He noticed on the back of Karl's left hand, a trace of a scratch that appeared to have healed.

Karl continued toying with the cup as he looked at Captain Mahoney.

"So, what do you want me to write?" Mahoney nodded to Logan, indicating the detective was to initiate the confession of the maniacal killer.

Steve Logan cleared his throat and took a deep breath. He wanted this long awaited confession to be precise and accurate. They had worked long and hard, and everything had to be addressed. The entire day, into the evening, the details of the bloody crime scene, everything!

Steve turned the pad to face him. He took his pen from his shirt pocket and wrote on the top of the blank page:

Friday, October 1, 1954. He glanced at the old clock on the far wall and added, Time: 6:50 P.M. Then, he noted all the persons present, Chief McNamara, Captain Mahoney, Detective Raymond Gage, and Detective Steven Logan.

He wrote in bold letters: The Confession of Carl T. Chapman.

Karl leaned over the table and said in a controlled voice, "That's Karl with a K, detective and the T stands for Theodore."

The detective ripped off the sheet, crumpled it into a ball and tossed it into the nearby wastebasket. He started over, repeating the same information he had previously written, only when he got to the name of the suspect, he turned the pad to Karl.

"Here, you fill in your name Karl. You'll be doing most of the writing from here."

In a childlike scrawling, Karl printed his name across the paper.

"What do you want me to write?" He asked.

Just then, the buzzer sounded. It broke the silence and startled everyone in the room.

Ray lifted the receiver from the wall. "This is Gage."

"I have Mr. and Mrs. Chapman here at the desk. Mr. Chapman says he wants to talk to somebody about his son, Karl Chapman." Replied the officer at the desk.

"Tell him he'll have to wait." Ray answered. "We'll be with him in a few minutes."

"Says he's not going to wait. He's hopping mad Ray. I think somebody better get out here to calm him down."

"Okay, Mike, tell him I'll be right there." Ray replied and placed the receiver back on the hook.

Ray related the conversation to the Chief.

"I'll handle this. You get on with this business."

The Chief left the room. After the Chief left the room, Ray nodded to Steve, indicating that he should continue.

"So, what am I suppose to write?" Repeated Karl.

The Captain interrupted.

"Don't write anything just yet, Karl. Let's just talk for a few minutes. Tell us about the day of the murders. In your own words, take your time, and just tell us what happened that day."

Karl replaced the pen on the table. He sat, relaxed and seemed to be at ease with his captive audience. He took a deep sigh, and began the confession that would chill the most seasoned law enforcement officers.

Occasionally, one of the detectives, or the Captain would ask a specific question. Karl would answer, not missing a single detail. He needed little prompting. The deeper he got into the story, the more excited he appeared to be.

Chief McNamara emerged through the security door and approached the distraught parents. He introduced himself and tried to be as considerate as possible to the elder Chapman's.

"I demand to see Karl!" Shouted John Chapman. "What is going on? I need to see him!"

The Chief was sympathetic but he did not give up any ground.

"He's being questioned, Mr. Chapman. I'm afraid you'll have to wait. Now, you can go home and I'll notify you as soon as we have something to tell you, or, you can wait here. But I must tell you, it could be a very long wait. I suggest you go home."

"What are you trying to 'get' Chief? What do you mean by something to tell me?"

This was the most difficult encounter he'd ever had with parents of a young suspect. He decided there would be nothing to be gained by skirting the issue. Mr. Chapman was not one to be handled gently. Mrs. Chapman stood sheepishly by her husband's side. She looked frail and frightened. Her husband was a full six feet four inches tall, with a bulky build. Marge Chapman was a mere five feet three inches.

"We are questioning Karl in regards to the Clarke/Rosen murders. We have evidence that leads us to believe he is responsible for the two deaths. Karl has not denied any involvement, and with his confession, along with the evidence we have in our possession, we will be prepared to charge him with the double homicide."

"Are you out of your mind? I'll see about what you can do and not do with my boy. You haven't seen the last of me tonight, Chief." Mr. Chapman was shouting.

He snatched his wife's hand and led her through the double doors leading out of the station.

Chief McNamara shook his head in dismay. This is going to be a nightmare. He poured himself a hot cup of black coffee and left instructions at the front desk.

"We are not to be disturbed, Mike. I don't care who it is!"

"You got it Chief." Answered the officer at the desk.

The Chief returned to the interrogation room. He pulled a chair away from the table and placed it up against the wall. His vantage point was behind Karl.

Ray Gage stood beside the Chief. Logan and Captain Mahoney sat at the table with Karl. By now, Karl was talking continuously. The detectives hardly questioned him. He voluntarily related each step, detailing the atrocity without any display of emotion. He was unburdening the secret he was able to carry without any suspicion for nearly two weeks!

He had watched the police at work for almost two weeks. He saw them making their way up and down the neighborhood streets, including Lynndale St. They went from house to house checking and rechecking families for clues. They visited the school. Never did he give any sign of suspicion.

Karl began to ramble. Steve asked him to slow down, and speak clearly, for the record.

"Okay, okay," Karl replied, "I was home until around 9:00, then I went for a walk. It was raining.

"Where did you walk, Karl?" Asked Steve.

"I took a walk up the street, up to Archer Boulevard." Chapman stated.

"I walked to the house where Lynn was babysitting. It was really raining hard!"

"Have you ever been there before?" Asked Logan.

"Yeah, I've walked by the house plenty of times. I used to go by and look into the window when Lynn was babysitting.

Usually on Saturdays. She always babysat on Saturdays."

Finally, Captain Mahoney asked, "Where's the weapon Karl? Where can we find the knife?"

"It's at my house. It's wrapped up with the clothes. They were a mess. I just rolled them up with the knife. They're in the bottom of my closet." Karl answered in a soft tone.

Ray and Steve looked bewildered. They had searched Karl's room. It was practically pristine! How could they have missed 'a bundle of bloody clothes'?

The Chief hurried from the room. He dispatched a mobile unit to get to the Chapman's at 51 Lynndale St. They were to pick up the bundle. A search warrant would not be necessary. Probable cause would be sufficient in this instance.

The Chief knew he was pushing the envelope a little, but he hoped it would work. He was worried about the state of mind Mr. Chapman was in when he left the station. He worried Mr. Chapman would search for anything connecting his son to the murders. He had no way of knowing what the father would do if he discovered this evidence.

The police unit radioed they were en route to the Chapmans. The press was swarming, pressing for the news.

Chief McNamara would eventually make the statement that would scream across the Saturday Morning Stanfield News.

The reporters, TV cameras, photographers shouted questions, snapped photos and recorded statements of the Chief.

The morning headlines would be sensational! Reporters followed the squad car that was dispatched to the Chapman's residence. The squad car lead a caravan down Archer Boulevard, and turned onto Lynndale St.

Two patrolmen walked to the front door and rang the bell. The reporters spilled from their vehicles, and cameras rolled. Flashbulbs flashed, and reporters frantically scribbled notes. This was the story of the year and nothing would be left out.

John Chapman appeared at the front door. He was visibly angry and shielded his face from the intrusion of the media.

"Mr. Chapman?" Asked one of the patrolmen. "We have instructions to remove a certain piece of evidence from your residence."

"What the hell are you talking about? I was at the station, I talked to the Chief. He said nothing about searching my house. What right do you have?"

"The Chief has issued this order under 'probable cause'. It seems your son has confessed to the double homicide of Lynn Clarke and David Rosen. He has disclosed the location of the murder weapon and the clothing. We are instructed to obtain them from your home and deliver them to the station. Now, may we come in?"

John Chapman agreed to let the police in. The two patrolmen stepped inside and Chapman slammed the door behind them.

Brenda was not at home. Anticipating an incident similar to what was now occurring, John had made arrangements for Brenda to be out of the home and spend the night with her aunt.

"I don't know what you think you're going to find here. Help yourself, I can assure you everything is in order." John Chapman spoke to the officers.

"We've been instructed to look into your son's closet. Would you mind showing me to Karl's bedroom?" The officer asked John.

Marge Chapman stood silently behind her husband. She was visibly shaken, and remained silent. One officer followed John Chapman to Karl's upstairs bedroom, while the other stayed with Marge Chapman just inside the front door.

The sounds of the media could be heard. They were not leaving without a story, and who could blame them? They worked tirelessly with the police and now it was about to pay off. This would be the biggest story ever printed in the Stanfield News.

While all the frenzy of the press, TV cameras, photographers and reporters filled the front lawn of 51 Lynndale St., the residents across the street, at 48 Lynndale St. peered out from behind the closed drapes. They had no idea what was to be the greatest shock of their lives. Second only to the death of their daughter.

Within a few minutes, the patrolman descended the stairs carrying a bag, clearly marked EVIDENCE. It was a bulky bag.

John Chapman followed the officer downstairs, still maintaining a steel composure. He said little. He was dumbfounded, but it didn't show. He was not convinced that Karl had anything to do with this horrific crime. Surely, there would be an explanation, and when he was finally allowed to speak to his son, he would find out what it was.

"When do I get to see Karl?" Demanded Mr. Chapman. "I have a right to talk to my boy!"

"You'll have to take that up with the Chief Mr. Chapman. We're just following orders."

"Well, you tell your Chief, I'll be there in ten minutes, and I want to talk to him when I get there! Do you understand that officer? I want to see the Chief, when I get to the station, and I won't take no for an answer!"

"Yes, sir, I'll give the message to Chief McNamara," the patrolman respectfully answered.

The two officers hurried to the awaiting cruiser they had arrived in. The media rushed to them. The patrolmen did not comment. The reporters raced to the Chapman's front door, only to be ignored. They snapped pictures of the Chapman home, noting it was directly across from the Clarke's house.

By now, Phil Clarke was on the telephone asking to speak to Logan or Gage. He was told to leave a message and the detectives would return the call when they were freed up.

Once Mr. Clarke gave his name to the officer, he was put on hold. In a few minutes, Ray Gage took the call.

"This is detective Gage. May I help you?"

"Detective, what's going on? I have the media swarming all over the place. Two officers called on the Chapman's across the street. They left carrying something and the reporters were all over them. What is going on?"

Mr. Clarke was shouting into the phone. He was getting more and more aggressive, and needed some information.

"Mr. Clarke, we believe we may have the killer. We're not absolutely positive, but we've got substantial reason to believe this nightmare just might be over."

Ray felt the family of one of the victims deserved to be kept abreast of anything that could lead to the arrest of their daughter's killer.

"I don't understand, what does that have to do with the Chapman's? Oh my God! It can't be, not John!"

Mr. Clarke felt weak. He had to sit down. Elaine had a puzzled look on her face as she watched her husband's face turn ashen.

"Are you saying........" he couldn't bring himself to say the words.

"Yes, Mr. Clarke, we're questioning Karl Chapman right now. I haven't released the name, but we're pretty sure we're on the right track. I will keep you informed, but I really have to go now. Please take it easy, and I promise I will call or stop by before the night is over."

"Karl?" Phil Clarke hadn't even thought of Karl.

"You're questioning Karl?"

"Yes, we have evidence that should be sufficient to make the arrest tonight."

After a brief silence, Phil Clarke replied. "Okay, Detective. I'll hang up, but I will be waiting to hear from you. What do I tell the reporters? I know they will be at my door any minute."

"Just tell them you have no comment, or don't answer the door. They may try to reach you by phone. You don't have to speak to them you know. They will respect that, I'm sure."

Ray tried to put Mr. Clarke at ease as best he could, although he realized the news he had just delivered was shocking to say the least.

By the time Ray finished his conversation with Phil Clarke, the two patrolmen were arriving at the station.

Ray met them at the front desk. They carried in the bulky package they had obtained from Karl Chapman's closet.

Ray was curious. "Where did you find it?" He asked.

"On the floor of the kid's closet. It was shoved back in a corner. Couldn't see it at first. But we moved a long coat that was hanging there, and that's where it was." The officer responded, handing the detective the bulky package.

"Did you unwrap it?" Asked Gage looking into the evidence bag.

"No sir!" Answered the officer. "It's just like we found it."

"Good, how did it go with Mr. Chapman?" Gage asked.

"Well, he wasn't too pleased. God, the media was everywhere Ray. This is the hottest story they've ever covered. You think this kid is the killer? Think the search is over?" Asked the officer.

He was excited. The entire police department had clocked unheard of hours and devoted their time and effort for nearly two weeks. Around the clock the search continued, and now, it looked like their efforts were about to pay off.

"Looks that way. Good job, Tommy." Gage gave the officer a pat on the shoulder.

"I'd appreciate you keeping this close to the vest, until the Chief decides how to handle it with the media."

"No problem, boss." Replied the officer. "We going to be reading this in the morning news?"

"I suspect you probably will, but until then, 'no comment'!"

Ray Gage walked to the evidence room. Once there, he reached for a pair of rubber gloves from the dispenser on the wall. He pulled them on. Slowly, he pulled out the blood stained clothing. A chill ran through him. As he untied the bathrobe cord, he felt perspiration beading on his forehead. His hands were trembling. Sully was behind the 'cage'.

When Ray had entered the room, Sully greeted him in his usual cheerful manner. Ray did not acknowledge him. He was absorbed in thought. Sully watched the detective, as he set the cord aside. Slowly, and carefully, the detective started unrolling the soiled clothing.

The center of the bundle was still damp! It had been so tightly wrapped, and it had a stench. The smell of death. Ray stepped back and wiped his forehead with his handkerchief.

"What you got there Ray?" Asked the plump Sargent, walking toward the detective.

"Sully, my pal, this is what we've all been looking for. You're looking at the murder's clothing, and if I'm not mistaken, the knife that butchered Lynn Clarke and David Rosen. Keep close watch on this stuff. I've got to get back in there. Don't let anyone near this stuff."

He stripped off the gloves, tossed them into the basket and returned to the interrogation room.

Back on Lynndale Street, the reporters continued their efforts to get comments from the Chapmans. John Chapman would not respond. He concealed himself in the house, with all the curtains drawn. Mrs. Chapman was on the verge of a collapse. She was sobbing.

John Chapman paced back and forth in the spacious living room. He lit his pipe and held it clenched between his teeth. He was seething. He was accustomed to being the man in control of any given situation. This situation was getting out of hand and for the first time in his life, he wasn't sure of what to do about it.

He looked over at Marge. She was curled up like a child on the sofa, whimpering.

John was never one to display emotion. He knew his wife needed a strong shoulder to lean on. That's what his role was. He had to be the strong one. He was the head of the household, and in his mind, he must take complete control. There would be no sign of weakness on the part of John Chapman.

The four men in the interrogation room exchanged perfunctory glances. They were astonished that the boy was displaying such a casual attitude. It was frightening to these seasoned detectives.

The person who had single handedly held the entire city in fear recounted the deed without hesitation. He showed no emotion. It was a chilling experience to listen to the details Karl Chapman shared with his interrogators.

Karl continued, " I just wanted to keep her company, you know, just wanted her to let me in and keep her company while she was babysitting."

He lit another cigarette and continued. "I tried to think of something that would make her let me in. I figured she was probably not allowed to let anybody in, but I thought, she'd open the door to tell me that, and I'd scare her."

Steve was puzzled. This kid wasn't making any sense! Why would she let him in? And this scheme he was talking about, 'scaring her' just didn't make any sense, but he let Karl continue.

By now, Ray Gage was writing the words of the maniacal teen. Karl had exhibited difficulty writing and was not able to keep up with his own rapid speech.

"So, I got dressed up in heavy clothes, and a hat. Then I walked to the Rosen's around 9:00, maybe later. I don't remember, but it was dark and real rainy. When I got there, I could see her in the living room, so I tapped on the window.

She looked to see who it was, and she opened the door. I had the knife wrapped up in a piece of paper, and tied with that string you guys found.

She didn't see the knife because I had it hidden sorta up my sleeve at first. I told her I wanted to come in and she was really snotty. You know, like I was some kind of creep or something! So, she started to shut the door, right in my face. Well, I got really mad about that, and pushed the door open. She kept saying, 'Get out, what are you doing here? Get out, you jerk'

I took the knife out of my sleeve so she could see it. She started to scream so I grabbed her."

The four men listened in astonishment as Karl related the gruesome details of the murders.

"I don't know what happened, I just couldn't stand to hear that screaming, so I stabbed her." Karl paused a few minutes and looked at each officer, Logan, Mahoney, Gage and the Chief. He searched the expressions on their faces. Their faces were blank.

"Can I get a Coke?" He asked.

"Sure, Karl, anything else?" Answered Ray Gage.

"Yeah, I could use a candy bar. Got any?"

The detective couldn't believe what he was hearing. No sign of remorse, sorrow, or even denial. They were stunned!

"I'll get it," Steve replied. The detective stood, stretched and headed for the door.

"Anyone else want anything?" He asked.

"Yeah, I could use a coffee," answered Captain Mahoney.

"I think we could all use a break, what'd say?"Asked the Chief.

They'd been sitting for several hours and the only one that failed to show any sign of tiring was Karl Chapman. He was still eager to tell all the details, and continued to enjoy his astonished listeners.

"Karl, we could all use a break. You mind? Just relax for a few minutes."

"Sure Detective. I guess I'm not going anywhere, am I?" Answered the teen.

John Chapman was an imposing man. Six feet three inches tall and 235lbs. He was a lineman by trade. Twenty three years with the company. Seawood Electrical Contractors, one of the largest in the Northeast.

He had started with the company as a 'grunt', eventually becoming a first class lineman. Now, he was a Foreman, with a 12-man crew. The company had been good to John Chapman, and enabled him to provide a comfortable living for his family.

That was of utmost importance to John. Provide for his family, and all else would fall into place naturally. It was difficult for Mr.

Chapman to conceive that the result of his hard work and high moral standards would be Karl, a maniacal killer.

The Clarke's were in utter confusion. They called relatives and close friends conveying what Ray Gage had related to them. It was beyond comprehension.

The media had given up any hopes of being granted an interview with either family. They headed back to the station, where they would gather in the press room. First, calls were made to the editor in chief. The presses would surely be held, if necessary, for this breaking news!

Steve went directly to the evidence room. Ray was not far behind him. Both detectives pulled a pair of plastic gloves from the dispenser.

Steve looked at the clothing Ray had laid out on the long table. A large brown jacket was laid out on the adjacent table and finally, a six-inch blade bayonet. The dried blood of the two victims was encrusted in the handle.

Raymond Gage watched in silence as his partner, piece by piece examined the clothing. Again, Ray shivered. How horrible this scene must have been. It was the same chilling feeling he had experienced the night he arrived at the scene.

He instructed Sully to keep an eye on the evidence. No one would be allowed even into the room, until further instructions. Sully assured him the clothing and the weapon would remain untouched.

The two detectives stripped off the gloves and disposed of them into a waste basket on their way out of the room. The media had crowded in the hallway and fired questions at the detectives. Ray raised his hands indicating he needed quiet and their attention. The reporters were silent, holding their pencils to their notebooks waiting for the news.

"Gentlemen! We've all worked very hard on this case. I know you are anxious to be brought up to date on the latest developments. You will be, but you have to be patient. I can tell you we have a suspect in custody, and it is likely he will be charged this evening".

Simultaneously, the barrage of questions spewed forth.

"What's his name? Is he a local person? Did he know the victims?" The questions were strung end to end.

Again Ray raised his hands and the hall was quiet.

"I can tell you he is an 18-year-old student, at Lincoln High School. Yes, he was acquainted with Lynn Ann Clarke. We are questioning him right now. I have to get back inside. The Chief and Captain Mahoney will keep you up to date on any developments.

You will have your story for the morning edition! Thank you, that's all I can tell you at this time. Now, please make yourselves comfortable in the press room. We have a job to do.

The press grumbled, but were confident they would get their story. It was just a matter of waiting. Several of them raced to the pay phones inside the station. Calling editors, producers, and broadcasters. The sound of coins dropping into the public phones echoed throughout the hallway.

Photographers checked their supply of film. Cameramen sat close by their reporters, and reporters made sure their supply of writing instruments were in tack. Now the waiting. But it would be worth it. The biggest story in most of their careers!

When the detectives returned to the interrogation room. Karl was waiting, anxious to continue his ghoulish account of the murders. He chewed on a candy bar, and began talking. This kid wasn't leaving out a single detail.

The detectives, Chief McNamara, and Captain Mahoney hardly asked a question. The words just poured out, in a flat, unemotional tone from Karl Chapman.

"And then after I did her, I heard this kid crying." He was saying, speaking rapidly, but very concise.

"It was the Rosen kid. So I went to his room. He saw me, and kinda crawled into the corner of his bed, up against the wall. I didn't want him to identify me, so I stabbed him."

"How many times, Karl?" Asked the Chief.

"I don't remember, several times, I know." Answered Karl.

"Then what did you do Karl?" Asked Steve Logan.

"Well, I was going to leave, but, when I got to the living room where Lynn was, she moved. I thought she was still alive, so I hit her with the handle of the knife, and stabbed her some more." He answered with a flat affect.

"How many times did you stab Lynn?" Asked Steve.

"I don't know, I told you, I wasn't counting, several times!"

Finally the question everyone was waiting for.

The Chief tapped Steve Logan on the shoulder, indicating he wanted to take his seat directly in front of Karl.

"Karl, why, why did you do this? What were you thinking? I thought you liked the girl, and you didn't even know the boy. Why?"

"The boy knew me. He's seen me before." Karl replied.

"What do you mean? You've been in the Rosen's before?" Asked the Chief.

"Yeah, when my sister babysat. I'd walk over there to watch TV with her. The boy was still up sometimes. He knew me. And he would have been able to tell I was there that night."

The detectives were stunned at this piece of information. Until then, they had assumed the boy couldn't have possibly identified Karl. Now, this made a little more sense.

Karl was silent, for the first time since the interview had begun. He wasn't showing any signs of tiring. He was pumped up.

He thought for a few seconds and replied, "I didn't want to hurt her, honest, I didn't want to kill her. I just went there to scare her. I thought if I scared her, you know, like a joke or something, she'd see it was me, and let me in."

Karl spoke in an even tone, although he was starting to rant, speaking rapidly. He seemed to get excited the more he talked about the horror.

"But, she opened the door, and I guess I did scare her, but she started screaming, I just lost it and started stabbing her. She kept screaming, and I finally got a good hold on her and stabbed her again and again, until the screaming stopped.

She kinda slumped up against the wall. That's when the kid started crying."

"Then what Karl? You said you really liked her. You've known her all her life, why do such a horrible thing to someone you liked? Can you see why it's hard for me to understand?

Try again Karl, tell me the truth. Did she make you angry? Did you two date and she didn't want to see you anymore? Tell us Karl, what really made you 'lose it'?" The Chief was truly baffled.

He really could not buy that motive.

"I told you. Oh! Man! I just lost it!" Karl replied. "I didn't want to hurt her, but she just kept on screaming! I didn't expect her to scream!" Karl was really trying to convince the Chief and all in the room, but the Chief just wasn't buying it!

The Chief got up and walked to the Captain. The two men walked to the far end of the room.

"What do you make of all this Jack?" Asked the Chief. "You've heard everything I have, you believe the motive?"

"Not even close." Replied the Captain.

"I say he was in love with the girl. She didn't want anything to do with him. This kid is not even close to being 'normal'. He couldn't take the rejection. Let's face it Chief, he went there with a knife for God's sake. He planned on killing her. I think it was a case of if she's not mine, she won't be anybody's."

"I have to agree with you Jack. But to butcher a girl? And the little boy? What kind of a depraved person could do this?"

"You said it, Chief, a depraved, psychopath, just like the doc described. He fits that profile to a T!"

"We've heard enough. This kid is going down. You ready? I'm going to my office. You give Gage and Logan the word, and meet me there. We'll go over how we're going to address the media. Let's do this close to the book. We don't want any technicalities out there to screw this up." The Chief left the room.

The Captain returned to the group at the table.

"I need to go to the bathroom." Said Chapman.

"Can I use the restroom?" His demeanor hadn't changed throughout the hours of interrogation. He appeared to be tiring, but showed no remorse, no regret and no sorrow. Truly a monster!

"Sure, Karl. We could all use a break. Just hold on for a minute. I'll get an officer to escort you." Ray complied.

He used the wall phone and requested an officer to the interrogation room.

"Sargent, you mind taking Mr. Chapman to the restroom. Use the side door. We don't want a media frenzy."

"Sure Sarge, want him cuffed?" Asked the officer.

"What do you think, Karl? Do we need to cuff you?" Asked Ray.

"Nah, just let me take a piss will you?" Answered Karl.

The Sargent lead Karl to a door installed for the sole purpose of moving suspects in and out, undetected by the media.

Once they exited the room, Steve took a deep sigh. He stood, and stretched. Ray leaned back in his chair and put his feet up on the table. The Captain addressed both detectives.

"He's all yours boys! Ray, keep writing. Make sure it's all there, all of it, and charge him with the two homicides. Make sure he signs that confession. Steve, you witness both Ray's and Chapman's signatures. We don't want any mistakes here. I'll take care of the media."

"You guys process him, and we'll get him down to State Street as soon as possible. Nice job! Now wind it up." This was a good day for the Captain!

"I'll catch up with you later." He said, and turned to leave the room.

"Captain," Ray continued, "What about the parents? You want them to see Karl tonight? How do you want to handle that? I can tell you the father is hopping mad. He's not going to be easy to deal with."

"Nope, Chief says nobody tonight. Let the kid stew for awhile. I'll deal with the father. The Chief talked to him earlier. I know what you're saying. You just take care of that maniac. Don't worry about Pop! You've got enough to handle.

I'm going to take a look at the evidence. Chief McNamara is waiting in his office. It's his turn in front of the cameras! You know how he likes to deliver good news!"

The Captain left and headed to the evidence room.

Karl rolled up his sleeves and removed his watch. He placed the watch on the sink and bent over. He splashed cold water over his face and neck. The officer stood by the restroom door, allowing the boy some privacy inside.

Karl tucked in his shirt and adjusted his belt. He appeared to be preparing for another round with the detectives. He reached in his back pocket and removed his comb, and primped for the anticipated cameras that would be swarming around him. He knew he would be arrested. He didn't seem to care.

The Sargent delivered Karl Chapman back to the room where the two detectives waited.

Ray and Steve had called for sandwiches to be brought in, they would arrive at any moment.

"Got you a couple sandwiches Karl. You must be hungry?" Asked Ray.

"Yeah, I'm starved. Thanks! Heard from my folks yet?" Karl asked. "Can I call them?"

"The Chief has talked with them. I think they're coming down here, but the Chief says to wait until tomorrow for anyone visiting."

Ray was hinting at the eminent arrest. "You'll have to read what I've written, and sign it. It's everything you've told us, just look it all over. When you're done you'll have to sign it. We want to be sure we've got everything the way you told us. You okay with that Karl?"

"Sure, I don't write very well. I don't spell too good, but if you wrote what I said, then I won't have to read it." Karl replied.

"Yup, got it practically word for word, Karl. Now, have a seat." Ray directed Karl to the chair he had occupied for the past several hours.

Once the boy was seated, Steve stated, "We're arresting you Karl. You'll be charged with the murders of Lynn Ann Clarke and David Rosen." Steve added. "Do you understand what's happening here Karl?"

"I suppose so. I figured that was what would happen." Karl replied in a soft voice.

"Just a few more questions, about what you did after you left the house."

"Well, I went home. It was still raining real hard. I cut through the backyards on my street. When I got to my house, I sat out on the porch for awhile. You know, to think."

"What did you think about Karl?" Asked Steve.

"I had to think of what to do next. I had blood all over me. I was soaking wet from the rain, and I had the knife in my pocket. It even cut me! So I just sat there for awhile to think."

"After you thought about it, what did you do?"

"I just went in the front door. My mother was in the living room and didn't see me. I just went upstairs and took all my clothes off in the bathroom. Man, there was blood everywhere! I had to clean it all up and find someplace to stash the knife and clothes. Then I went to bed. I remember, I was real tired." Karl responded in a calm controlled tone.

"Did you know your mother and Brenda went over to the Clarke's to get the little girl?" Asked Steve.

"Nope, never heard anything. I sleep pretty sound." Karl replied.

The detectives had heard enough.

"Got anything else you want to tell us?"

"No, I told you everything. I did it. Did you find the knife? Did you get the bundle of clothes?" Karl answered, in a matter of fact tone.

The three sat at the table. Ray nodded.

"Yes, Karl, they've been delivered here. We'll run some tests on them. See what comes back. Where'd you get that knife Karl?" Ray asked.

"It's a German bayonet. WWI vintage. Got it at the Army Surplus store down on Elm Street, couple of weeks ago."

"What did you buy it for Karl? Were you planning on using it on Lynn?" Steve interjected. Karl didn't answer.

"I just don't get it Karl. I just don't understand, why!" Steve Logan was not as patient as his partner.

He was visibly discussed at the sing-song attitude of this savage killer.

"Did you think about Lynn a lot Karl? You know, did you think about how it would be to put your arms around her and maybe do a little necking? You must have thought about that Karl.

You said you liked her, do you think she liked you the same way?" Steve was pushing, trying to get this depraved demon to respond.

Karl didn't change his story, nor did he change his cool demeanor.

"Well, we have your explanation of the motive, we have opportunity, and we certainly have the means. You're in for a long haul my friend, and it's not going to be pleasant. That, I can assure you." Karl's eyes glared at Steve.

It was the first revealing sign of his insane persona.

Ray knew all too well how his partner could blow up, and he didn't want any senseless harassment of the suspect. This had to be by the book, and so far, there were no kinks. Everything was rolling pretty smoothly, considering what they were dealing with!

"Well, Karl, I want you to read what I've written. If you don't understand something, just ask. Sometimes my writing can be hard to read. Just read it, and if it's all there the way you told it, I want you to sign it at the bottom." Ray turned the pad around so Karl could read his confession.

Karl picked it up and started reading.

"I'll be right back." Steve Logan said.

The sandwiches and beverages were brought into the room and placed on the wooden table.

The Chief had stopped by the evidence room. He was examining the weapon and looking over the bloody clothes. He felt a wave of nausea come over him. The clothes were covered in blood. Particularly the jacket. From the cuffs of the sleeves to the shoulder was almost entirely blood . The Chief could only imagine the scene. The victims' blood was still encrusted in the handle of the bayonet. A few strands of hair were meshed in the blood. They were pieces of Lynn Ann Clarke's hair.

"I've got to get with the Captain, he's waiting in my office. That crowd out there is going to get ugly real soon if we don't feed them something!" The Chief said to Sully, indicating the press that were pacing up and down the hallways.

By then, they knew who the suspect was, where he lived and that he would be arrested. They were also advised by their superiors, that they had to get the go ahead from Chief McNamara before their stories could be printed. The name could not be disclosed unless the Chief gave permission.

When the Chief entered his office, the Captain was already on the phone talking to the Editor in Chief of the Stanfield News.

"Yes, I'm about to release all the information to your reporters. Yes, we will be processing the suspect soon, and he will be transported to State Street."

State Street was the location of the Hampden County Jail. There, Karl Chapman would await his arraignment.

Ray Gage and Karl Chapman remained in the interrogation room and quietly ate hamburgers and drank Coca-Cola. Ray watched as the boy kept his head down reading the statement and devouring the sandwiches. He picked his head up only to gulp the cola.

Ray was physically repulsed as he recounted Karl's confession over and over in his head. He tossed the half-eaten hamburger back on the wrapper, stood up and kicked the chair. The abrupt gesture of anger on the part of Ray startled the boy. He jumped, and Ray looked at him. Now, he saw the face of a monster. Clear face to face with him. This kid is a paradox, Ray thought. Ray wondered if Karl was really insane. He'd have to be, he thought. But sane or not, this kid was not going to walk.

"Looks okay to me, where do you want me to sign?" Asked Karl.

"You sure you read it all? Take your time, make sure it's right." Ray knew Karl hadn't had time to read the hours of writing. He was sure he hadn't read past the first page.

"Yup, looks like it's all here." He replied, taking a gulp of the cola.

Suddenly, Karl spoke, "Hey, Detective, you got kids?"

This one question made Ray seethe! The gall of this kid, to ask a question like that! Without acknowledging the scathing question, Ray picked up the black wall phone.

"Mike, this is Ray Gage. Send an officer down here. I've got a suspect here that needs processing. Chapman, Karl T. That's right." Ray listened for a few minutes as the Sargent informed him that Mr. John Chapman had arrived a short time ago, and was demanding to see his son.

"The Chief said no interruptions, Ray. What do you want to do?" Asked the Sargent.

"Tell him someone will be with him in a few minutes. Does Logan or the Chief know he's here? And what about the mother, she here too?" Asked Ray.

"No, he's alone. Haven't seen Logan or the Chief. Think they're in the evidence room. I can tell you, the press is busting at the seams. Guess they got orders to sit tight, but don't know how long that's going to last!" The Sargent relayed to Gage.

"Don't worry about that. Are they in the press room? Did they talk to Chapman?"

"Nope, got Mr. Chapman sitting at your desk. Figured that would keep him away from the media until you figured out what to do." Answered the Sargent.

"Good move! I'll be there in a few minutes. Meanwhile, get that officer down here and get this kid out of my sight!"

Just as Ray was placing the phone on the receiver, an officer appeared in the doorway.

"Sargent Rollins, this is Mr. Chapman. He's about to sign a confession. I'd like you to witness his signature, and mine also."

"Sure Ray."

"Karl, sign right there." Ray instructed trying to keep his temper from flaring. He'd had enough of this kid glove treatment, and was holding back displaying his feelings toward this ruthless killer.

Ray leaned over the table and examined the signature of the teen. It was barely legible. A third grader could have done a better job. He signed just below and handed the pen to Sargent Rollins.

"Just sign below the two signatures." The Sargent complied.

"Take him down to processing. He's being booked for the murders of Lynn Ann Clarke and David Rosen."

It was the first time Ray actually heard the words, and they sounded good to him. Arrest for the murders of Lynn Ann Clarke and David Rosen. The nightmare was over. At least that part of the nightmare. What would unfold in the coming months would prove to be the continuance of the living nightmare!

Ray remained in the room alone. He mentally reviewed the eerie confession of the teen. He became angry. He got up, paced in the small room, trying to think of anything that made sense to him. He couldn't fathom the mind set of Karl Chapman.

Of course he was insane, but to live with this senseless slaughter? Damn, he attended the funeral! If that weren't enough, if that wasn't ghoulish enough he served as a pallbearer at her funeral! He offered condolences to the family, and listened to the terror of his fellow students! It was incomprehensible to the detective. He felt sick.

He went to the restroom. As he splashed water on his face, he caught a glimpse of himself in the mirror. The mirror reflected a middle-aged detective showing signs of exhaustion. Dark circles under the detective's eyes, the result of eighteen to twenty hour workdays, and the inability to sleep. His shoulders were aching and his head was beginning to pound.

"Well, Ray," he spoke aloud to the grim reflection in the mirror "we've got the monster. We finally got him!"

He returned to the interrogation room, rolled down his sleeves, and buttoned the cuffs. He slipped into his jacket and draped his tie around his neck.

Ray approached the Sargent at the front desk.

"Mr. Chapman still in there?" He asked, indicating the direction of his office.

"Yup, he's stewing. I brought him coffee about half an hour ago. He says he's not leaving until he gets to see his kid."

"Well, that's not going to happen tonight. Kid's being processed right now. Chief says no visitors until tomorrow. He'll be transported down to State Street soon as he's finished being booked." Ray replied, and headed toward his office.

As he entered his office, John Chapman stood and approached the detective.

"It's about time! Christ, I've been sitting here for hours. I want to see Karl. Where is he?"

Ray introduced himself, but John Chapman wasn't interested in any introductions. He wanted to see Karl, and he wanted to see him now!

"Have a seat, Mr. Chapman." Ray suggested, pulling a chair toward the desk.

"I don't want to have a seat, Detective! I want to see my son! Now, what's keeping me from seeing him?" Mr. Chapman was shouting.

181

Ray walked to the windowed wall that separated his office from the front desk. He pulled the Venetian blinds and closed them to the view of all.

"Mr. Chapman, I have orders from the Chief. You'll have to wait until tomorrow to see Karl. He is being processed and charged with the double homicide of Lynn Ann Clarke and David Rosen. He will be transported to State Street Jail." Ray explained to the angered father.

"You can't keep me from seeing my own son. He's not a murderer! He couldn't have killed those kids! I want to see him!" John Chapman was showing signs of breaking down. Ray repeated his orders.

"I want to talk to the Chief. I want to talk to the District Attorney." Mr. Chapman responded.

"I'll get the Chief, Mr. Chapman, but you'll have to get yourself under control. This isn't getting you anywhere. Now, excuse me, I'll see if the Chief can talk to you." Ray left the office.

Ray walked down the hallway directly to the Chief's office. As he entered, he found Steve Logan, Captain McNamara, and Chief McNamara all seated, discussing the horrific confession they had listened to.

"Chief, the father's in my office. Wants to talk to you. I think you should get down there. This guy is about to get out of control. Really upset!"

"Okay, Ray. Did you wrap up the confession? Did the kid sign it?."

"Yes sir, he sure did. I dotted every I and crossed every T. Sargent Rollins witnessed both signatures. It's all on record now."

"Good job Ray. I'll be back in a few minutes," he addressed the three men in the room. "Then, we'll talk to the press. I'll make a statement, and Jack, you can field the questions. Okay?"

"Okay with me." Replied the Captain. "They'll want pictures of the kid, what do you think?" He asked the Chief.

"Don't see why not, they've been waiting long enough, don't see any reason they should be denied pictures." Answered the Chief as he started out the door.

"Well, Mr. Chapman," the Chief started, as he entered Ray Gage's office. "I appreciate your patience." The Chief continued.

"I understand you've been here quite awhile, and I also understand you want to see Karl. Well, that's not going to be possible tonight."

"Why not? Why can't I see him? Gage says he's being charged with murder!"

"That's correct, Mr. Chapman. Double homicide. He's confessed, he's signed a written confession. We have the weapon and the bloody clothing he was wearing. Now, I suggest you go home, and you'll be able to see him tomorrow. He'll be held at the jail downtown."

John Chapman's shoulders seemed to slump. He looked down at the floor. He looked like he was defeated. He was distraught, and beaten. This was not something John Chapman was accustomed to.

"This may take some time, Mr. Chapman." The Chief began.

"I must tell you, the press is pretty blood thirsty out there. We've been holding them back until the booking process is completed, but they'll get the story for the morning edition." He informed Mr. Chapman.

"What can I do, Chief?" Mr. Chapman pleaded. "What should I do?"

"For tonight, Mr. Chapman, I'd suggest you go home, and be with your wife. There's nothing you can do here, or for Karl right now. You need to be with Mrs. Chapman." The Chief answered in a sympathetic tone.

" I guess you're right. Mrs. Chapman is not a very strong person. She's with her sister right now. I'm to pick her up. She was expecting Karl to be released. I don't know what to do."

"Just be with her, she's going to need your support from here on. Call the jail in the morning. They will be able to give you instructions, and appropriate time to see Karl. Now go get your wife, and I'll talk with you in the morning."

The Chief felt empathy for the father of the monster he held just a room away. He hated to even imagine how the mother would take all this. But his thoughts quickly turned to the victims' families. What was worse? From his point of view, all parties were dealing with grief and sorrow. He couldn't begin to imagine the suffering all families were brought to bear.

"I'll take you out the side door. You don't want to be exposed to the media." The Chief suggested as he picked up Mr. Chapman's jacket, and directed him to the door leading to the rear of the station.

"Thank you Chief, I'll talk to you in the morning." Mr. Chapman replied, and with the anonymity of a faceless citizen, walked slowly to his car.

The Chief returned to Gage's office. He pulled the Venetian blinds up and saw the multitude of reporters and cameramen. He took a sigh and pressed the button on the phone to his office.

"Logan here," came the reply.

"Hi Steve, this is the Chief. How's the processing going? Is Chapman ready to be transported to State Street?" Asked the Chief.

"Just about there, Chief." Answered the detective. "You headed this way?"

"Be right down. The father's gone home. Got him calmed down. I'm going to call the Rosen's. Give them a heads up. Don't want them getting the news in the paper."

"Good idea. We'll wait for you before we face the media." Logan hung up the phone.

"Hello?" A woman's voice answered.

"Hello, this is Chief McNamara. Is Mr. Rosen available?" Asked the Chief.

"Yes, just a moment Chief," answered Mrs. Schaefer.

"This is Ben Rosen." Came the reply.

"Yes, Mr. Rosen. This is Chief McNamara. I'm calling to let you know we believe we have the killer in custody."

There was a silence. "Mr. Rosen, are you there? We believe we have the killer. We're processing him right now!"

"Oh my God! Thank God! Who is it Chief?" Asked Ben Rosen.

"His name is Karl Chapman, a neighbor of the Clarke girl. We have the weapon, and the clothing and he's confessed. We've got him Mr. Rosen, we've got him!" The Chief repeated.

"Karl Chapman? That's not possible. He was one of the kids that worked part time in the summer at the market. It can't be him. I thought you were looking for a mental patient, or someone like that."

"Mr. Rosen, it's him. I wanted to let you know what we had so you wouldn't hear it first on the news, or read about it in the morning paper." Replied the Chief.

"Thank you for the call. Thank you very much. I have to go now." Answered Mr. Rosen.

"You're welcome, ah, well, feel free to call me if you need to."

The Chief was puzzled. He expected a different reaction.

"I will, and thank you again for the call." Ben Rosen hung up.

The Chief was dumbfounded. He stood with the receiver to his ear for a few more seconds. He wondered if Mr. Rosen had grasped the information he was conveying to him. Well, that's it, what else can I do, he thought.

Ray Gage had already confirmed the arrest to the Clarke's. They too, reacted strangely. They were overwhelmed. Of course, they would be. The news was bittersweet. Their senses were probably numb. They needed time to have the news of the arrest become a reality. Surely the news broadcasts and the morning paper would serve to verify the Chief's notification to the two grieving families.

In reality, three grieving families. The Chapman's would endure their own kind of hell.

The Chief headed for his office to join the others. They would emerge together and the Chief would make the initial statement to the eager awaiting press and TV news reporters. The TV would get the jump on the breaking news the Stanfield Morning News would carry.

When the Chief arrived at his office, the Captain had notified the processing officer that they would be there momentarily to escort Karl Chapman out and expose him to the cameras.

Karl was photographed, fingerprinted and placed in leg irons and handcuffs. These restraints were standard procedure for any capital crime suspect being transferred. It was particularly necessary under these circumstances, with the news frenzy they were about to face.

Karl Chapman continued to display little if any emotion. He courteously complied to any directives throughout the booking process. He appeared to be exceptionally calm and cool.

All officers that came within contact of him were chilled at Chapman's demeanor. What could possibly be going through his

185

mind? Is he comprehending any of this? One couldn't help but wonder.

"Okay, gentlemen, show time!"Announced the Chief.

The two detectives straightened their ties, and followed Captain Mahoney and Chief McNamara to face the hungry reporters. From another entrance, Karl was led out, flanked by two patrol officers.

The Reporters rushed toward Karl and his escorts. Lights to accommodate the TV cameras were flipped on and the cameras were rolling. Karl raised his manacled hands to shade his eyes, from the blinding lights only to have the officer pull them down. His head remained downward, as he shuffled through the mass of media. The two officers were dwarfed beside the gangly teen. His lips were pursed, and he responded to no one. He was being moved as quickly as possible to the awaiting patrol car.

Once Karl was secured inside the cruiser that would deliver him to the jail, the reporters turned to the Chief. The Chief raised both his arms gesturing for silence. The reporters hushed and the Chief began his statement.

"Well, we've all waited for some positive news, I believe we have it. This afternoon, we were lead to believe we have in custody the person responsible for the savage killings of Lynn Ann Clarke and David Rosen."

"We have notified the families of the victims. The suspect has provided us with his written confession and has lead us to the murder weapon as well as the clothing he was wearing the night of the murders. He was an acquaintance of the Clarke girl. Actually, a neighbor of the girl. Both resided on Lynndale Street. He is a student at Lincoln High School."

The reporters shot questions at the Chief. The Chief was hesitant to disclose too much until Chapman was officially 'booked'.

The reporters would dig and uncover most of the news that would hit the morning edition of the Stanfield News.

Meanwhile, Karl Chapman was delivered to the Hampden County Jail, State Street, Stanfield, MA

Saturday Morning October 2, 1954 Stanfield News:

KARL CHAPMAN, 18 HELD IN MURDERS OF GIRL, BOY

Neighbor of Slain Girl was Arrested Late Yesterday, Knife Reported Located

Victims' Families Informed of Killer: Police Bring Bloody Clothing to Station

An 18-year-old boy was arrested late yesterday in the Clarke/Rosen murders.

Arrested was Karl Chapman, son of Mr. And Mrs. John Chapman of 51 Lyndale St. Neighbors described the teen as a "gentle boy". The high school boy was employed, part time during summer vacation, at the R & S Market, owned by the Rosen family.

He was described as an acquaintance of Lynn Ann Clark. The 14-year-old babysitter who was hacked to death with 4-year-old David Rosen.

It has been reported that Chapman went 'berserk' and killed the babysitter, then the young boy for fear he may be identified.

Police were seen taking blood-stained clothing from the Chapman's home on Lynndale St.

Thread found in the youth's home matched that discovered in the Rosen's residence after the murders had been committed. Parents of the boy rushed to the police station to help him if they could. Police Chief Paul McNamara stubbornly refused to allow the parents access to the teen.

The article was very lengthy, describing how the murders had occurred and disclosing the incredible details that had unfolded during the police interrogation. The reporters uncovered the grizzly fact that Karl Chapman had actually participated in the girl's funeral, serving as a pallbearer. This was beyond anyone's comprehension. Chapman had attended school with the grieving students. He had offered his condolences to the distraught family, attended the funeral and served as pallbearer! Furthermore, the teen had been employed over the past summer by Ben Rosen. He was a stock boy at the R&S Market which was located only blocks from Lynndale St.

It was also reported that the teen would be held at the State Street jail and scheduled for arraignment on Monday.

As Karl sat somberly in his cell, he showed no signs of distress. He ate well, and reportedly slept well. He was described as a 'model prisoner'.

The entire city took a collective "sigh of relief" upon reading of Chapman's arrest. The ubiquity of fear had been lifted. Now they faced the 'after shock' of discovering the identity of the savage killer. They had expected a maniac, a mental patient, anybody but the 18-year-old neighbor of one of the victims.

John and Marge Chapman arrived at the jail around 9:00 A.M. on Saturday. The couple pushed through the crowds of reporters and cameramen, not commenting to anyone.

As they approached the officer at the desk, Mrs. Chapman clung to her husband's arm. Her eyes were swollen from sobbing throughout the previous evening, but John Chapman showed no sign of what he was experiencing. He was dressed in a dark suit, crisp white shirt and a conservative tie.

John carried a package with him. It contained a change of clothes for Karl, but the deputy sheriff insisted it be left at the desk. Nothing was to be delivered to the prisoner without inspection and approval of the Sheriff. The parents were granted a very brief visit with Karl.

After only a few minutes, Mrs. Chapman, with the aide of her husband, was led out. She was sobbing uncontrollably and Mr. Chapman thought it best she leave. The couple again pushed their way through the media. Flash bulbs flashing, microphones looming overhead and reporters shouting questions. Again, the Chapman's refused any comment, and headed directly for their awaiting car.

The Chapman's returned home. Camped out on the front lawn were reporters and newsmen from the local TV Station. It was impossible to avoid them. Brenda was not at home. She remained at her aunt's. They were thankful for that.

Mr. Chapman pulled past one of the media's cars parked in the driveway. He drove the car as close to the door as possible. He shut the engine off, and in an instant, the sedan was surrounded. John Chapman forced his door open and immediately went to the passenger side to assist his wife out of the car and into the house.

The shades and curtains had already been drawn shut. What do these people want from me? He thought. He peeked through the blind in the front room. The thought of the Clarke's directly across the street made his heart sick. How would they ever go on? How would the Clarke's ever go on?

Mr. Clarke's black sedan was parked in the driveway. Directly in front of the Clarke's house was another car. It was not familiar to John Chapman. Good, he thought, someone is with them.

Mrs. Chapman went to bed. The phone started ringing, and Mr. Chapman removed it from the hook. He knew it wouldn't be anyone he wanted to talk to. He would call Brenda after he attended to Mrs. Chapman.

Mr. Chapman went to his wife. She was laid across the bed and staring at the flower wallpaper. He tried to comfort her, but he couldn't find the words. Mrs. Chapman had nothing to say. She just stared blankly.

Beside the bed was a small personal telephone directory. John reached for it hoping to find their family doctor's number written in it. He couldn't remember the name. His mind went blank, so he leafed through the small pages until he finally saw, written in his wife's perfect penmanship, Dr. Charles Neilson, RE8-5700. He repeated the number over and over in his head as he proceeded downstairs to the telephone.

"Hello, this is John Chapman," he began. "Is the doctor available?"

A lady replied, "I'm sorry, the doctor is not in on Saturdays. Is this an emergency?"

"Yes, it is. My wife, Marge Chapman, well, she, is very ill." John replied.

He didn't know how to describe his wife's condition. He was certain she was in need of medical care.

"Please leave your telephone number, Mr. Chapman. The doctor is on call for emergencies, unless you would prefer to go to the hospital." The operator replied.

After a short pause, John Chapman answered, "No, I would prefer to talk to the doctor, thank you. My number is RE8-5005. Please give him this message as soon as possible. I'll be waiting for his call."

"Yes sir, I'll do my best. In the meanwhile, if you change your mind and ....."

John Chapman hung up the phone. He was making every effort to keep control of the situation, but his resources were limited. The sharp ring of the phone startled him.

"Hello, this is John Chapman," he answered, expecting the doctor to reply. Instead, it was the TV Station, asking questions faster than John could even comprehend.

"No comment! No comment!" John screamed into the phone and slammed it into the cradle.

Now, he realized he would have to answer the calls. He was expecting the doctor. He would have to field all calls until he heard from the doctor. If he had thought it through, he would have given Marge's sister's number. She would have explained the circumstances and she could have sent the doctor directly to Lynndale St.

The phone continued to ring. John was beside himself. He looked outside. The media crowd that had been there upon their arrival had noticeably disbursed.

He returned to his wife. Marge had not moved from the bed. She looked as though she had nodded off and John thought that might be the best for her. Surely the doctor would be able to do something for her. Marge was not emotionally strong. She was very dependant upon John to carry any burden, but, John was already growing weary.

John Chapman filled his hand carved pipe with his special blend tobacco. He lit it and took a long puff. He began pacing across the dark green carpeted living room.

As John worried about his family, Karl Chapman sat in his small jail cell. His dinner was delivered. Two large cheeseburgers, a large drink and a bag of chips. He sat on the thin mattress of his bunk and devoured the food.

The Police Department was pulling all the paperwork together. They had sent the bloody clothing, with the murder weapon to the crime lab in Boston, via the courier. The crochet thread that had been delivered to the Grouse Mills, there in Stanfield was surprisingly simple to match.

The foreman examined it, and declared it was very possibly, a match. He said he was no scientist, but because of the inferior quality of the thread, it was obvious even to him. The thread had been manufactured by American Thread. Because of the drying process used during the war, the thread was of inferior quality.

It was likely an older person would have this particular batch of thread. This would be the evidence that would be presented at trial. The thread had been the link, but the bloody clothing and the weapon would surely be sufficient evidence at trial. The trial that would decide the life or death of Karl Theodore Chapman.

'A THREAD OF EVIDENCE'

PART II

Saturday PM, October 2, 1954 Stanfield News

Special Edition*
CHAPMAN CLAIMS MURDERS BEGAN AS 'JOKE'
Teen Shows No Emotion, Is Eating Well, and Sleeping Well
Parents of David Rosen extend sincere condolences to the Chapman family

Benjamin and Gail Rosen publically extended their sincerest condolences to Mr and Mrs Chapman, family of their son's brutal murderer.

The eighteen year old, is accused of murdering 14 year old Lynn Ann Clarke and 4 year old David Rosen is reported to be eating and sleeping well. The hulking, six foot three, 180 pound defendant has been quiet and calm since he was arrested and awaits arraignment scheduled for Monday morning.

"The enormity of the crime has not affected his appetite," Deputy Sheriff Johnson was quoted.

Earlier today, John and Marge Chapman visited their son at the State Street Jail where their son Karl Chapman is being held. Mrs. Chapman was seen being led out in tears shortly after their arrival.

District Attorney Martin O'Neil has declined comments until Monday's arraignment. He was quoted as saying, "I don't buy the motive. I don't believe this was simply a prank gone bad. This was a premeditated act. I believe several motives are possible." With that short statement, the D.A. asked that no further comments be made by his office, the Sheriff's office or the Police Department until the arraignment had taken place on Monday.

The article continued recounting the murders, and recapping all the news that had been printed in recent days.

Mr. Rosen extended his sympathy to the Chapmans.

"I can appreciate just how they feel," he said.

Mr. Rosen spoke in a low voice, almost a whisper. He spoke to the press and expressed his intention to call Mr. and Mrs. Chapman.

Mr. Rosen told the press that they have not stepped a foot into the house and never will. He was very bitter towards Karl Chapman, but seemed to have empathy for Karl's family. He referred to Karl as 'that kid' and went on to say how he had ruined the lives of three families.

He was a very sad man, as he revealed that Brenda, Karl's sister had actually babysat for the Rosen's in the past. His heart was very saddened.

Sunday October 3, 1954 Stanfield Sunday Republican:

CONFESSED KILLER AWAITS ARRAIGNMENT
Thread Was the Major Clue in Solution of Murders
Chief Credits 'Teamwork' and Singles out Captain Mahoney
and his Detectives for Tireless Efforts
(A Picture of the Chapman house was spanned across three columns*)*

It was in this trim home at 51 Lynndale St, directly across from the 14-year-old victim's family, that detectives found the evidence that led to the arrest of Karl T. Chapman, 18 and the solution of the murders of Lynn Ann Clarke and David Rosen. A carbine type bayonet, the clothes worn by the killer, and the crochet thread found at the scene of the murder all were uncovered in this house, where Chapman lived. It was here that he had gone about stone-faced while police passed his door every day in a frantic search to track down the killer.

(On page 4, side by side, a picture of the two victims)

David and Lynn Ann were healthy happy children totally unaware that a killer stalked outside. Then, a youth with murder in his heart struck swiftly and surely with a knife and life for them ended suddenly and tragedy and fear was born in a city that was shocked as never before.

When asked to explain why he killed a young girl, who knew him well as her neighbor and an innocent baby, Karl Chapman simply replied "I don't know."

Will a trial solve this riddle? The tragic drama is over for these two victims. For Karl, the awareness of possible sudden death by a current of electricity is just beginning.

At 6:10 A.M., Ray Gage woke. He rolled over and wrapped himself around Linda. He nuzzled the nape of her neck. She smelled good. Linda moved closer to her husband. There was little doubt, the Gages would be sleeping in this Sunday morning.

Steve Logan sipped his coffee while Katherine remained sleeping. Steve, being a creature of habit for over two decades waited for the morning paper. He heard the thud of the heavy Sunday Edition hit against the front door.

The detective that had worked diligently, side by side with his partner, Raymond Gage, basked in the sprawled headlines before him. He read every word.

Still amazed at the apprehension of Karl Chapman. It was a real stroke of luck! He recounted the interrogation that had sent chills through him, as well as all others that had witnessed the gruesome details Karl Chapman had related. Detailed, and cold.

The facts were beyond comprehension. A neighbor, a classmate. What kind of a monster was he? The worst imaginable. The worst of the worst. And to think, he'd been right under their noses. He'd even been questioned the morning of Lynn Ann's funeral and gave no indication of any reason for suspicion.

He thought about the impending arraignment. Chapman would be charged with double homicide and he wondered if the D.A. would seek the death penalty. Surely, if there was a case deserving of the death penalty, this was it!

He flipped through the paper. The news of Debbie Reynolds and Eddie Fishers' wedding. Below, an article announcing the break up of Marilyn Monroe and Joe DiMagio.

With the Chapmam case still looming, Logan found the Hollywood news almost blasphemy. It seemed that the world should stop turning, and the sun should be hidden behind ominous clouds. But, the articles served to bring back reality. Regardless of the tragic events occurring in Stanfield, life went on everywhere, and the world kept spinning.

His thoughts turned to the families. John and Marge Chapman. He could only imagine what they were faced with. After a trial, their son could possibly face the electric chair.

The Rosen's. Beyond comprehension. The loss of a 4-year-old. The victim of a senseless, horrific murder. Little David Rosen, robbed of everything he could have only dreamed of in his short life.

And finally, Phil and Elaine Clarke. The loss of a 14-year-old daughter who fought and succumbed to the brutality of a depraved monster.

Katherine entered the kitchen. Steve welcomed the interruption. The proliferation caused by the double homicide consumed him. Katherine stood behind his chair and leaned over to deliver a kiss on Steve's neck. She looked at the newspaper spread on the table before him. The headlines were blaring.

Katherine knew when it was wise to keep her silence. She gave Steve an assuring squeeze and made her way to the freshly perked coffee.

"So you're finally getting a day home? It's been almost two weeks since you've had a day off."

Steve did not reply. Katherine sat across the table. She picked up the newspaper and began reading the lead story.

Steve had told Katherine the whole story and the detailed atrocities Chapman had revealed to him. Now, the reporters brought the details into the homes of all the citizens of Stanfield.

Katherine glanced up at her husband. He appeared older. This case had taken its toll on the senior detective. She wished she could comfort him. He had taken this case on and it had consumed both him and Ray Gage.

Monday October 4, 1954 Stanfield News

CHAPMAN WILL FACE CHARGE OF MURDER TODAY AT ARRAIGNMENT
Confessed Killer 'Calm' When Viewing Body of 14 year Victim
Unemotional Prisoner Appeared Languid Before Police Caught Up With Him

Tagged as the most unemotional killer ever taken into custody here, Karl T. Chapman before his arrest exhibited iron self control as his friends cried over the slaying of Lynn Ann Clarke and David Rosen. Chapman at no time ever gave any hint of concern.

He is said to have appeared languid as he went to a funeral home and viewed the body of Lynn Ann. The same was true when he acted as a pall bearer at her funeral. He was calm and composed at all times.

Since his arrest, his composure has been unshaken. According to police he has shown no visible remorse, despite the scheduled arraignment in court today.

The cell of Karl T Chapman , confessed knifer has been guarded 24 hours since his arrest last Friday said Sheriff David Lungdren.

The accused high school boy has taken his meals in his cell at all times and has not been allowed to mingle with other prisoners. He won't leave his cell until "sometime next week" the sheriff said.

At that time, Chapman will be allowed a half-hour of exercise daily. The exercise will be taken with a guard, away from other inmates.

By nine o'clock, Karl Chapman was led into the courthouse. The father of the teen, John Chapman was present for the arraignment. The teen was charged with the murder of Lynn Ann Clarke, baby sitter and David Rosen, the 4-year-old in her care.

Mr. Chapman remained stoic inside the filled courtroom. The proceedings were swift.

Karl appeared unemotional, as he was led into the court flanked by two Deputy Sheriffs. He was seated with his attorney, Eugene LaBonte who had entered the plea, "Not Guilty" on the part of his teenage client.

It was the standard plea in the Commonwealth of Massachusetts. His confession, notwithstanding, the Commonwealth had the burden to prove guilt. The defendant was automatically assumed innocent until the prosecutor had done his job.

Karl stood expressionless before the packed courtroom and in a firm voice, pleaded 'not guilty' to the most atrocious crime in the history of Stanfield.

Mr John Chapman, father of the teen along with a curious crowd which included about 50 teenage girls, looked on, as the tall, gangling Chapman entered a technical denial to two individual murder charges.

Surprisingly there were no emotional outbursts by the spectators.

Detectives Steve Logan and Raymond Gage were present. Neither the Clarke's nor the Rosen's were present for the arraignment.

After all the preliminary procedures had taken place at the arraignment, the judge ordered a preliminary hearing to be scheduled for Monday, October 11. With that, the court appearance was ended.

Karl Chapman was led from the courtroom manacled to another prisoner who, unlike Chapman covered his face and avoided the limelight. Chapman, looked downward but still showed no emotion. He was returned to the Hamden County Jail, State Street, where he was to remain until his next court date, October 11.

The detectives sighed. This was the first step to the inevitable conviction of the monster they had tracked down and finally apprehended. Maybe now, the world would begin to start turning again.

In the days to come, the news turned to the on-going, nationally publicized Dr. Sam Shepard Murder Trial. It was new fodder for the press. The Ohio doctor accused of killing his young wife. Ohio was dealing with their own atrocities, and the nation picked up the story.

John Cameron Swazie, the famous newscaster reported the doctor's upcoming trial. The jury selection for the Shepard case took weeks, the trial would take months.

The Shepard trial dominated the headlines in the Stanfield News, at least twice a week, but the citizens of Stanfield continued to search for any information regarding the Chapman case.

Friday, October 8, 1954 Stanfield News:

CHIEF MCNAMARA PRAISES DETECTIVES IN SLAYER ARREST
Captain Jack Mahoney Commended for 'Miracle' in Chapman Case

Police Chief Paul McNamara today commended Captain Jack Mahoney, head of the Detective Bureau, the lead detectives, Sgt.. Steven Logan and Sgt. Raymond Gage, as well as every member of the bureau for their work in the apprehension of the alleged killer of two innocent children.

The chief presented the commendation to Chief Paul McNamara so that he might in turn relay the message to all detectives and see that it be entered in the official records of the police department.

The commendation read as follows:

"On September 25, 1954, two innocent children, Lynn Ann Clarke and David Rosen were murdered at 425 Archer Boulevard, and their assassination became the object of the greatest manhunt in the history of the City of Stanfield. Every officer of the Detective Bureau of the Stanfield Police Department devoted his entire effort, energy and time to bring the guilty culprit to justice. Sgt. Steven Logan, sharing the lead with his partner Sgt. Raymond Gage under the command of Captain Jack Mahoney contributed brilliant detective and police work in the apprehension of a person who has been charged with this double murder."

"In my estimation, the solution of these crimes was nothing short of miraculous, and there are no words in my vocabulary adequate to describe my gratefulness to the members of the Stanfield Police Department who worked on this case. I not only commend each and every one of these great officers but offer them my personal salute for this marvelous accomplishment."

"Through their untiring efforts, while at the same time completely disregarding their personal comfort, these exceptional men have earned the sincere gratefulness of the entire population of the City of Stanfield."

"I wish at this time to officially commend each and every member of the Detective Bureau for his part in the solution of these serious crimes. This commendation is to be read at all roll calls and returned to the executive secretary to become a part of the Stanfield Police Department's official records."

Katherine Logan read the article and glowed with pride. Steve read it and humbly replied, "None of this would have been possible without that piece of thread. It was dumb luck that I picked it up. The footwork of the patrol officers, the hours of questioning by all the detectives. It was a real team effort."

The successful arrest was bittersweet to the detective. Two children were dead, and an odious teen refused to react. This just seemed to get under Steven Logan's skin.

Linda Gage reacted about the same as Katherine Logan. Ray, on the other hand praised the efforts of his partner, and credited him with determination and undying tenacity.

Ray admired his partner, and looked to him as a mentor. He felt very fortunate to work with such a brilliant detective. Over the years, Steven had brought Ray from an impulsive rookie, to a polished detective who exhibited natural instincts and confidence in 'gut feelings'. They were a good team. They had demonstrated it time after time, and the Chapman case spoke volumes.

As the weeks passed, the citizens of Stanfield began to show signs of getting back to the lives they were accustomed to.

The Chapman's had arranged home tutoring for Brenda. Their lives were a living hell. The proximity of the victim's home was disturbing to both families.

Within days of the arraignment, a 'For Sale' sign was placed on the Clarke's front lawn. They were unable to offer any condolences to the Chapman's. The Clarke's were seldom seen by neighbors, and declined any opportunity to be interviewed or make a statement to the press.

Of all the Clarke's, nine-year-old Barbara seemed to be holding it all together. Her parents made every effort to maintain normalcy within the household. Barbara was attending school, and attending her weekly 'Brownie' meetings. She attended family counseling with her parents once a week. Elaine was from a large family and they were very supportive.

She was heard to say, "With all the support we have, we are living a nightmare. I can't begin to imagine what Karl Chapman's family must be feeling."

That was the closest conveyance of concern that was ever heard from the Clarke family.

Sunday, October 10, 1954 Stanfield Sunday Republican

MANIACAL KILLER'S ATTORNEY FACES STORM
Attorney Eugene LaBonte Attacked for Trying to Defend Confessed Knife Killer

It was learned today that Attorney Eugene Labonte, defense counsel for confessed killer Karl Chapman, was badgered by the aroused residents of Stanfield. LaBonte has received critical telephone calls and letters.

LaBonte, handling his first major criminal case said today he has to "sneak around corners to avoid blasts from angry people who feel the accused slayer doesn't deserve the protection of the law."

More than 100 critics have telephoned or written the harried defense attorney to protest against his defense of the Chapman youth. Most criticisms, he said, begin with an amazed, "Are you defending HIM?"

Attorney LaBonte was living his own nightmare. The citizens of Stanfield were outraged that a confessed maniacal killer would be deserving of a defense attorney.

LaBonte was a family man, and had been a member of the bar for only three years. He was young and inexperienced, but none the less, was retained by John Chapman. He believed in due process and had taken his oath to defend. Never had he imagined the hatred that would be spawned within the community.

When he was asked about the attacks upon him, he replied,

"The majority of people are willing to go along with the process of the law and the protests of his defense are from an emotional, upset minority."

Eugene LaBonte tried not to let the criticisms bother him and made every attempt to explain to the people that it is a case of every person "presumed innocent until proven guilty."

This was a very difficult concept for LaBonte to convey to the citizens. After all, Chapman had confessed, and the majority of people found a trial a difficult pill to swallow.

The young attorney was tolerant and exceptionally understanding to the concerns of his critics. He explained,

"The state has a case to prove. Every person, no matter what he is supposed to have done is entitled to the benefit of representation of counsel. That is my job, and I intend to do it to the best of my ability."

He addressed the countless reporters with statements of his beliefs as a member of the bar association.

"What would happen if attorneys refused to defend people? What if the defendant were your brother or son?"

He found that usually cooled them off a little bit.

LaBonte was faced with a barrage of rumors as well as criticisms. Rumors included a request for a change of venue. That was unsubstantiated, and Eugene LaBonte addressed the reporters, making it perfectly clear it was completely a rumor. He did believe it might be impossible to hold a fair trial for Chapman in Stanfield, but that he had no intention to make a motion to move the trial to another city.

Eugene LaBonte was conferring on a day to day basis with both his client and John Chapman. Marge Chapman was not emotionally able to visit with Karl, let alone be privy to any decision making regarding the case.

Tuesday, October 12, 1954: Stanfield News:

KARL CHAPMAN IN COURT FOR HEARING ON SLAYING OF BABYSITTER AND CHILD
Local Courtroom is Jammed for Legal Step Leading to Grand Jury action: Police Tell of Wounds in Victims' Bodies

Karl Chapman was expected to be bound over to the Grand Jury without bail yesterday morning. Judge Mathews found probable cause during the preliminary hearing into the Clarke/Rosen murders. Chapman replied, "no sir" when asked if he had anything to say. Details of the bloody murders were unfolded by a pathologist and detectives today as confessed killer Karl Chapman was brought into a jammed District Court for hearing expected to end with the case being bound over to the Grand Jury.

The courtroom was filled to capacity. Over 100 spectators were turned away.

The robed Judge Mathews took the bench and all were seated. It was 10:30 when Karl Chapman was seated at the defense table, flanked by Eugene LaBonte and an additional member of the defense, Attorney Melvin Bonner.

Because of the inexperience of LaBonte, the court appointed an additional attorney. Melvin Bonner would lead the defense and Eugene LaBonte would be second chair.

The Commonwealth requires that an attorney representing a defendant in a capital murder case possess a minimum of 10 years as a member of the Bar Association. Eugene LaBonte had but three years. He was a graduate of Harvard Law, and upon receiving his degree, visited Europe. His purpose for his visit was to attend the famous Nuremberg Trials. The 1949 infamous trials would surely serve to enhance his knowledge of criminal law

LaBonte intended to practice criminal law, and the Nuremberg trial was an incredible experience for the young attorney.

Melvin Bonner, on the other hand, had sixteen years before the bar. He had never tried a capital case. He was a civil lawyer, but he had the experience in years that the law required.

Judge Mathews cited Chapter and Section of the General Laws of Massachusetts and directed that the district attorney issue a call for the special session of the grand jury.

Mr. Chapman, father of the defendant was present in the court. Karl was dressed in a brown suit, white shirt and brown tie. He sat unemotionally throughout the testimony of three witnesses.When the chief was asked about the motive, he briefly looked through his notes and then replied,

"The defendant claimed he just wanted to scare the girl."

He continued reading directly from his notes, "The boy reported, 'I walked down Archer Boulevard and I could see Lynn in the Rosen's house. I tapped on the window. Lynn was sitting on the sofa, reading a book. She looked out and saw it was me and went to the front door and opened it. When she did, I walked in and she saw the knife in my hand. I just wanted to scare her, but she got mad and started to scream'."

The Chief continued,'I grabbed her and stabbed her. Then I heard the baby cry and went to his room and stabbed him. After that, I saw Lynn Ann move so I went back and stabbed her some more'."

The courtroom was silent as the chief recounted the actual words of Chapman's confession.

Phil Clarke, and his wife Elaine were absent from the courtroom. The Rosen's were not in attendance.

When the hearing ended, Karl Chapman was again lead from the courtroom. He was not the image of a depraved murderer. He looked like a fine young man. His face remained stoic, and unemotional. One could only wonder what his thoughts could possibly be. He was returned to the County Jail to remain until the Grand Jury convened.

The District Attorney, surrounded by the media announced that he would be calling a special session of the Hampden County Grand Jury to hear the case and hand down the indictment. He explained that it was his belief that a special session of the Grand Jury to hear the evidence in the case would be in the best interests of the public. It would serve to provide early termination of the case which has had such an impact on the community.

Martin O'Neil was never one to pass up an opportunity to look favorable before the press.

He added, "This special sitting is the first in 35 years. I want a quick hearing on these murder charges. I have been given authorization for the special session by His Honor Judge Mathews."

The Grand Jury would hear the evidence to be presented by the District Attorney, and once they handed down the indictment, the trial date would be scheduled to be heard in the Superior Court.

Karl spent his days in a cell, by himself. He was constantly supervised. He continued to eat well and slept without any problem. By now he was allowed newspapers and magazines. He was escorted outside twice a day for recreation. The guards provided headphones for him to listen to music as he whiled away hour after hour, day after day.

Mr. Chapman, LaBonte and Bonner continued to visit him on a daily basis. All other visitors were limited to once a week. It didn't matter, nobody came.

On November 19th the Grand Jury handed down the indictment. It was literally handed to Karl Chapman. The guard passed a single piece of white paper through the bars of his cell.

The indictment sealed any doubts. Chapman was to stand trial in Superior Court for two separate murders in the 1st Degree. This capital crime was punishable by death, unless the jury recommended mercy. If mercy was recommended, it was mandatory, life in prison, with no possibility of parole.

Karl read the indictment and tossed it onto the bunk. He went to the small barred window of his cell and stared outside. What was he thinking? Could he possibly imagine he would never be free again? If convicted, he would, at best, spend the rest of his life behind bars.

The youth continued to be held without bail. His attorney, Eugene LaBonte, or Melvin Bonner visited with him every day, and insisted the youth could offer no reason for committing the crime.

When queried by the media, the attorneys insisted that during questioning, he remained calm and rational, complacently smoking while his attorneys hurled question after question at him. His replies remained soft spoken.

The attorneys would only confirm that Chapman was well known to Lynn Ann. He lived with his father and mother and sister Brenda in a modern house directly across the street from the Clarke family.

Another mystery that detectives Logan and Gage could not seem to get resolved was how Chapman was able to obtain entrance into the house. It was a mystery to them. After questioning many friends and the Rosen's, they all agreed that Lynn Ann, while baby sitting, was known to have refused admission even to members of the Rosen family on occasion.

Chapman claimed in his interview that he knocked on the window, Lynn recognized him and opened the door. With the knife already in hand, he admitted that he savagely attacked her as soon as the door was opened. He stabbed her several times.

After repeated questioning, the teen never wavered. His story of the night of the savage carnage remained precisely the same.

Shortly after the court date, October 12, a moving van pulled into the driveway of 48 Lynndale Street, the home of the Clarke family.

The 'For Sale' sign remained staked into the front lawn, but the Clarke's were moving. It had been agony, day after day, walking out of their house and facing the murder's house across the street. They purchased a house in the Breckwood area of Stanfield. Phil hoped this would help Elaine get back to some type of life. Barbara would be attending another school.

Elaine had talked with the director of the Sunshine Nursery School and officially resigned from the job she had loved, but couldn't continue. Phil worried about her spending time alone at home, but she seemed to be doing better.

The Clarke's managed to keep one secret from the press. Elaine Clarke was pregnant. She had conceived in August, only weeks before the tragedy had struck. She was so stricken with Lynn Ann's murder, the possibility of her being pregnant was not even considered. She had not discussed it with Phil.

Shortly after the arrest, Elaine Clarke visited her family doctor. The doctor considered medication to help her sleep and keep her calm, but he hesitated when he asked if there was a possibility she may be pregnant.

Two days after a thorough examination, the doctor informed Elaine she was pregnant and her 'due date' would be mid April. Elaine had mixed emotions but they soon faded when she broke the news to Phil. It was the first time since Lynn Ann's murder she saw a smile and the genuine warmth return back over his face. The doctor was very optimistic about a new child in the family. The doctor believed having more children may be exactly what was needed to help the healing process. Elaine was not 'showing' her pregnancy, and the timing of the move fit right into the plans of starting life over, without Lynn Ann.

The tenants upstairs from the Clarke's remained. They were elderly and had lived in that house before the Clarke's had. The downstairs would remain vacant until the house was eventually sold.

The Rosen's house was completely vacant. The posted 'for sale' sign remained in place since September. Real Estate agents continually made appointments to show the house, but nobody made any offers. The Realtors were convinced the potential buyers were simply curiosity seekers.

As the weeks passed, the Stanfield News turned to other lead stories.

Steven Logan and Raymond Gage went on to other cases. The cases paled compared to the Chapman murders. They were grateful for that. It would be a long time before they wanted to take on another case like that one.

It was far from over for them. They would be called to testify at the trial, and contribute all their findings in an effort to secure a guilty verdict. They believed it couldn't go any other way, but they would be sure this maniacal savage would never see the light of a free day again for the rest of his life!

Tuesday, October 19, 1954 Stanfield News:

CHAPMAN CASE DELAY GRANTED
Lawyers Given 30 Days to File Defense Motions: Youth Pleads 'Not Guilty' As the Indictments are Read in Open Court
Attorneys Melvin Bonner and Eugene LaBonte asked the judge for 30 days in which to "prepare motions." The judge asked District Attorney Martin O'Neil if he had any objections. The District Attorney said, "no, your honor."

The judge then granted the motion, which would prevent the start of the murder trial before November. Attorney Bonner gave no indication of the type of motion he would present to the court. He had said earlier, however that he may petition for a change in the trial site.

The indictments read today charged Chapman with willful murder. The jury selected for his trial would determine the degree of culpability if any.

This was the third appearance for Chapman in court. The Grand Jury consisting of 17 men and three women returned two sealed indictments after a four-hour session in which District Attorney O'Neil called upon Dr. Paul A. R. Chapman, medical examiner and several policemen to testify.

When the indictments were read, they did not affect the appearance of Karl Chapman. He had listened to the charges.

In part, the indictment read: On September 25, 1954, Karl T. Chapman did assault and beat Lynn Ann Clarke and by that assault and beating did murder the said Lynn Ann Smith. The second count was the same with the name of David Rosen inserted.

The District Attorney was swarmed by the media once again. He indicated that he had no idea when the Chapman murder trial would be held. The 30-day motion was scheduled to end just a few days before two other murder trials were scheduled to begin.

D.A. Martin O'Neil also stated, that the length of those trials would prohibit scheduling of the Chapman trial. He indicated that the Chapman trial would have to be put over to February, or possibly later. There was a regular criminal session slated and the Chapman case may be delayed until March.

The reporters pressed on. Some had not been accommodated inside the courtroom and quizzed the D.A. for more information. The D.A. raised his hands in an effort to silence the inquisitive reporters and delivered the information regarding proceedings that had just ended inside.

He began, "It appeared that the defendant showed more interest than in previous appearances. He has abandoned the 'head-down' attitude when his attorneys successfully were granted a 30-day period to file motions. Chapman looked interestingly around the filled courtroom.

John Chapman, the father of the teen did not attend today on advice of the defense counsel. Chapman was manacled in two rings attached to a belt tied behind his back. He stood erect and looked straight ahead when the assistant clerk of courts read the indictments. In a clear voice, Chapman replied, 'Not Guilty'."

With that brief statement, the District Attorney drove off, abandoning the reporters at the curbside in front of the courthouse.

Again, life in Stanfield, Massachusetts continued to resume it's normal pace. School activities were scheduled. People went about their daily routines, shopping, going to movies, out to dinner, and yes, even babysitters were permitted to provide service to those who were in need.

Lisa Jansen slowly got back to school activities. She was a regular on the cheerleading squad, just as Lynn Ann had predicted she would be. That was on the last day of her life. Lisa continued to go over and over the last time she saw her friend. It was a thought that would haunt her for a long time.

She couldn't help but think about how close she came to stopping by the Rosen's that night. She had stayed home to attend to her younger brother that night. Her parents had arrived home at about 9:00. She had given it some thought to keeping Lynn Ann company, but because of the torrential rains, she decided to curl up and watch TV at home.

Lisa also thought about the times she had babysat with Lynn Ann. She remembered how Lynn would always let Daniel get up after David went to sleep. Why had she not let him up that night? She would never know. Maybe if she had, she would be alive today. These thoughts haunted her over and over.

Brenda was dealing with her own horrors. Her brother, a murderer! How would she ever get over the stigma? How could she have lived with him and never noticed the monster in her midst? She was close to Karl, he was her big brother. Karl was so affectionate to Brenda. He was so protective of her. She couldn't fathom how this could be true.

When Brenda was a young child, she was stricken with spinal meningitis. Karl spent more time with her than anyone. He played games with her, read to her. If he thought no one was paying attention to her, he'd talk to her and play with her. He would go out of his way to make sure she wasn't being left out of anything.

Brenda tried to recall anything that would make this make any sense. She just couldn't. Karl, Lynn Ann and Brenda were planning on attending Mass together on Sunday morning, the day after the murders! Lynn Ann had stopped by the Chapman's house on her way to what would become the 'murder house'.

Brenda was also very concerned for her mother. Marge was a very frail woman. Brenda also knew, her father would be very difficult, and unreachable. She felt abandoned, and sought refuge at her mother's sister's house where she spent most of her time.

She was home tutored in the mornings, and she would walk to her aunt's at noon. Sometimes she'd stay late, and her uncle would bring her safely home after dark. She couldn't bear seeing the Clarke's. It was a blessing to Brenda when the Clarke's moved out. She hoped someday she would be able to visit them, but she thought that was unlikely.

Thursday, October 28, 1954: Stanfield News

ERNEST HEMINGWAY WINS NOBEL LITERATURE PRIZE
Swedish Academy Decides to Honor U.S. Writer
Prize Amounts to $35,000 USD

This type of headline, served the citizens of Stanfield for the weeks to come. Normal, every day non-sensational news. The kind Stanfield was accustomed to.

Occasionally the Dr. Sam Shepard case would appear in the headlines. His trial was ongoing.

Friday, October 29, 1954: Stanfield News

MARLON BRANDO ENGAGED TO WED FRENCH GIRL
Josiane Berenger

The public was still interested in what was happening in Hollywood. Occasionally Hollywood would make the headlines.

Monday, November 8, 1954: Stanfield News:

SENATE BEGINS SPECIAL SESSION ON JOE MCCARTHY
Censures Fight Due to Begin by Wednesday

The public was always looking for controversial news that came with the Joe McCarthy 'Witch Hunts'

Wednesday, November 10, 1954: Stanfield News

MOTHER VISITS CHAPMAN - YOUTH NOT AFFECTED
Father, Defense Counsels Only Other Who Have Talked With The Boy

The mother of confessed-killer Karl Chapman has recovered sufficiently from the shock of her son's arrest to visit him at the County Jail, it was learned today.

Mrs. Chapman has talked with Karl "two or three times," according to jail officials. They said the accused high school boy showed no emotion when he met her, and that Mrs. Chapman remained composed.

The boy's mother was stricken with grief and placed under doctor's care after Karl was arrested for the bayonet murders of Lynn Ann Clark and David Rosen.

Throughout the weeks of his detainment in the County Jail, Mrs. Chapman, John Chapman, Attorneys Melvin Bonner and Eugene LaBonte had been the only visitors for Karl. All the visits were held in the jail lobby with a guard present.

The jail authorities were reporting that only psychiatrists employed by the Commonwealth had talked to the defendant. Attorney LaBonte would however, make arrangements to have Karl examined by private doctors.

Attorney Bonner along with Attorney LaBonte were called out of town for a seminar. During their absence, The Massachusetts Department of Health appointed Dr. Eldridge Singlinger, of a nearby State Mental Institution and Dr. Frederick G. Klopper, the Director of Mental Health in the Northampton State Hospital to examine Karl at the jail.

Because Massachusetts has a "Briggs Law," it is mandatory that all persons in Massachusetts accused of a capital offense be examined by two psychiatrists. Dr. Singlinger arranged to have social workers investigate Karl's family history and school behavior. This would include interviewing teachers, friends and relatives.

Upon their return, the two attorneys were informed of the pending examinations. With this information, the following headlines appeared.

Stanfield News: Monday November 15, 1954

MENTAL TEST WILL DECIDE CHAPMAN TRIAL
Results Will Not Be Made Public; Trial Not Likely Before February

Whether Karl Chapman goes on trial for his life in the bayonet murders, hinges on mental examinations made by two state appointed psychiatrists. The decision will be made when the doctor's reports, which will not be made public, are forwarded to the clerk of the Superior Court. If the court decides Chapman's mental condition is such that he can stand trial, preparations for the murder hearings will be held.

If on the other hand, the defendant is judged insane, arrangements will be made for commitment to a mental institution.

As with all other breaking news stories, the District Attorney was again in the spotlight. The press surrounded him with microphones held high and a barrage of questions. The D.A. had become quite accustomed to this display and in his usual 'matter of fact' manner addressed the press.

"Release of the results of the tests might result in the development of a 'prejudicial attitude' which would jeopardize the defendant's right to due process of the law," he began.

"There is nothing more I can tell you at this time." Martin O'Neil ended the interview abruptly. When O'Neil said,

"I have nothing more to say," that was the end of the interview.

The reporters then rushed to the jail to gather any information they could regarding the demeanor and behavior of Karl Chapman.

The jailers were all in agreement, the prisoner continued to act the part of a model prisoner, with his behavior apparently 'normal' in every way. They related to the press that Karl reads books from the jail library, listens to the radio and eats heartily. He has displayed no emotion during frequent visits by his parents.

In the meanwhile, LaBonte and Bonner were arranging for private psychiatrists to examine Karl.

StanfieldNews: Friday, November 27, 1954

TESTS SHOW CHAPMAN IS SANE
Youth, 18 Will Go To Trial Probably in February in Double Murder Case
Details of Sanity Investigation Not Made Public

Two other murder cases come up before youth can face Superior Court. The District Attorney has received notice that the 18-year-old high school youth is not suffering from any mental disease or defect that would affect his criminal responsibility.

The reports were in. Karl Chapman was declared legally sane. Dr. Eldridge Singlinger spoke to the reporters and was quite emphatic, Chapman was sane. He had concluded this after his examination of the teen in jail only a week ago.

The defense team was furious!. They felt it was highly prejudicial, and intended to make a motion to delay, to allow time for private psychiatrists to examine Karl. They were confident the motion had merit and would be granted.

The finding that Karl was sane put his life into the hands of the jury which would hear the case. It meant if he was found guilty of first degree murder, only a recommendation of clemency by the jury would save him from the electric chair.

With this information, the way was paved for all the preparations for trial. The media labeled the trial 'the most atrocious' crime in the history of Stanfield.

Because of the other two murders that had been slated, Karl Chapman's trial would be pushed into early 1955.

Steve Logan continued to visit the Clarkes to lend the support they needed. Each time the trial was 'delayed' the victims' families grew more weary. The Rosen's had virtually become reclusive. They would not allow Ray Gage to visit in spite of the many efforts the detective made. Steven Logan also asked to visit with them. They refused. The detectives knew the victims' families would be called to court to testify at the trial. The longer they stayed to themselves, and refused the support of the department, the more difficult this ordeal was sure to be.

Throughout the month of December 1954 the Stanfield News ran coverage of the Dr. Sam Shepard Murder Trial in Ohio. The Shepard case was covered nationally, and with the Chapman case still awaiting its court date, it was fodder for the local press.

Politics entered into the news. With elections underway, the political battle for the elected District Attorney's seat was becoming heated.

Stanfield News:

HIT ON CHAPMAN, DA SAYS RIVAL INEXPERIENCED
Neophyte LaBonte falls for GOP 'Get Tough' Line

District Attorney Martin O'Neil, candidate for re-election on the Democratic ticket, today gave his Republican opponent, Attorney Eugene LaBonte the retort. LaBonte alleged that O'Neil was playing politics with office in the baby sitter murders. The District Attorney was challenged by the young attorney. Martin O'Neil has held the office of District Attorney for twelve years. Three terms, unopposed. When he was elected in 1942, it was by a plurality of 33,000 votes, the largest margin in the history of the office. He pointed out that Attorney LaBonte has been a member of the bar for a mere three years and was not qualified, under the rules of the Superior Court, to be appointed as a defense counsel in a murder case. He pointed out that this would be a hindrance, should he be elected to the District Attorney's position. He added, "Isn't it not equally important to the client?"

The article went on to reiterate that Eugene LaBonte would remain on the case, but would be second chair. The counsel of record would be Melvin Bonner.

The office of the District Attorney in the Commonwealth is an elected position, and the impending trial, notwithstanding did not prevent the campaigning from its usual heated debates.

Occasionally, a small news article would appear in the Stanfield News. Little bits and pieces of information to keep the Chapman case in the forefront of everyone's mind.

The two murder trials that were scheduled, were taking place. One in January, one in February. Both would be convicted and sentenced. The Stanfield press covered both trials, but the trials seemed to be whetting appetites for the Chapman trial.

In January there appeared a small article on page four of the Stanfield

Two Ex-Cops Reside Next Door to Killer

Two well known retired policemen live on Lynndale St, close to the homes of Lynn Ann Clarke and Karl T. Chapman, charged with murdering the 14 year old babysitter and little David Rosen, on September 25, 1954.

Sgt. Martin Dumaine, a former detective, lives at 63 Lynndale Street, just a few houses down from the Clarke's and Chapman's. Charles J. Arnold, who won international fame as the country's leading ticket passing patrolman, lives further up the street at 121.

The reporters were interviewing anyone and everyone who would talk to them. They were trying to get a feel of who this Karl Chapman really was. They interviewed Karl's teachers. His Geometry teacher talked about how 'normal' Karl was just a week ago.

"I corrected one of his geometry papers just last week and he had 100 percent!"

They spoke to neighbors. One neighbor in particular had lived next door to the Chapmans for fourteen years. She talked about incidences she'd witnessed regarding the humanitarian nature of Karl Chapman.

"I've seen him care for a bird with a broken wing. I've seen him petting little kittens and play with the younger children in the neighborhood. He was a gentle boy."

Another neighbor recalled the day of the murders. Karl had been in her home, with her son and some of his friends, watching TV and showing no sign of being agitated, or 'disturbed'.

"He was at my house the Saturday after the murders. He didn't behave any different than the week before." She said.

When asked about Karl's family, she had only high praises for Mr. and Mrs. Chapman.

"Nicer parents never lived." The neighbor shook her head in disbelief. "I feel so badly for the family. You just could never have imagined this would happen to them."

When questioning Karl's pastor, Father Francis O'Connor, he stated, "I was crushed, totally crushed by the news. We were talking about it at supper, that poor Chapman family. We agreed there are things worse than death."

The general opinion of those interviewed, who knew Karl well, was shock and disbelief. It was beyond their imaginations that Karl Chapman could be capable of such a horrific deed.

Stanfield News: February 21, 1955
(Karl Chapman's 19th Birthday)

DEFENSE REQUEST FOR DELAY, DENIED
March 7 Date Stands for Opening of Trial - Baby-Sitter Murders

Youth's Lawyers asked more time to prepare defense: Judge Grishbaum to preside at case involving the deaths of girl and child.

Karl T. Chapman, 19 today, lost the first round of a battle lawyers are waging to save him from the electric chair in the brutal murders of a baby sitter and her child ward here last September when Judge Albert Grishbaum of Greenfield rejected a defense plea that his trial be delayed.

It was another blow for the defense. Bonner and LaBonte claimed they would need more time to prepare for the capital crime, two counts of first degree murder. They requested that the trial be delayed until April or May. They claimed the grounds to be that they needed more time to have psychiatric tests. It became apparent they were bolstering an insanity defense.

Another interesting point that was presented. The defense offered that a delay should be granted in light of *Detective Magazine* stories that were inflammatory to the public's mind against Karl Chapman.

When the motion for more time was filed, the judge had said he would "sleep on it" before arriving at any decision.

District Attorney Martin O'Neil took a solid stand opposing any delays.

The judge was not convinced and handed down the decision from Boston, where he was sitting. Judge Grishbaum ordered Karl to stand trial before him in Hampden County Superior Court on March 7. This was the original trial date that was set by Justice Mathews of the Superior Court.

In the meanwhile, Karl continued to be confined to the Hampden County Jail under constant surveillance. He was not advised that his ordeal would proceed on schedule. The defense attorney had explained to the court that their plea for a delay centered primarily on the contention that a psychiatrist for their side planned a Florida vacation and would not be available.

The argument fell on deaf ears. The District Attorney was immediately on his feet.

"The defense has had adequate time to prepare a case and nothing will be gained from a delay in the trial."

Martin O'Neil had dug his heals in and would not be swayed. He announced his intention to proceed as planned, that Karl Chapman would be tried for first degree murder on two counts in the brutal deaths of Lynn Ann and David.

The District Attorney continued, reminding the court, of The Commonwealth's psychiatrists who had examined Mr. Chapman in jail had turned in reports saying he is sane. They had abided by the 'Briggs Law'. Under this set of circumstances, prosecution for first degree murder virtually is automatic. It would still be up to a jury to establish the defendant's guilt or innocence, however. The judge's decision to deny the delay stood.

Toward the end of February, the Stanfield News was beginning to feel growing pains. It was then, they offered two daily editions of the Stanfield News to the public. The price stayed the same, five cents. The morning edition would be the Stanfield Morning Union, the evening edition would be the Stanfield Evening News, and the Sunday edition would remain, The Stanfield Republican.

To be added to the newspaper were separate sections for each of the surrounding cities and towns who had no newspaper serving them at the time. There would be a West Stanfield section, a

Westfield section, and so on. It was favorably received by the readers, and just at the eve of the upcoming Chapman double murder trial. The coverage of the trial would prove to be extensive and thorough.

Monday February 28, 1955; Stanfield Union News:

An article appeared just days before the much anticipated trial was to begin:

Single Stenographer Will Serve at Chapman's Trial

The decision to have only one stenographer serve at the Chapman murder trial came after it was announced that budget cuts would be unable to carry more than the one stenographer. The economy move startled officials. They protested the decision by citing the 1912 murder trial that had four typists...

The defense councils were outraged, and rightfully so. It seemed that every major decision from the court was pro-prosecution, but this one affected both sides. They felt the trial would be hampered by the cut of court stenographers. It was Judge Albert Grishbaum who made the final decision. This was another set back of the overhaul trial. It was the first time in 50 years that only one stenographer had been used for a murder trial in the Superior Court.

In past trials, including the most recent ones, only a month before, two stenographic machine operators and sometimes extra typists had been used. Under this system, transcripts of the previous day's testimony were available to the prosecution, defense and the judge an hour before the next session of court.

With but one stenographer recording testimony in the Chapman trial, these transcripts would not be available. In order to study the record of the previous day, the prosecution and, or, defense would have to arrange with the single stenographer to make up a transcript of the particular portion of testimony desired.

No official explanation of the cutback was offered, but it was believed it was the result of a recent economy drive. It was also believed that this decision would surely extend the length of the trial.

It was quite ironic that the stenographic reduction was made in connection with the trial of a murder case that had stirred more public interest than any in the history of Stanfield.

It was concluded, that the defense, the prosecution as well as the judge would have to make their own notes of testimony for the most part.

A diligent young lady worked in the office of Melvin Bonner. She was quite proficient in shorthand, and taking dictation. Melvin Bonner scheduled Miss Lewis to be placed at the table with the defense and take notes of the proceedings as closely as she was able.

A short article appeared below the fold of the front page.

Chapman Still Enigma As His Trial At Hand

The accused murder remains a puzzle even to lawyers mapping insanity defense. The mystery of just what makes up Karl Chapman will be probed from all angles beginning Monday when the 19-year-old youth goes on trial for his life for the most atrocious crime in the history of the city...

The article continued on referring to the emotional makeup of Karl. He had defied analysis by experts and non-experts since he confessed.

It seemed that everybody following the case agreed with the newspaper's description of Karl. Steven Logan and Raymond Gage had been baffled at the composure of this youth. They had discussed it over and over since the arrest, and could not conclude any rational reason for his irregular behavior. Seasoned police, including the Chief were equally puzzled. They would remain that way throughout the upcoming trial.

The detectives reflected on the night the butchered bodies had been discovered. They had speculated about the murderer, his state of mind and motivations. They, as well as the entire Stanfield Police Department were briefed by specialists in the field of psychology. They were given profiles of what type of person they were scouring the streets of Stanfield for. All kinds of theories were considered, none made any sense.

Since the arrest and the weeks leading up to the trial, the Stanfield News ran article after article, almost on a daily basis. Of all these news articles, none favored the defendant. The reporters used every conceivable descriptive word in their vocabularies to describe Karl Chapman. They described him as maniacal, depraved and yet, they pronounced him sane, according to the state examiner's reports. This was hard to comprehend, and it was devastating to the defense.

To the average 'outsider' these articles would appear to have been highly prejudicial. However, no effort was made by the courts to seize 'trying the Chapman case, or dissuading the public through the media.'

The trial would be merely a case of following procedure.

The defense's greatest challenge would be to offer evidence that Karl was not guilty by reason of insanity. If this were not allowed, the defense was faced with the burden of convincing the jury to have mercy on Karl and spare his life. It was a day to day uphill battle for Eugene Labonte and Melvin Bonner.

The District Attorney, Martin O'Neil was popular throughout the city as well as the entire county. This case would put him at the pinocle of his career.

Martin O'Neil was tall in stature and his manner was intimidating to even the most seasoned defense attorney. Eugene LaBonte was particularly intimidated by the veteran prosecutor.

Martin O'Neil's impeccable style, right down to his unconventional alligator cowboy boots. Western style, custom-made suits became his moniker. He swaggered when he walked taking full control of 'his' courtroom.

Tuesday, March 1, 1955: Stanfield Morning Union

BOTH DEFENSE AND DA CLOAK CHAPMAN MOVES
Secrecy Surrounds Plans for Legal Battle in Murder Trial

Both the prosecution and defense said today they are ready for the opening of the murder trial of Karl T. Chapman on Monday. District Attorney Martin O'Neil, who will prosecute the case for the Commonwealth, was quoted as saying, "We're all set."

Attorney Melvin Bonner, chief counsel for the defense was quoted,
"We're ready for trial"...

Melvin Bonner commented on the decision of the court to deny his motion to delay. He said, repeatedly, whenever given an opportunity to speak to the media, that he'd wished they had more time, but his motion had been denied and he would be ready anyhow.

Melvin Bonner and Eugene LaBonte had worked fervently seven days a week. They visited Karl at the jail almost daily. Each attorney had dropped all other pending cases in order to prepare the defense for Karl.

Neither the prosecution, nor the defense would disclose how many witnesses they intended to call. Melvin Bonner confirmed he had a private psychiatrist examining Karl, but refused to give the name of the doctor, or if he would even be called on to testify. Bonner was tight lipped. He was determined his case would be kept secretive. He confirmed his daily visits to the defendant, but would not disclose the nature of their conversations.

At every turn, the defense met with opposition. The courts were not giving any ground to the defense, and the media was continuously influencing the public, which consisted of the potential jury pool.

The efforts of the defense were diligent and gallant, but in reality, they would ultimately fight to keep Karl Chapman from dying by electrocution. The last person in the Commonwealth of Massachusetts to be put to death was in 1947, only eight years earlier. This would be the fight of their careers.

Monday, March 7, 1955 Stanfield Evening News

CHAPMAN ON TRIAL FOR LIFE
Hundreds Wait in Line for a Chance at Seats, Jury Selection Slated to Begin

Several venire men were excused early as Judge Albert Grishbaum opened the case of youth charged with murder of baby sitter and boy. One of the largest crowds in the history of Hampden County Superior Court began jamming into the courthouse as early as 7:15 this morning for the murder trial of Karl T. Chapman.

By 11 AM, an estimated 200 people were lined up in the second floor corridor outside the courtroom where the now 19-year-old defendant is on trial for his life...

The judge began the proceedings at 10:30 A.M.. Some of the spectators had waited more than three hours. They would be in for a longer wait than they could have anticipated.

First order of business would be addressing the 96 venire men that had been called. From them a murder jury would be selected. They were seated in the courtroom for the roll call.

The venire men, or potential jurors, remained seated in the courtroom as the judge asked those who had excuses to come forward one at a time for a bench conference. A total of fourteen indicated they had something to discuss with the judge.

The Hampden County Superior Courthouse was buzzing with activity. Lawyers, prosecution aides, courtroom attendants, deputy sheriffs as well as the media scurried all over the building. All had an assignment and all were in preparation of the trial.

The spectators would not be allowed into the courtroom until all pre trial matters had been conducted. This included the selection of the jury.

The same air of tension permeated the area outside of the courthouse. Motorists vied for parking spaces and pedestrians paused to look at the impressive structure where a lengthy legal battle loomed.

The task of interviewing each one of the 96 men and women would be a laborious one. The judge began by asking if anyone had any purely personal reasons that they felt should excuse them from serving. Eleven replied. They were sworn and one by one approached Judge Grishbaum's bench. It was apparent to all, that they had substantial reasons, for all were excused. Two were excused because they were over the age of 65. The other nine were simply excused and no reason was offered to the public.

After the eleven were excused and exited the courtroom, the judge declared a brief recess. The remaining venire men were escorted to the grand jury room adjacent to the courtroom.

The court officers opened the main doors to admit the spectators. From both directions in the corridor, men and women jammed to get into the room. Only 80 seats were available. There were more than 200 that had been waiting. The remaining seats inside the courtroom were reserved for police officers, witnesses for the Commonwealth, some psychiatrists who would be listening to the testimony and Mr. and Mrs. Chapman, the parents of the accused. Seats were also reserved for the families of the victims. The Chapman's were accompanied by Mr. Chapman's brother. They would be Karl's only family members to appear throughout the trial.

The task began. It was the practice in murder cases of this kind to inquire into the type of work of the prospective juror, as well as whether he would be conscious of any prejudice for or against the defendant, or the Commonwealth. Also, and most important in a case such as this, if the prospective juror had any religious belief that would preclude a finding of guilty in a case which might involve the death penalty.

The district attorney sat at the prosecution's table along with an assistant district attorney. Melvin sat at the defense table, accompanied by his co-defense council Eugene LaBonte and Miss Lewis, the stenographer from his law firm.

Melvin Bonner stood immediately after all had taken their respective places in the courtroom. He stated to the judge,

"The defense is proceeding under protest because there has not been sufficient time to adequately prepare a defense." Bonner had been publicly stating this whenever he could find anyone to listen.

The judge stated that the protest could be part of the record but, unless it appeared in the form of a motion, the court need not take action. He refused to take a 'mere' statement.

Subsequently, Bonner filed several motions with the court. All but one were immediately denied.

The judge granted the motion for copies of all autopsy reports to be delivered to the defense council. Among the motions that were denied were, a motion to commit Karl to a mental institution for 30-days observation, and countless motions to delay.

Tuesday, March 8, 1955 Stanfield Evening News

CHAPMAN JURY IS COMPLETED
30 Brought From Street On Unusual Court Order as 1ˢᵗ Panel is Used Up

By noon, the murder jury was still short two. Surprised citizens were summoned by deputies to be examined. Two alternates were also needed. After the unusual procedure of sending deputy sheriffs into the street to 'round up' prospective jurors today, the Chapman murder trial jury was completed early this afternoon...

Judge Albert Grishbaum had addressed both the defense and the prosecution at the onset of jury selection. He ruled that each would be allowed 28 challenges without reason instead of the usual number of 14, because two murder indictments against Chapman were being heard simultaneously.

Many of the venire men were excused by the judge because of previously formed opinions. Others were excused by the judge because they had opinions or beliefs on capital punishment. It was imperative they secure a death penalty qualified jury.

The judge was not about to tolerate any further delays. He selected two deputy sheriffs in the courtroom. As the deputies approached the bench, they were instructed to go out to the streets, into coffee shops, and return with 30 citizens to be prospective jurors. This order was unprecedented!

The citizens of Stanfield showed shock and surprise, but none gave signs of objection.

William Jackson was approached by one of the two deputy sheriffs. He was one of the first selected and plucked off the street. Mr. Jackson displayed somewhat of a sense of humor over the ordeal. When he arrived at the courthouse, he joined the others that had been randomly picked just as he had.

He struck up a conversation with one saying, "Brother, was I surprised. I was standing at Sargent and Main Streets enjoying a good cigar, when this deputy came up, flashed his badge and informed me I was going to be on the jury panel." He chuckled as he related his experience which was similar to the other twenty- nine.

The thirty chosen to form a new ventire after the original panel of 96 was exhausted with only 10 jurors selected, were added to 20 jurors shifted from the civil sitting of Superior Court.

Of the twenty civil jurors examined for murder trial duty, sixteen were excused by the judge, two were challenged by the defense and one by the prosecutor. One was accepted.

Finally, the jury was completed. It consisted of 12 men with varied occupations. The murder trial jury was compiled of: One chemical foreman, a sales engineer, a tire builder, a reeler operator, an accountant, a checker, and a service manager. In addition there was a retail purchasing and sales manager, a garage parts man, a time and method analyst and a retail manager. Two alternates were also selected. One general contractor and a dentist.

With the jury in place, the trial would get underway the next day. The trial that would uncover the most heinous details and rock the entire community.

It was observed that the local coffee shops where the sheriffs made many of the surprise selections of jurors were practically abandoned the following day. Word had gotten out that patrons of the place had been tabbed for jury duty. Many regular customers stayed away until the panel was completed. The names, addresses and occupations of the selected jury were listed and appeared on the front page of the evening paper.

Defense councilors Melvin Bonner and Eugene LaBonte met with the District Attorney inside the courtroom. They talked over the trial of Karl Chapman for the Clarke/Rosen murder set to begin. Both sides would have dramatic roles as the high school student, who has stated he doesn't know why he killed, tries to beat the electric chair .

When asked it he was fully prepared to proceed with trial, Melvin Bonner replied,

"Yes, we are confident, and have prepared for this day. Although we would have liked more time, we have worked diligently, putting all else aside. We are prepared to go ahead."

The District Attorney was asked a similar question. He replied,

"The people of Stanfield are counting on me to put this case before a jury as swiftly as possible. They are depending on me and my staff to secure a guilty verdict. We are prepared to do exactly that!"

Now, the day the trial was about to begin, the defense recounted all the motions they had filed only to be denied. They had considered a change of venue. This was discussed with John Chapman, as was the entire strategy of the defense. John Chapman was opposed to the venue change. He gave no reason for his point of view, but was clearly opposed to moving the trial.

Karl Chapman sat at the defense table. He showed more interest than he had since his arrest. He scanned the jurors one at a time. John and Marge Chapman were also present.

Wednesday, March 9, 1955 Stanfield Evening News

STATE ASKS CHAIR FOR CHAPMAN
Premeditation is Alleged in Murder of Children DA Tells Crime Details

Martin O'Neil stressed the brutality in the stabbing deaths of baby sitter and boy. He described the attacks as cruel and savage.

Karl T. Chapman, 19, sat stone faced barely moving a muscle in Superior Court today as he heard the District Attorney give a dramatic recital of how he literally butchered a 14-year-old girl and a 4-year-old little boy. He went on to describe the bayonet used in a cruel and savage outburst of premeditated murder last September 25......

Martin O'Neil spared no details when he addressed the jury. His opening statement was bold and direct. He told of the vast amount of blood in the home and a "pool" of blood in which the four-year-old David was found, by his mother. He described how little David tried to escape from the attack by crawling between his bed and the wall.

The District Attorney paced before the sitting jury. He displayed anger, and disgust toward the defendant. He delivered his opening statement with a vengeance, sparing none of the graphic details of the horrendous crime.

He charged the jury, proposing to prove beyond a doubt that the gangling iron nerved youth, seated in a four-sided prisoner's cage, deserved to be convicted and sentenced to die in the electric chair.

The prisoner's cage had been installed the night before after the court had been adjourned for the day. It consisted of four sides and a top, looking like a 'portable jail cell.' In the center of the 'cage' was a straight backed wooden chair. Karl was provided with a small table and a writing tablet. The cage was located in proximity to the defense's table.

The District Attorney continued, and Karl Chapman was devoid of any outward trace of emotion on his always set features. At times he watched the D.A. and then his gaze returned to the general vicinity of a certain spot on the floor in front of the cage. He had fixed his eyes on this spot and would continue to do so throughout most of the trial.

The Commonwealth of Massachusetts' Superior Court is one of the few that adhere to the old British protocol, in that the witnesses are required to stand. A chair is provided, for special circumstances, but generally, the witnesses stand. There is no 'box'. Instead it is a witness stand which provides a metal bar for the witnesses to hold on to if they choose.

After he concluded his opening statement, Martin O'Neil called the first witness for the prosecution. He called Mr. Charles Latham. Mr. Latham had reported seeing a tall man on the porch of the Rosen's house at about 9:30 the evening of the murders.

As Mr. Latham was approaching the witness stand, the assistant D.A. placed a large floor plan of the Rosen's house on an easel.

The District Attorney began asking Mr. Latham about the floor plan.

Before he could finish, Eugene LaBonte was on his feet.

"Objection, your Honor!" He demanded.

"I don't see how he can testify, when the jury cannot see the floor plans."

Judge Grishbaum questioned the jurors. They concurred. They could not see the floor plan because of the glare of the ceiling lights.

The judge replied, "He can testify, but it may not do much good." The judge suggested that Mr. Latham's testimony be suspended until arrangements could be made which would allow the jury to see the floor plans. The prosecution did not object.

The next witness, Mrs. Grace Newman, took the stand. She testified that she, and her husband were on their way home from a ride when the radio reception became poor. Mr. Newman stopped the car to raise the aerial.

The District Attorney showed Mrs. Newman a picture of the Rosen's house.

"Yes, that's the house we stopped in front of." She replied.

"I saw a man standing at the door. I noticed he was fairly tall."

In the cross examination of the witness, Eugene LaBonte questioned Mrs. Newman regarding her ability to see the home from the car. She had testified that it was raining very hard. Mrs. Newman answered the defense attorney in a soft, but confident tone.

"I could see the tall man wearing a hat and a jacket because the house was well lighted."

Then she continued, "My husband and I went home and after reading of the murder the next day, we returned to the Rosen's home before going to the police."

Mrs. Newman was excused, and Mr. Charles Newman was called. Mr. Newman confirmed the testimony of his wife.

Eugene LaBonte took the opportunity to cross examine Mr. Newman.

He asked, "Did you see anyone walk by or pass while you were stopped in front of the Rosen's home? Did the 'tall man' move?"

Charles Newman answered the defense attorney with a simple "No sir."

Mr. Newman was excused and the prosecutor called his next witness to the stand.

"The Commonwealth of Massachusetts calls Mrs. Myra Pratt." Came the booming voice of the prosecutor.

Mrs. Pratt was a neighbor of the Chapman's. She and her husband were called to testify. She told the court that she and her husband were sitting in their basement television room on the night of the murders. They heard 'running footsteps' in their driveway between 9:30 and 10:00 P.M..

She was sure of the time, she said, because "The Ed Sullivan 5th Anniversary Show was on television." The show aired at 9:00 until 10:00 every Saturday night.

She continued with, "I'm sure whoever ran in the driveway was going from Lynndale St. to the garages in the rear. I went upstairs, turned on the back lights and then went out front to turn on the porch light, but saw no one."

After the District Attorney finished with the witness, Mr. LaBonte cross examined the witness. He asked if the basement had windows on the driveway side, and she replied,

"No." He asked if Mr. Pratt had been out that night and she replied,

"No." After this brief cross examination, he excused the witness.

Mr. Pratt was also called by the prosecution and simply confirmed the statements of his wife.

The Saturday night pastime of watching television programs and listening to the radio played an important part in the testimony of many of the witnesses. Several set the times of incidents connected with the murders by the programs that were on.

Alfred Swift, a college student, and also a resident of Lynndale St. testified that he too heard 'running footsteps'. He said they sounded as though they came from Lynndale St. sidewalk from the direction of Archer St.

LaBonte cross examined the student.

"Did you talk over your testimony with police? Did they refresh your memory about the footsteps?"

Swift replied, "No they did not."

When asked about the time, he stated he had been studying from 8:30 until 10:30. He heard the footsteps about half way through that time period.

He added, "I remember, Gunsmoke was on the radio. It comes on at 9:00.

The next witness for the prosecution was Lisa Jansen. Lisa stated she had known Lynn Ann for at least seven years. She was her best friend. She recounted their last meeting. Lisa was visibly shaken, but kept her composure.

During her testimony the jury fixed upon the young girl. They were visibly sympathetic to her account of the last time she was with her best friend.

The prosecutor asked if she knew the defendant.

"Yes, I know Karl," she replied in a voice just above a whisper.

"Did you ever hear Mr. Chapman comment about the murder of your friend, Lynn Ann?" The prosecutor asked.

"Yes, he only said that she must have known the killer. He didn't say much of anything else. When we would talk about it, Karl would walk away."

"Did Lynn Ann ever talk to you about Karl Chapman?"

"Yes, she told me one time when she was babysitting for the Rosen's Karl tapped on the front porch window, but she refused to let him in. She said it was very late, like after midnight. She didn't seem afraid. She joked about it with me the next day."

"Thank you Lisa." The prosecutor concluded his direct.

The defense declined any cross examination of this witness. Lisa exited the courtroom accompanied by her parents.

As each witness was called, questioned and cross examined, Karl Chapman failed to show any sign of 'understanding or memory'. His face remained stoic. Not once did he move a single muscle that could be observed, with the exception of blinking his eyes.

The first witness to be called after the noon recess was Detective Raymond Gage. The prosecutor asked the detective to describe to the jury what took place during the interview, before the arrest.

Detective Gage began, "The defendant described to me how he had the bayonet type knife covered with a piece of brown paper, tied with a blue piece of crochet thread."

He continued to describe the demeanor of Karl Chapman throughout the questioning.

"I asked him why he killed the girl. He replied, he just wanted to scare her and that she screamed and he just lost it. He also explained he killed the boy to avoid identification."

The detective then went on to testify that the defendant was very specific and detailed his every move.

"Mr. Chapman told me that he stabbed the girl several times. He also delivered a blow to her neck with the handle of the weapon. He told me that upon his return from the boy's bedroom, he thought the girl was still alive so he stabbed her some more."

The detective showed signs of hesitation as he delivered his gruesome testimony. He avoided the eyes of Mr. Clarke who was seated in the front row behind the prosecution. How painful this must be for him. The horror of the details.

The prosecution pressed on, and Ray obliged. He confirmed that Karl had told him he returned home by way of a railroad track near their homes. He ran between two houses to avoid passing under the street lamp.

By the time Raymond completed his two hours of testimony, it was nearing 4:00 P.M..

The judge declared the court adjourned for the day, to resume the following day at 9:30 A.M. instead of the usual time of 10:00. This judge was bent on placing this trial on a fast track, and making every effort to move it along.

Thursday, March 10, 1955: Stanfield Morning Union

MURDER TRIAL UNDERWAY
Prosecution Moves Swiftly Through Witnesses' Testimony
The prosecution moved through a total of eight witnesses yesterday before the court adjourned for the day at 4:00. The defendant, Karl T. Chapman, on trial for his life sat in the prisoner's cage and displayed no sign of emotion....

The article continued, reporting the testimony of each of the witnesses, but dedicated a large portion of the article to the unbelievable and puzzling composure of the defendant.

The reporters described the sorrow and pain on the face of Phil Clarke. It was heart wrenching. Mrs. Clarke did not appear on the first day of trial. The Rosen's were also noticeably absent, although Mr. and Mrs. Schaefer were present on their behalf. Mr. Rosen's sister and her husband sat directly behind Mr. Clarke.

Mrs. Schaefer sobbed during the detective's testimony. Mr. Schaefer was seen placing his hand on the shoulder of Mr. Clarke, a silent gesture of support for the grief stricken father of Lynn Ann Clarke.

The Chapman's were also present. They sat toward the rear of the courtroom. They focused on their son, caged like a vicious animal, displayed before the crowded courtroom. They too were experiencing their own pain and anguish. Mr. Chapman showed no emotion. Mrs. Chapman daubed her eyes with a handkerchief. She held her husband's hand throughout the day.

Karl sat in the cage, never acknowledging his parents, or any of the witnesses. He sat perfectly still, throughout the proceedings of the day. He focused on a discoloration in the marble floor. He never reacted to the gruesome details being presented to the jury. He was in his own private world. A world that was closed to reality. One wondered if he understood the consequences he would face should he be convicted! These 12 men would hold his very life in their hands. Life in prison, or death by execution!

After the judge retired from the bench, Karl was led out, manacled and shackled by a deputy sheriff. His head was bowed as he shuffled out of the courtroom to be returned to the jail. He was allowed to wear a suit and tie while in the courtroom. When he was returned to the jail, he would change into the customary prisoner's jump suit.

Friday, March 11, 1955: Stanfield Union

'SNUB' HINTED DEATH MOTIVE
Chapman's Sister Said Not Included In Clarke Girl's Pajama Party

Lynn Ann Clarke's father is scheduled to testify, it was learned late yesterday. The district attorney confirmed late yesterday that both the father of the slain babysitter and the father of the four-year-old boy are scheduled to testify. The girl's father is expected to testify to the prosecution's theory of motive for killings...

The prosecution refused to accept the motive given by Karl Chapman. Karl insisted he just wanted to 'scare the girl'. Martin O'Neil stated that was not the motive, and he would disclose a more believable motive. The prosecutor intended to present evidence that the reason for the brutal slaying of the babysitter was because his sister, Brenda, had not been invited to a pajama party only three weeks before.

The court convened at precisely 9:30 A.M.. The robed judge took his place at the bench and gestured for all to be seated. He then ordered the defendant to be brought in. Through a side access, Karl Chapman was lead into the courtroom.

He was dressed in a brown suit, white shirt and a solid colored tie. His hands were manacled and his feet were shackled. His head remained bowed. Two deputy sheriffs lead him to the prisoner's cage that he had occupied throughout the trial. After he was placed in the 'cage' the shackles and manacles were removed and he sat erect on a plain, straight backed chair.

The court was brought to order and the prosecutor called his first witness of the day. Called to the stand was Patrolman, Dwight Mitchell.

Dwight Mitchell was one of the two officers first to arrive at the murder house on September 25, 1954. He was asked to describe the scene.

"What time did you arrive at 425 Archer Boulevard?" Asked the prosecutor.

"I arrived at 11:55 P.M., Saturday, September 25," he replied.

"And in your own words, can you tell us what the circumstances were when you arrived at the crime scene?" The prosecutor asked.

Officer Mitchell pulled a small notepad from the breast pocket of his blue-black uniform shirt. He flipped a few pages and began.

"Upon arrival at the murder scene, there were four persons sitting on the front steps. My partner, Patrolman Keith Mathews, stopped to question the people on the porch. There were two women and two young boys. I proceeded into the house."

The prosecutor interrupted, "Was the door open when you arrived?"

"Yes, the door was open. I proceeded into the house. The small foyer was dark, and the floor was covered with shattered glass. The female victim was on the floor sort of between the hallway and the living room area.

I approached two men in the kitchen area. One was Mr. Benjamin Rosen, father of the male victim and the other Dr. Gordon Frazier. In the living room, seated on the sofa, was Mrs. Rosen, the mother of the deceased boy. She was holding the boy."

As the officer testified, over 20 crime scene photos of the bodies and the condition of the home were introduced. Officer Mitchell continued, "I inquired if anyone else was in the house, and the doctor replied, 'no'. The ambulance arrived immediately behind me. The paramedics entered and were led to both the victims. They left a few minutes after it had been determined both victims were deceased."

"What did you do next officer?" Asked the prosecutor.

"I exited the house and directed my partner to stay with the people inside. I called for back up."

After a number of other questions regarding the procedure that the officer followed, the prosecutor returned to his position at the table.

Eugene LaBonte stood and walked to the witness stand.

"Was anyone allowed into the house after you arrived?"

"No sir, the only persons in the house when I called for backup were the Rosen's, Dr. Frazier and my partner, officer Mathews."

"Were there people gathering outside?"

"Yes, a small number of neighbors were outside."

"Did you question anyone? Did you question the people outside? Any of the onlookers?"

"No sir, I returned to the house. I questioned the people inside. My partner questioned the people that remained on the porch."

"No further questions." With that short cross, the judge excused the witness.

The following witness was Officer Keith Mathews. He was questioned by the prosecutor and then cross examined by Eugene LaBonte.

The next witness for the prosecutor was Steven Logan.

"Detective Logan, you were present when the defendant was picked up at school, and subsequently brought to the police station for questioning?"

"Yes sir, my partner and I picked up Mr. Chapman at the Lincoln High School and brought him into the station for questioning."

"Approximately, if you know, Detective how many suspects were apprehended and brought in for questioning on this case?"

"I'm not sure, I would say 85, maybe as many as 100." The detective answered.

"Given your experience as a homicide detective, Sargent, is this an unusual number of suspects in a murder case?"

"Yes sir. I believe, at least in my career, it is a highly unusual number of suspects."

"Were any of these suspects, after questioning arrested, or even detained?"

"Yes sir. Some were detained pending results of lab tests. They were subsequently released."

"Why, was Karl Chapman questioned? What made him a person of interest?"

The detective explained how the investigation proceeded. He explained that all suspects had been released after the evidence had been returned from the lab and failed to incriminate anyone. It was then that he and the entire detective division were forced to start all over again. Retrace the steps they had taken, re-examine all the evidence, particularly the small piece of crochet thread that had been discovered at the crime scene. They had conducted door to door searches throughout the neighborhood, but concluded they should retrace their efforts.

Logan continued, "With the theory that the crochet thread was an intricate part of solving the crime, they concentrated on that one thread of evidence."

Then he related the manner in which he was lead to the Chapman's residence, through the information he had gathered from Mrs. Wayland, the defendant's grandmother.

He explained that the thread of evidence was powerful enough to interrogate Mr. Chapman for the double homicide.

He testified that in a short time after apprehension of Karl Chapman, a voluntary confession was obtained. Finally, Martin O'Neil asked the detective to describe the demeanor of Karl Chapman throughout the interrogation.

The crowded courtroom was silent. Steve Logan offered a mental picture of the defendant during questioning. Mrs. Chapman sobbed. Mr. Chapman turned and looked directly at his caged son. Karl did not look at his parents. He continued to fix his stare at the mar in the flooring.

"The defendant did not appear emotionally upset. He smoked and when he lit his cigarettes, his hands were not trembling. There was no indication of any remorse."

Steve Logan continued his testimony, with minimal objections from the defense.

"This thread of evidence you refer to, detective. Please explain to the jury where that came from."

"I picked up the blue crochet thread at the scene of the murder. It was on the floor, in the foyer." The detective replied. " I brought it to the attention of the Rosen's as well as the Clarke's. Neither family had any knowledge of where it could have come from."

"Again, Detective, when you found this thread, nobody had been allowed into the house, with the exception of law enforcement and officials of the department. Is that correct?"

"Yes sir. No one was allowed inside. Not even the media. We directed the backup officers to cord off the area outside. The spectators were not allowed within 50 feet of the house."

The detective's testimony lasted most of the morning. Eugene LaBonte cross examined him and after a long grueling session, Sargent Logan was excused.

Witness after witness was called. The prosecutor did not belabor any. He was swift and to the point with the witnesses. He was well prepared.

Eugene LaBonte cross examined most of the witnesses. Some were passed by the defense. Melvin Bonner would be on his feet when the defense's case was to be presented.

The Pathologist, Dr. Henry Swanson, was of the Harvard School of Legal Medicine. He was called in the afternoon session.

238

The Medical Examiner, Dr. Paul Chapman had performed the autopsy and subsequently had written his reports of his findings. Dr. Chapman was questioned and the autopsy photographs were presented.

The District Attorney took each 8 x 10 photo and placed it on the evidence table, in view of the jury. The doctor's testimony drew audible gasps from the courtroom which consisted of mostly women.

Eugene LaBonte approached the witness for cross examination. The doctor recited his credentials which were of the highest standard.

Eugene LaBonte: "Can you give an exact time of death?"

Dr. Chapman: "Not more than 5 minutes after the mortal wound was inflicted."

Eugene LaBonte: "Which wound caused Lynn Ann Clarke's death?"

Dr. Chapman: "A stab into the heart. However, there were at least 5 non-fatal wounds delivered prior to the fatal stab wound. A total of 38 stab wounds were detected. In my estimation, at least 32 of them were delivered post mortem. The doctor continued,

" She also suffered a broken neck. The result of a powerful blow to the neck.

The male victim was stabbed a total of 28 times. In my opinion, and after close examination, the boy died as the result of the first stab, through the heart. Twenty- seven stab wounds were delivered post mortem. He also suffered a fractured skull.

Eugene LaBonte: "Was there any evidence of sexual assault?"

Dr. Chapman: "No sir, no evidence of that nature was found." The doctor explained the flesh under Lynn's broken fingernails. "She fought her attacker, at some point she must have scratched him."

Eugene LaBonte quickly reminded the jury, no scratches were detected on the defendant.

"How do you explain that, Doctor?" He asked.

"The scratches, from the time they were inflicted until the time the defendant was apprehended, could in fact, have healed enough so they would not be detected."

For the record, LaBonte repeated, "Let the record show, there were no scratches on the defendant at the time of his arrest."

After several follow up questions by the defense, the witness was excused.

The witnesses that followed each gave an account of the murders. The lab worker that had tested the bloody clothing. He also discussed the murder weapon and the bloody sheets and carpet taken from the scene. He spared no details of his findings.

Every piece of bloody clothing was placed in clear view of the jurors. The prosecutor was determined to depict the defendant as the worst of the worst.

Again, at 4:00 the judge adjourned and announced court would convene the following day, at 9:30.

The jury exchanged glances, and the lawyers asked to approach the bench.

"Your honor," began Martin O'Neil, "We were not aware of the court's intension to proceed with this trial on Saturday. This is highly irregular, and unexpected."

Melvin Bonner shook his head in agreement with the District Attorney.

The judge simply replied, "Well gentlemen, there has been enough delay in getting this case to trial. I see no need to drag it on unnecessarily. That is my decision."

The attorney's were about to object when the judge ordered them back to their respective places in the courtroom. He then turned and addressed the jury.

"I know this is an inconvenience, and I appreciate your cooperation. I believe a Saturday session is necessary and I will expect you here tomorrow morning. You'll assemble in the jury room as usual, at 9:00. Court will be called to order promptly at 9:30. Thank you gentlemen, now you are dismissed."

The jury rose and exited silently through the side door that led to the jury room.

The defendant was chained and led out of the courtroom, as the lawyers gathered their paperwork. It would be a very long evening.

Saturday, March 12, 1955 Stanfield Morning Union:

JUDGE ORDERS SATURDAY SESSION
Fathers of the Victims Expected to Testify Today

The judge made an unprecedented decision yesterday. To the surprise of all, including the jury, Judge Albert Grishbaum announced court would be in session on Saturday. He instructed the jury to report to the courthouse at 9:00 today, and the trial of Karl T. Chapman would continue. The judge was reported to say he would not tolerate any unnecessary delays, and that the trial would proceed as he directed.

The decision to hold court on Saturday threw everyone into an uproar. Preparation by the prosecutor to call his next witness to the stand would be very difficult. He had intended to call the father of Lynn Ann Clarke, as well as the father of David Rosen.

Saturday was the Sabbath for the Jewish faith. He would contact Mr. Rosen to inform him of the judge's decision. Mr. Rosen would comply, these are "extenuating circumstances" he would say.

Up until then, the Rosen's were not present in the courtroom. Martin O'Neil was not accustomed to being thrown a curve from anyone. He was seething, but there was nothing he could do.

At 9:30, the judge took the bench. The jury was led into the crowded courtroom. The defense and the prosecution were at their places and Karl Chapman had already been led to his place in 'the cage.'

Mr. and Mrs. Chapman were present. They had been given a few minutes to visit with Karl before the judge entered into the room. Karl was unshaken, and listened to his mother's words. Mrs. Chapman tried to hide the tears that seemed to be never ending. Karl gave her a sheepish grin. He said not a word to his mother. Mr. Chapman stood a step behind his frail wife. He placed his hand on her shoulder, indicating it was time to take their seats among the spectators.

Ben Rosen sat directly behind the prosecutor. Beside him was his sister and her husband, the Schaefers. Mrs. Rosen was not in attendance. Mr. Clarke sat directly behind the Rosens. He was accompanied by his brother Michael. Michael had accompanied his brother each day Phil attended the trial.

The judge called the court to order.

"Please call your next witness, Mr. O'Neil."

"The Commonwealth calls Mr. Phillip Clarke," came the stern voice of Martin O'Neil..

Mr. Clarke walked to the witness stand. The spectators were silent. Mr. Clarke stood and raised his left hand as he rested his right hand on the bible. He was given the oath, and softly replied, "I do." Mr. Clarke looked past the prosecutor, and fixed a glare on the caged defendant.The prosecutor asked him the usual questions for the record.

"Mr. Clarke, what was your relationship to the victim?"

"Lynn Ann is...excuse me, was my daughter." Mr. Clarke choked on this reply. He cleared his throat. The prosecutor handed him a small cup of water, and waited patiently for his witness to gain his composure.

He then continued and managed to speak in a clear tone, responding to the District Attorney's questions.

Martin O'Neil asked Mr. Clarke to describe his daughter to the jury. Mr. Clarke seemed to be at ease when he talked about Lynn Ann. For a few minutes, he seemed to revel in the image he was delivering to the attentive jury. He was describing his daughter as any proud father would. He brought her alive in the minds of the jury. He humanized her. That was exactly the message the prosecutor had hoped he would deliver. Lynn Ann Clarke was a real, vibrant young girl.

When Phil finished, Martin O'Neil went on to disclose his theory of motive. Through this witness he would prove to the jury that Karl T. Chapman planned the murder of Lynn Ann Clarke, for failure on the part of Lynn to invite his sister to a pajama party only weeks before the murder.

He would call witnesses, who would testify to the relationship Karl had with Brenda. They would explain to the jury, how protective Karl was of his sister. To the point of being obsessive.

O'Neil: "Mr. Chapman, do you recall an incident in early September of last year in which your daughter Lynn Ann had a pajama party?"

Clarke: "Yes, I do. It was the Saturday before Labor Day."

O'Neil: "Where you present when this so called pajama party was held in your home?"

Clarke: "Yes."

O'Neil: "What did you observe?"

Clarke: "There were five friends, classmates, of Lynn's."

O'Neil: "Was Brenda Chapman present?"

Clarke: "No, she was not. I don't believe she was invited."

O'Neil: "Why was Brenda not invited."

Clarke: "I don't know. I assume it was because all the girls were in Lynn's class from last year, Brenda was a year ahead of Lynn. That's the only reason I can think of."

O'Neil "What did the party consist of?"

Clarke: "The girls had dinner and they put mattresses and blankets on the floor. Before they went to bed they talked and generally had a good time."

The district attorney's questions then brought out that Mr. and Mrs. Clarke were present the night of the party with the exception of 45 minutes to an hour when they went for a walk.

Mr. Clarke said he helped the girls arrange the mattresses and pillows on the dining room floor, and the girls went to bed around 12:00 to 1:00.

The questioning then turned to the night Lynn Ann was waked and the funeral on the following day.

Phil Clarke told how Karl had visited the funeral home to see his daughter's body and later acted as a pallbearer at the funeral. It was the most dramatic testimony of trial.

Mr. Clarke appeared flushed and swallowed several times, but managed to remain composed as he answered Martin O'Neil's questions. He focused on the defendant seated in the 'dock' about 25 feet away. Chapman did not look up.

Phil continued, saying that Brenda, Karl's sister had visited many times in the Clarke's home. When asked if Karl had ever been inside the house, Mr. Clarke answered, "No, not to my knowledge."

This was the first time Mr. Clarke had seen Karl Chapman since the brutal killing of his daughter.

The prosecutor finished his direct questioning. The defense passed the witness.

By the time Mr. Clarke's testimony was completed, it was near lunch. The judge called both the defense and the prosecution to the bench.

"Do you have another witness to call that will not take up much time? We have time to hear another witness, if it is brief."

"No your honor, I would like to wait until after the lunch break. My next witness is Mr. Rosen. I anticipate it will be lengthy.

The judge announced court was adjourned until 1:00. The jury was led out in the customary manner, as was the defendant.

During the break, the defendant was placed in a 'lock up' within the courthouse. The defense councils took advantage of the break to speak with their client.

The spectators attending the trial were seen looking over at the young defendant sitting in the cage. Several women in the same age bracket as Karl's mother stared at Karl and turned away shaking their heads.

As the spectators entered the courtroom they invariably looked around the room for the defendant and after spotting him, they would give him an 'up and down' inspection. Even the 'turn-away' crowd that remained in the corridor would get an occasional glimpse at Karl when he was brought back and forth from the lockup. He was transferred in manacles and shackles until he was inside the cage. Two sheriffs were seated on each side of the dock at all times.

At 1:00 the court reconvened. When all parties had been seated, the prosecution called Mr. Benjamin Rosen to the stand.

Mr. Clarke remained seated in the courtroom. Again, the courtroom was silent, as the father of the slain boy approached the witness stand. Millie and Tom Schaefer were present in the courtroom as they had been every day since the start. Mrs. Rosen did not attend. She was far too emotionally unstable to come face to face with her baby's killer.

Mr. Rosen stood at the witness stand.

"Mr. Rosen, how are you related to the victim?" Asked the prosecutor.

"I am his father, I....was his father." Replied Mr. Rosen. Mr. Rosen's voice faded often. Preliminary questioning of the murdered boy's father involved the Rosen family's acquaintance with Lynn Ann Clarke and her duties as a baby sitter.

"How was Lynn Ann's demeanor when she arrived at your house the night of the murders?" Asked the prosecutor.

"I don't know what you mean. Lynn Ann was always very cheerful. She loved the boys and Mrs. Rosen and I thought of her as a pleasant young lady. David and Daniel, that's my six-year-old boy, always looked forward to Lynn Ann's arrival. She was exceptional with the children."

"So, Mr. Rosen, you had no reason to believe Miss Clarke was apprehensive, or appeared to be frightened of anything that night?"

"No sir, not at all." Mr. Rosen replied.

The prosecutor lead Mr. Rosen to the night of the murders.

"Mr. Rosen, what did you observe when you arrived at your house on the night of Saturday, September 25th?"

"I pulled up to the front of the house. I let my wife out, and she went to the door."

"Was the door open?" Asked the prosecutor.

"No." Replied Mr. Rosen.

"Tell us what happened next, Mr. Rosen." The prosecutor prodded.

"Well, I was waiting in the car, you know, for Lynn to come out. The next thing I remember is my wife screaming. It was terrible. She screamed, 'Ben, Ben, my God!'."

Mr. Rosen was visibly shaken. He paused. The prosecutor poured a glass of water and offered it to Mr. Rosen. As he accepted the glass, midway through his testimony, he asked the judge if he could sit in the chair provided at the witness stand. The judge granted the request and Mr. Rosen sat. He looked beaten.

"Take your time, Mr. Rosen, please continue." The prosecutor spoke softly to the bereaved father.

"I jumped from the car. I don't think I even shut the car off. I ran into the house. I found Lynn Ann on the floor. "

"Where was she, Mr. Rosen?"

"She was in the front hallway."

O'Neil: "What position was she in?"

Rosen: "She was huddled face down. There was blood all over."

At this point, Mr. Rosen faltered and his voice came down to a whisper. The judge addressed the witness,

"I understand this is very difficult Mr. Rosen, but you must speak louder for the jury to hear you."

O'Neil: "Where did you go then?"

Rosen: "I ran to David's room. My wife, Gail, was lying across the bed atop of David. It was terrible. She was moaning, crying, wailing. I don't know, it was just awful."

He sipped the water and continued, "I ran to Daniel's room. That's David's brother, my other son. He was alright. I held him tightly for a moment, then I saw my wife running down the hallway, carrying David in her arms."

"Did you see anyone in the house? Was the killer in the house?"

"No, nobody was there."

O'Neil: "Then what happened?"

Rosen: "I called the doctor."

O'Neil: "The doctor? Mr. Rosen, why the doctor?"

Rosen: "My wife kept shouting, 'David is alive call the doctor!' I just didn't know what to do, so I called Gordon Frazier. Dr. Frazier is our family doctor. He's also a friend and lives close by."

The prosecutor continued the questioning. Finally, after Ben Rosen described the horror he had witnessed that night, the prosecutor asked,

"Do you know Karl Chapman? Have you ever seen the defendant before today?"

Ben answered, "I believe he was employed for a short time at one of my stores, but, no, I've never met the boy."

Throughout his testimony, Mr. Rosen set his eyes on the defendant, only 25 feet in front of him. His face was a portrait of strain and emotion.

During the questioning, two deputy sheriffs moved to the front of the cage, positioning themselves between the defendant and the witness, blocking Mr. Rosen's view. Judge Grishbaum interrupted the testimony and ordered the deputies to step away.

The prosecutor completed his direct examination and offered the witness to the defense for cross. The defense declined cross examination of Ben Rosen.

The judge excused the witness and Mr. Rosen shuffled out of the courtroom. Millie and Tom Schaefer raced after him. Mr. Clarke and Michael Clarke stayed in the courtroom the remainder of the day.

Because of Mrs. Clarke's pregnancy, she did not attend the trial. She was expecting the baby in April, and at eight months pregnant, she chose to stay out of the public eye.

Phil Clarke sat through the testimony of the State Police Chemist who had examined all the evidence at the State Police Crime Lab in Boston. Lynn Ann's clothing was displayed before the jury, along with little David Rosen's blood soaked pajamas and slippers. The oriental carpet that Lynn Ann was found lying on was also exhibited.

The murder weapon was entered for identification, but not an exhibit. It was described by the chemist as 11 ½ inches in overall length with a blade 6 ½ inches which at it's widest was 7/8ths of an inch. On the blade, the chemist found traces of human tissue and in the crevice between the blade and the hilt, were found traces of human blood.

On an adjacent table Karl Chapman's clothing. His father's jacket and the hat he wore. The denim jeans and blood soaked shirt. All on exhibit and entered into evidence.

At the end of the chemist's testimony, O'Neil abruptly stated,

"Your honor, the Commonwealth rests."

There was a murmur in the courtroom. Reporters rushed out to get the story into the evening paper. The defense was left 'flat footed'.

The psychiatrists were not called. Although, they would remain in the gallery. The prosecutor was confident his presentation of witnesses and evidence was sufficient. He still reserved the right to call additional witnesses during rebuttal.

It was clear to all that Karl Chapman's case was not a matter of guilty or innocent. It was stipulated, he had committed the murders. The challenge was for all intents and purposes, to establish murder in the first degree, punishable by death. The defense would surely pursue the insanity defense. Not guilty by reason of insanity. This verdict would insure commitment to a mental institution and spare Karl's life.

The defense had an arduous task before them, and much sooner than they had anticipated!

Melvin Bonner requested a bench conference. The judge complied, and both sides approached.

"Your honor, I would respectfully request two days to prepare my defense."

The prosecutor objected. "Your honor, Mr. Bonner has had several months to prepare. I see no need to delay."

The judge pondered for a few moments and said he would think about it in his chambers, and give him a decision before he adjourned the court. With that statement, he declared a short recess, and retired to his chambers.

After only ten minutes, the judge reappeared in the courtroom.

"The defense has asked for a two day delay. After careful consideration, I must deny his request."

"But your honor!" Melvin Bonner was on his feet.

"Mr. Bonner, I have made my decision. This trial will proceed as scheduled."

The judge turned slightly to face the jury. "You are directed to return to this courtroom at 9:00 Monday morning. Then he charged the jury with the usual admonitions. Thank you and enjoy your Sunday."

He turned and faced the crowded courtroom and announced that court was adjourned until 9:30 Monday morning. At that time, the defense was to be prepared to present their case. He ended with a slam of the gavel that echoed throughout the marbled courtroom.

After the judge had returned to his chambers, the jury filed out. The spectators lingered, not wanting to miss the defendant being prepared to return to the jail. Mr. Clarke left the courtroom immediately, and declined any comment to the public or the media.

Martin O'Neil and the assistant D.A. gathered up their paperwork. O'Neil briefly chatted with a court officer on his way out, delivering a friendly slap on the back. He had an air about him. An air of confidence that permeated throughout the courthouse.

The defense attorneys went through the motions of gathering up their paperwork. Miss Lewis was already out of the courtroom and headed for the office to transcribe the notes she had taken throughout the day. Melvin Bonner would want them that evening. He had to contact witnesses, and prepare his questioning for Monday. He was literally caught off guard by the surprising closing of the prosecution's case.

Eugene LaBonte agreed to meet with Melvin early Sunday morning. They would go over their strategy and prepare a witness list. Miss Lewis would assist in contacting the witnesses. Late Saturday afternoon was not an ideal time to be contacting anyone, but they had to make a gallant effort!

Saturday, March 12, 1955 Stanfield Evening News:

PROSECUTION RESTS ITS CASE
Defense Expected to Begin Their Case Monday Morning
Insanity Plea is Indicated, Mother of the Defendant Expected to Testify

To the shock of all, District Attorney Martin O'Neil rested his case. The prosecution examined the two fathers of the victims, the State Police chemist and presented the evidence, which included the bloody clothing of Lynn Ann Clarke, the Rosen boy and the defendant, Karl Chapman.

Mr. Clarke kept his composure while being questioned about the pajama party occurring only weeks before the murder of his daughter. The defense declined to question the father of the girl.

Mr. Rosen testified. He was visibly shaken and quite emotional as he recounted the horror he witnessed upon discovering the butchered bodies of Lynn Ann Clarke and his young son, David Rosen.

To the surprise of all, the prosecution did not call the two psychiatrists who had interviewed Chapman and had submitted reports, although it was noticed that the psychiatrists remained in the gallery and listened to all the testimony. The prosecution may call the doctors upon rebuttal of the case....

It was anticipated that Marge Chapman would be one of the most important witnesses. Melvin Bonner would put her on the stand and her testimony would be crucial to the insanity defense. He called her to his office early Sunday morning.

Mr. and Mrs. Chapman arrived at the office of Melvin Bonner at 9:15 Sunday morning. Miss Lewis was prepared to take notes, and Eugene LaBonte had prepared a list of questions that would be asked. They wanted to give Mrs. Chapman a 'run through' of her pending testimony.

The veteran attorney was fully cognizant of the difficulty he would face. Mrs. Chapman was emotionally frail. She would have to hold up long enough to get her testimony out loud and clear to the jury. She would have to unveil all the 'family skeletons'. This would be the most important story she would ever relate to anyone. This was the testimony that only a mother could convey, and Melvin was taking full advantage of any sympathy she may extrude from the jurors.

Throughout the day, the defense team shot questions at Mrs. Chapman. On numerous occasions she broke down and cried, "I can't do this, I can't. It's too painful!"

Mr. Chapman was uncharacteristic from his usual hard facade. He comforted his wife in a way that amazed the two defense attorneys. This was a good sign. She finally had won the support of her husband.

They took several breaks throughout the sessions, and finally at the close of the day, Bonner and LaBonte were feeling far more optimistic than they had earlier. They were confident they had done everything humanly possible to prepare for the Monday morning court session.

At 4:15, the Chapman's left. They headed straight to the jail for a brief visit with Karl. Upon their arrival, they handed a freshly cleaned blue sport jacket, a crisp white shirt and a pair of khaki trousers to the jail attendant. These were to be given to Karl for his Monday morning court appearance. The attendant in turn handed

John Chapman the brown suit and shirt that Karl had worn in his previous appearances.

Karl was seated in his tiny cell. He didn't hear them approach, he was wearing earphones, listening to his favorite music, and eating his jail house dinner.

Mr. Chapman entered the cell and removed the earphones from his son's head. The teenager stood immediately in the presence of his father. John gestured for him to sit down, and he cleared the newspapers on the bunk allowing room for his wife to sit beside her son.

Mr. Chapman lit his pipe and started pacing back and forth, drawing heavily from the pipe.

"Karl, we've been to Melvin's office. Your mother will be testifying tomorrow. It will be very difficult, but Melvin feels it must be done."

Karl watched his father and listened intently. He seemed to sit up straighter in his father's presence. Marge Chapman reached for Karl's hand and gave it a squeeze. He did not reciprocate. His eyes were fixed on this giant of a man he called 'Dad'. The parents visited briefly. Karl had little to say. He displayed no interest in the trial which held his life in the offing. He sat, listening to his father's assessment of how the trial was going thus far. How he believed that Melvin Bonner would be excellent in his defense, and that he was optimistic, that after Karl's mother testified, there would be no doubt, Karl would be found at the least, a person of diminished capacity.

If the jury were to return a verdict of 'not guilty by reason of insanity', it would spare Karl the electric chair, and possibly allow him his freedom after several years of commitment in a mental facility.

Karl shrugged his shoulders, indicating, 'whatever you think is best Dad.' He had become accustomed, from an early age to look to his father for decisions, and not to disagree with John Chapman. His father ruled the Chapman family. This general observation was confirmed by the submissive Mrs. Chapman's behavior. Brenda, although a bit more rebellious, also regarded her father's authority as stern to say the very least. Brenda customarily counted on her mother's interception instead of having to confront her father directly.

After the short visit with Karl, the Chapman's left. They stopped at Mrs. Chapman's sister's to pick up Brenda. Brenda was very quiet and becoming more and more withdrawn. It was a concern, but their concern for Brenda's changes were paled against the overwhelming concern for their son's life in the hands of twelve strangers.

Monday, March 14, 1955 Stanfield Morning Union

CHAPMAN DEFENSE EXPECTED TO BEGIN
Defense is Expected to Begin With Testimony of Early Childhood and School Records

After the Commonwealth rested its case on Saturday, the defense is expected to open its case by calling to the stand, two psychologists that have conducted interviews with the defendant.

The two doctors are expected to offer testimony to Karl Chapman's mental state of mind at the time of the murders, as well as history of his mal adjusted youth.

Also expected to be called are teachers, friends and relatives of the defendant....

The reports were brief and unclear at this point. Because of the sudden and unexpected end of the prosecution's presentation, it was not known the exact order of defense witnesses to expect.

At 9:30 the court was called to order. All parties were in their respective places within the courtroom. Mr. Clarke was present, accompanied his brother and the Schaefer's. The Rosen's were not present.

John Chapman and Marge Chapman were seated in the same place they had been during the previous days of the trial. They were in close proximity of the 'cage' their son was forced to occupy.

Melvin Bonner delivered his opening statement. He approached the jury and greeted them with a warm smile and an amicable "Good morning, gentlemen."

"I intend to bring before you a total of 11 witnesses. These witnesses will offer testimony regarding Karl Chapman's life. We will chronologically uncover the true Karl Chapman through childhood friends, teachers, psychologists and the boy's mother, Mrs. Marge Chapman.

You will hear testimony that will tell you about Karl's behavior before the terrible crime, and the days that led up to it. You will also hear testimony of Karl's behavior following the night of September 25th."

Mr. Bonner's opening statement lasted a short 15 minutes.

"The defense calls its first witness." Announced Melvin Bonner. "Mr. William Talbot."

Mr. Talbot was the Supervisor of Guidance of the public school system of Stanfield. Mr. Talbot approached the witness stand carrying several manila folders under his arm. He was to produce the school records of Karl Chapman.

He began with grade 2, where Karl had attended the Franklin Elementary School at the age of six years, seven months.

He continued, "Karl had passed all his grades satisfactorily, with the exception of writing. He had a difficult time with writing. Eventually Karl was given what is called "auxiliary service" because of his apparent inability to learn to read and write. At this time, it was noted that Mr. Chapman lacked consideration for other children, did not play well, and did not spend his time well. All school reports indicate the same weakness, up to his second year in high school."

Under continued questioning by Melvin Bonner, the witness testified that in early years in school, Chapman was about 2 ½ years above the average height and below the average in strength.

At this point, the district attorney called a bench conference and the judge ordered a brief recess so that the Commonwealth could examine the records for the purpose of agreeing to their admissibility or to challenge, if necessary.

The recess was very brief and the district attorney did not challenge the testimony of Mr. Talbot.

The defense resumed the questioning of Mr. Talbot. His testimony proved to be very lengthy, as well as the cross examination of the district attorney.

As the noon hour approached, the judge adjourned until 1:00. Again, the defense attorneys visited with Karl in the courthouse lockup. They went over all the pending testimony. Karl did not contribute to his defense in any way. He listened, but did not offer anything.

It was noted, one woman was seen eating her lunch in the Superior Courtroom. After three days, she was ordered by the judge to refrain from this activity in the future.

Also, present in the gallery was a writer sent from a national news magazine. He was sent to do an article on the psychiatric testimony.

There was considerable speculation when Mrs. Chapman, a potential witness was allowed to remain in the courtroom while other defense witnesses were on the stand. Witnesses ordinarily are not allowed to stay in the courtroom until after they have testified. When the District Attorney brought this to the judge's attention, Judge Grishbaum made a special ruling allowing Mrs. Chapman and medical experts to remain in the courtroom.

The court reconvened at 1:00. Mr. Talbot took his place at the witness stand and the prosecution continued the cross examination.

The cross examination was very lengthy. There were several objections by the defense and many bench conferences. By the time the testimony of the Supervisor of Guidance was completed, it was 2:30. The judge looked to the defense.

"You may call your next witness, Mr. Bonner."

Bonner and LaBonte conferred for a few minutes. They had intended to put the psychiatrist on the stand, but they hadn't anticipated the testimony of Mr. Talbot to be so lengthy. They decided to call the next two witnesses, out of order and save the psychiatrist, Dr. Slattery on the following day.

Bonner stood and called his next witness. A neighbor of the Chapman's.

"Mrs. Dion, are you acquainted with the defendant, Karl Chapman?"

"Yes, the Chapman family have lived next door to me for 14 years."

Bonner: "How would you describe the defendant?"

Dion: "Karl has always been a kind and gentle young man.

In the 14 years I've watched him grow up, I don't recall a single instance that he ever caused any problems in the neighborhood. He was always helpful. In the winter he would shovel my walk without me having to ask."

Bonner: "How did you feel when you heard that Karl had been arrested?"

Dion: "My goodness, I was shocked! Everyone in the neighborhood was. I couldn't believe it. He would have been the last person on earth that I would ever have thought of."

Bonner: "So, it was completely out of the character of Karl to display any type of anger, or harmful behavior? This was not his normal manner? He was not cruel, or abusive by nature?

Dion: "No sir, not at all."

Bonner: "Thank you Mrs. Dion."

The prosecutor passed the witness. The defense called the next witness. One of Karl's high school teachers. The questions and answers were similar to the previous testimony of Mrs. Dion. Bonner was attempting to establish that Karl was normally a gentle, non-violent young man that suddenly 'went berserk'.

At the conclusion of the teacher's testimony, the judge called the defense and prosecution to the bench.

"Can you have your next witness on and off the stand within ½ hour?"

"No your honor, I don't believe that is possible." Replied Melvin Bonner.

"How would you prefer to proceed, councilor? Do you want to call your next witness now and continue the testimony at the start of tomorrow's session? I'll leave that up to you."

"Thank you your Honor, I would prefer to call the witness at the start of tomorrow's session. The witness will be Dr. Slattery. I would like to question this witness without interruption, if it pleases the court."

The judge gave the jury his usual admonitions and then announced, "Court is adjourned until 9:30 tomorrow morning."

The judge slammed his gavel. The court officer ordered, "All rise." The judge retired to his chambers and the court was officially adjourned for the day.

Reporters rushed from the courtroom, hurrying to meet their deadline for the evening edition of the Stanfield Evening News.

The television reporters attempted to get live pictures of the parents of the defendant as well as the victim's father, Mr. Clarke. Mr. Clarke shielded his face from the cameras and simply repeated his usual phrase, "No comment, please, no comment."

The Schaefers escorted Mr. Clarke to his car, positioning themselves between him and the cameras.

Monday, March 14, 1955: The Stanfield Evening News:

INSANITY PLEA INDICATED BY OPENING STATEMENTS MOTHER TO TESTIFY
Chapman Said Problem Boy Defense Begins Testimony on Early Conduct

The defense began with testimony on the early conduct of the defendant. School records were produced and testimony came from Mr. William Talbot, Supervisor of Guidance for the Stanfield Public Schools.

Mr. Talbot told the court of the behavior of the defendant. He reported that Karl Chapman was having difficulty adjusting and learning as early as second grade. The boy's mal adjustment continued to accelerate throughout his school years, up to and including his second year of high school. Karl Chapman, now in his third year of high school is accused of brutally stabbing 14 year old Lynn Ann Clarke and David Rosen, the 4-year-old boy in her charge.

If convicted, Karl Chapman may face the electric chair. Attorney Melvin Bonner will proceed with an insanity defense to save his client from death...

The article reported the testimony of the day's primary witness, Mr. William Talbot. It also described Karl Chapman as a cold, unemotional enigma. Karl remained stoic throughout the day. He showed no change in expression, and continued to gaze at the floor. A writing tablet was provided but Karl took no notes. He never picked it up, not even to doodle. He sat straight without shifting positions. He was stoic and appeared to be drifted into another world. This would continue throughout the remainder of the trial.

The jury was unusually attentive. They clung to every word of the witnesses. They took avid notes. Their feelings and reactions to the testimony were clear by the varied expressions on their faces. Never did the jury appear to be detached in any way.

This was a group of twelve men who intended to take their duty with utmost responsibility. This was a case that would ultimately come down to each one, deciding the fate of the teen age defendant.

Steven Logan and Ray Gage were seen in the courtroom daily. They stopped in whenever their schedules would permit. Other members of the detective bureau, and many off duty patrolmen were present.

The law enforcement of Stanfield took particular interest in this case. They had all participated in some manner, in the apprehension of Karl Chapman, and now they wanted to see the teenager tried and convicted.

Chief McNamara was rarely seen at the trial. He was confident a guilty verdict would be handed down by the jury, and hoped they would not be a merciful group. He had seen the anguish Karl Chapman had imposed on three families. He had witnessed the flat affect of the boy. No indication of remorse, or sorrow. This was not a case of mercy for a young man that had simply 'lost it' and now, was contrite. No, this was a cold savage that deserved to die for his demented, depraved actions.

The Chief kept his convictions to himself. He did not want to taint or influence the department with his personal feelings.

Melvin Bonner and Eugene LaBonte returned to their office immediately after court.

Miss Lewis called the local delicatessen and ordered food for the defense team. She proceeded to the small kitchenette off the office and prepared a fresh pot of coffee. This would be another long evening of preparation, as they had become accustomed to.

Miss Lewis then retreated to her desk in the small reception area of the office suite. She busied herself with the laborious task of transcribing the testimony of the day. She had turned out to be invaluable to the defense. She was eager and tireless.

Monday, March 14, Stanfield Evening News:

DEFENSE PUTS MOTHER ON STAND
Says Her Father, Uncle Both at State Hospital; Karl Ill as a Child

The boy's relatives suffered epilepsy, testified his mother. Mrs. Chapman described Karl Chapman's childhood health and school problems. Mrs. Chapman took the witness stand today in a dramatic attempt to save her 19-year-old son from the electric chair. Mrs. Chapman remained composed as she testified about the mental illness of her father and uncle and of the health and behavior problems with Karl as a child...

Melvin Bonner began the questioning.

Bonner: "Are you Karl Chapman's mother?"

Mrs. Chapman: "Yes I am."

Bonner: "How long have you lived at 51 Lynndale Street?"

Mrs. Chapman: "Fourteen years."

Bonner: "Besides Karl, who else lives at 51 Lynndale Street?"

Mrs. Chapman: "My husband John and my 16- year-old daughter, Brenda."

Bonner: "Would you describe Karl as a kind brother to Brenda?"

Mrs. Chapman: "Yes, very."

Bonner: "Did Karl ever mention the matter of Brenda not being invited to the pajama party that took place at Lynn Ann Clarke's home?

Mrs. Chapman: "No, I don't recall that he ever did."

Bonner: "In your own words, Mrs. Chapman, can you tell the court about Karl as a baby?"

Mrs. Chapman: "Karl was born on February 21, 1936. He was a very big baby. He weighed 10lbs. 9ozs. and was 24 ½ inches long. In his early years, he had a sinus gland condition, eczema, earaches and nosebleeds. He often required medical care."

Bonner: "Did Karl have any other physical ailments?"

Mrs. Chapman: "No, except he never slept."

Bonner: "What do you mean?"

Mrs. Chapman: "He always had a hard time sleeping. He was always restless. The trouble with Karl's eczema and ears lasted until two years ago." She paused, and looked in the direction of her husband who was seen giving her a soft look of encouragement.

She continued, "Karl grew very rapidly and gained four inches in the last two years."

Mrs. Chapman told of her concern for her son, to the point that she wrote a letter to Mrs. Sarah Wright, principal of the Franklin St. Elementary School. She asked that the boy be examined in a psychological laboratory.

Melvin Banner read the letter in the court.

In part, the letter said, "We are sorry it is necessary to write this, but we feel there was a slip up in his first year of school. Karl is known to be ahead in arithmetic and backward in reading and writing."

"It seems to us that we are forever punishing Karl, for something. We have taken things away that he likes and put him to bed without supper. We have spanked him.

I can't understand what makes him act the way he does. At times he's sweet, but at other times he often makes noises and jumps around.

He is not malicious or destructive and we have good reports of his behavior at Sunday School. That's why we can't understand it."

Finally, Melvin Bonner launched the questioning that would bolster an insanity case.

Bonner: "What is your father's name?"

Mrs. Chapman: "Ralph Wayland."

Bonner: "Did he suffer from any illnesses?

Before Mrs. Chapman could reply, Martin O'Neil called a bench conference and then the question was repeated.

Mrs. Chapman: "Yes, he did."

Bonner: "Will you tell us what it was?"

Mrs. Chapman: "Epilepsy."

Bonner: "Were you ever present when he had an epileptic fit?"

Mrs. Chapman: "Yes."

Bonner: "Tell us what you observed."

Again, the district attorney was on his feet, and said he was satisfied with the answer without a description, but after another bench conference, Melvin Bonner was allowed to repeat the question.

Mrs. Chapman: "His eyes seemed to go back in his head and he would fall on the floor."

Bonner: "Did you observed this more than once?"

Mrs. Chapman: "Yes. Over a period of 10 years."

Bonner: "Did anyone else in your family have illnesses?"

Mrs. Chapman: "Yes, my uncle, Charles Wayland."

Melvin Bonner continued questioning Mrs. Chapman about her father and uncle and the mental illnesses they suffered from. Mrs. Chapman testified that her father died in the Northampton State Hospital. Her uncle was also committed to the State Hospital until he also died.

Melvin Bonner then shuffled through papers, allowing the testimony of Marge Chapman to resinate with the jury.

As Marge Chapman testified, she never looked at Karl. While his mother was on the stand, Karl maintained a poker face and never looked directly at her. His only moves were quick side glances in her general direction.

Melvin Bonner was very considerate of the nervous middle aged woman. He spoke softly to her. Her responses were thoughtful, and cautious. As she answered Mr. Bonner's questions, Martin O'Neil stood.

"Your Honor, please ask the witness to speak up. We can hardly hear her. I doubt the jury can hear her."

The judge turned to the frail mother seated to his right.

"Please try to speak a little louder, Mrs. Chapman. It's important you are heard by the jury."

Melvin Bonner then changed his questioning, bringing Mrs. Chapman directly to the night of the murders, and after.

Bonner: "Was Karl Chapman home on the night of September 25, 1954?"

Mrs. Chapman: "To my knowledge, Karl was home all evening."

Bonner: "Who was in the home that night?"

Mrs. Chapman: "I was, my sister stopped by earlier in the evening. I think she left around 8:30. My daughter, Brenda was out with a friend. She came home just before 11:00. My husband was out of town, an emergency, power line down in Connecticut."

Bonner: "Again, Mrs. Chapman, was Karl home?"

Mrs. Chapman: "He was in and out of the room."

Bonner: "How did Karl act after September 25?"

Mrs. Chapman took a deep sigh and continued. "He acted perfectly normal after September 25th."

Bonner: "Did you notice anything different in his eating or sleeping habits?"

Mrs. Chapman: "No, he ate well, he's always had a big appetite, and he seemed to sleep well also."

Bonner continued questioning Mrs. Chapman. It was a lengthy direct examination by the defense. Mrs. Chapman showed no signs of fatigue. Occasionally, Karl glanced in her direction and his face reddened slightly. With the exception of the slight flushing in his face, there was no sign of emotion from the iron nerved teen.

As the morning session concluded, so did the direct examination of Mrs. Chapman. The prosecution would begin its cross after the lunch break.

The judge adjourned until 1:00.

The 'turn away' crowd remained in the hallway just outside the courtroom. They waited for a chance to see the defendant, being led to the lockup. For hours, they gathered in the hallway while others sat inside, listening intently at every word of testimony. Perhaps they would come to understand what motivated Karl Chapman to commit this horrendous act.

The afternoon session was called to order at precisely 1:00. Judge Grishbaum was very adamant about schedules being adhered to.

The prosecution began his cross examination. Mrs. Chapman had not yet been excused. She sat wringing her hands in her lap. The small woman was obviously nervous, anticipating the prosecution's questioning.

Surprisingly, O'Neil was courteous towards the mother of the defendant. He was thorough, and precise. Mrs. Chapman soon showed signs of comfort with the line of questioning, which was far more brief than anyone could have predicted.

When the prosecution finished with the witness, Melvin Bonner asked for a redirect. He asked Mrs. Chapman a few clarifying questions.

Bonner: "Mrs. Chapman, do you love your son?"

Mrs. Chapman: "Yes, I do, very much."

Once Melvin Bonner was satisfied, the judge excused the witness.

Mrs. Chapman stepped down from the witness stand. For the first time she looked at her son seated in the cage. They exchanged glances, and Karl lowered his head and resumed his fixed stare at the floor.

Mrs. Chapman took her seat with her husband in the galley. Mr. Chapman reached for her hand and held it throughout the remainder of the afternoon session.

Melvin Bonner called the next defense witness. This witness was the best he had to offer and the defense case hinged on the testimony of Dr. Charles Slattery.

"The defense calls Dr. Charles Slattery." Dr. Slattery, was seated in the rear of the gallery. He had been allowed to remain in the courtroom during the testimony of the other witnesses.

Dr. Slattery took the witness stand. He was very professional and confident. This case was one of many occasions he'd been called to testify in a capital case.

Melvin asked for the doctor's qualifications. The doctor offered his qualifications which were impressive and impeccable. It would be difficult to underestimate this doctor's testimony. The doctor's testimony finished the afternoon session, and would be continued to the next day.

The judge adjourned the court at 4:00. After his usual admonishment to the jury, he stepped down from the bench, and all were free to leave. Of course, with the exception of the defendant who was manacled and shackled and escorted from the courtroom.

Tuesday, March 15, 1955 Stanfield Morning Union

CHAPMAN CALLED MENTAL CASE
Youth Cried for Four Days Defense Calls Psychiatrist to Testify

Dr. Slattery, a noted psychiatrist began his testimony for the defense. The doctor stated that the teen "cried for four days in lonely remorse after murders." The psychiatrist testified said Karl Chapman exhibited 'Murder Themes'.

The defense played a trump card in the murder trial when they introduced the testimony of a Harvard psychiatrist. The doctor testified that the defendant is suffering from schizophrenia and psychomotor epilepsy. Dr. Charles Slattery gave his testimony before leaving the stand for the recess...

Dr. Slattery continued his testimony upon return from the noon recess. He revealed that he had tested the defendant at the Hampden County Jail shortly after his arrest. The doctor went on to explain that Karl Chapman's crying was not done in the open, but alone. His testimony was the first indication during the trial, or since the arrest that the 19-year-old ever showed any signs of remorse after the bloody slaying.

When the prosecutor cross examined the doctor, the doctor testified that "Chapman cried for about four days after the crime for which he was eventually arrested for. He told me that he doesn't cry openly, but alone."

The doctor continued. He told me, "I'm not nervous now because there's nothing to be nervous about. It's done now, I can't do anything about it."

The "Murder Theme" was introduced as the prosecutor pressed further to de-emphasize any support to an insanity defense.

Dr. Slattery described Karl's 'indifferent' attitude during the tests when the witness said, "As he gave responses, and murder themes, Chapman showed lack of emotion considering the situation the boy was in at the time."

Martin O'Neil jumped at the term "Murder Theme" and asked the doctor to explain the meaning of the term.

"This was in his story on one of the three TAT (thermatic perception tests)"

The doctor further explained that Karl was shown a picture of a woman partially exposed in bed with a man, fully clothed, walking away. Chapman gave the following account,

"This guy may have done something that he's sorry for now. It's just that he walked in on the scene and he can't look at it any more."

"It's just that it's somebody he liked who had a disease or something and died or was sick and died from it. He could be crying because she died.

He could have killed her, but didn't realize what he did until it was too late. It could have been beyond his will power, I guess. He couldn't stop himself. After it was all done, he was very sorry for it."

The spectators were noticing the similarity to the tragic events of the recent murders.

When Melvin Bonner approached the doctor on re-direct, Dr. Slattery repeated the story.

Bonner asked his witness to expand a bit further on the tests he conducted on the defendant.

"Well, I asked Mr. Chapman why the man killed the woman. The boy replied, 'it could have been an argument, it could have been anything. It must have been something to make him flip his lid. He couldn't help it'.

The doctor continued, "I asked what he thought would happen to the man? The boy said, 'He'll get caught and be punished for it'."

At one point during his testimony, the doctor was asked about the popular concept of the ink blot tests which he had used on Karl during one of his two visits.

He explained to the judge that considerable publicity had been given to these tests through the press and he was concerned that there was damage of impairing the future usefulness of these tests. They are accepted by psychologists all over the world, he said.

Martin O'Neil was quick to ask, "Why would you bring them into the court, if they were so secret?"

The witness replied, "I didn't think they would be given the publicity they have received."

The judge thought a few moments, and directed his reply to the witness,

"The jury is entitled to all evidence introduced here. It would be unfortunate if this system is impaired, but we, nonetheless, must give the jury a chance to know all about it. Jurors are ever in a position to appraise the testimony of medical men, therefore, they must have the right to understand what these tests are about."

The prosecutor reminded the doctor that he had placed the IQ of the defendant at 102.

O'Neil: "Doctor, according to your previous testimony, you placed the IQ of Karl Chapman at 102. Is this an average IQ?"

Slattery: "It is within the average range."

O'Neil: "What is the average range, doctor?"

Slattery: "90 to 109"

The doctor was becoming restless. Martin O'Neil was at his best. He asked the doctor what percentage of the population enjoyed this rating.

The doctor agreed to review a book on the subject of IQ matters and from that he agreed with the district attorney that 48% of the population could be so rated.

Now the district attorney was coming in for the kill.

O'Neil: "How many times did you visit the defendant for these tests?"

Slattery: "Twice in one day."

O'Neil: "Did you identify yourself to him?"

Slattery: "I do not recall."

O'Neil: "Did you tell him you were from the Northampton State Hospital?"

Slattery: "I cannot say."

O'Neil: "Did you tell him the purpose of the tests you were about to give him?"

Slattery: "I explained to him there were certain tests I was going to make."

O'Neil: "Doctor, did you tell him why you were giving him these tests?"

Slattery: "No."

The district attorney was bearing down on the witness. The doctor was showing signs of nervousness and occasionally wiped his brow with a handkerchief. He asked for a glass of water. The prosecutor continued.

O'Neil: "You knew he was charged with a very serious crime?"

Slattery: "Yes."

O'Neil: "Did you tell him you were giving him these tests to report to someone?"

Slattery: "I don't recall."

It was at this point, the prosecutor asked the doctor to select three of the cards which by popular concept depict a person or persons, or part of a person.

The doctor turned in the witness stand and addressed Judge Grishbaum directly. He pleaded with the judge not to reveal the popular concept of any of the test cards.

His plea fell on deaf ears, and Martin O'Neil took the cards that the doctor handed to him.

The first card was displayed to the jury, and the doctor was asked to identify it as the card that Chapman had identified as a Halloween mask.

The doctor declined to say that it could mean to him a Halloween mask on the grounds that he had received so many answers from subjects that his interpretation might be colored by his interpretation.

When pressed for an answer, he said the most popular concept of that card was either a butterfly or a bat.

O'Neil quickly swung the questioning to perception tests, which according to the doctor, required the subject to make up a story about the picture which included the events that led up to the picture, what was happening in the picture, how it turned out and the appearances and emotions of the people reflected in the picture.

The picture the district attorney selected was one of an older man with his arm outstretched, standing over a younger man reclining on a couch.

He asked, "What did Karl Chapman tell you about this picture?"

The doctor replied, "I can't think of anything except that maybe it's a soldier who has become exhausted by the trip. It is his father standing over him trying to see if he's really there. Sometimes people see things only in a dream, and reach out to see if it's only a dream. The father wants to make sure that it is real."

After a lengthy session that lasted the entire afternoon, the judge called the defense and the prosecution to the bench.

"Gentlemen, this witness will have to be held over until tomorrow morning. The hour is late, and I would like to adjourn for the day."

Neither the defense, nor the prosecution had any objections to the judge's decision.

As they returned to there places in the court, the judge admonished the jury, and called the court adjourned until 9:30 AM, Wednesday morning.

Tuesday, March 15. 1955 Stanfield Evening News

MENTAL EXPERT QUIZZED, D.A. ATTACKS THEORY
Chapman Was Mentally Ill On Night Of Murders
The defense put Dr. Charles Slattery on the witness stand for the entire day. Dr. Slattery is a notable Harvard Graduate and well respected in the field of psychiatry. Martin O'Neil attacked the doctor while testifying to the results of several tests he performed on the defendant at the Hampden County Jail. The district attorney challenged the reliability of the 'secreted' tests. Although the doctor showed signs of protest when asked to divulge popular concepts of his tests, Judge Grishbaum insisted he share all the results to the jury...

The reporters showed no mercy for the doctor's concerns and his attempts to protect the tests and the popular concepts of the potential subjects.

By now, the defense was shaking their heads and wringing their hands with frustration. They were counting on the doctor's testimony to lay the groundwork for the insanity plea. This was all they had to safe Karl from the electric chair.

The jury must find the defendant not guilty by reason of insanity. Martin O'Neil was knocking that theory down, piece by piece.

Bonner and LaBonte would be working around the clock to plan their next strategy. They were running out of time, and they were failing to gain any ground.

At the end of the day, Bonner and LaBonte visited Karl at the jail. They quizzed him regarding the tests, and how they had been presented to him. Karl could offer no assistance. He remained the disinterested party he had been since the beginning.

The district attorney was basking in the aftermath of a very good day. He was determined the defendant would not be declared insane. He still had his psychiatrists sitting in the gallery, listening to all the testimony, and he still reserved the right to call upon them at rebuttal. Martin O'Neil was in a very good place, and he was very confident.

Wednesday, March 16, 1955: Stanfield Morning Union:

DOCTOR TESTIFIED CHAPMAN'S MENTAL ILLNESS CURABLE
State Tries to Weaken Defense Illness Contention

After a lengthy testimony by defense witness Dr. Charles Slattery yesterday, the doctor concluded that the illness, schizophrenia and psycomotor epilepsy could possibly be cured. The District Attorney wrung this testimony from the Harvard Medical School doctor yesterday who took the stand for the defense and gave the first direct testimony that the accused was mentally ill. The doctor added that this mental condition stood a good chance of responding to treatment...

The court was called to order promptly at 9:30. All stood as Judge Grishbaum took the bench. He announced to the court, there would be a slight delay, and he would like to see all the councils in his chambers.

The jury was not in place, and the judge motioned that the defense as well as the prosecution were to follow him into chambers.

The judge explained that it had been brought to his attention, last evening, that juror #5, the accountant had suffered an appendicitis and was taken to the emergency room last evening.

He will be replaced, and the trial will continue uninterrupted.

This was the first occasion since passage of the law providing for two spare jurors in murder trials that its value had been proven in the Superior Court of Hampden.

The short recess ended, and the twelve of the thirteen jurors were brought into the courtroom.

The murder trial had evolved into a battle of minds over a mind. It appeared definite, now, that to save the defendant, defense attorneys Melvin Bonner and Eugene LaBonte must convince the all male jury that Karl was insane the night of the murders of Lynn Ann and David.

The prosecution called 18 witnesses in 2 ½ days to present its case. The defenses witnesses with lengthy psychiatric testimony, cross examination and rebuttal would substantially slow this pace.

Many persons following the case were puzzled. How could Chapman plead not guilty when police produced two separate copies of his signed confession? The answer was clear, in the Commonwealth, a plea of not guilty is mandatory on a charge of first degree murder. This procedure is based on the premise that a defendant is presumed innocent until proven guilty.

Another ironic fact came to light, and was discussed in the hallway during the breaks. If, Eugene LaBonte had been successful in the election of the District Attorney only a few months before, LaBonte would have been prosecuting the very case he was defending now!

Doctor Slattery was called to resume his testimony.

When asked about Karl's sexual prowess, the doctor testified that Karl had been reluctant to discuss possible sexual urges. He testified that Karl did reveal that when he was a freshman three girls refused him dates. The doctor was responding to questions that were asked during one of his two-hour long visits with Karl.

When asked what this indicated, the doctor explained,

"The refusal to divulge anything on this angle, might have been a possible factor, or cause of the crimes."

The question of sex in the murders was raised for the first time. The doctor spoke to the jury directly now. He seemed to be more at ease, facing them. He explained that all natural motives, including sex, were suggested to Chapman when he was under psychiatric examination.

The doctor was walked through the entire question and answer session that had been conducted by him to the defendant. Finally, the doctor was asked directly,

"Did the defendant's refusals to talk about a certain angle of the crimes indicate to you that there was no disorganization present?"

The doctor answered, "Yes."

O'Neil: "By the way Doctor, in your previous testimony, do you recall stating that the defendant claimed he 'walked around for about an hour' before committing the crimes?"

Slattery: "Yes, I remember that."

O'Neil: "Did you ever check with the parents of the defendant as to the accuracy of this statement?"

Slattery: "No sir, I did not."

The prosecutor then swiftly changed the line of questioning, again addressing the subject of epilepsy. He produced a book written by a renown expert in epilepsy. He asked Dr. Slattery his appraisal of this expert.

Dr. Slattery replied, "He is probably the world's greatest authority on epilepsy."

O'Neil: "I refer you to page 13 of this book, which deals with psycomotor epilepsy, and does this not state that during such seizures, there are spasms?"

Slattery: "Yes."

O'Neil: "Did Karl Chapman tell you he'd had spasms?"

Slattery: "No."

O'Neil: "Did the defendant ever mention having convulsions?"

Slattery: "No."

O'Neil: "Does it state here, that the subject may act automatically and appear to be confused or stupid?"

Slattery (hesitantly): "Well, if that's what appears in the book, I'd have to say yes."

O'Neil: "Did this young defendant, at any time Doctor, say that he felt confused?"

Slattery: "No."

O'Neil: "At any time, in your opinion, did Karl Chapman appear to be stupid?"

Slattery: "The whole story indicates that Chapman specifically was not aware of everything that was happening."

O'Neil: "Doctor, when you talked to him, was he confused?"

Slattery: "He was confused to details."

O'Neil: "Did he not give you almost complete details of what transpired on the night of September 25th?"

Slattery: (almost inaudibly) "Only three or four of the details."

The prosecutor had done his homework and quickly turned his attention to another publication by the recognized expert.

O'Neil: "Do you agree with the opinion that there is a ratio of 40 to 1 against inheritance of tendencies toward epilepsy?"

Dr. Slattery agreed with this opinion. Then the doctor continued, offering that Karl had told him, "I remember the hand striking, but, I thought it belonged to somebody else."

O'Neil then asked the doctor about a cure for epilepsy. The doctor responded, "Yes, there is a cure."

O'Neil: "Do you believe there would have been a cure in this case?"

Slattery: "I think there would have been a good chance, yes."

O'Neil: "In the matter of schizophrenia?"

Slattery: "I think there would be a very good chance of a cure."

O'Neil: "When a person is in a seizure of schizophrenia, does he not lose memory of details?"

Slattery: "No, he may suffer no lose, partial, or complete. There is nothing positive about it."

The district attorney concluded his cross examination of Dr. Slattery displaying a recent magazine article.

O'Neil asked, "Dr. Slattery, I have a recent issue of the New England Journal of Medicine. Did you contribute an article to this publication?" The doctor confirmed that he had.

"Is it entitled, the "Clinical Definition of Love?"

"Yes it is," replied the doctor.

"Isn't it in respect to psycho analysis?" Asked the prosecutor.

"It is in respect to my total training." Replied the doctor.

"No further questions." The District Attorney completed his questioning. He was confident he had made his point.

"Mr. Bonner?" Asked Judge Grishbaum.

Melvin Bonner picked up the re-direct questioning addressing an earlier point that had been raised by the prosecution.

"Dr. Slattery," he began. "When asked in earlier testimony can you recall and repeat to the jury the definition of the word 'insanity'?"

"The word insanity is not used by medical men. It is however, used in the law in the difference between right and wrong."

Bonner: "In your opinion, was Karl Chapman insane at the time of the murders?"

Slattery: "Based on my medical knowledge and experience, I would say Mr. Chapman was definitely mentally impaired."

Melvin Bonner then turned the subject of the results of the electroencephalographs referred to in the trial as EGG.

"Dr. Slattery, why did you suggest a third EEG test of the defendant. Wasn't two sufficient to get accurate results?"

The doctor answered, "I ordered a third one, because it was brought to my attention that the subject had been taking barbiturates to help him sleep. When the third test was ordered, the subject had been taken off the drugs three days before the test to obviate the possibility that the drug may induce an excess of negative brain waves."

"Thank you doctor." Replied Bonner.

"No further questions."

The judge excused the witness, and adjourned for lunch.

Melvin Bonner and Eugene LaBonte went directly to their office. They wasted no time, they had to make a decision. Would Karl Chapman take the stand in his defense? They weighed both sides, and it didn't take long, they agreed, the defendant would not be taking the stand. When the court convened at 1:00, the defense stood.

"Your Honor, the defense rests its case."

The courtroom was buzzing. The defendant looked directly at the defense table. It was the first indication he was actually paying attention to what was going on around him.

Throughout the trial, he had been placed in the 'cage' and sat hour after hour devoid of all emotion. The statement from his attorneys surely got his attention. He looked frightened, for the first time since his arrest.

Mr. Chapman leaned forward. He was seated directly behind the defense table.

After a short conversation, he leaned back, folded his arms and appeared to be angry, but he remained silent, pursing his lips and glancing at Karl. Karl did not catch his glance. Mrs. Chapman was not present.

The Rosen's had not attended the trial. The only appearance of the Rosen's was the day Mr. Rosen was called to testify.

Mr. Clarke attended all but this day. His wife was not feeling well, and he was weary from the daily trial proceedings. He decided to remain with Elaine.

Gordon and Millie Schaefer never missed a day. They were there representing the Rosens, sparing them the anguish. Mrs. Brazzini, the Rosen's neighbor was seen occasionally in the gallery.

Wednesday, March 16, 1955 Stanfield Evening News

CHAPMAN TRIAL NEARING CLOSE
May Be Given to Jury Sometime Tomorrow State Expert to Testify

To the surprise of all, the defense rested it's case this afternoon. The prosecution is expected to put on its rebuttal witness tomorrow. It has been learned the rebuttal witness is to be Dr. Frederick Klopper, a state psychiatrist who has interviewed the defendant on several occasions. At the conclusion of the doctor's testimony, the prosecution is expected to rest his case...

The courtroom was astonished that the defense rested so abruptly. It was doubtful they had convinced the jury that Karl Chapman was insane at the time of the murders. Melvin Bonner was not optimistic and Eugene LaBonte had all but thrown his hands up.

The defendant was not in the least helpful, and Mr. Chapman had become alienated from the defense team when he sat day after day, watching Martin O'Neil gaining ground. He was prepared for the worse.

In his mind, the worse would be, Karl would receive a guilty verdict and be sentenced to life in prison without any possibility of parole. He never considered the death penalty.

Steven Logan and Raymond Gage were present in the courtroom throughout the testimony of Dr. Slattery. They walked away feeling confident that his testimony was not in the least convincing, and Karl Chapman was doomed.

Unlike Mr. Chapman, the two detectives never considered the sentence would be life in prison without parole. They were convinced, Karl would receive no mercy from this jury. They would recommend death by electrocution.

Karl remained calm and unaffected by the overall proceedings. The trial literally held his life in the balance, and yet he continued to sleep well, and ate with his usual insatiable appetite.

Mr. and Mrs. Rosen were reportedly taking the appropriate steps to adopt a child. They had moved to nearby Connecticut, and were anxious to put the trial behind them, and start their lives over. Mrs. Rosen became active with the adoption procedure.

Daniel was enrolled in a new school, and the notoriety of the September 25th murders had begun to subside. At least outside of the City of Stanfield.

Mrs. Clarke was looking forward to the arrival of a new baby, expected in about one month. Barbara was excited, and Phil Clarke was back to work full time, with the exception of the time he would take to attend the trial.

Karl Chapman was not the focus of the victims' families. They refused to allow his demise to consume their lives or add to their grief. They put Karl in the abyss of their minds, and began getting on with their lives.

Thursday, March 17, 1955: Stanfield Morning Union

D.A. EXPECTED TO CALL EXPERT TODAY
It is expected the testimony of Dr. Frederick Klopper will be the final testimony of the Chapman murder trial. The trial of Karl Chapman, who's life is held in the balance, could end today with the Commonwealth's main witness. When District Attorney Martin O'Neil was asked today,

"How do you feel about your case?" The district attorney answered with a confident smile, "I believe we've done our job, we've represented the Commonwealth, and the case should go to the jury tomorrow. I'm sure the jury will do the right thing, and return a guilty verdict without recommendation of mercy...."

There was no question the district attorney had every reason to believe he would prevail in this case. The defense had virtually no where to go with this case. They were carrying the burden of Karl's life. Life in prison, might be the best news they would be able to deliver to Karl. The only decision that would be favorable and considered 'a win' would be not guilty by reason of insanity. That would carry a recommendation of commitment to the State Mental Facility, and a possibility of release. It was not a likely possibility, but Karl would be allowed to live a reasonable life.

Thursday, March 17,1955: Stanfield Evening News:

D.A.'S EXPERT WITNESS, CHAPMAN NOT MENTALLY ILL
Dr. Frederick Klopper Declares Youth Not Victim of Epilepsy

Judge Albert Grishbaum announced this afternoon that "all evidence is closed" in the case of Karl T. Chapman on trial for two murders, as the case moved swiftly to a close. Dr. Klopper declared, "Karl Chapman is not a normal person" although he has no mental illness. Dr. Klopper, state neuropsychiatrist, admitted during cross-examination today at the 19-year-old's murder trial in Superior Court. Dr. Klopper gave his opinion that Chapman is "possibly maladjusted" during cross-examination by defense Attorney Melvin Bonner...

The prosecution called his rebuttal witness, Dr. Frederick Klopper, PhD. Dr. Klopper's credentials were impeccable. He was a graduate of Harvard. He held a position on the board of directors at the Northampton State Hospital, taught classes at Harvard and continued his private practice. He couldn't have been a more impressive witness in this case, and he was the prosecutor's rebuttal witness.

Included in the extensive questioning by the D.A., the doctor established the point that Karl was, at best, maladjusted. The doctor formed his opinion based on questioning of the defendant's emotional reactions after the bloody murders.

After the prosecution questioned its expert witness, Dr. Klopper, the defense cross examined.

Melvin Bonner asked the doctor if in his opinion a normal, healthy American boy "could perpetrate these crimes with the mere motive of being angry because his sister was snubbed."

The doctor answered, "Yes." He immediately followed this affirmative reply with,

"Chapman is not mentally ill, but is maladjusted.." He brought up the testimony of the defense's witness, Dr. Charles Slattery, challenging the defense witnesses's diagnosis, psychomotor epilepsy.

Dr. Klopper stated that if Chapman were a psycomotor epileptic at the time of the murders and in a seizure at the time of the murders, he would not have remembered all of the details he had given.

The defense council pressed further. The doctor stood his ground and repeated that at no time did he find any evidence of this rare type of epilepsy.

Again, Bonner pursued this point to bring out from Dr. Klopper that there could be a partial amnesia during this type of epileptic seizure. The doctor declared, positively there is no memory at all while victims are in such a psychomotor seizure.

He added that during a three-hour period of questioning at the jail, one of the victims was referred to by the doctor as "Miss Clarke" and Chapman adopted the same use of Lynn Ann's name in his answers.

Trying another approach, Melvin Bonner sought to bring out that daydreaming was a symptom of schizophrenia, but the doctor rejected this interpretation.

Feeling frustration, the defense attorney tried to bring out from the doctor his interpretation of a man wishing he had a million dollars to spend in Florida at the present time. Dr. Klopper said that this was better described as wishful thinking, a more acceptable description than daydreaming.

After two hours on the stand, Melvin Bonner 'passed the witness'.

The prosecution had no need for a re-direct examination of this witness. The doctor's testimony was powerful, and Martin O'Neil was not about to disturb what appeared to be the most convincing expert testimony he had ever experienced in a capital case.

Court was adjourned following the prosecution's rebuttal witness.

Friday, March 18, 1955 Stanfield Morning Union:

FINAL ARGUMENTS EXPECTED TODAY IN DOUBLE MURDER TRIAL
Judge Rejects Defense Move, Insanity Plea Denied
After all witnesses were heard, the court was recessed early yesterday afternoon. Judge Grishbaum rejected the defense motion to enter an insanity plea. The judge ordered the trial of the defendant recessed until 9:00 Friday morning. The final arguments will be presented at that time.

Although the motion was formally denied by the judge, the issue of Chapman's sanity or insanity would be left to the jury to decide, despite the testimony of Dr. Slattery, defense expert.

Melvin Bonner brought attention to the judge in the matter of Singlinger, who had testified for the prosecution. Dr. Singlinger had testified that he never personally examined Karl, but that he had supervision of 1600 epileptics at the state institution.

Basing his opinion merely on a study of Chapman's history, test results and on the testimony he was allowed to listen to in court, Dr. Singlinger said the defendant was not suffering from any form of epilepsy during the commission of the crime. Melvin Bonner argued that this testimony should not be considered by the jury.

He claimed that the admission from Dr. Singlinger that he had never even met the defendant should not be admissible. He claimed that Dr. Singlinger testified as an 'expert' and that his testimony was not that of what the court considered 'expert' testimony.

The doctor had also declared that complete loss of memory was a part of this rare type of epilepsy and that Karl had remembered all the details of the murders. Bonner felt this was very inflammatory, and could prejudice the jury. He also stated that there was no evidence of hallucinations or delusions, which would be present in that type of illness.

The entire case for the defense was based on the claim Karl suffered schizophrenia and psychomotor epilepsy, something Martin O'Neil, representing the Commonwealth vehemently denied.

Several bench conferences continued through the morning session, and into the afternoon. Most concerned the defense council's insanity plea. The judge would not be swayed, and insisted, insanity or sanity would be in the hands of the jury. He concluded that, "all evidence is closed."

Friday, March 18, 1955 Stanfield Evening News

CLOSING ARGUMENTS BEGAN TODAY IN THE CHAPMAN TRIAL

D.A. Demands Death Verdict, Defense Insists Chapman Insane

Spectators in a packed courtroom sat tensely as the defense attorney, Melvin Bonner and the prosecutor, Martin O'Neil argued main points in the trial in which the chief issue had been Chapman's sanity or insanity...

The defense spoke to the jury. For the most part Melvin Bonner spoke in a mild manner, in tones that at times could not be heard beyond the jury

.He told the jury that Karl could not distinguish right from wrong the night he murdered Lynn Ann Clarke and David Rosen. The crime was "the act of a demented mind." He repeatedly hammered that there is reasonable doubt that the defendant did not know right from wrong. As the defense labored to save Karl's life, Karl showed no emotion. Mr. and Mrs. Chapman looked straight ahead.

Phil Clarke buried his head in his hands.

Melvin Bonner continued telling the jury he would not appeal to their emotions. He spoke at length on the American tradition of justice. He accused the prosecutor of appealing to the juror's emotions in referring to the brutality of the crime and referring to the murder weapon as bayonet.

As he worked into the insanity defense, Bonner said the days when law called for "an eye for an eye and a tooth for a tooth" disappeared 3,000 years ago.

"We don't punish the body - we punish something much higher," he said. "We don't punish animals - they don't know what they are doing."

Melvin Bonner positioned himself directly in front of the jury. In a gentle voice, he said, "Gentlemen, you all know the defense in this case is insanity. You, the jury will decide whether this boy is sane or insane, not the experts or witnesses who took the stand."

The defense attorney's closing argument was lengthy, and compelling. He addressed every portion of the witnesses testimony. He challenged the prosecution experts, and reiterated the testimony of Dr. Charles Slattery, expert witness for the defense.

He urged the jury to first consider what happened at the time of the crime, not what occurred before or after.

"It all boils down to the fact that on that night, did the defendant have the mental ability to determine right from wrong?"

He referred to the testimony describing schizophrenia and commented that Karl couldn't prevent himself.

He boldly stated that the act was committed because of an irresistible impulse, not intellect, not intent, not even reason. He went on to convince the jury that Karl had a split personality and was suffering an epileptic attack at the time of the dual murders.

He made reference to Dr. Jekyll and Mr. Hyde. He stated that Chapman's ability to be a good Boy Scout at one time and lose his grasp on reality at another time was the same thing.

Bonner then addressed the 66 lacerations. The fact that most of the 66 lacerations were in one place on the bodies showed "no design". He said that was significant that there was no aiming at the heart or genital organs.

Then, addressing the prosecutor as "my brother" he accused Martin O'Neil of 'laughing off' the butterflies and ink spots.

"These tests, gentlemen, were an honest search to find the defendant's hidden emotions."

Bonner quoted the prosecutor. He added that the prosecutor contended Chapman was a "sophisticated 18-year-old boy" who could curb his emotions. Melvin continued, "A hardened man like 'Machine Gun Kelly' could do this, but not Mr. Chapman."

He continued explaining Karl's failure to dispose of the weapon and his service as a pallbearer at Lynn Ann's funeral. He stated that behavior could only be the product of a split personality.

He dwelt at length on the fact that the 'very competent and experienced district attorney, as well as seasoned detectives', were unable to find a real motive.

In his final statement to the jury, Melvin Bonner's last words were. "I looked at the picture of my two sons this morning. When arriving at the courthouse today, I looked at Karl Chapman and said to myself, 'There but for the grace of God stands my son'."

After delivering this poignant statement, he concluded his closing argument and walked to the defense table.

He looked to Mr. and Mrs. Chapman. He hoped to detect a favorable, perhaps even an encouraging look on the faces of Karl's parents. They did not meet his glance.

Eugene LaBonte reached over to move the chair beside him, allowing his co-counsel to be seated. Melvin removed his glasses, rubbed his eyes slightly and took his seat.

Karl remained phlegmatic throughout the proceedings wherein he heard himself denounced as a brutal killer on the one hand and a confused, irrational boy on the other. He did not react to either description.

The judge addressed the court,

"The defense has completed its closing argument. The court will take a recess for lunch, and upon returning, the prosecution will deliver the closing argument for the Commonwealth."

With that announcement, the judge ordered the jury out and retired to his chambers.

It was noted, a total of seven motions for a directed verdict of innocent by reason of insanity were filed. All were denied.

After an hour, the courtroom was packed again. Spectators were still spilling out into the hallways where they would remain throughout the session. The jury was led in by the bailiff and the judge took his seat.

He called the court to order and asked that the prosecutor proceed with his closing arguments on behalf of the Commonwealth of Massachusetts.

Martin O'Neil stood, walked to the jury box and greeted them with a cordial "Good afternoon, gentlemen."

His manner quickly changed. His opening remark came across loud and demanding.

"First degree murder, without recommendation of mercy. This, Gentlemen of the jury, is the only verdict that you should consider."

In a vigorous point-by-point attack on defense arguments for Chapman, Martin O'Neil engaged in a bitter denunciation of the efforts of defense expert witness Dr. Charles Slattery.

The matter of ethics had been alluded to briefly by Melvin Bonner in his summary for the defense and O'Neil, in a ringing voice declared,

"And they bring up the question of ethics in this case."

He went on to say that it was not until early in the beginning of the case that "the shrewd Dr. Slattery" decided to add psychomotor epilepsy to his previous finding. And it was not until after the visit of Dr. Slattery, did the matter of being impelled toward Lynn Ann on the murder night as "steel drawn by a magnet" had entered into any of Chapman's replies to questions.

O'Neil was sparing nothing. He rebuked the testimony in the matter of the difficult birth of the accused. He accused the defense of injecting this into the minds of the jury that he might have suffered a brain injury.

"I believe the Commonwealth has proven Karl Chapman guilty of murder in the first degree by reason of deliberation, premeditation and with malice aforethought, and with extreme atrocity and cruelty.

This was proven by the fact that Chapman had taken his father's hat and jacket on the rainy night for a disguise rather than protection.

He carried a concealed bayonet. This is extreme indication of premeditation."

He continued. "Let's face it, Gentlemen, teenagers today can't be induced to wear hats."

The prosecutor was becoming animated and considerably louder as his argument mounted against the defendant. Again he attacked the credibility of the defense expert witness Dr. Slattery.

He reminded the jury that Dr. Slattery had attributed Chapman's sharp memory of details of the crime and the events that preceded and followed it to 'confabulation'. In other words an ability to try to fill in forgotten details.

"Well, Gentlemen," he continued, standing directly in front of the jury, "the defendant remembered the last words of Lynn Ann. Her last words were, "Karl, what are you doing here?"

He turned and pointed directly to the defendant seated in the cage and said, "I am going to change two words, '**Karl, what were you doing there**'?"

"Only he knows the answer to that. Why did he go in there?" The prosecutor's voice was booming!

"He went in to kill, that's right gentlemen, kill! Not to frighten her! Else, why didn't he just rub his fingers against the window pane? That would have frightened a young girl."

Next, Martin O'Neil addressed the matter of Lynn Ann's funeral. He reminded the jury that Karl had been pall bearer at Lynn's funeral because he didn't want to arouse suspicion by declining.

"He didn't throw the knife away as an expert had stated a plotting criminal might do, because that would be the one act which would have led the police to him within a few days of the crime. Karl T. Chapman was rational enough to know that!"

And in closing, Martin O'Neil was as abrupt as his opening.

"We know when the crime was committed. We know who committed the crime. We all heard the testimony of Dr. Klopper, Karl Chapman was legally sane.

What we don't know for certain is why? Was it anger, lust, love, revenge? It is not the responsibility of the Commonwealth to establish motive, as my brother has alluded to.

We may never know the 'why'. But we do know for certain what happened on the evening of September 25, 1954. Karl Chapman, with premeditation did butcher two young people. Lynn Ann Smith and David Rosen are dead and Karl Theodore Chapman, with malice in his heart killed them!"

"The only reasonable verdict you can return, Gentlemen, is guilty of two counts of first degree murder. No recommendation of mercy."

After the prosecution had completed his summation, the judge asked the defendant to rise. He faced the six foot three defendant and said,

"In this type of case, you have the privilege of saying whatever you want without making a sworn statement, do you have anything to say?"

In a soft, controlled voice, Karl Chapman answered. "No sir."

The judge called the defense councils and the prosecutor to the bench. They briefly discussed what the charge to the jury would include, as well, as what would not be included. At this time, the judge advised that he omitted manslaughter from one of the possible verdicts.

"In this case, there is no evidence that would justify a finding of manslaughter. In this case it's either murder, or not."After the lengthy discussion, the councilors returned to their respective tables and waited for the jury charge.

The judge swivelled his chair, positioning it to allow a straight ahead, full view of the all male jury. His charge to the jury was direct and precise. He gave the jury the option of returning any of these verdicts:

- Conviction of first degree murder, death in the electric chair
- Conviction of first degree murder, with a recommendation that the death penalty should not be imposed, life imprisonment, with no possibility of parole.
-Acquittal
-Acquittal by reason of insanity

The judge began his charge to the jury,

"Make true deliverance of this prisoner who is in your charge. You have got to throw away any and all prejudices or sympathies. Our basic passions that we have must be set aside..."

The judge stated the standard admonishments to the jury. He explained that there must be a unanimous decision. They were to take their time, discuss the case amongst themselves and deliver a fair and just verdict.

If one or more of the jurors felt a need for clarification of the judge's instructions, or needed a reading of any part of the testimony, they were to request it in writing and hand the note to the bailiff.

He recited all the legal jargon that is standard in charging the jury. In closing, the judge said,

"You twelve men are the final arbiters. Deliberate wisely, considering all the testimony you have heard over the past eleven days."

The thirteenth juror, the alternate, was excused and allowed to leave. The Insurance investigator was selected as foreman. He was one of the jurors that were brought in from the street by the deputy sheriffs because of the shortage of prospects.

Upon rendering a unanimous verdict, they were instructed to signal the court by ringing a buzzer three times.

The jury filed out of the jury box. Each displayed a somber look. The life of Karl T. Chapman was in their hands after an 11-day trial.

The judge notified each side that they would have a one hour notification once the jury notified him they had reached a verdict.

After the judge dismissed the court and left the bench, the prisoner was shackled, and led from the courtroom. The spectators waited until Karl, escorted by two deputy sheriffs was out of sight.

Slowly, the courtroom emptied, with the exception of the defense attorneys.

Bonner, LaBonte and Miss Lewis remained at the defense table. It was difficult to comprehend that the trial had come to an end, and now the waiting. It was quiet in the hallows of the ancient marble floored courtroom.

Melvin shuffled papers around, putting them back into order. Eugene LaBonte gathered the stack of notebooks Miss Lewis had compiled throughout the trial, along with the corresponding transcripts she had typed. It had been a long journey, and now the finale would be left to the twelve men seated only one room away.

It was 3:15 P.M., on Friday. It was likely, a Friday verdict would be delivered. If not, the jury would be sequestered until they reached their decision.

Reporters paced in the hallways. The banks of telephones on the far wall of the downstairs lobby were all occupied.

Spectators were milling around throughout the building. The tension was in the air. The Chapman's were nowhere to be seen. Phil Clarke had left the courtroom soon after the judge had charged the jury.

He needed to be with Elaine. He had no opinion of what the fate of Karl Chapman, the killer of his daughter, should be. Nothing would bring Lynn Ann back, but he hoped that Karl would be 'put away' in respect for the safety of all.

There was no doubt of his guilt. The question was, would the jury recommend mercy? It was anyone's guess.

Four hours and twenty six minutes later, the buzzer sounded three times, indicating the jury had reached a verdict. It was 8:35 P.M., Friday, March 18, 1955.

Saturday, March 19, 1955 Stanfield Morning Union

CHAPMAN GUILTY IN 1ST DEGREE
Mandatory Electric Chair Penalty Will Be Result of Verdict; Leniency Not Asked By Jury

The schoolboy killer was found guilty of premeditated murder of baby sitter and child here, six months ago.

Karl T. Chapman, 19, was found guilty of 2 counts of murder in the first degree, without recommendation of mercy, by a jury in Superior Court late yesterday.

This verdict calls for a sentence of execution in the electric chair...

The grim faces of the jurors gave an ominous hint of what they had decided. After reading the roll of jurors, the clerk of courts called,

"Karl T. Chapman." The defendant answered, "Here," firmly but quietly.

Judge Albert Grishbaum ordered, "Have the defendant stand." Chapman stood. The clerk then turned to the jury.

"Have you agreed on a verdict?"

"We have," the foreman answered.

"What say you, Mr. Foreman?"

"Guilty."

The courtroom buzzed, after the verdict was announced.

The judge ordered, "Silence in my courtroom!"

Then he addressed the jury directly. He called attention to the fact that there were two separate charges of murder, one for the murder of baby sitter Lynn Ann Clarke, and the other for four year old David Rosen. The jury answered guilty of both charges, with no recommendation of mercy.

Mrs. Chapman slumped forward in her seat. Mr. Chapman put his arm around her and lowered his head. Karl's face remained immobile and without expression as it had through most of the trial.

The judge thanked the jury and commented,

"I realize you have had a pretty hard task." With that comment, the trial ended and the jury was excused.

Mr. Clarke held his head in his hands and wept. Michael Clarke handed his brother a handkerchief .Gordon Schaefer, seated beside the grieving father laid his hand on Mr. Clarke's shoulder.

As Mr. Clarke reached for the handkerchief, a deputy sheriff approached the slumped man. The deputy bent down and whispered in Mr. Clarke's ear. Without hesitation, Mr. Clarke rose and rushed from the courtroom, leaving Millie and Gordon Schaefer to wonder what was so important that would call Phil Clarke out of the courtroom at such a critical time. Michael rushed out behind his brother.

Phil Clarke raced to Mercy Hospital. Mrs. Clarke had been admitted only an hour earlier. By the time Phil arrived, he was informed that his wife was in satisfactory condition, but, had given birth prematurely, and the baby had not survived.

Phil Clarke crumbled and was led to the doctor's lounge. He lay on the leather sofa. The doctor sat across from him and explained that Elaine was doing well. Phil sobbed. The tension of the 11-day trial, finally the verdict, and now, the death of a baby was just more than he could take.

He pounded the wall, and screamed, "Chapman has killed two of my children! He's killed my baby, just as sure as he killed Lynn Ann!"

Michael wrapped himself around his brother in an attempt to force him onto the sofa. The doctor consoled Mr. Clarke, but it was clear the man was broken and it would take time for him to maintain his composure and be able to visit his wife.

At the courtroom, Karl stood unblinking as he heard the fatal words sentencing him to die by the passage of a current of electricity through his body. His parents, who had bared family secrets in their all-out fight to save his life from the death penalty sat behind 'the cage'.

Mrs. Chapman wept uncontrollably. Mr. Chapman attempted to console his wife, while trying to keep his own emotions at bay.

The reporters, some with photographers, scribbled notes while flashbulbs popped, until the judge ordered all cameramen out of the courtroom. They obliged the judge's order, but some left with photos that would make their way into the lead story.

The morning edition ran a collage of photos chronologically depicting the brutal double homicide.

The pictures span across the entire page, starting with photos of the victims, Lynn Ann Clark and David Rosen.

The next photo showed pictures of David's casket being placed in a hearse, then of mourners gathered around the small grave site.

A picture of the long bayonet used in the slaying. was beside a picture of Karl's parents and then a picture of Karl being escorted into court. Finally a rare picture of Karl Chapman sitting in 'the cage' inside the courtroom.

It was noted that the Chapman trial photos had set a new record. The pictorial coverage of the trial was the greatest of any Western Massachusetts news story, with the exception of the 1938 hurricane.

By actual count, 90 photographs of trial participants, crowds and the trial setting appeared in the Stanfield newspapers from the opening day to the verdict delivery. It was the largest number of photographs used in any regular edition on one story. The flood pictures had appeared in a special pictorial supplement.

Saturday, March 19, 1955 Stanfield Evening News:

NEW CHAPMAN TRIAL ASKED
Defense Readies Appeal; Says Time Insufficient To Test Youth's Sanity

Melvin Bonner rapped the state's insistence on "speedy trial". Bonner will petition the judge for a new trial, and insists he will appeal to the Supreme Court if denied it.

The councilor for the convicted murderer, announced today that a motion will be filed in the Hampden County Superior Court for a new trial. The appeal motion will be heard by Judge Albert Grishbaum, the judge that presided over the trial which ended with a jury verdict of guilty of murder in the first degree, and no recommendation of mercy which carries the mandatory death penalty...

The defense councils, Melvin Bonner and Eugene LaBonte wasted no time to file their appeal. Eugene LaBonte announced that if the appeal was denied, it would be filed with the Massachusetts Supreme Court.

The appeal would be based upon the contention that the findings of the jury were against the weight of evidence and errors in the trial.

Eugene LaBonte also claimed that the defense did not have sufficient time or opportunity to arrange for further brain wave tests, electroencephalographs (EEG's) that would have established the insanity of Chapman.

He said that an indefinite 'stay of execution' was in effect until the defense was prepared to argue the appeal to the high court.

"Mr. Chapman has been deprived of his constitutional rights as an American because of the insistence of the prosecutor of a swift, speedy trial. This deprived the defense the chance to establish the insanity of the accused youth." Eugene LaBonte stated before the throngs of media personnel.

LaBonte went on to explain that more brain wave tests would establish that his client, Karl Chapman was not guilty, by reason of insanity. He insisted that the testimony of the two medical men brought in by the defense, should be fortified with more testing.

Meanwhile, Phil Clarke stayed with Elaine at Mercy Hospital. Barbara was about to be dealt more heartbreaking news. Elaine Clarke seemed to be handling the news of the still born child better than the doctor had anticipated she would. She consoled Phil, and offered to break the news to Barbara 'in her own way.'

The Schaefer's had delivered the news of the verdict to the Rosen's. They displayed very little interest in anything concerning the nightmare of September 25th. They did agree with the verdict, but were not comfortable with the death sentence that would be imposed.

Karl Chapman remained impassive, John and Marge Chapman visited him shortly after the verdict was delivered. They wondered how Karl would handle his sentence to be put to death by electrocution.

Karl maintained the unruffled calm that had characterized him throughout the trial.

The guards at the jail remarked that there had been no change in him whatsoever. They couldn't understand it either. He continued to eat and sleep just as he had before the sentencing. The guards were instructed to maintain a twenty-four-hour vigil on the convicted murderer. Although Karl did not display any sign of suicide, the order was put in place, as a precaution.

The Sheriff was instructed to take Karl from Hampden County Jail and deliver him to Charleston State Prison on Monday morning. A warrant of commitment would be obtained from the clerk of the Superior court.

After Karl was delivered to Charleston, it was expected he would be confined in the death house at the prison.

He would be allowed to bring with him whatever personal articles he had with him at the time of his initial incarceration and what had been brought to him since then.

The sheriff had agreed that Karl's parents would have unlimited visitations over the weekend, if they desired. No request for visitation came from John or Marge Chapman.

Sunday, March 20, 1955: Stanfield Sunday Republican

CHAPMAN DEATH CAN BE FIRST IN NEW CHAIR
Modern Prison Has Latest Electrocution Equipment;
Last Execution in 1947

Karl T. Chapman, 19, in addition to being one of the youngest persons in state history to be sentenced to the electric chair, may also be the first to be executed in the chair installed in the new Massachusetts State Prison at Norfolk.

Chapman, sentenced to death on two murder counts after he was found guilty by a Superior Court jury of the stab-slaying of Lynn Ann Clarke, 14-year-old baby sitter, and her 4-year-old charge, David Rosen is expected to be taken to the prison Monday, from Hampden County Jail to await execution...

The Sunday Republican carried a brief headline story of Karl's fate. It lacked the sensationalism readers had come to expect. The article described the new electric chair, and that Karl could be the first to put it to use.

Karl would not be the youngest Massachusetts man to die for his crimes. In 1942, an eighteen year old was put to death in the old State Prison in Boston. The last execution to take place in the Commonwealth occurred in 1947. Two men, one 35, the other 31, were put to death for the slaying of a Massachusetts Marine.

John and Marge Chapman gathered Brenda from Mrs. Chapman's sister's and returned home after their brief visit with Karl. They would not visit him again before his transport to Charleston State Prison on Monday morning.

Monday, March 21, 1955: Stanfield Morning Union

12 KILLED, 23 HURT ON PLANE
Many Critically Injured in Springfield, MO Crash; Cause Is Still a Mystery

A terrible vibration was felt as Convair came in for landing. The mud was so bad ambulances were delayed for 2 ½ hours. No fire was reported on the plane.

An American Airlines plane threaded its way through darkness and rain toward a landing field crashed last night, killing 12 passengers and injuring 23.

The twin engine Convair crashed in a pasture about two miles north of the Springfield Airport. Wreckage was scattered over 300 feet. The plane carried a 3-member crew and 32 passengers. All the survivors were injured...

The Stanfield Morning Union made no mention of Karl Chapman's trial, verdict or sentence of death.

The newspapers had moved on, so it seemed. After six months of every conceivable aspect of Karl Chapman's crime.

Lengthy articles along with pictures of the victims had been the featured stories, almost daily for the past six months. Now, it was over, except for a short article on page 4.

Chapman Trial Bills Reach $8,480
With Expected Demand for Transcripts, Cost May Hit $12,000

Bills totaling $8,480 had been recorded in the office of County Treasurer's office. Not all known bills have yet been received and it is estimated that the cost will reach $12,000.00

The payroll for officers of the court, entertainment of the trial jurors, transportation and meals for the officers are now fixed at $4,520.

The payrolls for jurors were $2,566.00 and for the lone court stenographer, the present bill for services and expenses is $400.00 Yet to be determined and submitted is the bill for transcripts. Up to now, the official court stenographer has had no order for transcripts but with appeals in the offing, it is certain that the official documents will be ordered in the near future.

These come at the rate of 25 cents a folio for the first copy and 10 cents for additional copies. Folios run about three to a page and when completed the county will have another sizable bill for the prosecution's copies.

Not all of the bills for experts used by the state have been received and the total of $670.00 already submitted may fade considerably before the week is over.

Now, it appeared the biggest aftermath of the most publicized trial of the City of Stanfield was the accounting! After months of coverage, the only article to appear on the morning immediately following a guilty verdict and subsequent death sentence was the reports of how much it would cost the county.

Monday, March 21, 1955: Stanfield Evening News:

CHAPMAN LEAVES HAMPDEN COUNTY JAIL
Convicted Murderer Heads for Charleston Prison

Only six people came to see convicted youth enter a car for trip to Boston. Chapman still showed no sign of emotion over the death sentence. His face was a mask, as usual as the sheriff whisked him out the front door of the jail to the awaiting chauffeur-driven black automobile.

Precisely six people, none who were identified, stood outside the jail to watch Chapman depart. Chapman's parents were not at the youth's departure from Stanfield for the last time.

A woman took in the scene from a second floor window of an apartment house near the State Street Jail.

It was 9:30, when Karl was taken to the vehicle that would take him from his hometown for the last time.

There was a cold March wind blowing, and Karl wore a suit, and heavy overcoat. The sheriff was in civilian clothes and accompanied the prisoner in the back seat of the black automobile.

A chauffeur drove young Karl Chapman to Charleston, the death house. The 19 year old's first chauffeur driven trip, and it was to keep an appointment with the executioner at Charleston State Prison.

Whether he would get the supreme penalty was still a matter to be determined, but, he was, to all intents and purposes leaving Stanfield forever.

John and Marge Chapman, were not at the jail to see Karl leave. No other principals of the trial were present. His attorney's were absent, and there were no friends or acquaintances of Karl's at his departure. Only six strangers, curiosity seekers.

The car pulled out of the jail's parking lot, turned left, and headed east. In the front seat of the automobile was a cardboard carton tied with a piece of twine. The carton contained the personal effects he was allowed to take with him to the cell allotted to him. There, he would wait out the hours, days, and weeks that would lie ahead while his attorneys carried on a last ditch legal fight to save him from the electric chair.

Karl leaned back in the seat, anticipating a long ride. He remained expressionless. His attitude appeared to be that of resignation. Perhaps his courage was holding up based on the possibility of a new trial, or at the very least, a commutation of the death sentence, which had not been carried out since 1947.

The death house was opened for the new arrival. Karl arrived at the Charleston State Prison in the charge of Sheriff Lundgren.

After a brief processing, he was lodged in Death Row which was the notorious Cherry Hill Section of the prison.

The guards took up a 24 hour vigil over Karl. They were ordered to observe his every breath as the time of his execution drew closer.

Karl's attorneys were preparing motions for a new trial and vowed to appeal the jury verdict if the new trial were to be denied. Not until the last appeal was exhausted would the date for the execution be set.

The overcoat and suit, all clothing down to his socks gave way to the gray prison ticking of the Charleston inmates.

Karl Chapman would be alone in Death Row, which had not seen another occupant in many months. He maintained the curious calmness that had marked his attitude since his arrest even to the doors of the Death House.

Karl's immediate family were allowed to visit him at the discretion of the prison authorities. The only others would be his attorneys, chaplain, guards and other official personnel of the prison.

Karl would be fed regular prison food, which would be brought to him by guards. He would take his exercise in the prison yard under the eternal vigil of the guards. Other prisoners would be out of the yard when Karl was occupying it for the simple 'airing' permitted to prisoners whom the death sentence had been passed.

The young prisoner would be permitted reading in his cell. The cell would contain all necessary sanitary facilities. The only times in which Karl would leave the close quarters of the cell would be for the exercise period.

These rules and regulations would remain in place for the entire duration of Karl Chapman's stay at the prison. Days, weeks, months and even years would pass, and the rules would remain in place. Karl would evolve from a high school teen, to a solitary man.

Karl was not permitted direct contact with any of the crime-hardened residents of the maximum security section of the prison. That very prison had erupted in violence only a month before Karl's arrival. Prisoners had held guards hostage over a period of 5 days. Charleston State Prison, Cherry Hill was no country club. It housed the most hardened criminals.

As the days, weeks and months passed, Bonner and LaBonte filed numerous motions for a new trial. The basis of these motions were numerous.

They declared, the court had denied a request for Karl to be committed for 30 days observation to determine his mental stability. This was denied by the Appellate Court. Insufficient time to prepare for trial, denied.

They brought attention to the fact that potential witnesses, including the professional experts were allowed to remain in the courtroom during testimony.

Prejudice caused by insisting the defendant remain in the 'dock' or 'cage' throughout the trial, in view of the jury.

Finally, a motion for a new trial was petitioned based on inadequate representation of counsel. This, of course was based on the fact that Melvin Bonner had been appointed by the court, and although he had the required years before the bar, he was not a criminal attorney and had never tried a capital case. The appeals were continually denied.

Karl Chapman remained in a private cell, on death row. He became an avid reader and spent most of his time reading books that addressed electronics and high tech products coming onto the market. He never changed his demeanor. He remained a quiet, cooperative model prisoner. He'd spend hours with the guards, playing chess. When he was very young, Karl enjoyed hours of playing chess with his grandfather. He became a worthy opponent and challenged the best players.

The guards grew to like Karl. It was probably the first time in his life Karl felt the comradery of male adults.

Throughout his incarceration, Karl's only visitors were his attorneys, only to deliver the news of another denial of their appeals. The attorney's soon 'gave up the cause' and their visits diminished to a mere once every three or four months.

With the exception of the attorneys, Karl had no other visitors. Upon his arrival, he was given an application, which allowed him to list acceptable visitors. This was standard procedure. Prisoners had the right to refuse or accept visitors. If the name was not on the prisoner's list, visitations would be denied. Karl had only three individuals listed. His father, mother and sister. There were no records indicating any family members ever visited.

When John Chapman paid his last visit to Karl at the Hampden County Jail in Stanfield, the day after the verdict was handed down, that was the last time he would see his son.

He made it clear to Marge Chapman that Karl would be severed from the family. Brenda was told she was not to contact Karl by correspondence, or by any other means. For all intents and purpose, John Chapman had declared his only son, dead.

He would not allow Karl's name mentioned. Karl's room was stripped to the bare walls and eventually, it became a 'sewing room' for Marge. Brenda returned to Lincoln High School, and was to 'bear up' the best she could. That was the order handed down from John Chapman, and it would be adhered to without exception, or further discussion.

The Clarke's had gone on with their lives. They were in their new home and within a year of the trial, Mrs. Clarke gave birth to twins. Two boys! On the third day after their births, one failed, and died. Again, Phil Clarke raised his fists and declared another death in his family caused by Karl Chapman.

The surviving twin thrived, and soon Elaine arrived home, carrying Phillip Michael Clarke. Brenda was ecstatic, and Phil was observed walking a little less bent and smiled that warm smile more frequently.

One Saturday afternoon, Elaine and Barbara were busy doing the regular Saturday cleaning. Brenda was dusting, Elaine was fussing with the baby. Phil arrived home from a ball game and sat in the living room.

Across from him, on the mantle was the picture of Lynn Ann smiling. He stared at the picture for several minutes. Then he looked around the room. She was everywhere it seemed. He hadn't realized it, but pictures of Lynn at every age were still decorating the walls. He called to Elaine, and Barbara. Both appeared in the doorway. Elaine carried little Phillip, and Barbara stood by her side.

"I think it's time," Phil stated. "I think it's time we put Lynnie away. We need to put her away, and put some happy pictures in here."

"But Phil, what's wrong with you? These pictures are all we have left!" Elaine declared.

"No, honey, they're not. We have Barbara, and Phillip. We need to cherish what we have, and lay to rest what we have lost."

Elaine handed the baby to Barbara and went upstairs. Phillip patted Barbara gently and smiled that warm smile.

"Don't worry honey, it's going to be fine." He said, and followed Elaine upstairs.

"I didn't mean to make you cry. I've been giving it a lot of thought, and I think I'm doing the right thing. Lynn is in another place now. We're still here. Let's keep her memory in our hearts and not on display. Our family is different now. Lynn would not want our house to become a shrine in her honor. It's the right thing to do Elaine. Please think about what I'm trying to say."

With that, Phil returned downstairs and took the baby from Barbara. He sat back on his chair, and Barbara curled up with him and her little brother.

"I understand Daddy. I miss Lynnie too, but little Phillip never even knew her. She would have just loved the baby. Don't you think?"

"Yes, honey, I'm sure she would have." He turned to the baby and gave him a gentle squeeze. He reached for Barbara's hand and then silently he spoke to God.

"Please forgive me for all the times I've cursed you. Thank you for the years you gave us Lynn Ann, and thank you for the family I have today."

The next morning, Elaine woke earlier than usual. She made coffee, and spent the quiet early morning hours seated in the living room. By the time Phil came downstairs, Elaine had removed all the pictures of Lynn Ann.

When the Clarke's had moved from Lynndale St., the chore of cleaning out Lynn's room was heart wrenching. After several weeks, Elaine, with the help of her sisters had removed all of Lynn's belongings. Elaine had selected some special mementos and placed them in a cedar chest.

Now, she opened the cedar chest for the first time since it had been placed under the window in the dining room. She placed the pictures on top of the raincoat and loafers. She closed the lid. Silently, she was able to say goodbye to Lynn Ann.

The Rosen's did not proceed with the adoption plans. They raised Daniel and kept little David's memory alive through Daniel. They encouraged Daniel to talk about his brother and the memories he had of him. They were able to find comfort in Daniel's memories.

Eventually. Mr. Rosen sold his share of the business to Gordon Schaefer and opened his own accounting firm. Daniel became an excellent student and a fine athlete.

Mrs. Rosen became an active member of the school organizations, and life went on in the Rosen household.

The Chapman's did not fair well. Brenda became more distant, and hardly talked to her father.

Marge was plummeting into a clinical depression. She went from doctor to doctor, none seemed to be able to help. John continued to work. He would return from work and soon his casual drinking accelerated.

Alcohol became his means of coping. He was a violent man when he drank. Brenda soon learned to retreat to her room, and Marge simply took more pills. It was a vicious environment.

Four months before graduation, Brenda quit school. She was pregnant. Quietly, she married Paul, her high school sweetheart, and the father of her baby. Paul had graduated and worked as a mechanic for a garage in Stanfield.

Soon after, Marge became so disabled, she was committed to the Northampton State Institution. The very hospital her father had died in years before.

John Chapman remained at 51 Lynndale St. The window shades were kept drawn. He became reclusive.

Brenda tried to visit, but was turned away. She never tried again. She visited her mother, but could not bear to see her mother in the state she was in. Marge failed to recognize Brenda. Marge was in a world of her own.

In May, 1956, just a little over a year after Karl was delivered to Charleston, Governor Stanton vigorously debated whether to commute to life imprisonment the death sentence of Karl Chapman.

The trial, he noted, had focused on Karl's sanity and additionally noted that Judge Grishbaum repeatedly rejected motions for additional psychiatric testing.

Karl's sentence was deferred pending motions of a new trial and an appeal to the State Supreme Court.

After all the appeals were exhausted, Governor Stanton asked that the Massachusetts Commissioner of Mental Health examine Chapman. The commissioner found Karl to be legally sane, but stated that he was schizoid and emotionally flattened.

The doctor's diagnosis did not rise to the level of insanity according to the law. It was considered a personality defect, not a mental illness.

Based on the findings of Dr. Slattery, the Governor again recommended that the sentence be commuted to life imprisonment. He stated, "No rational explanation could be given for the horrific crimes."

He went on to say, "Because of Chapman's abnormal and questionable personality condition, and lack of any prior criminal offenses, society would not benefit from his execution."

The Governor made it perfectly clear that he was not apposed to the death penalty in general.

It took over a month for the council to reject the governor's plea for commutation. One council member refused to consider the request on the grounds that Chapman had been declared sane at the time of the murders. The council did however, grant another six-month respite to allow the defense attorney to pursue an appeal to the State Supreme Court.

Karl had various advocates, including a major Boston newspaper. The Attorney General, Albert Goldman continued to push his pro-death penalty belief.

The Attorney General had an agenda. He was gearing up for the gubernatorial race. He made several speeches about killers and commutations. He was well received for calling attention to murders who escaped the death penalty because of 'executive action.'

The Attorney General, in one of his more colorful speeches stated. "We should dust off the cobwebs that have grown over the electric chair." He added, "'No one goes to the chair in Massachusetts,' is becoming a slogan among criminals."

This was to be the Attorney General's platform in the upcoming election.

In October, 1956, authorities moved Karl to Walpole Prison's death row and scheduled his execution for December 1, 1956.

As a last ditch effort, Governor Stanton asked that the Council hear testimony of Dr. Ivan Shultz, a distinguished New York psychiatrist who had examined Chapman.

The Council agreed to hear the doctor's testimony.

In early November, the doctor spoke confidently to the council. He concluded his testimony with, "He didn't know right from wrong - he didn't have the capacity to know." Dr. Shultz continued, "We would be compounding the wrong by sending a sick boy to the electric chair!"

The day following the doctor's testimony, the Council delivered the news. They had voted six to three in favor of the commutation. One of the opposing members angrily stated,

"Commutation of Karl Chapman's death sentence will declare open season on children."

One of the prominent Boston newspapers praised everyone who had worked to save Chapman's life. The paper published the following commentary:

"What stands out vividly today is the fact that Massachusetts has finally decided to keep a life rather than take one. An unimportant life, too, a warped and crippled life, a life of little value to the boy himself, a life that will now fritter away in the bleak inconsequence of prison existence. But Massachusetts has chosen to keep even such a lesser life, and by that choice has imbued all human life with a special consecration. Even the affront of murder of two children has not moved us to execute."

Karl Chapman's sentence was commuted and the official documents of the commutation were signed by Governor Walter B. Stanton.

Incorporated in the commutation, was a resolve by the Governor's Council. It stated that there be included in the record a request from said Council to all future Councils that the defendant, Karl T. Chapman never be considered for further pardon, parole or commutation.

In 1984, the death sentence was abolished in the Commonwealth of Massachusetts.

In the 1980's Karl was again transferred. This time to the newly constructed Massachusetts Correctional Institute at Shirley, MA. There he remained until his death on September 26, 1996. He was incarcerated for a total of 41 years.

Karl Chapman's remains are buried on state property. His funeral was attended by, the Warden, a Priest and one guard, who enjoyed playing chess with Karl.

"Mercy for the Guilty is Cruelty to the Innocent"
-John Adams

ABOUT THE AUTHOR

Joanne Connors-Wade is a native of Massachusetts. Writing has been a lifetime passion of hers. She equates writing a story to participating in an exciting adventure.

Although *A Thread of Evidence* is her first published book, Ms Wade is the author of several unpublished works which she has shared with friends and family. She enjoys a challenge and becomes engrossed in extensive research which she believes is the key to credibility within a story, whether fiction or non-fiction.

A Thread of Evidence is an example of a fictional story which adheres as closely as possible to the actual event that it was inspired by. Ms Wade draws on her personal recollections of the 1954 crime and utilizes it as a springboard for the intriguing story that unfolds and is delivered to her reader.

Presently, she lives in Central Massachusetts with her husband and has begun creating her next book which she hopes to publish within the year 2005.

Printed in the United States
31167LVS00005B/46-48